The Choice

The Choice

DOMS OF HER LIFE:
HEAVENLY RISING (BOOK 1)

by
Shayla Black,
Jenna Jacob,
and Isabella LaPearl

THE CHOICE
Doms of Her Life: Heavenly Rising (Book 1)
Written by Shayla Black, Jenna Jacob, and Isabella LaPearl

This book is an original publication by Shayla Black, Jenna Jacob, and Isabella LaPearl

Copyright 2018 Shelley Bradley LLC, Dream Words LLC, and Tale Spin LLC
Print Edition

Edited by: Shayla Black and Amy Knupp of Blue Otter
Proofread by: Fedora Chen and Kasi Alexander

ISBN: 978-0-9911796-3-3

Dedication

Of all the relationships in life,
sisterhood is one of the best.

Authors' Note

DOMS OF HER LIFE: Heavenly Rising is a serialized story told over multiple full-length books. This is the second collection in the DOMS OF HER LIFE series. The first, Raine Falling, is complete and can be read for deeper enjoyment of Heavenly Rising, but is not necessary. The timelines of these collections intersect, however. We will refer to events in Raine Falling, but they don't affect the outcome of anything in Heavenly Rising.

If you have not read Raine Falling and would like the backstory of those characters, here is the reading order:

One Dom To Love
The Young and The Submissive
The Bold and The Dominant
The Edge Of Dominance

Lastly, the events of DOMS OF HER LIFE take place prior to 2018.

We hope you enjoy the journey!

Shayla Black

Jenna Jacob

Isabella LaPearl

CHAPTER ONE

Thursday, March 21

"Excuse me. Can you repeat that?" Across his small living room, River Kendall stared at her as if she'd lost her damn mind.

Heavenly Young feared she had.

Nerves twisting her stomach in a fierce knot, she drew in a deep breath and tried again. "Would you be willing—I-I mean, if it's not too much trouble—to, um…take me to bed?"

"That's what I thought you said." River shook his head with slack-jawed shock. "You're kidding, right?"

She fidgeted. In her imagination, this conversation had been much easier—and less awkward. River had proven he would do any halfway-decent-looking woman. She hadn't expected him to suddenly need a reason.

Maybe coming here and risking their burgeoning friendship had been a mistake.

"Of course I am." Heavenly stood. "I'll take my bad jokes and go."

"Sit down." He waited, brow raised, until she complied on shaking legs. "What the hell is going on?"

She refused to burden him with the ugly truth that she'd far rather have sex with a friend than the odious and inevitable alternative. This "favor" was already asking a lot. "Nothing."

"If that were the case, those words would *never* have come out of your mouth. Why do you want to have sex with *me*? I'm assuming that's what you meant since you didn't mention a nice tucking in with hot cocoa and a bedtime story."

Yes, River probably saw her as a kid, far more like a little sister than a lover.

She felt guilty for compounding an impossible request with a lie, but her options had dwindled to almost none. While convincing him

1

to help her wouldn't solve all her problems, it might make one of them more bearable. "I was feeling lonely and thought we could...you know..."

He leaned forward on his elbows and peered at her. "Are you attracted to me, Heavenly?"

How did she answer that without insulting him? "I like talking to you. We enjoy some of the same TV shows. You're nice."

"Nice? I'm not hot for you, either, by the way."

Even better. "Well, I'm only asking for a one-time thing. Since you're popular with the ladies, I thought maybe I was missing out."

"No. Hell no." He jerked his head. "Double fucking no."

In truth, she hadn't been looking forward to the actual deed with him, just in knowing it was done. But he'd turned her down, so it was time to make her exit.

She stood again and headed for the door. "Okay. Sorry to have bothered you. Have a good day."

River wrapped his hand around her elbow and hauled her back to the sofa. "Don't Rebecca-of-Sunnybrook-Farm me. You don't get to ask me for sex, wave toodle-loo, then walk out without a damn explanation. I thought we were friends. Are you in trouble? Do you need help?"

Heavenly was tempted to confess her situation to River. He would lend a hand if he could. Neither her conscience nor her pride would let her take more from him than an erection.

"Not at all," she lied with a smile. "I just thought it would be nice to have some no-strings fun. But you're not interested, so forget it."

His snort told her that wasn't going to happen. "Let's set aside the fact that we're not attracted to each other and that you're putting me in a really awkward position. I'll just ask the obvious question: If you want sex, why not go to Beck or Seth? If they aren't scratching your itch, I'm sure they'd be more than happy to."

Yes, but it didn't matter now. Unfortunately, hearing dreamy Dr. Beckman's and seductive PI Seth's names in the same sentence with sex started fires she couldn't put out. Before she'd met them, Heavenly never imagined burning with need for one man. But these two enemies who had pursued her relentlessly both set her ablaze. Her feelings for them dazzled her, confused her...conflicted her.

She couldn't tell either of them she was on the verge of starvation and homelessness, especially now.

Instead, she'd chosen to ask River for this favor because he was safe. But he was also right. Her proposition would put him at odds with Beck and Seth, who were both his friends. She didn't want that.

"It was just a passing thought."

"Bullshit. You came to my apartment, speech rehearsed, but you couldn't bring yourself to look me in the eye while asking me to sleep with you. You blushed like a fire engine the minute I mentioned Beck and Seth. So quit stalling and talk."

The truth was too complicated. "Nothing to say except I overstepped the bounds of our friendship and I'm sorry. I really have to go."

Her humiliation would fade sometime in the next century, right?

When Heavenly wriggled from his grip, River stood and blocked her path to the door, blue eyes pinpoints of confrontation. "Sit your ass down. You've BSed me, lied to me, dodged me, and tried to placate me. Let's try the truth. Why do you want sex, but not from Beck or Seth?"

She sighed. "You know if I chose one over the other, it might incite nuclear war."

"Valid point," he conceded. "But if they found out I'd done you, all that toxic fallout would rain down on my head. Not to mention the fact that me defiling Raine's bestie would piss my little sister off."

Heavenly winced. She should have thought of that, too. "You're right."

"Why not ask Beck and Seth to do you together? I think they'd bury the hatchet, at least temporarily, for that."

She'd fantasized about them touching her together, especially late at night when she let her fingers roam a forbidden path inside her panties. But to believe that would ever happen was absurd.

"I can't." Not after what happened the last time she'd spoken to them.

"Why not? It worked for my sister. She's really happy with Liam and Hammer."

"Raine is, and they're devoted to her. They'll make great parents. But asking both Beck and Seth for a physical relationship wouldn't stave off the war."

"How do you know until you try?"

Heavenly wished she'd never started this conversation. Since River obviously wasn't going to give her a quick tumble, she wanted out. Unfortunately, he stood like an immovable mountain between her and the door.

"You're missing the point. I want something without attachment. Beck and Seth have both been trying to tie me down for months."

A little grin played at River's lips. "More than you know."

Heavenly frowned. Obviously, he found that funny for reasons she didn't grasp. "So you see my problem?"

"Let me get this straight." He shot her a skeptical glance. "You want to fuck? Just once? And never to do it again?"

When he put it that bluntly, her proposition sounded terrible…but not as bad as the alternative. "Absolutely."

"No, you don't. You've never fucked a day in your life, sweetheart."

"Why would you think that? I'll be twenty-three next week."

"Uh-huh. And still a virgin, I'll bet."

Oh, time to end this conversation. "Why are you getting so personal?"

"Because you asked me to get naked and stick my dick inside you," River quipped. "I think that's pretty personal."

She tried not to wince. "Sorry. It was stupid. I'll just go."

"So you'll forget this crazy idea of hooking up?"

Heavenly said nothing. It was better than lying.

He sighed with frustration. "If you're going to look for someone else, at least keep me posted so I can be sure you're safe."

"I'll be fine." Heavenly was relieved when he stepped away from the door and let her pass. "See you next week at Raine's."

River sent her a quelling glare. "Yeah. I'll definitely see you then."

Saturday, March 30

HEAVENLY DODGED RIVER'S phone calls and texts for a week, even telling Raine that everything was fine when she'd asked on her brother's behalf. But she couldn't avoid him tonight unless she bowed out of the birthday bash Raine was throwing for her. Not only would that raise questions, but it wouldn't stop River from demanding answers. Problem was, Heavenly still didn't know what to say. Over the past week, the inevitable had become imminent, so unless he changed his mind, her only choices were to brace for the unthinkable or burn bridges.

She rang Raine's doorbell, relieved when her bestie answered with a big smile and a hug. "Come in. I'm glad you're here. River is dying to see you."

Heavenly gulped. "Here I am."

Concern lined Raine's face. "Beck and Seth have also asked about you twenty times. Are you ready to see them?"

It was going to hurt so bad… "Sure."

Raine didn't look convinced. "Are you doing any better since we talked?"

"Much," she fibbed, then glanced down at Raine's swelling stomach. "Wow, those little ones are growing!"

"I know. Sometimes I'm not sure if they're twin babies or twin Godzillas." She stroked her baby boulder and dropped her voice. "What's even funnier is, I can't tell whether Hammer or Liam is more turned on by the pregnant thing. Go figure."

Heavenly didn't know how to respond. "That's…great. I never thought you'd be this happy when we first met. You were in such a dark place."

Raine's face turned solemn. "Thank you for being there that day at the hospital. And thank you for being my friend since." She sniffled suddenly, her big blue eyes filling with tears. "And if we don't stop being mushy, I'm going to sob like a hormonal mess and ruin my makeup."

When she laughed again, Heavenly joined in. "No more mushy, I promise. I'm just glad to see you."

"Me, too. Wine?"

She rarely imbibed, but she'd probably need the liquid courage tonight. "Please. Is it in the kitchen?" When Raine ambled in that direction, Heavenly stopped her. "I'll get it. You sit."

"Oh, not you, too. Liam and Macen say that constantly. I'm pregnant, not helpless."

"There you are, love. I've been looking for you," Liam crooned behind Raine, his Irish lilt sounding happy as he wrapped his arm around her, giving her gently distending belly a rub. "Heavenly is right. Time to get you off your feet. The obstetrician says you need rest."

Raine groaned. "I've only been upright for three minutes. It's a party…"

"Which means it will be a long evening, and you should pace yourself." Liam spoke the words as if they were a suggestion, but Heavenly had the distinct impression otherwise. "I'll get her wine." He turned in her direction. "Good to see you, little one."

Before Heavenly could reply, strong fingers wrapped around her arm. "Don't trouble yourself, Liam. I'll get her a drink."

River.

She had to face him sooner or later. And if she could think of the right white lie, maybe things between them would go back to normal. Ish, anyway.

"Thanks." She faced Raine's brother. "I'd like something white and fruity. As soon as I visit with Raine, then—"

"Let Liam settle her in the living room first." River's grip tightened. "You come with me."

The Irishman nodded, sending her one of those unnerving stares. "A grand idea."

River hauled her to the kitchen. What was it with these men? Every single one of them was bossy. Beck and Seth were the worst—powerful and larger-than-life. Bold. Sexual. Determined. *Way* beyond her experience.

Gosh, she really had to stop thinking about them.

Out the kitchen window, she glanced wistfully into the backyard and spotted the pair of them standing with Pike, Dean, and a few other guys she knew in passing, holding brews and laughing. Thank goodness Beck and Seth were occupied. Nothing would be worse than them overhearing River ask her embarrassing questions.

With a guiding hand, Liam led Raine to the sofa. When they reached a waiting Hammer, the men situated her in the middle of a cushion and fluffed pillows under her feet.

River dragged Heavenly to a quiet corner near the refrigerator and snatched the nearest bottle of wine. As he poured, Liam passed through on his way to the backyard. Then she and River were alone.

Raine's big brother shoved a glass of thick red vino in her hand. "So, did you find someone to fuck your brains out?"

She recoiled. If she gave him an equally blunt answer, would he stop this mortifying inquisition?

"Yes. It was easy." Heavenly punctuated her lie with a bright smile.

River glowered. "Tell me Beck or Seth finally manned up."

"He's someone you don't know."

One of River's dark brows shot up. "Where did you meet him?"

"Um…around."

"What does that mean? A park? A bar? A grocery store? A swingers' club?"

"Why does it matter? I found someone and it was lovely."

He looked skeptical. "Lovely? That's how you describe meeting a stranger, losing your clothes, and banging him?"

Heavenly bristled. "How would you describe a hookup?"

"Hot, sweaty, messy. Mind-blowing. Spine-melting. Earth-shattering." River snorted. "Never lovely."

"Sweaty?" She shuddered. "That sounds unpleasant. It was nice. I…tingled."

"Tingled?" He scowled. "Did your pussy fall asleep because he couldn't find your clit? Maybe you should have given him a map."

She nearly choked on her wine. "I found the experience perfectly satisfying."

"Sweetheart, you don't know squat about satisfaction." Raine's brother leaned in and peered at her, eye to eye. "Here's what I think happened: You haven't so much as flirted with another man. You don't understand why 'lovely' sex is bad because you've never had it. In fact, not only did you *not* have sex with this mysterious 'stud,' you haven't offered the virginity you asked me to take to anyone else."

"What. The fuck. Did you say?" Beck growled suddenly.

Heavenly glanced over her shoulder. Both Beck and Seth glared from across the kitchen. *Oh, no.*

"Get out," Seth snapped at River, hauling ass across the room. "Now. While you can still walk."

Dread burned her veins. She didn't have to wonder how much they'd overheard. Obviously, it had been more than enough. Tonight had just gone from mortifying to catastrophic.

River backed away, hands raised. "Hey, just so you know, I turned her down because I like my balls where they are."

"That's the only reason you're getting to keep them," Beck insisted. "Seth told you to get the fuck out."

"I'm leaving," River assured, then glanced her way. "Good luck."

Once he'd gone, silence descended. She was alone with the two men who had been tempting, confusing, and consuming her for months. They were going to demand answers.

This wouldn't end well.

Heavenly drew in a shaky breath, startled to find both now inches away, arms crossed over their chests. Aggression rolled off them, filling the tense air. Beck drilled holes through her with narrowed eyes, set off by a scathing slash of his mouth. Seth's seething stare was no less displeased. Unfortunately, she had nothing to offer the savage beasts except a smile full of trembling bravado.

Because the truth would change everything.

"Hi, guys. Can I get you a drink?"

CHAPTER TWO

"I DON'T WANT a fucking drink. I want to spank your ass until I get some answers." Dr. Kenneth Beckman tried not to snarl and failed.

God, the fucking betrayal… He itched to stretch Heavenly across his lap, yank her panties down, and paddle her sweet little backside until it flushed red. But when he fantasized about spanking her—which was all the fucking time—he made her count out every swat with his fingers deep in her pussy. The fact that he couldn't mete out punishment now frustrated him. Months of unfulfilled desire made him feel as if he was coming out of his skin.

Heavenly was his fucking worst nightmare rolled up in his hottest wet dream. If she had any clue how deep and dark his fantasies of her were, it would scare the hell out of her. She'd be even more afraid if she knew he was both a Dominant and a sadist.

Seth turned his way. "I was just thinking the same thing."

After months of biting rivalry, they finally agreed on something—not that Beck could spare a fuck about that right now.

"What the… Why in the holy, ever-loving hell did you…" Fury tied Beck's tongue in a knot too tight to speak.

"Offer River *fucking* Kendall your virginity?" Seth finished, teeth bared.

Beck gestured to the East Coast bastard. "What he said."

Wine sloshed in her shaky grip. "You shouldn't care if I'm a virgin anymore."

With one hand, Beck grabbed the glass and slammed it on the island. With the other, he pressed his thumb to her chin and forced her darting gaze to his. "Are you saying you're not? If you didn't give your virginity to River, who fucking took it?"

She better be as innocent as the day he'd met her or there would be hell to pay.

"My sex life is none of your business, Dr. Beckman." Heavenly wrenched from his hold.

"Is that what you think, Ms. Young?" He scoffed. "My fingers up your pussy should have told you otherwise."

Seth grabbed her by the wrist and hauled her too close for Beck's sanity. "He touched you?"

When she blushed furiously in answer, Beck smiled, remembering every passionate word he'd uttered while he'd plunged his digits deep and swallowed her moans with his kiss.

"So that's a yes." Seth bit out. "Well, as the other guy who's had his fingers—and tongue—inside you, I think I'm entitled to know who supposedly popped your cherry."

Beck had suspected the PI had done more than kiss her, but having his hunch confirmed infuriated him even more.

Heavenly tried to wriggle from Seth's grasp. "I didn't ask you who your first, um…sexual partner was."

"Mary Jo Bartkowicz in a stall inside the men's room at the White Castle. I was fourteen. Now it's your turn. Spill."

Her eyes flared wide, and she tore her gaze from Seth to Beck, as if she thought he was going to save her. *Fat chance.* He wanted this answer, too.

"Who did you fuck? We're waiting for an answer."

"No one you, um…know."

Beck grabbed both wrists and anchored himself in her face, inches from the quivering candy mouth he was hungry to taste again. "Let's try the truth."

Suddenly, Seth was behind her, his fist in her hair, tugging on the strands. He bent his considerably tall frame to murmur in her ear. "If you lie again, we'll find a quiet corner and prove our threats to spank you weren't empty."

Shit, they were all but outing themselves as Dominants. They might terrify her, but it was too late for decorum and restraint.

When Seth's silky threat sank in, her cheeks flared rosier. The pulse at her neck jerked faster. Her pupils dilated.

Beck cupped her face. She gave a startled gasp. Under her red T-shirt, her nipples stood stiff. The musk of her arousal tinged the air, making his cock throb. After four long months of wanting her, seeing that she still ached for him nearly brought him to his knees.

So did believing that the singular prize between her legs was still there for him to pluck.

There was just one problem… He and Seth were touching her at the same time, and she looked more aroused than he'd ever seen her.

Goddamn it.

"Spank me? I'm not a misbehaving child." Her voice sounded nervous and breathy.

"You're not, but that won't stop us from firing up your ass. Because let me tell you, little girl, no other man better be the one to make you a woman."

"That's for one of us," Seth insisted.

Knowing that Heavenly had offered her virginity to River, that Seth had touched *his* pussy, and that she wanted them both—Beck's control snapped. He didn't care that they were in the middle of a party and anyone could walk in on them. He didn't even care that Seth watched his every fucking move. He had to taste Heavenly or lose his mind. Later, he'd figure out how to ditch the other hard dick.

He lowered his lips toward her pale, graceful throat. And Seth—thank fuck—pulled her hair so he could stare into her eyes. It gave Beck more of her skin to explore. God, he was so close he could see every individual bump of her gooseflesh, feel the ragged pants of her breath. He could almost fucking taste her.

Suddenly, an obnoxious droning alarm buzzed at an ear-piercing decibel level around them, pealing from her back pocket.

"What the hell?" Seth snapped to attention and scanned the kitchen as if searching for threats.

Beck scowled. What was that annoying-ass sound?

Heavenly struggled free from their grasp and grabbed her phone. It fumbled in her shaking hands as she answered it. "Dad, what's wrong? Are you all right?"

Dad? Beck looked at Seth, who shrugged. He didn't like being in the dark, but at least his competition was clueless, too.

As she paced out of the kitchen, holding the phone in a white-knuckled grip, he and Seth followed, shamelessly listening to her every word. Out of the corner of his eye, he caught sight of Liam watching. The Irish bastard with the uncanny perception gave them a nod. This was the trouble Liam had warned them about, the threat that might tear her out of his life forever.

Like hell.

He didn't need Liam's urging to stay close. Until he knew that she and her father were all right, he'd be no more than half a step off her ass. The determination on Seth's face said he felt the same. Beck had mixed feelings about that, but he couldn't focus on those when Heavenly needed them.

"Did you already call 911?" She paused. "Good. Yes. I'll grab the first bus and meet you there."

"Bus?" Beck whispered.

"She takes it everywhere," Seth supplied under his breath.

The *city* bus? That filthy, urine-soaked, rapist-filled mode of transportation? Beck felt like he'd been punched in the solar plexus. How had he not known?

"Hang on, Dad. Please…" she sobbed, shoulders shaking. "I'll be there as soon as I can."

Fuck, she was ripping his heart out.

"Give me the phone. Let me talk to your dad. Medical condition?"

She turned to him, tears rolling down her face in watery paths. "H-he already hung up."

Beck stifled a curse and pulled her close. It said a lot that she wrapped her arms around him without a qualm. In fact, she gripped him so tight he could barely breathe.

As he held her, he shared a glance of concern with Seth, who whispered soft words of reassurance and caressed her back.

But nothing eased the anxiety pouring from her.

"Which hospital? We'll take you," Beck offered.

Heavenly sniffled. "Really? The VA. Please."

As Beck wondered why the hell her father was going there for an emergency, she spun from his embrace and dashed to the door. Seth took off after her, ignoring the gawking partygoers.

Nearby, Raine struggled to her feet. "What's going on?"

Liam eased his concerned girl back to the sofa. "Heavenly will be all right, love. They'll call later."

Beck didn't hang around to hear the rest. He sprinted outside, after Heavenly, into the night.

"I'll drive." Seth yanked his keys from his pocket and hit the fob. The second the vehicle pinged, Heavenly ducked into the backseat and shut the door. "Get back there with her and be a doctor. And I don't mean *play* doctor."

"Fuck you." Beck jumped in beside Heavenly and pulled her onto his lap as Seth climbed into the driver's seat and turned over the SUV's engine.

She curled against him, arms around his neck, and heaved in huge sobs as Seth peeled out of the driveway. As he shot down the road, Beck held her tight, wishing he could do something to take away her pain. She might not want him in her future and maybe he didn't deserve her, but at least he possessed the skills to help her.

"Shh. We'll get to him, little girl," he crooned. "Tell me what's wrong with your dad."

"H-he's had an autoimmune disease for eight years, but he wasn't officially diagnosed until about three years ago." She winced. "We've…talked about it before."

Beck froze. So many things suddenly made sense. "Your dad has Guillain-Barré?"

She nodded contritely. "I'm sorry."

For hiding? For lying? For hurting him? Or for sins he might not even know about yet?

"We'll talk about that later." He smoothed a soothing hand down her back when she fell into his arms again.

Months ago, Heavenly had begun peppering him with question after question about all things related to the disease, homing in on one "fictitious" patient in particular, which she'd claimed was a hypothetical case study for a research paper. *My ass.* Why hadn't she bothered to tell him she was talking about her father?

While the autoimmune disease was serious, it wasn't usually fatal. But her father had suffered for years, hadn't gotten proper treatment right away, and his extremities were already weakened so much he was largely unable to walk without assistance. Heavenly had cause to be worried. Normally, with good care it was possible to recover, but being over forty was another negative factor. The man probably needed nearly round-the-clock help. Was Heavenly his primary caretaker?

Beck began sorting through his mental list of good neurologists.

Seth glanced over his shoulder as he headed toward the freeway. "Um…guy who's only lived in LA for, like, five minutes driving here. Where's the VA?"

"Here." Beck plugged the address into the GPS on his phone, then tossed it onto the front seat. "Get us there in one piece, okay?"

Flashing him a caustic smile, Seth veered onto the freeway and accelerated.

Beck settled Heavenly against him once more. He comforted her with a kiss on top of her head, at her temple, against her shoulder while he whispered soft assurances he didn't feel. What would he find when he came face to face with her father?

Quick minutes later, Seth stepped on the brakes outside the emergency room. Beck would have grumbled at Seth's not-so-gentle stop, but a glance out the window said the ambulance had already arrived. EMTs were wheeling out an older, frail-looking man on a stretcher.

Heavenly wrenched the handle as Seth unlocked the doors. An instant later, she lurched onto the pavement, her feet pounding as she ran after the prone figure. "Dad!"

A COUPLE OF hours later, ER doctors had managed to stabilize Heavenly's father. His neurologist had never made an appearance, which pissed Beck off. At least the dipshit had sent instructions for a plasma exchange. With that underway and Heavenly's panic dissipating, Seth had taken her to find some coffee. Beck stood across the room, tablet in hand, and stared at the frail man only ten years his senior. Dread thudded in the pit of his stomach.

"So, Mr. Young—"

"Call me Abel."

"Right. Abel. Thank you for giving me permission to scan your chart. Like I said, I'm not a neurologist." But since Heavenly had been obsessed with her "case study," he'd researched the disease and talked to knowledgeable colleagues on her behalf. He knew more than he wished he did.

The dissecting stare Heavenly's father sent him almost made Beck

squirm. There was a lot wrong with Abel's body…and nothing wrong with his mind. "You might not specialize in my condition, but if you were playing poker, I'd already know you had a lousy hand. My own doctor barely talks to me. Give it to me straight."

God, he didn't want to do this, and any decent lawyer would tell him this consultation had lawsuit written all over it. But he had to be honest with Abel. It was the humane thing to do. Besides, Heavenly would never forgive him if he wasn't.

"First, it's clear you need a better neurologist. I know some great ones, any of whom can tell you far more than I can about the optimal treatment and—"

"I'm dying, aren't I?"

Beck hesitated, searching for the soft-shoe phrases he dished out to gravely ill patients and their families all the time. Nothing. He simply nodded.

Abel sighed. "I've suspected for a while. I've been trying to hold on as long as possible. Once I'm gone, Heavenly will be alone in the world."

The man's words knifed Beck in the fucking heart. Based on the mutual devotion he'd observed between Heavenly and her father tonight, Abel's death would undo her.

"No, she won't," Beck vowed, no matter what she thought. "I promise you that."

Abel scrutinized him with a glance. "I'm relieved, Dr. Beckman. You know, Heavenly talks about you all the time."

That sent him reeling, especially since she'd never once mentioned her father to him.

"Oh?" Beck was dying to know what she'd said.

Despite all the IVs and tubes crisscrossing his body, the older man laughed. "She speaks very highly of you, and I can see why. Not many colleagues would follow a co-worker late at night to another hospital to help and offer support."

The man was asking about his relationship with Heavenly without asking at all, and Beck tried not to look guilty. "She's a very bright nursing student with a promising future."

"Uh-huh. I saw the way you looked at her. Heavenly might be innocent, but I assure you I'm not."

Shit. "Your daughter is a beautiful woman."

There. That didn't sound like he was desperate to strip her bare and fuck her breathless.

"I agree. But where do you fit into this picture? I know Mr. Cooper has taken her on a few dates, so I'm not surprised he looks at her like a tasty snack cake he wants to gobble up. But I assumed your time with Heavenly was strictly professional."

Beck felt himself start to sweat. He'd never had to explain himself to a woman's father. And Abel didn't seem the type for candy-coated bullshit.

"I've been dating her, too." He met Abel's piercing blue gaze. "As for Seth… Well, I'm neither a quitter nor used to coming in second place."

That made Abel laugh. "Gumption and balls. I like that."

"The choice is Heavenly's, of course."

"But you're going to make sure she picks you?"

Beck nodded, though he knew damn well it wasn't that simple…

"You should know that she's been my sole caretaker since she was fifteen, so she hasn't seen much of the world. She needs to live, to enjoy herself. But she also needs protection, guidance…and a firm hand. She may seem sweet on that soft-spoken surface, but don't be fooled. She's got a spine of steel."

"Oh, I'm well aware."

Abel laughed again. "Since you're closer to my age than hers, I wondered if you'd already figured that out."

He didn't need Abel's reminder there was almost fourteen years between him and Heavenly. Beck never forgot. He was a perverted fuck—and he knew it. Usually, he embraced it. Right now? This was awkward as hell.

"Weeks ago. I'll do my best to make her happy," he promised.

Abel relaxed back against his pillows, a faint smile on his weathered face.

"My first priority is to make sure you get better care." Beck changed subjects. "Would it be all right if I made some arrangements?"

"I'll agree to anything that makes Heavenly's life easier, since I've been nothing but a burden for years. But I don't have any money."

"It'll be pro bono. I have friends in the medical community who owe me favors." Not entirely true, but he'd do whatever necessary to help Abel.

"Thank you. That's very generous." Abel sighed. "Is this damn treatment almost done?"

Beck scanned the monitor. "Sixteen minutes."

"How long do I have to live?"

His gut seized up. "I can't say for sure—"

"Ballpark." Abel wheezed. "Before Heavenly returns."

Beck didn't know for sure. "If we get you out of here and get you proper care, could be longer than you think. But you've had multiple relapses, which are uncommon. That's not promising. Your blood pressure isn't good. You're experiencing difficulty breathing, which concerns me most. You've got to be in pain."

"It consumes me every single day."

"That's a strain on your entire organ system, especially your heart."

Abel nodded. "You would know. Heavenly said you work a lot with tickers."

"I'm a vascular surgeon, but I've teamed up with cardiologists on a number of hearts. I intend to keep watch over yours."

"Thanks, Doctor."

"You can thank me by being with your daughter for as long as possible."

"I promise."

Conversation stopped when Seth guided Heavenly into the little room. Beck cursed under his breath because he already knew that was a promise her father couldn't keep.

IT WAS NEARLY two in the morning when Seth left I-10 eastbound and veered onto the 110. He stayed focused on the road…but his head was reeling. Until tonight, he'd had no idea that Heavenly lived with her father or that the man had such a vicious disease. What else didn't he know?

He purposely hadn't investigated the angel when he'd first met her because he hadn't wanted to trample on her privacy. He'd wanted to earn her trust. So he had only known what she'd wanted him to—almost nothing. And judging from the look on Beck's face, she'd done the same to him.

They'd both grossly underestimated her for the first—and last—time.

Christ, he felt like a dumbass. If he hadn't ignored the red flags or his gut instinct for months, he could have been lightening her load. And this night wouldn't have been a shit show.

Unfortunately, the crap kept coming.

While Heavenly accompanied the nurse wheeling Abel from the emergency room, he and Beck had trekked to the parking lot. Seth had pelted the doctor with questions about the man's disease. Since they were vying for the same girl, he hadn't expected more than a growled "fuck you." Instead, the smartass doctor had been surprisingly forthcoming about Abel's condition.

Fuck. When her father passed, it would crush Heavenly.

The only bright ray tonight had been the moments Heavenly turned to him for comfort. After thinking he might never hold her again, having her melt against him, face nuzzled into his neck, had been a dizzying relief. All night, the pang of his empathy had warred with the slow burn of his anger and tangled with the never-ending ache of his lust.

This woman had him tied up in knots.

Hearing that she'd let Beck put his hands in her panties hadn't thrilled him, but seeing her pant while she'd been between them troubled him far more.

On the other hand, could she be terribly attached to either of them? He had to wonder...

The GPS prompted him to exit the freeway in half a mile. From the passenger's seat, Beck scowled and grabbed his phone.

"This can't be right," he whispered, then cast a furtive glance to the backseat, where Heavenly was curled up against Abel, both in an exhausted sleep.

"Why?" He glanced at the device again. "This is the address she gave me."

Beck's scowl deepened. "Goddamn it."

Seth glanced at the street hugging the freeway. Pawn shops, bail bondsmen, and strip clubs lined the road. Boarded-up buildings and shady used car lots provided a backdrop for the flurry of police activity. Several squad cars with blinding light bars blocked traffic as cops contained a group of gangbangers in handcuffs, facedown on the sidewalk. A gunshot resounded nearby. The GPS told him to exit now.

"She lives *here*?"

The doctor stared at the phone again. "Point-six miles away."

In the backseat, Heavenly rustled and peered forward. "Exit here, take a right onto Figueroa. It's the third street past MLK Boulevard."

Feeling gut sick, he followed her directions. As he passed the bus stop, he realized her place was still nearly half a mile away. She walked that distance every day, at all hours, to catch her ride? How had she managed without being mugged, raped, or murdered?

When they turned down her street, the cracked road ran between dilapidated houses, all locked down with bars on their windows and doors, as if the inhabitants intended to ward off an imminent home invasion. In front of one rickety place, he saw a box of random trash and a ratty mattress. In front of another sat a sedan missing its rims.

"It's the big pink place on the left," she murmured.

The dive with the dumpster at the curb and "guarded" by rusted gates?

Beck slanted him a shocked gaze Seth totally understood. Sure, he'd been in neighborhoods like this. Once upon a time, he'd been a cop for the NYPD. But he'd never come to gang turf without backup. And he'd never cruised into the hood because the girl he dated lived there.

No fucking way he would leave Heavenly in this hellhole unprotected, but he couldn't exactly take her to his new one-bedroom bachelor pad, either. He'd have no room for her father.

As he eased the car to the curb and killed the engine, his thoughts raced. Maybe he should offer to sleep on her couch, gun at the ready. If he did, would his SUV still be intact when the sun rose?

When Heavenly eased from the backseat and helped her father out, Seth glanced at Beck, who was clearly doing similar mental gymnastics.

"If you have a couple of assault rifles, pass 'em out," the doctor mumbled. "We might need them to make it inside her place."

"No shit. I can't believe she lives here."

"Not for much longer."

Seth nodded. "You got that right."

As soon as he locked the SUV, he rushed to help Abel. Beck followed suit. They both wrapped a strong arm around the frail man and helped him to the wrought-iron gate. As a security feature, it was a joke. A good kick would send the decaying metal skittering across the walkway. But Heavenly dutifully inserted her key and turned the handle. The hinges squeaked as they ushered her dad into the shoddy courtyard. The gate slammed behind them with a rattling clang.

Christ, Seth had to believe Heavenly had some reason beyond her pride for concealing her father's health and her crime-ridden neighborhood. Neither he nor Beck had been able to persuade her to confide in them for months. He was loath to partner up with Dr. Dipshit…but would it take them both to finally get answers?

They led Abel along a chipped pink stucco wall, following Heavenly to the second apartment on the right. As she reached the door, she faltered at the sight of a bright orange notice on the door that read RENT OVERDUE. Heavenly ripped it down, crumpled the paper in her fist, and shoved a key into the knob.

"What's that about, boo?" Concern laced Abel's voice.

"Nothing, Dad. I've just been busy. I'll take care of it."

"Wait until tomorrow. You need rest, too."

"It's fine. Mr. Sanchez's lights are still on. See?" She pointed.

Her hand trembled.

Heavenly pushed the portal open and flipped on an overhead light. Cockroaches scurried to darkened corners of the painfully tidy studio apartment. A mussed hospital bed dominated the space. Water spots stained the ceiling. Paint peeled from the dingy walls. Seth feared what he'd find if he took a black light to the carpet.

The place was a shithole. And his angel *lived* here.

"Can you settle Dad on the bed? Then I'll adjust him until he's comfortable," Heavenly murmured.

Seth nodded, pressing his lips together in mute anger. It ticked up another notch when he spotted the lumpy pillow and thin, folded blanket stacked on the sagging couch against the wall. He had no doubt Heavenly slept there.

This reality got uglier with every passing moment.

"I know how to maneuver a hospital bed," Beck said as he and Seth helped Abel onto the mattress. "Relax, little girl."

"Actually, if you two don't mind staying with Dad for a few minutes, I'll pop across the courtyard and deal with last month's rent." Heavenly's voice shook.

With stress? Exhaustion? Embarrassment? Seth's gut coiled tight. Why was she paying the rent at two a.m.? He didn't like it.

"We'll get your dad settled in," Beck promised.

"Thanks." Heavenly's pensive expression was the last thing he saw before she hurried out the door.

He and Beck exchanged a concerned glance. Yeah, the doctor suspected something wasn't right, too.

Beck removed the older man's shoes. "Would you like something to drink?"

"Water, thank you. Clean glasses are in the cabinet to the left of the sink. Help yourselves." As Beck crossed the room, Abel regarded Seth, then gestured to a battered kitchen table. "Grab a couple of those chairs, make yourselves comfortable."

Forcing a smile, he dragged two spindle-backed seats beside the bed as Beck returned, balancing three full cups.

"Thank you for helping Heavenly and me tonight." Abel took a long gulp from his glass, fighting shaky hands. "We truly appreciate it."

"We're happy to," Beck assured.

"I wish we could do more." Seth hoped worry hadn't bled into his tone. The old man didn't need more concerns, especially about the safety of the daughter he relied on.

"I know this place isn't fancy. It's certainly not as big or homey as our farmhouse in Wisconsin. That's where Heavenly and I used to live. Before I got sick, we had a cozy kitchen, a big stone fireplace that would heat the whole living room come winter, and our own bedrooms. I miss that for her. She deserves more." Regret lined Abel's face. "Broke my heart to sell out when we couldn't keep up with everything. She loved living on the farm. We had three hundred head of dairy cows that made the best damn cheese in the state. When Heavenly was little, she used to name them all."

Seth could picture that. Her evasions aside, he'd seen her big heart.

"That sounds like a sizable operation."

"It was. How much has Heavenly told you?"

Not a damn thing. But Seth was determined to get some straight answers. "I'd appreciate it if you filled in the gaps."

"In other words, nothing." Abel sighed. "That girl… She's private, shy, and even more proud. You may have noticed she doesn't trust easily."

"We did," Beck grumbled. "Why is that?"

"Well, my wife left after I got sick, said she hadn't signed up to spend her life taking care of an invalid. Heavenly was just a teenager, in school and far too young to manage the spread by herself."

What kind of mother left her young daughter to shoulder such an adult role? "Heavenly must have taken that hard."

"She felt so abandoned after Lisa walked out. I'm afraid the experience taught her that those who should care most often don't give two shits. Unfortunately, she's had to shoulder most of the responsibility since. But Heavenly is a good girl. She's taken care of me all these years."

No wonder she handled everything on her own.

He darted a gaze over to Beck, who looked equally stunned by Abel's story. Heavenly's father was giving him more information about the girl in a few minutes than he'd managed to learn in months.

"After I sold the farm, I rented a little house in town for us. Eventually, my medical condition forced us to move to Milwaukee, then here. I wish the doctors back home could have diagnosed me properly before we had to move across the country. But the team in Wisconsin said the VA out here had more experience with my condition. Not so sure about that, and I don't much like LA."

Beck placed his hand on Abel's shoulder. "I promise I'll make some phone calls and set you up with the best neurologist in the city."

The older man smiled in gratitude. "I can't thank you enough. If your medical friends can't cover all the expenses, maybe we can pay some now that Heavenly got that raise at the hospital and started working so many hours. It's the only way we've been able to afford that gawd-awfully expensive medicine my doctor recently prescribed."

Seth schooled his expression. Heavenly had even fooled her father into thinking that a nursing student volunteering thirty hours a week at the hospital made a salary. He didn't blame her for not wanting to worry the sick man, but he also couldn't stop wondering… Other than the tips she earned working part time at that kids' pizza place, where was the money to pay the rent coming from? And if her cash flow was short, how was she paying now?

As the older man rambled on about the rising cost of pharmaceuticals, the hairs on the back of Seth's neck stood on end. Only one answer came to mind.

She'd offered her virginity to River because she'd wanted some control over her first time. And when Raine's brother had refused her sex… Shit, she'd been so rattled before heading across the courtyard because she'd known she would have to fuck her landlord to pay the rent.

Seth darted from his chair and bolted for the door.

Not a moment later, Beck scrambled to his feet, hot on his heels.

"You're leaving?" Abel sighed. "Well, nice to meet you boys…"

"We're going to check on Heavenly," Seth shot over his shoulder.

"Uh-huh," Abel mumbled as he drifted off to sleep.

Seth lurched out into the dark night. Beck followed. They peered across the shadowy courtyard. Seth tried to remember which apartment belonged to the landlord when a door along the far side slammed against a wall. He heard a cry, then caught sight of Heavenly, her pale hair whipping wildly as she ran toward them, panicked and sobbing—and frantically tugging her shirt over her bare breasts.

"You still owe me, *puta*." A guy who looked more like a beer-bellied gangbanger than a landlord chased after her, clutching her bra in his meaty fist. "You promised me that cherry pie."

As Seth raced to Heavenly and caught her in his grasp, rage—white and hot—enveloped every cell in his body. "Get inside."

She looked over her shoulder with revulsion and terror. "B-but—"

"Go!" Beck insisted. "We'll take care of this."

The moment she dashed to her unit and slammed the door, Seth charged toward Sanchez. "I'm going to fucking kill him."

"Not if I do it first," Beck growled beside him.

Here was something else they agreed on. Miracles never ceased. "We could make it hurt more if we did it together."

That was probably the only thing they would ever do together, and it was only happening because they both wanted Heavenly safe, protected, and sheltered. Plus, neither could wait to pulverize this shitbag.

Beck shot him a wolfish grin. "You're on."

CHAPTER THREE

Monday, November 26
Four Months Earlier

"SINCE MY SHIFT is over, and you're done with patients for the day, why don't you stop making me suffer and ask me out, Dr. Beckman?"

Beck bit back a quip that he knew a couple hundred ways to *really* make Kathryn Hitch, ER Nurse Specialist, suffer. Instead, he merely glared at the brunette with crazy eyes who'd cornered him outside the OR.

He had two hard-and-fast rules: First, he didn't date where he worked. Second, he didn't touch vanillas. As far as he knew, Kathryn wasn't part of the lifestyle. She damn well wasn't a member of Shadows, the BDSM club his friend Macen Hammerman owned, which had been his second home for the last seven years. He strictly maintained rules one and two because unleashing his kinky proclivities on the gossipy female staff would do irreparable damage to his professional reputation. After all, no one wanted a doctor who moonlighted as a sadist. Kathryn's unrelenting pursuit was strike three.

She was out.

"You know my answer," he said impatiently, shouldering his way past her.

"Your 'rule' about not dating co-workers again?" She followed, lower lip stuck out in a pout.

Her childish expression didn't do anything to soften his resolve, just his cock.

"Yes." He sighed. "Glad you remembered this time."

"I was hoping you'd changed your mind. Our conversations have been so meaningful."

The ones in which she'd chased him between surgeries and his office while he'd done his best to be civil but distant?

"You think so?" He raised a brow at her, which usually made savvy subs stammer and back down.

Once again, Kathryn proved she was neither submissive nor smart.

"I do. I want to tell you a secret." She leaned in. "I have a rule, too. I don't sleep with a guy on the first date."

Oh, so you and Dr. Manning were having your second date when you fucked him in the janitor's closet. Got it.

Slipping her hand into the pocket of his lab coat, she whispered, "But I'd bend that for you."

Usually, he encouraged a woman begging, but he was willing to get down on his knees to shut Kathryn up.

Beck brushed past her again. "That's not going to happen. I'm late. Excuse me."

Kathryn chased after him. "I know you're busy. But I won't give up on you."

Yeah, he'd already figured that out, just like he knew she pursued him because she wanted bragging rights as the first of the hospital's slut squad to bag and tag him.

Not in this lifetime.

Determined to escape, he ducked into an empty elevator and smirked as the doors shut in her face.

As he descended to the lower level so he could escape to the parking garage, he sighed in relief and eased a hand in his pocket. What the hell had she shoved in there? Phone number? Naughty note? Naked picture of her tits?

He felt something silky.

Frowning, he pulled the scrap free. A pair of her panties. Given how warm the slinky black satin was, Kathryn had been wearing them moments before slipping them into his pocket.

He fought not to puke as he pinched the waistband between his thumb and forefinger and ducked into the first empty lab on his left. When he flipped on the light with his elbow, he spotted a red bin on his right marked BIOHAZARDOUS WASTE.

Perfect.

With a shudder, Beck disposed of Kathryn's unmentionables, then scrubbed his hands raw in the nearby sink.

What would it take to make the delusional psycho back off?

Shaking his head, he shoved his way out of the lab and headed for his car. If he didn't leave fast, Kathryn would catch up to him again. No idea what other blatant shit she'd pull to get his attention—and he'd rather not find out.

As he marched around a corner, he accidentally plowed into a soft, feminine figure in pink scrubs. On impact, the little blonde gasped and stumbled.

He managed to grab her by the shoulders before she tumbled to the linoleum. "I'm sorry, miss. I..."

She raised fluttering lashes to him. Beck locked stares with the most startlingly blue eyes he'd ever seen. His train of thought fell off a cliff and died. Electricity sizzled through his veins. His heart chugged and pumped. Every muscle tensed. The hungry length between his legs roared to life with an urgency he hadn't felt in forever.

Who. Was. She?

He had no idea, but fuck... Peachy pale skin. Lush mouth. Cheeks flushing rosier with every moment he stared. And painfully young.

"I-I'm the one who's sorry. I was turned around and not watching where I was going, Doctor..." She dropped her gaze to the name stitched on his lab coat, then quickly backed out of his grip. "Oh, *you're* Dr. Beckman?"

Suddenly, she looked intimidated. So, his exacting reputation had preceded him. She was probably wondering how the hell to get out of his path. He was already trying to figure out how to get her into bed.

"We haven't met before." He damn well would have remembered her. "What's your name?"

"I'm Heavenly. Heavenly Young."

The name certainly fit—and underscored every reason he'd be terrible for her. Unfortunately, that didn't quash the growing problem in his pants, stretching and scraping against his zipper.

"Nice to meet you. You're new here?"

She nodded. "I'm going to nursing school online and volunteering for class credit. Today was my orientation."

"And you've already heard of me?"

She nodded again, her gaze dipping to the floor. The action was so naturally, unconsciously submissive Beck shoved down the urge to hook a finger under her chin and lift her gaze to his. This one would scare easily. He had no business thinking about her as anything other than a medical professional in training. Unfortunately, he still wanted to fuck her breathless.

Because he was stupid, Beck bent closer and inhaled her scent. Jesus, she smelled wholesome, like summer berries, humid breezes, and a thousand other sweet things he couldn't name. His knees nearly gave out. His cock jerked as if she'd stroked it.

"Don't believe everything you hear, little girl. I'm not the big, bad wolf."

Sure, plenty of people would disagree. But for Heavenly, he'd make an exception—just like he'd make an exception for the previous rules he'd given Kathryn.

"All right."

His reputation usually intimidated most, yet she now met his gaze straight on. So Heavenly might be shy but she didn't lack spine. *Interesting...*

"Excellent. Where are you headed?"

"The front entrance. But I've only managed to walk in circles for twenty minutes."

With a hospital under construction and half the elevators not working, he wasn't surprised. "I can help. Want an escort to the lobby?"

Her grateful smile was blinding. "That would be great. I was beginning to fear I'd wander the halls for a week. This is a big hospital."

"Once you get the lay of the land, it's not so bad." Grateful for any excuse to touch her, Beck wrapped his hand around her elbow and led her toward the entrance.

A pink blush stained her cheeks. It took all his willpower not to cup her face, simply so he would know what she felt like. Fantasies about putting his hands on the wet, aching parts of her filled his head. He imagined her breathless and begging for him...

His cock gave an approving lurch.

"Are you in your first year of nursing school?"

"Yes."

"Been tough?"

"It has, but it's worth the effort because helping people is a passion.

I just didn't realize how much I'd have to learn."

He smiled. "I remember feeling overwhelmed a time or two in medical school. If you ever need any help, just call. Here's my card."

When he pulled one from his pocket and set it in her palm, she raised her big eyes to him again. His heart fucking stuttered.

Get real, man, the voice in his head scoffed. *She might look as scrumptious as Little Red Riding Hood, but once she finds out you really are the Big, Bad Wolf…*

She'd run screaming in the other direction.

"Thank you. You're so kind."

Kindness wasn't in his vocabulary, but he'd try if it would persuade her to get naked. He'd also have to think of some way—any way—to run into her again. Because fuck his rules. He wouldn't stop pursuing Heavenly Young until she was his.

Thursday, December 6

"HEAVENLY, CAN YOU find Mr. Hammerman and Mr. O'Neill and update them on Raine's condition? Then show them where they can get cleaned up. No doubt they need it. It's been a damn rough morning," Dr. Beckman said, barely taking his concerned gaze off the battered brunette in the ER bed.

Heavenly couldn't stop staring at the woman, either. The black eye, the stitched lip, and the finger-shaped bruises circling Raine's neck broke her heart. Heavenly had heard the whispers that Ms. Kendall's father had beaten her—and that she'd had to kill him to survive. The horror and the shock of that stunned Heavenly. Her father was her person, the one who had always loved and encouraged her. How must this woman feel after being forced to take the life of the man who'd given her half of her DNA?

"Of course, Dr. Beckman," she murmured. "I'll be happy to."

And she was…but she couldn't stop wondering about his relationship with the victim. Obviously, Ms. Kendall was more than a mere patient because, despite not being her physician, he hadn't once left her side. After calling his staff to say that he had a personal emergency and wouldn't be in today—at least according to the hospital grapevine—he'd come flying into the ER and begun barking orders. He'd only let go of Raine Kendall's hand when he'd acted as a buffer between her and the police. He watched over her with solemn dark eyes and a clenched jaw, staring as if her pain was killing him. And he called her princess.

Was he in love with her?

As she left the room, Heavenly silently admonished herself. She barely knew Dr. Beckman, other than the short ten-minute conversations they shared almost every day when they somehow managed to run into one another. Her crush on him was stupid. Of course the sophisticated, hunky doctor was in a relationship. So what? She was here to learn, not find a boyfriend.

Unfortunately, that didn't stop her fascination.

According to the rumor mill, Ms. Kendall had stumbled into his office less than a week ago, seemingly distraught. He'd taken one look at her, canceled a whole afternoon of appointments, and shepherded her away almost immediately. Heavenly already knew he took his patients—and his career—very seriously. He wasn't the sort to slough off on a Friday just because. He'd also been absent on Monday and Tuesday, at least according to gossipy Kathryn.

Had Dr. Beckman spent that time with Raine?

Probably. She was obviously important to him. Heavenly knew her pang of envy was silly. But unlike creepy Dr. Manning, the gorgeous vascular surgeon had never asked her out. Sure, he'd shown her professional interest, patiently answering her questions via email the night before a test. Definitely kind of him. And she thought once that maybe he'd stared a bit longer than professionally necessary. But the consideration he'd shown her was nothing like the focus and dedication he'd given Raine Kendall this morning.

At the end of the hall, she dismissed him from her thoughts and entered the waiting room. "Mr. Hammerman? Mr. O'Neill?"

A tall, bearded man whose rumpled suit was covered in blood zipped toward her, humming with a pent-up impatience that made his frame taut and his eyes something just short of wild. Another restless stranger whirled her way, his shirt also stained crimson. He zeroed in on her with narrowed eyes, his handsome face sharp with demand. Their intent stares made her nerves jangle. She bowed her head without knowing why.

"Yes?" the one with the beard barked as if he wanted to shove past her and stalk through the door.

"Do you have news?" asked the clean-shaven man. He had an accent of some sort. Irish? Hard to tell when he sounded frantic.

How did they know Ms. Kendall? Given all the blood, maybe they'd rescued her. Were they Dr. Beckman's friends?

"Ms. Kendall doesn't have any major injuries. She's alert and talking. Dr. Beckman has been with her since she arrived. He's personally ensuring she's comfortable."

The Irishman let out a huge sigh of relief. "Our girl is okay?"

Their girl? Heavenly frowned. Were they her…brothers? They didn't look a thing alike, but she had no idea how else to interpret his question.

Heavenly nodded. "She'll be fine."

"When can we see her?" the first one demanded.

"Neither of you are family?"

"Technically, no. But…"

So they weren't her brothers.

The one with the beard gritted his teeth and sent the Irishman another frustrated stare. "Why hasn't one of us married her yet? That would have solved this."

They definitely weren't Ms. Kendall's brothers. Dare she hope one was the woman's boyfriend?

"That's a good idea," the other answered with a considering note in his voice and a wry stare. "We should do that. Are we going to arm-wrestle for it?"

They were kidding, right?

"Maybe you should flip a coin." A tall, blond god horned in between the two men, staring at her as if he'd like to eat her whole. She almost took a step back when he stuck his hand in her direction. "I'm Seth Cooper."

She slid her fingers against his palm. A furious blush and a wave of shyness overcame her. Gosh, was he ever gorgeous… "I'm Heavenly. Are you the patient's family?"

"Just a friend," Seth assured.

"She has no one else. We're like her family." The man on the left stroked his beard as if he had restless energy to burn.

"But you're not actually related or married?" Keeping family apart when they could comfort a patient was unconscionable. On the other hand, she couldn't violate hospital policy.

"One of us will marry her in the next ten minutes if we'll be allowed to see her." The Irishman's growl teemed with frustration. "Hell, we both would if it was legal."

Both of them? Heavenly had never heard of such a thing. Even more shocking, the growling man nodded as if he completely agreed. Were they...both Raine's boyfriends? Did that mean Dr. Beckman wasn't?

It didn't matter. Rumor was, he refused to date colleagues. She didn't have time for men, anyway.

Heavenly sent them an apologetic grimace. "I'm sorry. I don't make the rules."

The bearded man elbowed Seth out of his way. "What else can you tell us about Raine's condition?"

She shook her head regretfully. "I'm just a nursing student. I've only been in to give her ice chips and blankets."

"Do you know how much longer before we'll be able to see her?" The Irishman was hanging on to his temper by a thread.

"The police haven't finished with her, so I suspect it will be a while. In the meantime, Dr. Beckman asked me to escort you to a nearby lounge. You'll be able to shower there. Just let me know when you're ready."

The two men exchanged a glance, seemingly in instant agreement.

"Let's do it now," said the one on the left. "In case we're able to see her sooner, rather than later."

The Irishman nodded.

"Follow me." She used her badge to open the door to the secure area of the ER.

The two men followed her, each carrying a bag of clothes.

Before the door shut behind them, Seth called out to her, "Thank you, Heavenly."

She turned to him and smiled. He was almost too handsome to look at.

She'd never been attracted to a man until recently. Now she felt a pull to two? Were her long-dormant hormones suddenly awakening?

"You're welcome." Once Ms. Kendall left the ER, it was highly unlikely she would ever see Seth Cooper again. The fact that he tongue-tied her was no reason to be rude. "It was nice to meet you."

Then the door shut behind her, and she showed Mr. Hammerman and Mr. O'Neill where they could shower. They thanked her and disappeared to clean up while she checked another patient. Afterward, she swung by the nurses' station. Jennifer, the charge nurse, sent her to the waiting room again to pick up food someone had brought for the men.

Would she catch another glimpse of Seth? As she hustled down the hall, that idea made giddiness coil in her tummy. She'd never really flirted, but he seemed the sort who would let her—if she ever worked up the nerve.

Heavenly gave the door a gentle push. Seth rose to greet her, carrying two Styrofoam containers on a cafeteria tray.

A mere glance at him turned her palms damp and hot. The weight of his stare tempted her to look at him. She did and...oh, gosh. He made her dizzy. If she wasn't careful, it would be all too easy to trip on her own two feet and wind up in a heap on the floor.

"Hi. Is that for Mr. Hammerman and Mr. O'Neill?"

Seth cleared his throat, and even that sounded sexy. "Yeah, eggs and toast. They haven't eaten in hours, and they're going to need their strength today."

Good-looking and thoughtful. She took the tray from his grasp, intending to assure him the men would receive the food right away. But her stare lingered in places it shouldn't. He was so tall and he had strong legs and narrow hips encased in faded denim. And behind his zipper—

He was...erect. Oh, goodness. She gulped.

Was he having an involuntary male response? Or did he find her attractive?

Heat flashed up from her chest, straight to her cheeks. Her face was on fire—and getting hotter the longer she stared *there*.

Heavenly blinked. "Um, yes. I-I will. Of course. Right away."

On the verge of panting with both mortification and thrill, she turned and dashed to the electronic door, balancing the tray in one hand and reaching for the handle with the other. She nearly collided with the solid wood instead, only managing to jerk it open with trembling fingers through sheer will.

Oh, could she get any more ridiculous? For Pete's sake, she was twenty-two, not twelve.

Unfortunately, nearly a decade ago was the last time she'd had a "boyfriend," who hadn't even kissed her before he'd broken up with her. Seth Cooper obviously saw no reason to be self-conscious about his body. Then again, why should he?

He probably had lots of sex with beautiful women…and he must think she was a skittish, tongue-tied dork. He couldn't possibly be interested in her, and she shouldn't read too much into his reaction.

"Hey," he called to her. "Are you—"

Inept? Stupid? Klutzy? Heavenly didn't stay to hear the rest of his question. She let the door slam between them and ran.

SETH PACED THE ER waiting room, his gut in knots. It smelled faintly like puke, rubbing alcohol, and desperation. The news on the nearby television blared bullshit. He tuned it out, but the dude in the corner peering over a magazine who'd been watching their every move put him on edge. So did the waiting. Hammer and Liam had disappeared with the angelic blonde who'd given him a raging hard-on ten minutes ago, and he'd hung back to give his buddies alone time with Raine. Now he wished he'd followed. He could best help everyone by talking to Raine and dissecting CSI's preliminary findings. With his experience, he could break down the evidence and determine what, if any, legal trouble she might be facing.

He couldn't do squat trapped out here.

Whipping his phone from his pocket, he found Beck's contact info. He didn't know the guy well since they'd just met last week, but the doctor seemed okay.

Quickly, he tapped out a text. A little help? Stuck in waiting room.

Not two minutes later, Beck appeared and waved him inside.

"How's Raine?" Seth asked, following the other guy down halls crowded by medical carts and gurneys.

"She'll recover physically in a week to ten days."

But the doctor's bleak tone said his concern had nothing to do with her visible injuries. Seth understood. Raine was a strong woman, but she'd endured enough today to break even the heartiest soul.

Worry gnawed at him as he clapped eyes on Raine. She lay beaten and bruised, swollen and sporting fresh stitches, which didn't stop her from trying to smile in welcome. There was a trace of the fighter he knew. Seth shuttled his urge to kill Bill Kendall all over again. Liam and Hammer, watching over their girl with guilt wracking their faces, obviously felt the same.

Soft footsteps sounded behind him, and Seth craned around to find Heavenly carrying in a cup of ice chips. Hunger burned through his veins again. Though he liked women a bit older and more experienced, Heavenly made his heart rev full throttle. Parts south stood and saluted her again. He'd bet the attraction was mutual, and if she walked her gaze below his belt buckle once more, he'd be happy to whisper that every hard inch was for her...

"Well, hello again." He grinned her way.

"Hi." Her stare met his...but didn't stray below his waist.

She might not be looking—or touching—where he ached. Yet. But the day was young, and he'd be here for hours. He could work fast. He had skills. And if he could get his tongue on her...

Until then, he'd fantasize about sinking his fingers into the pale mass of the angel's hair and wrecking her elaborate braid as he aligned her pretty pink mouth under his. When she was breathless, he'd claim her lips. Of course, she'd melt against him, allowing him to slide his palms over her skin and prove she was as velvety as she looked.

Every hot-blooded, masculine cell in his body shouted *hell yes*.

In the hospital bed, Raine shifted and moaned. Shit, the woman had fought for her life this morning. He shouldn't be thinking about what was going on behind his zipper. He'd come from New York to help Liam with Raine. His sex life would wait.

Cup outstretched, Heavenly approached Raine on his right, then she sent a questioning glance Beck's way. Asking him for permission?

Granted, she sought to help a patient and Beck was the medical expert, but Seth didn't like her submitting in any way to the sadist.

Did she, outside the hospital? He would have sworn Heavenly had good girl written all over her…but he sensed something between those two.

The idea of this sweet thing bending to Beck's will and begging for his pain made Seth surly. Ridiculous since he'd met this woman ten minutes ago, and they'd exchanged a handful of words. She didn't mean anything. Hell, none of the girls he banged did. And he'd *never* want Beck's leftovers. But neither logic nor the mental caution tape stopped the instant flare of Seth's primal instincts.

When Beck nodded his approval, Heavenly set the plastic cup on the nearby tray and smiled at her patient.

"Thanks," Raine murmured.

"You're welcome. Do you need anything else?"

"I'm good for now."

Heavenly gave her hand a compassionate squeeze. "If you change your mind or want an ear, I'm here all day."

The angel had a kind streak. Most people he dealt with were criminals, cheaters, and dregs out for themselves. She was part of the good still left in this world. That made him not only want her but like her more.

When Heavenly hurried past him, an indefinable feminine scent wafted in her wake. She shifted a quick glance his way before scurrying toward the door.

She was leaving? Hell no. He might not have another opportunity to proposition her. And he wasn't giving up until he got his hands—and mouth—on her. After all, that sweet face and banging body desperately needed corrupting. He'd do a damn good job of it, too—even better if he could get a bead on her.

As a cop, then a PI, he could usually size people up in two minutes. But so far, Heavenly didn't fit into any of his neat mental categories. She'd yielded to Beck like a natural submissive, but this girl had fortitude he could feel. Seth wanted to strip her down, learn her. The instinct jolted him as if he'd shoved his tongue into a light socket.

What the hell? He'd done the relationship thing once—a lifetime ago. Now he stuck to flings, club sex, and one-night stands, giving zero fucks about anything except mutual pleasure.

Why should Heavenly be different?

Before she could leave, Beck cupped her elbow, staying her. Fury burst inside Seth at the sight of another man's hands on her.

Now he was *jealous*? What the fuck… Heavenly hardly belonged to him, and he'd bonded with the fair but firm Dom last week when Liam and Hammer had asked them to give a confused Raine guidance. So why the urge to break every one of the sadistic surgeon's fingers?

"Thank you for your help," Beck praised her.

That tender voice had come from Dr. Sarcasm-and-Pain?

"My pleasure. I told you I enjoy helping others." Heavenly sent him a warm smile. "Do you believe me yet?"

Heavenly was *flirting* with Beck? Did she have any fucking idea who—and what—he was? She couldn't. Unless he was reading her totally wrong, she was the kind of submissive who would unravel for whispered commands, not the lash of a whip.

When Beck released her with a grin, Heavenly headed out of the room. Hungry for one last glance, Seth watched, fixated on the sway of her hips. God, the things he'd like to do to that ass…

Damn, he'd told himself to shelve thoughts of sex. Epic fail on that.

"Whatever you're thinking about her, don't," the doctor growled. "And stop staring."

"You were gawking at her," he challenged with a raised brow. "Is she your sub?"

Beck glanced around furiously, then glared his way. "Don't mention that shit here."

Seth understood. The power exchange and the workplace didn't mix well. "Fine. Is she?"

Beck's jaw clenched. "I look out for her welfare around here. I mentor her."

In other words, no. Seth smiled. His day was looking up…

"But obviously not in the sack, and you're dying to. Dream on, buddy."

Raine groaned. "Not you, too?"

"I didn't do a thing." *Yet.*

"Make sure you keep it that way," Beck snarled.

"Fuck you." Seth would have said more, but they shouldn't be pounding their chests when his friends needed him.

He eased next to the bed, pausing beside Liam, and caressed Raine's inky hair. "You doing okay, little one?"

"Yeah. Thanks for being here."

Before he could ask if she was up to answering questions, the ER doctor arrived and glanced at the overabundance of visitors with a censuring scowl.

Beck gestured toward the door. "Let's give them some privacy, Captain America."

Yeah, Beck was a doctor and had the authority to toss him out. But his attitude rubbed Seth wrong. He shelved his annoyance because Raine didn't need their shit. Instead, he followed the doctor out with a glare.

Beck seemed oblivious as he addressed the trio around the bed. "We'll be back shortly."

Hammer's nod was somewhere between grim and grateful. "Thank you, guys. For everything."

Seth filed into the hall. He'd come back later and question Raine. Until then, he'd get his hands on the preliminary police report.

Beck followed him, closing the door. "I meant what I said. Don't pursue Heavenly. She doesn't need a player with Vaseline on his fly."

"Vaseline? Why the hell would I do that?"

"You fuck so many chicks, I can't imagine how else you get your zipper down that fast."

Since he'd come to LA, people had told him the doctor could be an asshole. Until today, he'd never seen Beck's puckered, bleeding side. Now he understood.

"And you're a monk?" Seth scoffed.

When he opened his mouth to point out more reasons Beck wouldn't suit Heavenly, local cop and Shadows member Dean Gorman sent him a text. Got the prelim report. Still at the hospital? I'll drop it by.

Seth tapped out a quick reply. Thanks. See you soon.

"Gotta go. Fuck off," he tossed to Beck, then headed down the hall.

Twenty minutes later, Dean had come and gone. Sipping coffee,

Seth flipped through the report in the half-empty cafeteria. Only cursory information since the investigation was only hours old. No reason the scene could be interpreted as anything other than self-defense...so far. He'd see what the next iteration held.

Without a crime scene to decipher, his thoughts strayed to Heavenly. After barely half an hour without the angel, he felt an inexplicable desire that still rubbed him raw. Why should he want a woman so seemingly innocent? She wasn't built for a quick fuck, and he didn't do more. Beck might be all wrong for her...but Seth was, too. He would return to New York, to his life, his business, and his family. No way was he spending the rest of his time in LA fighting with Beck over a female the way Liam and Hammer had squabbled over Raine.

All perfectly logical reasons to back off. But his dick was vetoing his brain.

What a dumb fuck.

Resting his elbows on the table, he sighed and pinched the bridge of his nose.

"If you have a headache, cutting a lime in half and rubbing it across your forehead might help."

Seth snapped to attention at the sound of Heavenly's soft voice. He looked up to find her holding a paper cup and smiling.

"Really?" he drawled. "What other sage medical advice do you have?"

The light trill of her laughter roused every male part of him again. "I don't know about sage, but it's a remedy my grandmother used when I was little."

"Since I don't have a lime to make my headache go away, maybe you'll sit with me until I feel better?"

Heavenly hesitated, then slowly slid into the chair opposite him. He restrained a celebratory fist pump.

"What other cures did your grandmother have?"

"Quite a few, though none most doctors would approve of. For instance, if you're having a coughing spell, take a washcloth and dip it in icy water..."

As she explained, he drank in Heavenly's guileless appeal. He cataloged her smile, the halo of her hair, her lightly flushed cheeks, the fidgeting clasp of her hands. He made her nervous, huh? Seth grinned and filed away that handy tidbit as he listened and let himself be charmed.

"And as unbelievable as it sounds, that helps, too." Heavenly smiled ruefully. "I probably shouldn't tout the natural remedies since I'm studying to be a nurse, but sometimes the old ways work."

"Sounds like you have a few tricks up your sleeve."

"I like to think so."

I have some, too.

He bent and ducked his head, forcing her to meet his gaze. The connection hit him like a gut punch.

She blinked his way. For an instant, the windows to her soul opened wide. He could almost taste her uncertainty, her tentative thrill. He saw it in the thready, thumping pulse at her neck. Every artless, delicious detail about her utterly reinforced his urge to drag her beneath him.

And instinct told him he'd better be fast. Beck might be reluctant to do more than lick his chops while eyeing the tempting morsel—something Seth found fucking hilarious—but the big Dom wouldn't wait long.

Before he could roll out a smooth line, Heavenly pushed her chair away from the table. "I should get back to work."

Without thinking, he stood and grabbed her hand. Desire zapped him, sending him reeling.

Holy shit. How much stronger would the sensation be when he touched her everywhere?

"Hey," he crooned. "I'm just making conversation. No need to be nervous."

"O-of course. I…um, just don't want to be late. The patients might need me and I'd like to be there for Raine. Excuse me."

He needed to say something—and speak her language. "Thanks for all you've done to help her. She needs the kindness you've shown her. I know Hammer and Liam appreciate your effort. I certainly do."

That made a little smile flit across her face. "It really is my pleasure. I can't wrap my head around what she's been through. It's none of my business, but her own father doing such terrible—"

"He was an abusive alcoholic who'd terrorized Raine for years. No one should have to endure what she has, but I'm glad she'll finally be able to live in peace."

"She seems very sweet." Heavenly cleared her throat and eased her hand from his grip. "You all appear to be very close. Have you been friends a long time?"

"With Liam and Hammer, yes. They're some of my oldest and dearest friends. I only met Raine a week ago, but she's a great girl who's perfect for my buddies."

The curiosity playing across Heavenly's face said she wanted to know more about their unconventional relationship...but was too polite to ask. "So...how do you know Dr. Beckman?"

Fuck me. Was she chatting with him to grill him for information about Dr. Dipshit?

"He's been a friend of Hammer's for years. They, um...have some common interests." If that's what one called restraining and whipping subs.

"Oh. Like golf?"

"Not exactly." And it was time to change the subject. "I'm guessing Raine will be staying here overnight?"

Heavenly nodded. "I peeked at her chart. I think they're worried about infection setting in, and since she's pregnant, they'll—"

"What?" Without thinking, he tucked a finger under her chin and lifted it. "Raine is pregnant?"

Apology tightened her face as she slipped free. "I-I thought every-one knew. I shouldn't have said anything. I'm so sorry."

"Don't be. Your secret is safe with me. Besides, Liam and Hammer will be thrilled." If they could process that motherfucking bombshell after everything else that had happened today. "I only mentioned Raine staying overnight because I planned to visit her tomorrow. Would you have time to have coffee with me on your break?"

She gave him a furtive shake of her head. "I've got to study for finals. But it was nice to meet you, Mr. Cooper."

When she would have passed him, he sidestepped, blocking her path. "Call me Seth. How about after your tests?"

Heavenly pressed her lips together before she gave him another negative jerk of her head. "I shouldn't. Good-bye."

And then she was scurrying across the clinical white tile toward an employee-only area as if her very fine ass were on fire.

A smart man would accept her refusal. But Seth already knew he wasn't remotely intelligent when it came to that woman. Nope. He was already making plans to regroup and try again, because giving up on Heavenly Young simply wasn't an option.

CHAPTER FOUR

THE FOLLOWING DAY was Friday, and all the crazies flooded the ER. It wasn't even a full moon, but she'd already seen a near-fatal drug overdose, a weekend warrior who'd done stupid things with a nail gun, two car accidents, an expectant mom in labor, and a party girl who'd been mugged while walking home from a rave. It was barely noon, and Heavenly was already exhausted.

As she passed the nurses' station, Jennifer stopped her. "Hey, you've got a visitor in the lobby."

Who? Her father couldn't make his way here without help. She didn't know her neighbors and hadn't made any friends, except maybe Dr. Beckman. But if he wanted to see her, he'd simply come to the unit.

"You're sure?"

"He asked for you by name."

Bemused, Heavenly headed to the lobby. Maybe a former patient had come. It was possible, but she really hoped—

Yes, there he was. *Seth.* She couldn't stop thinking about the man. He blinded her with his handsomeness, tongue-tied her with his charm, and overheated her with his smoldering stare.

"Hi." She tried to be professional, smile like a normal person. After all, he was just a man, and she'd known those all her life.

But none affected her the way Seth did. Well, except Dr. Beckman, but he merely helped her when she didn't understand something medical. Seth seemed determined to flirt.

"Hey, angel."

That grin of his was powered by megawatts of charisma. His low voice rumbled the growled endearment, exciting all her distinctly female parts. She resisted the urge to sigh at him like a girl over her favorite teen idol.

"Hi."

You already said that, dummy.

He grinned even wider. Gosh, he must be used to females bumbling and throwing themselves at him. What woman wouldn't turn into a puddle at the sight of him? Piercing green eyes, chiseled jaw, hard, wide shoulders... A dreamy sigh escaped her lips.

Get it together, girl. "Are you hoping to see Raine before they discharge her?"

"Actually, I came to bring you something." He turned and lifted a cellophane-wrapped basket from the chair beside him. "You said you were busy studying, so I thought I'd help in whatever small way I can."

He'd brought her a gift? Yes, and it wasn't small at all.

Heavenly took it, spotting so many thrilling goodies through the clear wrap she almost squealed. "This is for me?"

"Of course. You've helped Raine so much, I wanted to spoil you."

"I, um... Wow." She sank into the nearest chair. Tears stung her eyes. Blinking wasn't making them go away. He'd done something thoughtful, and she was blubbering? "Thank you. You didn't have to get me anything."

He sat beside her. "I wanted to. Open it."

Excitement bubbled up. What a thrill!

Heavenly plucked at the bow and tore away the cellophane. Chocolates spilled into her hands and made her mouth water. A few cans of Red Bull and some Emergen-C lined the front rim. Behind that, she saw ibuprofen, lip balm, and hand sanitizer. Oh, pens, pencils, and notebooks to make studying easier, which she needed and could never afford.

After she pulled those out, she found flavored coffee—an indulgence she never had funds for—and a coffee mug that read: THE MOTTO OF EVERY NURSING STUDENT—SORRY. CAN'T. GOTTA STUDY. She laughed, even as more tears gathered. Rolled up inside was a white T-shirt with a big red heart bisected by an EKG line. Above, it read: CUTE ENOUGH TO STOP YOUR HEART. Under the drawing were the words: SKILLED ENOUGH TO RESTART IT.

Heavenly gave Seth a sniffling smile as she met his gaze, then dug deeper. *Wine!* She squealed. She'd always wanted to try it, and he had seemingly read her mind.

Buried at the back was a purple clipboard with a built-in calculator she'd eyed for months.

"Oh, my goodness. Thank you! It's...everything. No one has given me a gift since high school graduation. But this is..."

When she blinked Seth's way, shock and horror crossed his face. The expression punched her in the chest. She knew that look. She'd seen it on others in Wisconsin after she and her dad had been forced to sell their farm and move to a cramped apartment.

Pity.

The gift that had made her feel so special now made her feel like a charity case.

Heavenly jerked her stare to the floor, her face burning with humiliation. She'd hoped that maybe he like-liked her. But no. He felt sorry for her. Gosh, that hurt.

She gathered the contents of the basket and pasted on the brightest smile she could manage. "This was very thoughtful. I appreciate it."

When Heavenly stood to escape, he gently pulled her closer. "Tell me what upset you. I only wanted to make you happy, angel."

"It's not you."

"I don't know what you're thinking, but I wanted to give you something because you've been on my mind."

Heavenly bit her lip. Of course he was going to say nice things. So had the people who'd knocked on their door last Christmas to give them a holiday dinner because they'd guessed she and Dad didn't have the money for a turkey and the trimmings. The gesture had been both welcome and crushing.

"I know you put a lot of thought into this basket. I appreciate each and every one of these items. Really."

Seth frowned, staring at her as if she was a puzzle he was determined to solve. Ugh, why wasn't she better at hiding her reactions? The last thing she wanted to do was guilt him. "Thank you so much."

He took her hand in his. "Look, we met under stressful circumstances. I'm sorry if I came on strong. You've been on my mind, and I want to get to know you. I'm new in town and—"

"Me, too." They had that in common. Maybe he hadn't meant the gift purely as charity, but a friendly offering. "I've only been here since August."

He gave her a wry grin, his dreamy eyes glinting with…mischief? Flirtation? "I've been here a week. My friends could use some time alone after what's happened and…I'd like to take you out to dinner."

So he likes me? Oh, his offer was so tempting. She wanted to spend time with Seth, flirt with him. Have a real first date with him.

But school, her father, and responsibility came first.

"I'd love to, but I volunteer during the day, then I take my lectures and study during the evenings."

"What about weekends? Can you spare time for breakfast? What about lunch on your day off? We can explore the city together. C'mon. I won't bite…unless you beg me to."

His coaxing made her feel warm and happy. Of course, her father would tell her to go out, be young, enjoy herself. But who would cook for him? Make sure he took his medicine? Help him to bed?

"C-can I check my schedule and let you know?" Maybe one of the VA volunteers would help.

If Seth did pity her, the last thing she wanted was to tell him her father's medical woes. Besides, was it so wrong to pretend for a few hours that she had a normal life?

"Absolutely. When you get free, call me. Here's my card." He dug into his pocket and handed her one. "I'm looking forward to spending time with you."

She glanced at it. The office address was in Manhattan. His title proclaimed him a private investigator and personal security specialist. Like a bodyguard? Wow.

"Have you dealt with dangerous people?"

His smile said he absolutely had. "Before I hung out my PI shingle, I used to be a cop for the NYPD."

She'd already noticed he could be watchful. But now she understood the barely leashed something mysterious under his surface.

"That sounds dangerous." And exciting. He'd seen things. *Lived* them.

"Sometimes. And sometimes, it really was a lot of driving around while drinking coffee at three in the morning to stay warm and awake."

"Why did you decide to become a PI?"

The playful smile slid off his face. "I like being my own boss."

That wasn't the reason he'd left the force. She'd dodged enough questions over the years to recognize the behavior. He didn't want to talk about it, and she wouldn't pry. Heavenly couldn't mind if he kept secrets when she had plenty of her own.

"I don't blame you. That sounds really appealing."

Especially now. Heavenly was sick of Kathryn, Marcella, and the other nurses treating her like a lower life-form. Granted, she was merely a volunteer now, but she was making straight As. It wouldn't be long before she'd be their equal—but better.

Until then, she'd handle the situation. Just like she'd done with persistent Dr. Manning...

"Is working here tough?" Seth asked.

"Mostly good, but there are challenging moments."

"Challenging, huh? I guess that means you work with Beck a lot."

"You mean Dr. Beckman?"

He nodded. "His friends call him Beck. I figured you knew that."

Heavenly shook her head, sad that he hadn't asked her to use his nickname. It fit him. Sharp. Strong. Straightforward. "No. I actually don't work with him much. I run into him a lot, and he's graciously agreed to help with some of the complicated material in my classes. But other than Raine, we haven't worked on the same patient."

"Probably for the best."

What an odd thing for one friend to say about another. "I've heard he can be demanding."

Her words amused the heck out of Seth. "That would be an understatement."

Did he think she couldn't handle it? "I'll be a good nurse. I could work for him."

"Oh, angel..." He shook his head. "I believe that. You'll be one of the best, I have no doubt."

But he still didn't think she should work for Dr. Beckman?

"Heavenly?" Jennifer called, sticking her head out the ER door. "You wanted to know when Raine Kendall was leaving. She should be gone in the next thirty minutes."

"Then I guess I'd better go," she murmured to Seth. "Did you want to say good-bye to her?"

"Actually, I'll see her back at their house."

Of course. Because they were friends.

Heavenly suspected Raine lived with Mr. Hammerman *and* Mr. O'Neill, because they both seemed comfortable with the fact they doted on her equally. Heavenly wasn't judging, just envious. What would it be like to have people she could count on so she didn't have to endure life's hardships alone?

"All right, then…" Heavenly stood and grabbed her basket. "Well, I've got your card."

"And you'll call me when you're free?"

She nodded. "I'll do my best."

Heavenly itched to go out with him at least once. Would it be so wrong to steal a few moments for some fun?

"I'll probably be in town for another week or two." He shrugged. "Maybe more. Let me know."

Carrying the basket he'd given her, she smiled at Seth over her shoulder, unable to take her eyes off him as she headed toward Jennifer and the open door. Except she nearly walked into it because the charge nurse had already gone.

Seth laughed. "Watch where you're going, angel."

Fighting a furious blush, she whipped her badge over the scanner, then scurried inside the secure area. How embarrassing. Was she destined to make an idiot out of herself every time she saw this man?

Shaking her head, she hustled beyond the ER and into Raine's room. There, she found Mr. Hammerman and Mr. O'Neill—she still didn't know one from the other—flanking Raine. Dr. Beckman stood nearby. The bruise surrounding Raine's eye had darkened and spread. The swelling on her lip had worsened. The finger-shaped marks around her neck were stark and unmistakable.

Just looking at the injuries Raine's father had inflicted pained Heavenly. Every day with Abel Young was hard. His illness kept progressing in new and frightening ways. But he'd never raised a hand to her in anger. He'd never even spoken a harsh word.

"Liam and I will fetch the car so we can take you home, precious," said the man with the beard.

"Thanks. I'm so ready to leave."

"I know you are," said the Irishman. "I promise, we'll take care of you this time, love."

"Liam, Hammer…" Consternation crossed her face. "You didn't

not take care of me yesterday. None of this was your fault."

Heavenly wasn't sure what Raine meant, but both men fell silent. The weight of their guilt was telling.

Beck filled the void with a hearty clap on the bearded guy's back. "Go on, Hammer. Get the car. I'll deliver the princess to the entrance. You've got her discharge papers. Call me if you have any questions." Then he turned to the Irishman. "Keep him in line, O'Neill."

"God knows he needs it," Raine drawled.

Everyone gave a stiff laugh, and the forced cheer tightened Heavenly's chest. These people wanted life to be all right again, but they knew the true blunt force of Raine's trauma had yet to really hit them.

With a nod, Mr. Hammerman turned toward the door. Mr. O'Neill was on his heels.

Raine caught sight of her. "Heavenly. Hi!"

"Hi," she murmured as all three men turned and stared. The rest of her greeting fell silent under the combined weight of their stares.

Mr. Hammerman and Mr. O'Neill murmured a thanks for Raine's care, then sidestepped to the exit.

Dr. Beckman frowned at the basket in her hands. "What's that?"

"Seth brought it to me as a thank you for helping Raine."

Something cynical crossed his face. "Of course he did."

Then he muttered something else under his breath she would have sworn was a four-letter word.

Raine clearly heard and repressed a smile. "He's a smart guy."

"That's enough out of you, princess. I'll see you tonight."

Heavenly was trying to figure out the undercurrent in their conversation when the doctor nodded her way. "Ms. Young."

Then he was gone. What had just happened?

Raine burst into laughter. It was stunted since she couldn't move her eyes and it must hurt to put pressure on her stitches. But the expression still transformed the woman.

"Oh, his face was priceless." Mirth danced in Raine's eyes. "What have you done to him?"

Heavenly blinked. "Nothing?"

Raine cocked her head. "Uh-huh. How long have you known Beck?"

Clearly not as long as Raine. "Not quite two weeks. You two seem close."

"He and Hammer have been friends for years, and he's known me since I was a kid. Beck is a good guy. He was my rock during a difficult time recently."

But he wasn't her lover? Heavenly was relieved. Not that it actually mattered. Dr. Beckman had only shown professional interest in her.

She set the basket on a nearby tray and sank into the chair beside Raine. "I'm happy you have such wonderful people in your life. You're very lucky, both to be alive and to have men who adore you."

"I know." Raine paused. "Thank you for taking care of me. And not judging me for loving Liam and Hammer."

"It's not my place."

"Not everyone here has been as understanding."

Raine probably meant Kathryn. The nurse specialist disliked any other woman who snagged an attractive man's attention. She would especially sniff her delicate nose at one who had two hot, successful-looking men seemingly wrapped around her finger.

Heavenly took Raine's hand in a tentative hold. "Life isn't always easy. If you're happy, what other people think shouldn't matter."

The black-haired beauty gave the brightest smile she could muster. "You're right. So...what do you think of Beck? He's very single."

Heavenly blinked. Raine was...matchmaking?

He's gorgeous, he's smart, and he makes me hot all over. "He's been very kind."

"Really?" Raine sounded surprised. "Has he asked you out?"

"No." And Heavenly wished he would. "We just work together."

"Right..." Raine sounded as if she didn't believe a word. "And what about Seth?"

Heavenly couldn't stop herself from blushing. "He's very thoughtful. And flirty."

Raine's smile widened. "I *know* he asked you out."

How did she know that? Was Raine trying to pair her with Dr. Beckman or Seth? Or...both? Surely she didn't imagine everyone would be able to balance her sort of unconventional relationship. Heck, Heavenly didn't have the time—or experience—to juggle one man, much less two.

She neither confirmed nor denied Raine's question. "He and the doctor don't seem to like each other much."

Raine reared back in surprise. "Hmm, I've never seen them not get along. But now that you mention it, Beck didn't seem thrilled Seth had given you that basket. And I take it Seth has said or done something that makes you think he doesn't like Beck?"

"A few minutes ago," she blurted, then bit her tongue. She wasn't a tattletale or a gossip. "Maybe they're just having a bad day. I shouldn't say anything. They've both been very nice."

"Nice? Oh, my god…" Raine shook her head as if she found that reply somewhere between interesting and comical. "If I wanted to see you again when I'm feeling better—you know, to say thank you for your kindness—how could I get in touch with you?"

Heavenly hesitated. Not only had she not dated during her teen years, she'd missed out on friendships. After she and her father had left the farm, she'd lost touch with the girls she'd been close to as a child. Making new friends in a new city had been intimidating. But here Raine was, offering her a bit of girl time.

Impulsively, Heavenly jotted her number down on a scrap of paper. "Here you go. I'm slammed most weekdays, but I can try to slip free on a weekend or something."

Before Raine could reply, Dr. Beckman appeared in the doorway again with a fifty-something nurse pushing a wheelchair. "Time to go, princess. Before Liam and Hammer tear apart the entrance waiting for you."

The other woman nodded, looking not just relieved to be leaving here but truly happy. She turned to Heavenly, scrap of paper in her hand. "I'll call you."

The doctor glanced between the two of them. Then his eyes narrowed. "Raine…"

She didn't seem put off by the warning in his voice at all. In fact, she stuck her tongue out at him. "See you later, Beck!"

With that, the older nurse rolled Raine away. Then Dr. Beckman turned all his scrutiny on her. His stare made her heart flutter.

She grabbed her basket of goodies and skittered past him. "Excuse me, Doctor."

AFTER A SUCCESSFUL valve replacement the following Tuesday, Beck strode into the hospital cafeteria for a drive-by at the sandwich counter. Before he could grab and go, he felt a familiar prickle at the back of his neck. Kathryn was eyeing him. Again. In fact, most of her desperate posse would jump him if he stood still long enough. He kept walking, refusing to acknowledge them.

"Dr. Beckman," Nurse Hitch called.

He gave Kathryn a vague, non-encouraging wave. She sent him a come-hither stare, crooking her finger at him. Beside her sat Marcella, who had slipped her phone number into his shirt pocket just last week while squeezing his biceps and giggling.

Beck rolled his eyes. These two needed to get their man-eating vaginas under control.

Jennifer, seated next to Marcella, had never seemed interested in anything except good patient care. He wished she'd teach the others to be professional.

"Join us, Doctor." Kathryn inched to the edge of her chair, wriggling like she was having an X-rated fantasy. "It's crowded, but you can share my seat."

"Or mine," Marcella piped up with suddenly visible cleavage. "It'll be cozy."

Or disease laden. A number of men had occupied their "seats," according to hospital gossip.

"No, thanks." If administrators, visitors, and fellow staff weren't watching, he'd tell them exactly where they could go. "Too busy."

He turned away, gauging the number of steps between his sandwich and the exit. Then he spotted Heavenly sitting alone at the back of the room, staring into a paper cup.

Why was she in a corner by herself?

After grabbing a plastic container with a turkey on rye, he paid and headed in her direction.

The closer he drew, the more his heart skipped and his palms grew sweaty. He was a grown man, for shit's sake. A surgeon. A sadist. Not some sappy boy who mooned over a girl. Yet every time he clapped eyes on Heavenly, that's how he felt. Even now, his blood pumped as if he were doing a hard-core workout. What he'd really like to work out was a dozen ear-piercing screams from this woman who had yet to notice him as a man.

Beck headed toward her, searching for something witty to say. As he weaved past a couple of tables, Dr. Richard Manning, a.k.a. Manning-the-Manwhore, plopped his tall frame in the chair directly across from Heavenly and leaned close.

If you touch her, you'll die a slow, painful death.

Heavenly blinked at the plastic surgeon. Beck tensed. She wasn't actually attracted to that soul-sucking pustule, was she?

He didn't know, and that pissed him off. Manning-the-Manwhore had plowed through most of the nursing and administrative staff. He'd definitely planted himself in Kathryn's "seat" more than once. Marcella's, too. The fact that he didn't look like a troll and was smoother than an oil slick made it easy for him to lure women to the nearest flat surface.

Now he had Heavenly in his sights.

Gnashing his teeth, Beck quickened his steps and ate up the distance between them.

"...It's the hottest new restaurant in the city. The view is amazing. The food is to die for. And you've never been?"

She shook her head. "I only moved here a few months ago."

"Ah." Manning smiled, pretending to give a shit. "Well, you'll have to let me take you to dinner there as a welcome to the city. The ambiance is almost as stunning as you. Let's go Friday night. I'll pick you up around seven."

Beck wanted to throttle the asshole, especially when Heavenly lowered her lashes and pink climbed up her cheeks. Was she actually buying this sack of shit's polished lines?

"Well, I—"

"Heavenly, don't disappoint me again. We'll have a good time. I'll open doors for you..."

Beck nearly crushed the sandwich container in his grip. It was either that or bash the bastard's head in.

Instead, he stepped up behind her and tossed his sandwich on the table between them. When she gave a startled jump, he cupped her shoulders and positioned himself in Manwhore's line of sight. "Hey, Manning. I don't usually see you in the cafeteria. Oh, but you're here because you're trying to sweet-talk Ms. Young into bed. Don't you think it's a little soon after the last nursing student you banged? I heard you gave her the clap."

Heavenly gave a startled gasp.

Manwhore smiled acidly. "You're a better surgeon than a comedian, Beckman." He tossed Heavenly a placating stare. "He's joking, of course. And doing it very badly."

Heavenly stiffened. Beck had no idea what she was thinking. Hell, he might be overstepping boundaries, but unless she told him to fuck off, he wasn't backing down.

"Actually, I'm not joking at all," Beck said. "Since Ms. Young has already turned you down, you should leave her alone. But hey, I'll bet Kathryn would do you in the janitor's closet again. Sounded like you two had fun. The whole floor thought so, anyway."

"Beckman!" Manning glared at him while maintaining a smile for Heavenly's sake. "Ms. Young doesn't appreciate your sophomoric humor. If you'd like to belittle our feminine co-workers and stoop to the maturity level of fart jokes, we can no longer be friends."

"Oh, we were never friends, tool." He maintained an affable smile, voice low. "I simply want Ms. Young to understand who's asking her out."

"She'll get to know me on our date. Now we're having a private conversation…"

"Were. It's over." Beck bent lower, barely shuttering the rage in his eyes. "If you're having trouble comprehending the word *no*, I'll spell it for you: N-O. It means she's not interested."

Manning stiffened. "If that's how she feels, she has a mouth. She can use it."

"Not on you. Maybe you should try thinking with the head up top for a change."

The other doctor leapt to his feet, chair scraping against the tile. "This is absurd, and I'm highly insulted."

"Stop harassing her, or I'll insult you more by slamming my fist in your face."

Manwhore's mouth opened and closed in silent shock. "Are you threatening me with violence? I'm sure the hospital administrator would love to hear about this…"

"*Now* I'm joking." He flashed Manning a smile that said one thing: *Not.*

"I can only think of one reason you'd tell Ms. Young these lies about me. You want her for yourself."

Well, aren't you perceptive, asswipe? Someone get the guy a prize…

For the last two weeks, Beck had masturbated to thoughts of Heavenly—all dimples and pigtails, big eyes and sweet pleas. What he wanted from her was probably far dirtier than anything Mr. Missionary-Position fantasized about. Sure, that made him a hypocrite. But he'd protect her from the skirt-chasing pricks of the world, even Seth, whom Beck had liked until the shitbag's eyes had glued themselves to Heavenly's ass.

"Don't you?" Manning goaded.

In her chair, Heavenly turned and studied him. Was she interested in his answer? The possibility made his dick stir and stretch.

"Of course you have nothing to say, Beckman," Manning challenged. "Because I'm right."

Beck scowled. "I'm just not dignifying your sexist bullshit with a reply. Try acting like an adult and a professional. Stop treating the workplace like a meat market and the nurses like pieces of ass."

Manning's eyes narrowed in silent threat. The dipshit wasn't scared, which was both stupid and regrettable. Beck had mad skills, honed over nearly two decades, at inflicting pain. God, he'd love to unleash those on the prick right now.

"You've got everything wrong. I provide guidance to the nurses." Manning puffed up. "I *help* them."

Yeah, out of their panties and onto their backs…

"If Heavenly needs help, she's got me. Don't speak to her, look at her, or even think about her. Or I'll tell HR *everything* about you."

And it was plenty.

Heavenly's lush mouth formed an *O* of shock. For a blinding moment, Beck itched to sink his fingers into her bun, cover her lips with his, and kiss her until she forgot every other man existed.

Manning pinned Beck with a deadly glare, then thrust his shoulders back with an infuriated huff at Heavenly. "I suggest you take your guard dog to the vet, Miss Young. He needs a rabies vaccination."

When the plastic surgeon whirled away, Beck couldn't resist an acidic parting shot. "Woof."

As soon as Manwhore had gone, silence fell.

With a sorry-not-sorry grimace, he slid into the chair across from her. "I didn't mean for that to get out of hand."

"Oh, my gosh. I'm so glad it did." Heavenly snickered. "That was funny, and I needed a laugh. Is everything you said about him true?"

"All of it."

"Really? He and Kathryn?"

Beck nodded. "Marcella, too."

"And the nursing student?"

"Oh, yeah. You're hardly the first he's offered to 'open doors' for."

She shuddered. "What a slime! I told him four…no, five times that I wasn't interested and I don't have time to date, but he just wouldn't get a clue."

Beck understood. Her excuse wasn't going to stop him, either. But dating? Hell, what did he know about that? With so many pain sluts willing to have no-strings sex, he'd never bothered.

"Manning isn't a very bright bulb," Beck drawled. "I'm not sure how he passed medical school."

"Maybe he got by on bluster and…" She bit her lip, as if she didn't want to say the obvious word.

"Bullshit?"

She flashed him a conspiratorial smile. "Exactly."

He laughed, fascinated by her beauty, her sweetness, her charm. Her everything.

Good god, where was his man card?

"Anyway, thanks for sticking your neck out," she murmured. "You're protective—of Raine, the underdog, even of me. It's really noble."

Beck almost choked. His friends would shit themselves laughing if they could hear her. "You're, um…welcome."

She propped her chin on her palm and sent him a speculative stare. "And yet…I have a feeling you can be a very bad man."

Heavenly was flirting? After saying she didn't date? Then again, everything about her was unpracticed. She probably wasn't even aware.

Oh, I would love to show you just how bad I can be, little girl.

"You might be right," he replied with a sly wink.

She stared at him from under dark lashes. "Should that scare me?"

"I'd never hurt you." *Unless you begged me to.*

Heavenly sighed. "I've never met a man like you."

"What do you mean?" *A kinky beast?*

"Interesting. Witty. Thoughtful."

"You left out charming, smart, and good-looking."

She laughed without an ounce of reserve. "That, too."

Beck mentally inventoried the smartass remarks in his repertoire, ready to roll more out to keep her smiling. "So where did you come from, Mars?"

"Ha! Actually, no. I'm from a tiny town in Wisconsin." He didn't miss the wistfulness that crossed her face. "Given the difference between LA and there? It might as well have been Mars."

"You're a long way from home, little girl."

"You keep calling me that. I'm not a child, you know."

"I didn't mean it as an insult. I'm just saying you're…"

Young.

Inexperienced.

Unjaded.

Everything he wasn't.

"Practically a baby and in over my head? I've heard that before." She shrugged. "Age is just a number."

She was wrong. That was a platitude the young spouted when they weren't too cynical to know better. But Beck liked her attitude. He couldn't wait to peel back that mysterious something about her that drew him and touch the woman underneath. Then he'd teach her about sex and pain and orgasm. About the feel of his hand on her lush backside. About the fit of his cock deep inside her pussy.

"If you say so," he drawled. "So, I've never been to Wisconsin. Tell me what it's like. I'm imagining a lot of snow and fields of cheese."

"The snow part is true enough, but cheese doesn't grow in fields, Dr. Beckman. And if you think I've been living on Mars, what planet does that make you from?"

He was thrilled she was already zinging one-liners back at him.

"Spoken like a true smart ass."

When she laughed, it lit him up. God, he had it bad for her.

"Well, damn. I was imagining a land of cheddar goodness. It's a shame. That actually sounds delicious." He winked, delighted when she laughed again. "The guys in Wisconsin must be nursing broken hearts and keeping themselves warm at night with memories of your kisses."

"Not hardly." The sparkle faded from her blue eyes. "Try never."

Never…what? Been kissed? Christ, was she completely untouched? "You're a virgin?"

Please say no. Please…

Heavenly merely bowed her head and blushed.

Definitely a virgin.

Holy fucking son of a bitch.

Beck didn't do virgins. That was another rule of his—and it was a hard one.

Time to shuttle his crushing disappointment and take a giant goddamn step back. He'd always suspected he was too old and too cynical for her. Now he knew it. If he unleashed his desire on Heavenly, he would utterly destroy the girl.

But damn it, she was the fresh breath of air he'd needed after choking forever. Where the hell would he find the strength to walk away? And how could he when she had a predator on her tail?

"I'm sorry for putting you on the spot," he finally murmured. "Don't be embarrassed. I'm a doctor, remember?"

"I know," she mumbled.

"Look at me." He spoke in the low, firm voice he used at the club.

As if unable to refuse him, she lifted her chin. His Dominant side leapt with joy. His cock swelled. And every other part of him wept.

"Your secret is safe with me. But I suspect I know why Manning won't take no for an answer. You still have my business card, right?" When Heavenly nodded, he went on without even thinking about the hours of self-torment ahead. "Good. Text me before you go to lunch in the future. I'll do my best to rearrange my patient load so you won't have to deal with Manning alone. Will you do that for me?"

"Do you really think he suspects that I'm a, you know…?"

"I'd rather be safe than sorry. Give me the power to protect you,

Heavenly."

She had no idea what those words meant in his world. If she did, she'd never agree.

"Of course."

Beck gripped the table. She'd turned herself over to him so quickly and perfectly. The hungry beast inside him wanted to gobble her up and savor every delicious morsel. He shoved it down.

"There you go, sticking your neck out for me again."

Because I'm a jealous prick. If I can't touch you, he won't, either.

"You're a good person. I'd be lucky to have a friend like you."

He'd be even luckier to have her as a lover.

Never. Ever. Stop dreaming...

"That's the sweetest thing anyone has said to me in a long time, Dr. Beckman. I think I'd be the lucky one."

"Well, I enjoy helping people." He tossed her own words back to her, forcing a wink.

She flashed him a watery smile that kicked him in the gut. "I feel better already, knowing I won't have to contend with Dr. Manning alone. Thank you." She shoved her water glass to the center of the table and eased her chair away. "I should get back to work."

"Wait." He slid his hand over hers. Just like every other time he'd touched her, that addictive hum razed up his arm, like the warm crawl of a morphine injection. He grasped for a reason—any reason—to prolong their conversation. The only thing he noticed was the lack of food on her table. No tray. No dirty dishes or silverware. "Have you eaten lunch already?"

"I'm not hungry. I've been grazing on the snack food at the nurses' station all morning. I just came down here to get off my feet."

Beck nodded, sliding a nonchalant stare to her threadbare shoes. These weren't the thick-soled kind most nurses donned to cushion the impact of walking and standing all day. He made a mental note to get her new shoes...and somehow convince her to wear them.

"Then stay for a minute and tell me why cheese doesn't grow in fields."

"You're so funny." She shook her head at him.

Without further prompting, Heavenly began explaining how cheese was made. Beck didn't tell her that he already knew. He got lost in the gentle lilt of her voice, even as he mourned the impossibility of ever being more than her friend and protector. He'd guard her from all the big, bad wolves, especially the biggest, baddest of them all—himself.

CHAPTER FIVE

ON FRIDAY, SETH felt his cell phone buzz. It wasn't his mother or his brother, Matt, who was looking after his business back home. He'd already talked to them this morning. He half expected a call from Liam, asking him to come cheer Raine up. The good news was, the LAPD had concluded—rightly so—that she'd acted in self-defense when she had killed her father. But now she was dealing with the residual trauma—anxiety, flashbacks, nightmares. She needed her men more than ever. Liam was her pillar, supportive and unbending. But Seth already saw cracks in Hammer's stoic facade. That worried him...but didn't surprise him much. Protectors took their failures hard. He ought to know.

Shaking off the thoughts, Seth scanned his display. An LA prefix. The number was unfamiliar.

"Hello?"

"Hi."

Heavenly.

The hair on his body prickled to attention. His dick, seemingly hardwired to react to her, thickened.

How was it possible she'd spoken one syllable, and he was already aching to fuck her?

"Good to hear from you, angel." He hadn't been sure the bright ray of sunshine would call.

"How did you know it's me?"

"You think I could forget your voice?"

"Um..."

Seth enjoyed rattling her, but he loved even more that she'd sought him out.

"So, I know it's short notice..." she began nervously.

He pounced. "Tell me you're free today."

"This afternoon."

Thank god. Now he could spend some time with her and figure out why the hell she fascinated him so much.

"Perfect. Any idea what you'd like to do?"

"Well, it's a beautiful day. What if we went to the park and soaked up some sun? I know one with a great walking path. Or we could sit and talk."

That would be great. He'd love it even more if he could have Heavenly sprawled naked under him, her peachy-porcelain skin shimmering in the sunlight. Imagining her spreading her thighs to reveal the blond down below dusting her swollen pussy was sweet mental torture that nearly had him groaning.

"What time?" he croaked out. "Give me your address. I'll come get you."

"I'm finishing a short shift at the hospital. If you want to swing by around twelve thirty, I'll meet you outside the visitors' entrance."

"See you then, angel."

"Bye."

Two hours before she put him out of his misery. He would have to think fast to toss together a memorable afternoon and pick her up on time. Heavenly might think they were simply hanging out, but as far as Seth was concerned, he was planning their first date. He intended to leave a lasting impression.

Whistling, he strutted across Shadows' parking lot and hopped into his rental, plans already forming. After stops at Williams-Sonoma and La Paloma Deli, he pulled up at the hospital as Heavenly stepped through the front entrance. The angel glowed under the vivid sunshine as if she had a halo…but her body was definitely made for sin.

Her dewy face was fresh and bare. A pink headband held back her hair, which cascaded in sunshiny waves around her breasts and flirted with the nip at her waist. He imagined wrapping his fists around it as he claimed her mouth and slid between her spread legs.

She ignored the people milling on the sidewalk and zeroed in on him. Their stares locked. Their connection slammed through him again. It didn't let up, even when she lowered her lashes in a demure sweep.

Damn, he wanted her surrender so badly he could taste it.

His stare wandered down her body. A sheer wrap the color of her blushing cheeks, trimmed in appliqués of little white daisies, hung loosely over her shoulders. When Heavenly smiled and raised her hand to wave, the lace hem of the white tank inched up, giving him a tantalizing peek of her bare midriff above a pair of denim shorts and strappy sandals.

God, she looked both sweetly adorable and fuckable.

All too soon, she lowered her arm, concealing the glimpse of skin. Without meaning to, she flirted. Teased. And hell, that kittenish expression, coupled with the hint of cleavage… Seth let out a groan. When every drop of blood in his body rushed south, he adjusted his fly.

It was going to be a long, hard afternoon.

She bypassed pedestrians, then stopped at the curb. A black sedan conveniently pulled away, and he steered his crappy midsize rental to take its spot.

As Seth hopped out of the car, Heavenly broke into a bashful grin. Her gentle bounce of excitement was contagious.

Fuck, why was he so into this woman he barely knew?

"I didn't keep you waiting, did I?" He wrapped her hand in both of his and smiled. He could look at her all fucking day.

"No. You're right on time."

"And you're absolutely stunning. I'm glad you called. I've been hoping to spend time with you."

On cue, a rosy blush stained her cheeks as she dropped her gaze to their joined hands. He crooked a finger beneath her chin and lifted her face. Her eyes were big and blue. Seth felt himself drowning.

"Don't be nervous, angel."

She sighed. "I hate that every emotion shows on my face."

"It's darling, like you."

Heavenly's lashes swept over her cheeks again. "How am I supposed to respond when you say things like that?"

"Smile and say 'thank you?'"

"All right." Her gaze bounced up to his, lips curling. "Thank you."

Everything about this girl reached between his legs and tugged hard. That didn't surprise him. But the way she managed to twist something in his chest did.

"You ready?" At her nod, he led her around his rental and tucked her inside. "Then let's go. I have a surprise."

Her smile brightened. "You didn't buy me another basket, did you?"

"Of a sort..."

"Seth!"

"This one's different," he promised as he pulled away from the curb. "We'll be sharing it."

"What do you mean?"

"Impatient?" He winked. "You'll have to wait and see."

Her brow furrowed. "I'm not sure I can handle two gifts in a week."

"It won't kill you. But if it does, I know this cute nurse volunteer..."

"Now you're just flirting." She sent him a chiding glance.

"Caught on to that, did you?"

"It was hard to miss." She pressed a melodramatic hand to her chest in jest. "And I'm not sure your intentions are honorable, Sir."

Oh, they're quite dishonorable, especially if you call me Sir again.

Seth grinned. "I'll get back to you on that."

She giggled.

Fifteen minutes later, they reached the park and scouted a spot beneath the shade of a huge oak tree. Heavenly spread out the checkered blanket he'd scrounged up, then she watched him set the wicker basket down before he settled beside her.

"A picnic? How exciting!" She lifted the lid and withdrew a bottle of wine, various cheeses, sliced meats nestled in wax paper, and warm, crusty bread. She oohed and aahed over small jars of olives, pickles, and other condiments. Last but not least, she plucked free two large slices of raspberry-almond tart. "Wow! There's enough food here to feed an army."

"I haven't been on a picnic in years, but when you called, I thought why not do it up right?"

"Where did you find such scrumptious goodies?"

"I have my talents. One of them is knowing where to find good grub." *Maybe you'd like me to introduce you to my other talents, too?*

He'd heard plenty over the years that he had a very talented tongue...

"Well, wherever you found lunch, it looks amazing. Should I dish us each a plate?"

The fact that she wanted to serve him should not make him harder, but... "Please."

He reclined against the trunk of the tree and watched her make him a sandwich. She took direction well, putting together his meal exactly as he requested it. Then she handed him a plate, along with a corkscrew and the wine.

"Could you open this? I don't know how."

He broke the seal. "Have you tried Chianti before?"

Heavenly shook her head. "I've never actually tried wine at all."

"Really?" Seth paused. "If you don't drink or have an objection, I also brought sparkling water."

She waved his concern away. "No, I just haven't had a chance to try wine. I've been saving the bottle you gave me for a special occasion."

"In that case, I might have one or two other things I'd like to introduce you to," he drawled.

Her eyes brightened as if the prospect excited her. "Like what?"

For starters, what would you do if I leaned in and kissed you?

Seth hesitated. He couldn't stay in California much longer, so today might be his only chance. On the other hand, his gut warned him she wasn't ready. If he scared her now, she'd never give him another opportunity.

Holding in a curse, he downshifted. "In good time. I don't want to spoil the surprise."

"Before today, I would have said I'm not into surprises, but I love this one so far."

Seth hoped that if—no, when—they did something more personal together, she'd love those surprises even more.

For now, he took the glasses, poured a generous serving into each, then handed her one. He lifted his own. "Well, then... To sunny days, new friends, and exciting surprises."

"I like that." She clinked her glass with his, then sniffed at the fruity aroma. "Do I sip this?"

Damn, she was so innocent. "Have you eaten yet today?"

She shook her head. "I usually skip breakfast."

While he'd love to see her without inhibitions and she might be a cute little drunk, he wanted her sober. "Then drink slowly, especially until we get some food in you."

With a cautious nod, she tipped the glass to her rosy lips and closed her eyes. Her throat worked. Watching her was a sensual experience, and Seth couldn't shake the feeling that he was somehow corrupting her.

Fuck, he loved that idea.

"Well?"

Her face lit up. "I like it. A lot."

"Good. Try it with some cheese."

They ate together, savoring the food and vino. When they were replete, they lazed in companionable silence, too full to move, and watched the other parkgoers around them enjoying the weather. People trekked the flowered walking path. Children laughed and played. The warm day had even tempted a few sunbathers.

She closed her eyes beside him and sighed softly. "I never do this."

"Do what?" He turned to her. "Come to the park? Or take time out for yourself?"

"Both. It's nice."

"Why not?"

She gave him a lazy grin. "Well, first, I'm originally from Wisconsin. We don't do picnics in December."

"Isn't this weather insane? But in a good way." He held up his hand as if he could capture the sun. "Believe me, days like this in New York are in May or September, but December? We're huddled around a fire watching football or something."

"I don't know if I can get used to all this warm sunshine. I always thought if I had the chance to escape the snow, I would. But now...I think I'm missing the seasons. There was no fall here, no changing leaves or crisp breezes. I miss snowmen and ice skating. I'm beginning to wonder if Christmas will feel like Christmas if it's eighty degrees."

He grimaced. "Good question. If I ever moved here, I'd definitely miss the big tree at Rockefeller Center and, stupidly, freezing my balls off at Times Square on New Year's Eve."

"New York sounds fascinating. I've always wanted to go. In fact, I plan to explore the big world one day."

He heard the yearning in her tone. "You should. Maybe you could start with New York?"

"Maybe. Is that where you'd rather be?"

"Yes and no. I miss my family, but I like the company here. I have to admit being able to hit the beach almost year-round is sweet. But I'm pretty sure a big quake will send this whole hunk of land into the ocean someday."

Heavenly cocked her head. "You're afraid of earthquakes? Hmm. It never occurred to me to worry about that."

"Afraid is a strong word. I'd say concerned."

She laughed. "No. You're totally afraid. It's…cute."

"Cute?" He raised a brow at her that dared Heavenly to say that again.

"In a very manly way, of course."

"That's what I thought." He sat back, enjoying the easy conversation between them. He liked that she wasn't nervous anymore. He especially liked the way she kept stealing glances at him between her sips of wine. "So if California isn't for you, why did you move out here?"

Suddenly, she wasn't smiling anymore. "A couple of reasons, mostly school."

"Couldn't find a good one to attend in Wisconsin?"

"Something like that."

Her vague answer set off his internal alarms. "Don't you attend nursing school online?"

Heavenly froze, then nervously began tucking away the leftovers in the basket. "I do, but it's a long story and I'm monopolizing the conversation. You haven't told me much about you."

Heavenly was a terrible liar. The Dom in him wanted to growl his displeasure and find delicious ways to make her atone. The cop in him wanted straight answers. Had her parents kicked her out? Had she followed a boyfriend here? Neither of those scenarios rang true, but there was a reason she'd moved. And she didn't want to say why.

"I don't mind long stories," he countered. "I've got all the time in the world for you."

"I'm boring. Tell me how you met Liam and Hammer. Have you

always lived in New York? What kind of cases do you work as a PI?"

If he called her out again for her desperate change of subject, his gut told him she'd cut the date short.

"I met Liam and Hammer through mutual friends." He glossed over the truth since revealing the fact they'd all bonded at Graffiti, a Manhattan BDSM club, would also reveal his kink. "They lived in New York then. Hammer moved here eight years ago, Liam just a few months back. Let's see... What else? I was born and raised in Brooklyn. My father was a cop. He died in the line of duty when I was sixteen. My mom still lives in the house where I grew up. All of my brothers have spread out but still live between New York and Boston."

"All of them? How many?"

"Five, including me. We're a loud Catholic family."

She gaped. "Oh, my goodness. That sounds chaotic. And wonderful. I don't have any brothers or sisters."

Seth filed that information away. "It was a lot of fighting and roughhousing, teenage hormones, and smelly feet—at least according to my mother."

That made her laugh. "Are you the oldest? Youngest?"

"I'm the oldest, so I ended up kicking a lot of younger-brother ass over the years. And that's enough about me. Now, tell me about you."

"Wait! What kind of cases do you work?"

"Mostly cheating spouses, some embezzling business partners." He shrugged nonchalantly but looked her straight in the eye. "I'm good at spotting dodgers and liars."

As those words sank in, she swallowed. "Oh. What about—"

"My turn." He cocked a brow. "Were you born in Wisconsin? Do you live alone? What about your parents?"

Her eyes went wide, then the windows guarding her soul slammed shut so quickly he almost heard the audible click. "Well, I was born in Wisconsin. There's not much else to tell."

Bullshit. Before he could confront her evasion, a bright red ball landed with a *thwack* on the blanket between them.

When Heavenly reared back, Seth grabbed the ball as a couple of little boys came panting up to them. They looked beyond eager, and as he stood, he couldn't help but smile.

"Who wants it?" He tossed the ball up a couple of times, making them wait.

"Me!" the towheaded scamp on the right said.

"It's my turn, not yours. You kicked it out of bounds." The other boy frowned.

"How about I give it a kick? You can both chase it."

When he did, they ran after it like a pair of eager puppies. Then he turned and sat beside Heavenly again.

She smiled softly. "You like kids?"

"When they're someone else's and I can give them back. So what were you saying before we were interrupted?"

"That I'm beat after a long week and I should go home. I have to study for finals."

As if on cue, the sun dipped low and a chilly wind blew leaves across the grass, signaling an end to their date.

Damn. He'd overplayed his hand. Normally, he was a patient man. In his profession, it paid to be. He should have been able to coax Heavenly into talking. Like an idiot, he'd given in to impatience. Sure, he could investigate her and probably learn most everything in ten minutes or less. But he wanted the satisfaction of earning her trust, of her offering him her truth. Besides, if she found out he'd violated her privacy, she wouldn't forgive him.

The question was, could he manage to win her over before the holidays? He didn't know, but his gut told him that if he had to choose between opening Heavenly up and going home for Christmas, he should stay.

"All right. Thank you for coming with me today, angel. I hope we can get together again." He wouldn't give up unless she flat out told him no.

"I'd like that." When he stood and offered his hand, she let him help her to her feet. "Gosh, there's so much leftover food."

"I don't have any way of keeping it where I'm staying. Want to take it home?"

"Are you sure?"

"Absolutely. Take the basket, too. Maybe we can use it another day."

She smiled. "That would be great. Thank you."

"Can I drop you off at home?"

Heavenly shook her head. "The hospital, please. I left some books in my locker I need for studying."

He opened his mouth to assure her that he'd wait and drive her when she'd collected everything. But he'd already pushed her past her comfort zone. Instinct told him he had to back off...for now.

Shoving down his itching curiosity, he lifted the basket with one hand and held hers with the other as he led her to his car.

He might not have figured her—or this crazy attraction—out today. But he would. No way was he giving up.

ON MONDAY AFTERNOON, Beck sat across from Heavenly in the hospital cafeteria, fixating on the lush bow of her lips and wondering if Seth Cooper had already kissed her.

"When you didn't text me for lunch on Friday, I worried Manwhore was bothering you again. I asked around, and Jennifer said you left at twelve thirty." He pinned her with a stare. "Were you studying? Or did you do something fun?"

Yes, he wanted information. He'd spent all weekend gritting his teeth because he knew she'd gone somewhere with that smooth-tongued bastard. As he'd left the hospital's parking garage that evening, he'd seen Seth drop her off. Their good-bye might have looked like a mere hug and a chaste kiss on her forehead, but there'd been nothing platonic about Seth's stare as he watched her walk away.

"I went on a picnic." Her cheeks turned pink, as if the memory had her blushing.

What the hell kind of picnic had that been, the sort where Seth spread her out on a blanket and made a feast of her body?

Beck tried not to growl. "By yourself?"

"No." She focused on the water cup in front of her. "Seth asked me out the day he gave me the gift basket. I said yes."

"Isn't he thoughtful?"

Heavenly blinked at him and smiled, making it obvious she'd missed his dripping sarcasm. "He is. We had a nice afternoon. I even drank wine for the first time."

Had that prick gotten her drunk so he could take advantage of her?

Beck gripped the edge of the table, biting back a demand that she stay away from Seth. He couldn't. Heavenly wasn't his. But Seth had plowed through a whole bunch of panting subs his first few days in LA. Hard not to hear through the walls that the guy enjoyed dishing out spankings. Seth liked the screamers, too. And now the douche wanted to bag Heavenly? Not on his watch.

"Did you like it?" Beck ground out.

"I did. Everything was delicious. I haven't enjoyed myself that much in a long time."

Her starry-eyed expression made him want to punch Seth Cooper ugly.

"Are you planning to see him again?" *Say no. Fucking say no.*

"I think so. He's fun to be with. And he put so much thought and effort into all the little touches."

With his hands? With his tongue? Beck gritted his teeth. She probably meant Seth's attention to detail…but his subversive brain played an image of the bastard lowering his head between Heavenly's pure white thighs. Beck nearly lost his shit.

"You're scowling. Is something wrong?"

"Don't be disappointed if it doesn't work out between you two. He's going home to New York soon. You should be careful."

She frowned. "I-I thought Seth was your friend and he'd be safe to date. Was I wrong?"

The litany of reasons Seth would be terrible for her rolled through his brain. Captain America might not have a sadistic streak, but that hardly meant he was a saint. Then again, every one of the reasons Seth wasn't good for Heavenly was doubly true for himself. Unfortunately, logic didn't stop Beck from wanting her. And if Seth had managed to seduce her, he'd skip the man-to-man chat and rip the asshole in two.

"I only met him a couple of weeks ago. But he's been…very popular with the ladies since coming to LA."

"He's already dated other girls here?"

Beck smiled tightly. "I don't know that I'd call it dating."

"Oh." She looked crestfallen. "I guess I shouldn't be surprised. He's handsome. And charming. He made me laugh and… Of course other women would find him as hard to resist as I do."

How difficult had it been? Too hard to bother?

At the thought, Beck's stomach turned and he pushed his sandwich away, untouched. "If you need me to tell him to back off—"

"He's not bothering me. But if he's really, um…busy and he's going back to New York soon…" She sighed glumly. "Well, it was just nice to have fun for a change."

That shut Beck up and broke his heart all at once. He'd love to show her fun, but he doubted she'd enjoy being strapped to a cross while he introduced her to the joys of impact play.

Shit. Time to change the subject before he crawled across the table and did something they'd both regret.

"So, have you talked to Raine since she left the hospital? By the way, if she says anything bad about me, don't believe it." He tried to lighten the mood with a wink.

"I'll ignore every word." She flashed her dimples. "I have talked to her. She invited me to a get-together at her house on Wednesday." Heavenly slanted a glance his way. "Will you be there?"

Did she want to know because she was curious? Or because she was interested? "I will."

Her face lit up. "Thank goodness. I almost turned Raine down, since I usually can't get away in the middle of the week. But I'll wrap up my classes for the holiday break tomorrow night. And if you'll be there, I won't have to worry about not knowing anyone."

Unfortunately, unless Seth hauled his ass back East, that fucker would be there, too… Hopefully, once he left for Christmas, he'd fuck off for good.

"Don't worry, little girl," Beck assured. "I'll be beside you." *Super-glued to your side every moment.*

Her smile turned even wider. "Thanks. You're such a good friend."

Just like that, his mood—along with his dick—deflated.

He'd been relegated to the fucking friend zone? Yep. And he had no one to blame but himself. Still, that didn't stop him from wrapping his fist around his desperate cock every night while he fantasized about taking her hard and dirty to the breathy soundtrack of her pleas.

He forced a smile. "Well, you can never have too many of those."

Heavenly absently stroked the side of her water cup. "It's been so long since I've had any, so I really value the time you spend with me. I know you're busy—"

"Unless I'm elbows deep in a patient, I'm never too busy for you."

He meant that, but he'd had lunch with her almost every day for a week and he was only more desperate to touch her. Still, if all he ever had with Heavenly was conversation, that was better than having no part of her at all.

"I'm really grateful, but I don't want to cause problems," she murmured. "I-I mean, if you have a girlfriend or someone spec—"

"I don't." And if he was merely her "friend," why did she want to know his relationship status?

Heavenly looked surprised…but distinctly not unhappy. "I just assumed you would since you're, um…good-looking and successful and really, really nice."

Nice? He'd been called a lot of four-letter words, but never that one.

She dropped her gaze, suddenly fascinated with the scarred Formica table between them. "Now that I think about it, Raine mentioned you were single…"

So, she was interested in him as more than a friend. Jesus… What the hell was he going to do? Resisting her was getting really fucking hard. Because so was he.

Beck scowled. "Raine meddles."

"She communicates."

He snorted. "Should I be worried?"

"No, silly. We just like to see the people we care about happy. I know she thinks the world of you."

Was Heavenly saying she cared about him, too? "She's the little sister I never wanted."

Heavenly laughed. "She feels the same."

The quiet between them hummed with awareness. Had Heavenly ever imagined him as the lover who could teach her the joys of raw, primal, deep, consuming sex? Or had her sheltered little fantasies even progressed beyond kisses?

Beck mentally jerked on the reins of his libido by extracting an envelope from his pocket. "When you mentioned you were writing a paper on Guillain-Barré Syndrome, I did some research and talked to Dr. Litchfield, who's the head of neurology."

Heavenly plucked up the envelope and eased it open with glee. She scanned the information he'd printed off for her, along with several medical journals with articles about the disease. Her baby blues went wide. "This is great. Thank you so much!"

"You're welcome. I didn't know much about the disease when you first asked, but I do now. You picked a rare and ugly disorder to focus on."

Her happiness faded into a somber nod. "The way the virus strikes with little or no warning is frightening. But the way it assaults the patient's immune system, which turns against the nerves, is even more terrible."

Beck agreed. "I'll keep wading through my medical journals for more articles and bring you what I find."

"I would really appreciate that. I want to know as much as I can."

"You're welcome." Picking up his sandwich, Beck finally took a bite. He watched Heavenly pore over the documents as he washed down his food with a gulp of coffee. "How's your paper coming along? Shouldn't you be turning it in soon since the semester is ending?"

"What?" She didn't lift her head, just kept drinking in the words on the page. "Oh, it's…good. I've got a few days. Online classes have a more flexible schedule… It's taking a little extra time because I've decided to make this a case study. I'll learn more that way."

She was dedicated. And compassionate. She really would make a great nurse. Beck vowed to do everything he could to help her.

"Great idea."

She kept reading. "Thanks."

He gently grazed his fingers over her delicate knuckles to get her attention…and for the pure pleasure of touching her. When she lifted those big blue eyes to him, Beck held in a groan. "Are you sure you won't let me buy you lunch?"

"I'm positive. As usual, I got full on the goodies at the nurses' station."

Still, he felt guilty for stuffing his face every day while she sipped water. "Those 'goodies' probably aren't healthy. You need protein, fruits and vegetables, and complex carbohydrates, little girl."

Heavenly lifted her chin in a defiant tilt. "I learned about the food pyramid in grade school, Dr. Beckman. I'm just not hungry."

God, he'd love to slide his fingers into her hair, bend her over the table, and rip away her pastel-green scrubs before he spanked the sass out of her. After she counted, begged, and cried, he'd curl her onto his lap, hold her tight, and reassure her…right before he fucked her raw.

Down, boy. Down.

Seconds later, Heavenly's stomach let out an audible growl. She ignored it. Beck wasn't fooled. He didn't know what she was up to, but she sure as hell wasn't going hungry.

Without a word, he pulled out his wallet and plucked out a twenty. Gripping her wrist, he shoved the money in her palm and curled her fingers closed. "You *will* get yourself something healthy to eat now."

"But—"

"It wasn't a request." He dropped his voice and pinned her with an expression ripe with displeasure. "Go."

"You don't have to—"

"I do. We're done discussing this."

The sleeping Dominant inside him stretched and roared. Beck mentally tightened the leash on his dark side.

Begrudgingly, she rose to her feet, resolution stamping her face. "Just this once."

Beck raised a brow at her. *We'll see about that.*

As she walked away, he watched the smooth sway of her ass.

"Ahem." The not-so-subtle clearing of a woman's throat caught his attention.

Reluctantly, he dragged his stare from Heavenly and peered up, half expecting Kathryn or one of her slut squad. Instead, he found the hospital's nursing administrator standing over him.

He stifled a guilty grimace. "Good afternoon, Nurse Lewis. Can I do something for you?"

"I'm sorry to interrupt your…lunch." A knowing smirk curled the corners of her mouth. "I wanted to thank you for watching over Ms. Young this past week."

Bridget Lewis said the words like he was a gentleman.

Beck shrugged, playing it cool. Heavenly was merely a volunteer now, but if she wanted a future at the hospital, Bridget could either make that happen…or make her life hell. "Well, I remember my first year in med school. It's a lot to deal with. I'm trying to help Ms.

Young learn while she juggles her duties here."

"Of course," she said in a tone that told Beck they both knew better. "Heavenly is a sweet girl. She'll make a good nurse. She's smart, dedicated, and an extremely hard worker. I see a lot of potential in her." Bridget shot him a shrewd stare. "It would break my heart if she left."

Left? "Why would she do that?"

"I thought she might have told you about the challenges she's been facing."

What else, besides being hungry, had she kept from him? "Actually, I'd like to hear about them from you."

The nursing administrator carefully weighed her words, and her hesitation amplified his concern. "Heavenly is great with patients but hasn't bonded with the nurses in her unit. Ordinarily, I wouldn't be concerned, but I've been made aware of some situations recently that give me pause."

Beck had no idea what she meant. Four lunches together, and Heavenly had told him nothing. "Really?"

"The surgical lube all over her locker could be written off as part of the grand 'welcoming' tradition, as could the unused catheters being stuffed inside."

He rolled his eyes. "The nurses should have gotten the hazing out of their system by now. She's volunteered here for a few weeks, and that's crap they usually pull in the first day or two."

"Precisely, and that stuff is harmless. But the pranks have escalated. More recently, someone rigged an aerosol can of deodorant to the door mechanism of her locker so that when she opened it, the spray blasted her face. Most disturbing, last Wednesday someone painted the word WHORE in red on the inside."

What the fuck? That wasn't mere hazing. "What's been done?"

"I only became aware of this whole situation a few minutes ago when Heavenly reported some money stolen from her wallet, which had been locked away."

Maybe that explained why she'd been prepared to go hungry…but not why she hadn't breathed a word about any of this to him. *Stubborn girl.* He was going to get some goddamn answers.

"Is the nursing staff bored in the ER? Do they need more to do?"

"Oh, they should be plenty busy. But if you're looking for a reason they've zeroed in on Heavenly, I've got some theories. First, she keeps to herself. Some may interpret her standoffishness as being haughty."

No one was less stuck-up than Heavenly. She was too sweet to be so misunderstood.

"What's your other theory?"

"That not everyone appreciates your marked interest in her."

Translation: either the other nurses were condemning Heavenly without really knowing her or they were jealous hags. His money was on the latter.

He'd only meant to protect her from Manwhore's advances. Granted, he'd been enjoying his lunches with her too much to stop. He certainly hadn't given a second thought to the jealous vipers and their petty reprisals.

"Do you know who's doing this to her?" Beck glanced at the slut squad. Kathryn watched him with a sharp stare.

Bridget followed his line of sight. "I have my suspicions but no proof."

If it would help derail Kathryn, he'd cry sexual harassment to HR, since she'd made umpteen passes at him. But she could easily deflect by accusing him in turn. If he confronted the bitch directly, she might get even more vindictive with Heavenly. But somehow, someway, he'd protect her. He had faced more cunning foes than a horny nurse pushing thirty and come out just fine.

"What can you do to stop this?"

"I'm going to let everyone in her unit know this sort of behavior is grounds for dismissal."

It wasn't a perfect solution, but maybe that threat would shelter Heavenly from more of the bitches' antics. If not, he'd come up with a plan B. "If the situation continues, please let me know."

"Of course."

Despite seething inside, Beck managed a smile. "Thank you. I appreciate that."

"Enjoy your lunch."

"One minute. Before you go… When did the nurses start bringing snacks to their unit on a regular basis? They never did during my rotation in ER, unless it was to celebrate a birthday or promotion."

She frowned, confused. "As a rule, they don't."

"What about today?"

Bridget shook her head. "This morning when I spoke with Heavenly about her missing money, I didn't see any goodies at their station."

So not only had Heavenly *not* mentioned being bullied, but she'd lied to him about the food as well?

Beck swallowed a livid growl. "Thank you for the clarification."

"Of course. Is there something special going on today that I'm not aware of?"

If Beck had his way, it would be Spank Heavenly's Ass Red Day. Instead of balloons, streamers, or a parade, the two of them would celebrate alone—in the dungeon. He'd throw her over his knee, yank down her panties, and slap her tender cheeks until she couldn't sit for a week. She'd learn the value of telling him the goddamn truth.

But he couldn't do any of that, and it was driving him fucking crazy.

Beck shook his head and forced a cordial expression. "None I can think of. Have a good day."

"You, too." As the nursing administrator walked away, Beck tried to tamp down his blazing anger. It wasn't easy. Why the hell hadn't Heavenly told him about her problems?

Across the table, she slid a tray onto the scarred surface, laden with roast beef, mashed potatoes and gravy, green beans, a hearty dinner roll, a side salad, a wedge of cheesecake, and a large soda. It was a sizable dinner for a big man. But lunch for a little girl? Either Heavenly had one hell of an appetite or, more likely, she hadn't eaten all day.

She spread her napkin in her lap and shoveled bite after bite into her mouth. The fucking truth had been staring him in the face. And didn't he feel like an asshole for not realizing that Heavenly wasn't just starving today, but every day?

The girl was broke. Why else would she work in shoes so unsuitable for the job? Or only have water for lunch?

Heavenly didn't need a hand merely with her case study; she needed basic necessities. He might never be her lover, but he could at least be her friend. If she thought he pitied her, she'd refuse his help. So he'd have to be discreet. Devious, even. Luckily, he was good at that.

While he was at it, he'd work on figuring her out. The woman was a puzzle. A conundrum. A maze. Trying to read her was like reading a technical manual in Braille. Still, something about her compelled him to understand.

"So…" he tossed out after a few forkfuls. "How are things?"

Heavenly carefully set her utensil aside before taking a long sip of her drink. Beck knew a stall tactic when he saw one but waited for her reply.

"What 'things' do you mean?"

"Oh, you know…classes, tests." *The bitches of east wing.* "Your volunteer work here at the hospital? Life?"

"Fine."

She lied to him without hesitation, without even blinking. No mention of anything vital like being tormented or hungry.

What are you going to do about it?

Nothing he could do…for now. But with a little finagling, he would ingrain himself in her life. Open her up. Earn her trust. Help her.

But if he got that close, what would stop him from taking her to bed? Beck feared nothing at all.

CHAPTER SIX

FAIRY LIGHTS TWINKLED like diamonds, casting a warm glow of welcome over the guests gathered on Raine, Liam, and Hammer's expansive back patio. Standing heaters and a big fire pit kept the crisp December air at bay. The trio had invited their dearest friends for this holiday party, and the cozy event was in full swing when Seth arrived.

He was damn happy for them. They stood close, never drifting far apart. Despite the still-visible bruising beneath her makeup, Raine looked positively radiant. Hammer and Liam were both puffed up with pride at their impending fatherhood. Their resilience amazed him. He knew too well the harsh reality of tragedy and what it took to survive the aftermath.

After everything they'd been through, they deserved this beautiful new home, good times, peace, and the joyful life they planned together. If all went well, they'd be blessed with a baby, too.

An unexpected pang of envy twitched in his chest.

Frowning, Seth stared at the amber liquid in his glass, gave it a swirl, then downed the last of the whiskey. When he glanced up again, the threesome's nearly tangible love still stared him in the face. That pang poked him once more. Christ, he hated this maudlin shit.

Maybe he shouldn't be surprised. He'd had nothing close to a meaningful relationship since... Well, for years. Completely his own fault. Eight years ago, he'd made a vow of singledom with good reason. It had been great...mostly. Tonight, he found himself wishing for more.

Unless he made drastic changes in his life, he'd never have it.

Footsteps behind him, a sudden, loud pop had him snapping around, every muscle tense. Gunshot?

Heart thundering, he scanned the gathering. Nothing but conversation and laughter—and one of Shadows' dungeon monitors, Pike, opening a bottle of champagne. Dragging in a breath, Seth forced himself to relax.

No one's getting shot tonight. Stand down.

Suddenly, someone clapped his back. Seth whipped around, hyper-vigilant again. God, he was always jumpy this time of year...

He felt like an idiot when he saw Liam standing beside him with a grin.

"It's a party, mate. No long faces allowed here."

Seth pasted on a smile. "Just lost in thought."

"Thinking about the past?"

"The future, actually." That would probably surprise the hell out of Liam.

His friend raised a brow. "I can guess what you're thinking about. Or should I say who?"

Seth followed Liam's line of sight and clapped eyes on Heavenly. No mistaking the angel.

She sat alone on the far side of the yard, her silhouette illuminated by the party lights strung between trees. The simple blue shift she wore accentuated her slender shoulders and the curve of her breasts. Her hair hung in loose waves that draped over her shoulders and down to her waist with a luster like spun gold. Her slender legs had him wondering how they'd feel wrapped around him. She wore the same sandals she had for their picnic. Hell, even her toes were cute.

He'd suspected she would be here, but seeing her was still a punch in the gut.

"I barely know her." And he shouldn't be thinking about her so constantly after two weeks, one date, and no kisses. But for some reason, he'd hardly been able to think about anything else since feeling the first inexplicable pull to her.

"Well, if you're not interested, I suggest putting your tongue back in your mouth," Liam teased.

"I didn't say I wasn't interested. She's really sweet. Maybe too sweet. I'd bet money she's a virgin."

To his surprise, Liam burst out laughing. "Is that your problem? You daft prick, that just means she's ripe for the plucking."

Maybe Liam was right, but... "My life is back in New York."

"Why can't you enjoy her company now?"

"Heavenly isn't the kind of girl you love and leave. Besides, if I stayed and 'plucked' her, could you really see her prancing around the dungeon in a corset, kneeling for me? Look at her..."

"I am. She just might surprise you."

He whipped his gaze back to his friend. "It doesn't make any sense."

"You think Raine made sense for me?" Liam laughed. "It's not about logic. Remember when you said I acted as though Raine had a voodoo pussy? You were right." He nodded toward Heavenly. "She's yours."

Seth rolled his eyes. "I've never even seen her pussy."

"You'd like to."

"I'm a guy. She's pretty. That isn't rocket science."

"No, it's biology. I'll bet you could sweet-talk your way into seeing her pussy. She likes you. I can tell. And you definitely like her." Liam sent him a considering stare. "What if she's the one for you, mate?"

Seth had begun to wonder the same thing. To hear his old friend echo his question was eerie. "I don't see how. I should already be back in New York since I promised my family I'd be home for the holidays. And once I leave this godforsaken state, I'm not coming back. And you know how I feel about relationships. So I really have no business with that girl."

Liam laughed. "Uh-huh. When did you say you'd scheduled your return flight?"

Seth had already put off making his reservation for too long. "Fuck off."

Liam gave him a knowing smile. "You're dragging your feet, and she's the reason. I have a hunch about you two..."

"Are you turning into your mother now?" Seth frowned. "It's downright scary, the way shit she says comes true."

"I'm not following in her footsteps. Just...sometimes I get a sense of things. And I've got one about you two."

"Well, worry about your own life. Doesn't Raine need a fresh water bottle? Or some slap and tickle?"

That made Liam laugh again. "All right. I'll fuck off for now. I reserve the right to give you shit in the future. I'm sure I owe you."

With that, his Irish buddy headed toward Raine and Hammer with sure, jaunty steps, leaving Seth alone with his thoughts—as well as a clear path to either the front door...or to Heavenly.

He hesitated. It would be logical to return to Shadows and book a flight home tomorrow, then see what kind of good-bye action he could finagle at the club tonight. But all he wanted was to cross the patio to the pretty blonde and do his damndest to seduce her. Besides, the poor thing was sitting by herself since Raine was currently busy being happy and playing hostess. Heavenly probably didn't know anyone else here. It would be rude to ignore her.

When he spotted a tray of champagne flutes on a nearby bar, he plucked up two and sauntered in her direction.

When he reached her side, she looked up and flashed him a cock-hardening smile. A sappy grin stretched across his face. Yeah, he was happy to see her. Seth knew it showed.

For the hundredth time, he wondered why Heavenly got under his skin. Smooth moves and banter came easily, and he usually had no problem segueing from a drink to a few kisses...to a sweaty orgasm or two. Right now, he felt tongue-tied. And unsure.

Damn, he was usually cooler than this.

"Hi, Seth." Her voice caressed him as she gave him a sweetly dimpled smile.

For a moment, he just stared at her glossy lips, dying to know if she tasted as sweet as he'd been imagining for nearly two long weeks.

"You look...fantastic, angel." He offered her one of the flutes, then bent to kiss her cheek. The scent of something fruity—strawberry?—coupled with a musk that was strictly her filled his nostrils. "Since you're sitting here alone, I thought you might want some company."

"That would be great. I was here with Dr. Beckman before he got called away for emergency surgery."

"What a shame." Inside, Seth mentally fist-pumped at his good luck. The night was definitely looking up.

"Yeah, I think he was looking forward to the party. He said he'd stay beside me tonight, but of course he went when duty called. He's a dedicated surgeon and a brilliant man."

Seth raised a brow. "I thought you didn't work with Beck that much."

"I don't, but..." She blushed. "He intervened when one of the doctors kept hitting on me. Since then, he's taken the time to spend lunch with me most every day. I really enjoy it."

He barely managed not to scowl. Beck was pursuing a virgin? It would be hysterical if it wasn't so fucking wrong.

"So are you two dating?" Or, god forbid, getting naked so he could bend her over his desk and plow into her?

She blinked, and her lashes swept down. "N-no. Dr. Beckman is a mentor. A friend."

Friend? Oh, that was priceless. He had a hard dick for her, and she considered Saint Beck her role model and pal.

Couldn't happen to a nicer guy...

Even better, the sadistic doctor obviously hadn't found the balls to ask her out, much less touch her. His evening was looking up.

Seth smiled. "But he left you here by yourself and..."

"Since I don't really know anyone else except Raine and her men, I decided to sit by the pool for a bit. It's peaceful."

"Want me to keep you company, angel?"

"I'd love that." She gestured to the chair beside her.

He took the seat opposite her instead. "I'd rather sit here so I can look at you. You really are gorgeous."

Heavenly blushed again. She did it often and well, and Seth didn't want to imagine her too jaded to give him such an innocent response.

She focused on the fluted glass of bubbly, holding the delicate stemware as though it were her anchor. "You're flirting with me again."

"I am."

"Dr. Beckman said you do that with a lot of girls."

Did he now? Asshole... "Beck doesn't know me well, angel. He's wrong."

Technically, Seth wasn't lying. Usually, he didn't need to flirt to get laid. In dungeons, women came to him. He didn't mingle with the fairer sex outside of BDSM. Too messy and complicated. Too...everything spending more time with Heavenly would probably be.

She suppressed a big smile. "Oh, okay. So what's in the glass you brought me?"

Leaning forward in his chair with a grin, he dropped his voice to a low, conspiratorial whisper. "Champagne."

"I've never had any." She looked wide-eyed and excited.

"Take a drink. See if you like it," he urged. "You'll have something else to add to your ever-expanding repertoire of new firsts."

A list he really wanted to add to in a meaningful way.

With a dimpled smile, she closed her eyes and took a tentative sip. "Well?"

Her eyes flared with pleasure. "Oh, I like champagne. Smooth and sweet. The bubbles tickle my nose."

"I thought you would. Look at you, being all adventurous."

She laughed aloud, and the musical sound hit him square in the solar plexus. "Not quite, but I'd like to be. I've got to get through nursing school first."

"Well, you've got to start expanding your horizons somewhere. You know, it's hard to figure out where you belong and what life might have in store for you if you never live a little. What's that expression? All work and no play makes Jane a dull girl…"

"I must be the dullest person on the planet," she groaned. "Nursing school really is harder than I thought. Good, though. I like the challenge. But I haven't had time for much else since I started. That's why I'm really looking forward to this winter break. A whole month without research papers and exams!"

"So you have time to spread your wings." And if he stayed, he'd love to help her spread other appendages, too. "I have some ideas where you can start. Want suggestions?"

"Why not? I have a feeling you'll give them to me, anyway."

"You're right, but I promise to make them good. We might not know each another well yet, but I'm a very good detective. I'll figure you out…"

She stilled. Her lips parted in a pantomime of a smile. "Have you, um…deduced anything yet?"

Why are you suddenly so nervous, angel?

Seth didn't want to spook her, like he had at the end of their picnic. She was beginning to open up, so he chose his words carefully. "Well, since you like to try new things, you've got courage. I also suspect wine could become one of your favorite indulgences."

She exhaled the breath she'd been holding. "That's probably true."

"And I know you'd love to travel and explore the world."

"I think about it *all* the time."

"Hmm… And on your travels, I can imagine you acquiring a slew of eager lovers, only too happy to satisfy your every desire." He dropped his voice and seized her stare. "Myself included."

Her blush deepened to a rosy glow. "I don't even have time for one man. What would I do with a slew of them?"

Heavenly might have scoffed, but under that she sounded almost wistful.

Seth leaned forward again, his hands dangling over his knees. He stared, his gaze deliberately direct as it traveled down her body. The longer he drank her in, the more her nipples poked the front of her dress. The more she fidgeted as if an ache settled between her legs.

Oh, this was getting good.

"I don't know about any other guy, but I know what I'd do if you were mine…"

Heavenly downed the last third of her champagne, then set the flute aside before tilting her face his way. Her heavy-lidded gaze nearly had him hurdling the table and closing the distance to kiss her.

"What?"

Her rapt, breathless curiosity made his cock jerk. "You wouldn't ever want for attention, angel. My hands, my lips, my body would be all over yours at every opportunity. You'd know I was thinking about you all the time and just how indecent my thoughts were."

She dropped her gaze and hissed in an indrawn breath. The air between them hummed. He focused on the slender column of her neck, watching in satisfaction as the throb of her pulse leapt frantically at her throat.

"Indecent?"

"Filthy. I shouldn't even repeat what I'd be thinking. It would shock you."

"T-tell me," she murmured. "I want to know what you'd imagine if you thought about me…in that way."

"Once we go down this path, there's no turning back. You'll know exactly what's burning through my brain every time I look at you. And you can't 'un-know' that. Are you sure you want me to go on?"

She bit her lip, crossed her slender legs, then toyed with one earring before stilling again. He waited and watched, every cell in his body tense and desperate for her consent.

The flush of color spreading up her cheeks only made him want her more. The buzz between them charged him like a live wire. He clenched his fists to keep himself from touching her. He just needed that one word…

But she made him wait, staring, her breath uneven as she licked her lips before finally whispering what he wanted to hear. "Yes. Please…"

The rest of his blood rushed south to fill his already engorged cock. "I haven't kissed you properly. Not yet. But you have no idea how badly I want to nip at those plump lips or how much I fantasize about tasting the rest of your sweetness."

She blinked, eyes wide, then swallowed and seemingly forgot to breathe. Her nipples hardened even more. "Seth…"

The palpable pull between them thickened. It had him beyond hard and desperate. Christ, when was the last time he thought he'd lose his mind if he couldn't have a woman? Especially one he'd never even touched?

"Once I showered you with kisses and love bites, you'd be aching to tear away your clothes and press your skin to mine, but I wouldn't let you. I'd want to undress you myself. And I'd take forever doing it. I'd reveal you one creamy, tantalizing inch at a time, kissing every newly exposed bit of skin until you panted and whimpered and begged."

She let out a ragged breath. The sound of it was an electric spark that lit up every erogenous zone in his body. She shifted restlessly in her seat again, her hands clasping and clenching in her lap. Her eyes were deliciously dilated.

"But you'd know how unbearably hard and aroused you'd made me, angel, because I'd lift you in my arms and drag you against me, wrapping your legs around my waist so I'd press my thick, hard cock—"

She gasped, the color in her cheeks deepening more. Even the shade of her lips had become a flushed red.

Fuck, she was absolutely stunning.

"I'm shocking you. Should I stop?"

The emphatic shake of her head was an urgent plea. "No. Tell me more."

The triumph spilling through him was liquid pleasure. "Mmm, where was I?"

"Um, my legs. Around your waist. You're...hard."

"I am." The smile he sent her sizzled with heat. "Once I had you pressed flush against me, I'd notch my cock against the swollen pad of your sweet pussy. Since there wouldn't be any more clothing between us, I'd grind against you, skin to skin. And I wouldn't stop until you told me in explicit detail what you wanted me to do next. Do you know what that is, angel? Do you know what you'd want?"

She wriggled on the bench, uncrossed and recrossed her legs. She licked her lips as if they'd gone desert-dry. "I-I don't..."

"Yeah, you do," he cajoled in a tone only she could hear. "Our bodies don't lie, and I can read yours."

Slowly, her lips parted. Her eyes went soft with arousal. Her hunger simmered just under the surface. He could almost feel it, taste it. She ached. She was wishing he would touch her. She wanted to know what it felt like to have his mouth, his hands, his naked body on hers.

The scent of her lust filled his nose and slid deliciously into his brain. So potent, so perfect, the fragrance seemed as though it had been engineered for him alone. *Christ...*

"Tell me you'd want it, Heavenly."

At his husky demand, she took a shuddering breath. "I...would."

"I know. But I wouldn't do anything more than press my dick against your pouting folds for a good, long while."

"You wouldn't want to make love to me?"

"Oh, hell yeah. I'd want to. I do right now," he admitted, leaning even closer, brushing his thumb back and forth across her palm. "But I'd make sure you were wet and needy for me first."

"How?"

Seth hadn't thought it was possible, but every visible inch of her skin flushed darker. God, this verbal foreplay was better than the last round of sweaty sex he'd had with a sub whose name and face he'd already forgotten.

"Well, I could use my fingers, but I'd much rather check your needy little cunt with my tongue..." The stunned breathlessness on her face and her fine trembling spurred him on. "I'd feast on you, angel, as if you were my last meal. I'd lap and lick at you, sucking in your clit and delving into your soaked passage until you came hard."

"Seth…" Her plea was sweet and shocked and aroused as hell.

"Angel?" he tossed back, already considering where he might be able to find them privacy inside the house. No one would notice if they disappeared for an hour…or five, right?

"I-I…"

Before she could wrap her brain around her thoughts and speak, her mobile phone blared between them, rude and insistent. She jerked in response, hands fumbling as she picked up the device and obviously tried to gather her wits.

Heavenly opened her phone and scanned the screen. Her lips parted and her eyes widened with a totally different emotion.

Alarm.

Suddenly, she shot up and darted away, calling to him over her shoulder. "I have to go. Sorry…"

What? No. She couldn't just go. Why the hell was she leaving?

Seth was mere seconds behind her. "Tell me what's wrong. What upset you, angel?"

"I can't stay. I'm sorry. We'll talk later. Bye."

He charged after her with longer strides—until Pike suddenly stepped in front of him, blocking his path. "Hey, Seth. I got a question."

"Later. I need to talk to her." He sidestepped the guy and gestured to Heavenly.

Pike grabbed his arm. "No, you don't. Beck wants you to stop sniffing around that girl like a dog in heat. So I told him I'd make you heel."

The pierced, tatted Dom's sly smile sent Seth's temper soaring. "You tell that asshole that lifting his hind leg and pissing all over her doesn't make her his. Now fuck off."

He shoved past Pike and jogged past the other guests, scanning for those blond waves and that bright blue dress. Nothing. He darted for the front door and wrenched it open, hoping to spot her. But when he searched up and down the shadowy street, it was clear Heavenly had disappeared.

"IF IT WOULD please you, Sir, this girl would happily join you in your private room."

Chastity's endorphin-drunk invitation made Beck tense. The submissive rode her natural high after the "punishment" she'd begged him for and now nestled her welted ass on his lap. Normally after a hard scene with his favorite whip, Beck would be loose and relaxed. He'd definitely be ready to take Chas or whomever he played with to bed, plow her deep and hard. He'd done it—and most of the subs here—many times.

Tonight, his cock was snoring.

He refused to close his eyes and pretend she was Heavenly. He might be a prick, but he wasn't completely heartless. Besides, he couldn't fool himself, even if he tried.

Grimacing at the hopeful lust in Chastity's eyes, Beck brushed sweaty red strands of hair from her face gently. "Not tonight."

What else could he say? He couldn't give her a good reason for his refusal. Hell, he couldn't even give himself one. Fixating on a blue-eyed virgin was a terrible fucking excuse.

When he'd come to Shadows tonight, playing with a willing pain slut had sounded like a fantastic distraction. He'd eagerly peeled off his lab coat, fully intending to let the sadist inside him stretch. Gratification that didn't come from his fist had sounded mighty nice, too.

That wasn't happening. All he could think about was having Heavenly in his arms.

Not happening. Sure, Heavenly might have submissive tendencies, but he doubted BDSM was even a blip on her radar. Hell, as sheltered as she was, she'd probably never heard of it.

Unfortunately, none of that stopped him from imagining her naked and panting and bound for him, her ass throbbing and red with his marks…

Yeah, he was a fucking perv. Everyone knew it, especially him.

"This girl understands, Sir," Chastity said. "Please excuse this girl for asking."

Somehow her soft acceptance only made Beck feel worse. She'd approached him to sate her need for pain, and he'd done it, wishing he was a thousand miles away the whole time. He couldn't bring himself to satisfy her in any other way.

"No apology necessary. You better now?" It wasn't Chas's fault that she wasn't the woman on his mind, and he refused to be a dismissive prick.

"Oh, so much… Thank you, Sir."

A peal of laughter across the room snagged his attention. Around the bar, a group of subs preened and flirted, all but rubbing their half-naked bodies against some Dom.

The big blond male turned his head, flashing a Hollywood smile. Seth. That motherfucker.

Of course he was here. Liam had put the guy up at Shadows while he was visiting. But why wouldn't he go the fuck away?

He'd love to whip out his phone and snap a couple of incriminating shots of Seth with his "harem" to show Heavenly. But Beck wouldn't break the rules of the club or bend his moral code for the bed-hopping bastard.

He'd love to know what had happened last night between Seth and Heavenly at Raine's party. It was definitely something. When Beck had asked her for a recap at lunch earlier today, she'd blushed profusely and dodged his question. While heading back to his office, he'd texted Pike for information. As usual, the DM had given him a smartass response.

They cozied up in a corner by themselves until she suddenly ran off. Seth chased her. I stopped him. You're welcome.

The ten texts he'd sent back for more information had all gone unanswered. Asshole. Why had Heavenly run off? Had Seth ever caught her? Had he seduced his way into her bed? Beck had no idea.

Biting back a growl, he tamped down his fury and handed Chastity the water bottle from the table beside him. "Will you be okay if I step away to take care of something?"

"Yes. Thank you, Sir."

"Feel free to stay on the couch and float a bit longer."

She sat up, gingerly making her way off his lap. "Happily, Sir."

With a nod, he watched her curl up with a serene smile and drift.

Guilty relief oozed through Beck's bloodstream as he tossed a soft cotton blanket over her.

Behind him, another burst of raucous laughter rolled from the bar. He whipped around with a scowl, glaring at Seth and his flock.

Really, fucker? Last night you were coaxing Heavenly out of her panties, and tonight you're handing out numbers to subs. Obviously, you pride yourself on excellent cunts-tomer service.

Rolling his eyes, Beck strode toward his private room. The slap of leather, along with cries and moans around the dungeon, usually soothed his nerves. Tonight, they only reminded him of what—and who—he'd never have, adding another layer of shit to the growing pile.

Before he could disappear behind the closed door, a firm hand gripped his shoulder. Beck stopped in mid-stride and spun on his heel. Hammer stood, staring, brow raised.

"Problem?" Beck asked.

"You tell me."

"No. And there shouldn't be with you anymore. Finally."

"What's that supposed to mean?" Hammer's brows knit together.

"You and Liam have Raine, that big 'ol house, and a baby on the way. Her old man is dead, Satan rest his miserable soul. Since you're living the dream, why are you here? Oh, god. Tell me you two morons didn't fuck up again."

"No," Hammer barked. "And I didn't stop you to talk about Raine. Why didn't you take Chastity to your room?"

Beck tensed. "Since when is fucking a sub after a scene a requirement?"

A smirk tugged one corner of Hammer's mouth. "Never. But in the past you rarely refused pussy. What's it been now, three weeks? I'll bet your hand is getting tired. Should I grab a bottle and meet you in your room for a chat?"

For the first time, the shoe was on the other foot. It felt too tight. "Unlike you, I don't have to be shitfaced to discuss my feelings. And I don't need an intervention."

"Good. Then I'll skip the booze and you can start talking."

"What is there to say? I didn't feel like fucking her." Beck forced himself to shrug.

"Your sudden celibacy wouldn't have anything to do with Heavenly, would it? And before you give me the bullshit denial rolling across your face, I saw your expression when you had to leave the party last night. I know you told Pike to make sure Seth didn't get too close."

"I don't trust him, and I wanted to make sure she was all right. Speaking of which, did you take her home for me?"

Hammer shook his head. "Never got the chance."

Beck's blood pressure soared. "Who the hell did?"

But he had a pretty goddamn good idea. He slid a glance toward the bar, teeth clenched.

"Not sure. But you seem awfully worried about Seth. Heavenly has you by the balls, doesn't she?"

He pinned his longtime pal with a furious glare. "Shut the fuck up."

Hammer chuckled. "I'll be a nice guy and tell you that Seth didn't take her home, either. So don't do anything stupid, like storm up to the bar and pick a fight. I'm not sure what happened between them. One minute they were talking, and the next, she was flying out the door. Alone."

"You didn't try to stop her?" Beck gaped.

"I wasn't sure she'd actually left until Seth came in cursing. He told me she'd gotten a text, read it, then pulled a Cinderella-style exit."

Beck mulled that. He'd seen Heavenly texting someone when he'd caught her alone, too, but she'd never used an incoming message as a smokescreen to escape him. What had Seth done to make her bolt, try to haul her up to one of Raine's guest rooms and leave the aftermath of her innocence all over the sheets?

"Did she tell Raine why she left abruptly?"

"She called this morning to apologize. Said that 'a friend' needed help." Hammer shrugged.

Friend? She'd never talked about any fucking friends. Well, besides him.

Beck needed answers from her. But first, he intended to make a few things clear to Sir Dick-for-Brains.

"Thanks," Beck snapped as he shouldered his way past Hammer and barreled toward the bar.

Hammer yanked on his arm. "Don't be stupid. And don't make me kick you out of the club."

"It wouldn't be the first time." Beck jerked free and stormed into the bar.

"You could keep all five of us in your thrall at the same time, couldn't you, Sir Seth?" Kristen, a curvy sub with pink hair, purred.

"I'm sure he could," Eden, a very active sub, offered with a sensual purse of her lips as she laid her hand on his thigh. "You're so good one-on-one, and we'd be happy to let you try us together."

Kat, Vinyl, and Glitter all nodded enthusiastically.

Beck shook his head. This guy got more ass than a toilet seat.

Seth plucked up Eden's wrist and lifted her hand from his leg. "Maybe I could have you all panting in less than ten seconds. If I wanted to."

Yeah, because you'd only last ten seconds…

At the chorus of eager female coos, Beck wanted to puke.

Seth merely grabbed his bottle. "Tonight, I'm just enjoying my beer, ladies."

Beck forced an affable smile as he approached. "Sorry, girls. You'll have to Top Master Seth from the bottom another time. I need to talk to him."

The subs' expressions ranged from guilt to disappointment as they scampered away.

Seth turned to him with an annoyed glower. "Hi, Beck. You're as welcome as poop in a punchbowl."

"Yeah? I wish like hell your parents had practiced birth control, but since they didn't do the world a favor and we're both here, you and I are going to have some words."

"Why are you up my ass? Didn't slicing Chastity open with a whip soothe your savage beast?"

His lack of satisfaction was none of Seth's business. Making the asshole back away from Heavenly was. "What did you do to Heavenly at Raine's party?"

The bastard sent him a smug grin. "We…talked."

"Is that code for getting her drunk and trying to take her to bed?"

"Is that what she said? I guess you two chatted over lunch since she told me you're great 'friends.'"

Beck seethed. He didn't need a fucking reminder that Heavenly had labeled him a pal. Knowing she'd told Seth only chafed him more.

"Back off."

"Why? You don't have any claim on the girl."

"The last thing she needs is a player like you. I've spent time getting to know Heavenly. If you'd bothered to do the same, you'd know how innocent she is."

"Oh, I know. And last night proved she's ripe and more than ready to give away her sweetly guarded virginity."

Beck's gut churned. "What the fuck does that mean?"

"She begged me to tell her what I'd do to her if she were mine. So I gave her every dirty detail of the things I'd do to her body with my fingers, my cock, and of course, my tongue. That woman has the most beautiful blush from head to toe when she's aroused."

Beck's blood rushed and pooled like a living volcano about to erupt. He didn't know what he wanted more, to knock out the prick's teeth or eviscerate him with the bar knife. "I'm going to kill you."

"Don't blow an artery, Doctor. I didn't touch her...yet," Seth drawled. "But I damn well intend to drag her beneath me and take every bit of her soft, lush innocence. Just so you know."

"Have some fucking decency. If you do that and run back to New York, you'll leave her in a million shattered pieces. She doesn't need that. She doesn't need you."

"And you think she needs you?" Seth cocked his head toward Chastity, who still lay curled on the sofa, glowing ass lined in angry red welts. "Do Heavenly a favor and fuck off. We both know she needs a man who can be gentle, and that's not you."

"I can be fucking gentle!"

"Don't kid yourself."

"You know what? I admit it. I'm all wrong for her. But have you looked in a mirror?"

Seth scowled. "You don't know me."

"Oh, please. You're as predictable as a B movie. And as one of Heavenly's friends, I intend to protect her from assholes like you. And if you hurt her, I *will* make you suffer. I know how."

"Bring it. I've flattened guys like you in my sleep. If you weren't so busy fisting your cock and playing her 'professional daddy,' you might finally see the only way you'll have Heavenly is in your dreams."

"Outside. Now! I'm going to rip your head off and shit down your throat."

Instead of leaping to his feet and stalking to the parking lot, Seth frowned. "Holy shit."

"What? Are you too much of a pussy?"

"No, you stupid bastard. I'd wipe the parking lot with your ugly face," Seth tossed back. "Listen to us. Don't you get it?"

"Get what?"

"The way we're fighting..." Seth waved his hand between them. "Doesn't this feel like Hammer-and-Liam déjà vu?"

Fuck. The jackass had a point. The two of them were heading down the same path they'd helped Hammer and Liam navigate less than a month ago. The difference was, those two had been friends for a decade before battling bitterly for Raine. Finally, they'd realized they needed to share her, but the war leading up to that truce had been ugly. More than once, Beck had been sure it would end in casualties. There'd certainly been enough curses hurled, fists thrown, and blood spilled.

He and Seth had zero history. They also had zero trust. And zero intention of sharing a drink, much less Heavenly.

"There won't be any fighting. There will be me protecting the girl and you fucking off."

"It must be tough to pretend you're so altruistic when your dick is that hard."

"Get your thoughts out of my pants."

"We can trade one-liners all night, but I've got your number."

"Yeah? Lose it. I'm going to make sure you never lay a finger on her."

"You can't stop me."

Beck cocked a brow at him. "Watch me."

CHAPTER SEVEN

*T*HANK *GOD IT'S Friday.*

Heavenly sat in the metal chair next to the nurses' lockers at the back of the ER and groaned in relief as she tore off the ratty athletic shoes that had long ago ceased to support her instep. The hole near the heel would soon become noticeable. Tomorrow, she'd have to find the time—and money—to search the second-hand shops for another pair, before she started her new job. Of course she'd rather spend the holidays with her father, in case this was their last together. That hurt, but she had to be realistic. And practical. Since the break from school afforded her time, she had to spend every possible moment making money to cover their mounting bills.

She'd never waitressed before, but she was willing to work hard. The tips at this place were supposedly generous—not surprising since the uniform barely covered the essentials. In time, she'd get over her self-consciousness. She hoped.

With a sigh, Heavenly opened her locker. Thankfully, she found her backpack and its contents untouched. Even better, the few precious dollars she possessed were still in her wallet.

During her first few days at the hospital, the nurses had played some harmless pranks on her, which she'd written off as hazing. But the following week, someone had painted a slur inside her locker. A few days later, her forty dollars for groceries had disappeared. Heavenly suspected Kathryn was responsible. The nurse specialist had become particularly petulant once Dr. Beckman turned attentive and protective.

Heavenly shoved her shoes in her backpack with a sigh and donned her sandals. As she made her way toward the street exit, she spotted Dr. Beckman in the lobby, lounging in one of the chairs and glancing at his watch. Was he waiting for someone?

She hadn't seen him since he'd left the party abruptly. The insecure part of her had worried he no longer wanted to spend time with her because he saw her as the little girl he always called her. She'd missed lunches with him, not because he made sure she ate every day, even in his absence, though that was nice. No, each moment she spent with him, she soaked him up like a sponge—his dissecting intelligence, his robust laugh, his cutting humor, his dark eyes that held a hint of the devil.

At the sight of him, her heart skipped a beat. "Dr. Beckman?"

His head snapped up, and he stood. "I was hoping to catch you. Sorry I haven't been at lunch the last couple of days. A few patients with difficult conditions and…"

He'd sought her out to apologize and explain? Oh, my gosh. She smiled in giddy relief. Having him near again made Heavenly's world feel right once more.

"How dare those life-or-death patients be so demanding?"

"Yes, well… Thankfully, they're going to live."

"Of course. They have you."

She shouldn't flirt when he didn't want more than a professional relationship, and she tried not to. But nothing changed the fact that he made her both gooey and shivery at once.

Then again, so did Seth.

And that baffled her.

For the hundredth time since Raine's party, the big blond PI's verbal seduction whispered through her head and made her ache.

When she saw him again, would he seduce her with more than his voice? Would he actually put his hands and his mouth on her? She'd loved the idea when she lay alone on her pallet at night, tuning out her father's gentle snoring as she touched herself and tried to find the mythical pleasure called orgasm. Of course, she thought of Dr. Beckman then, too.

"Heavenly?"

Feeling herself blush, she blinked up at him. The doctor watched her every expression.

Gosh, here she was talking to one man she had less-than-platonic feelings for while fantasizing about the other. It happened whenever she was with either of them. Why did she have *those* feelings for them both? What did that make her?

A ridiculous girl with pie-in-the-sky fantasies.

"Yes. Sorry. Hi."

Dr. Beckman stepped closer, dropping his voice. "Are you all right?"

"I'm good. Happy to see you."

"How have you been?"

"Fine. You?"

He studied her more intently. "I'm sorry I couldn't stay at the party. I heard you left abruptly, too. What happened?"

Raine's gathering had begun with so much promise...and ended so terribly when her father had called to say that he'd fallen near the kitchen and hit his head. "Nothing much. I didn't stay long because a friend needed my help."

"Before you left, I heard you and Seth were deep in conversation."

"Yes." She breathed the word more than spoke it. "We talked."

Now Dr. Beckman scowled. "Did he come on to you?"

Did he ever...

She tucked a strand of hair behind her ear and smiled. "He might have."

"And?"

Heavenly was capable of taking care of herself, but she adored the way Dr. Beckman protected her. Maybe that was simply his nature or maybe he just felt sorry for the shy girl. If he thought she was too inept to take care of herself, she didn't really want to know.

"Oh, don't worry. It wasn't creepy, like Dr. Manning. It was...nice. More than nice, actually." She sighed. "No one has ever talked to me like that."

She didn't think he'd mind hearing about her feelings for another man since he'd never given her any romantic vibes. Even when Dr. Manning had accused him of wanting her, he'd totally denied it. While Raine was fast becoming a friend, Dr. Beckman was probably the best one she had right now. He listened so well... She needed to appreciate the rapport they shared and stop wishing for more.

"How did he talk to you?" he demanded. "What did he say?"

She wouldn't repeat Seth's words. They were private, his gift to her. Sure, he'd likely just been flirting to pass the time at a party where he didn't know many of the guests, either. But his attention had meant the world to her.

"Things that made me feel pretty and special." Not to mention sexy, which she'd never felt until that moment.

The doctor's scowl deepened into something furious. Oops. He'd been clear about his opinion of the PI. Of course he wasn't happy she hadn't heeded his advice. Heavenly made a mental note not to mention Seth next time she saw Dr. Beckman.

"Um...I-I should go," Heavenly said, though she hated to leave him.

"Wait. Listen to me, little girl. You—"

A honking horn interrupted whatever he'd been about to say. When she glanced up, she spied a familiar rental car at the curb—and an even more familiar face peering out from the open window, golden hair glinting in the California sunshine.

Seth.

He waved. Her heart jumped. She sent him an excited smile in return.

Dr. Beckman whirled to peer out the glass, then zipped back to her, looking irritated. "Did you know he was coming?"

"No." Gosh, there was her breathless, dreamy voice again. "It's a complete surprise." But a nice one, so she shouldn't keep him waiting. "You're on vacation next week, right? Going to see family for Christmas?"

"Yeah." He raked a hand through his hair before sidestepping to block her view of Seth. "I'll be back on the thirty-first. You have plans for the holiday?"

"Staying here. I took a waitressing job to make some extra money. I have a silly uniform and I'll be serving a bunch of big ol' kids with sticky fingers." Not for anything would she embarrass herself and tell an esteemed professional like Dr. Beckman that she had stooped to working at a place like Bazookas. "Not fun, but it will pay a few bills." When Seth honked again, she smiled at the doctor before daring to step up on her tiptoes and kiss his cheek. "Have a great holiday. I hope we can resume our lunches when you get back. Bye."

Before she could see whether her impulsive peck had annoyed him, she turned and pressed her hand to her suddenly tingling lips. Shoving aside the useless wish that he would have kissed her mouth, she ran out the hospital's revolving door—and into Seth's waiting arms.

He'd exited the car and now leaned up against the driver's side. When he pulled her close, Heavenly's heart thudded all over again. "What brings you here?"

"You." He cupped her cheek, lifting her gaze to his. "Did you really think I wouldn't want to see you again after Raine's party?"

She'd hoped but hadn't dared to expect. Now she couldn't hold back her smile. "I'm glad you're here. Sorry about the other night, leaving so suddenly. I got a call from someone who fell and thought they were hurt. Turned out to be nothing."

"I'm glad everything's all right. Someone close to you?"

"Yeah. He's a sweet old man, doesn't really have anyone else to help him..."

She hated to be less than honest, but what else could she say? Maybe Seth was interested in her. Or the idea of her. Sure, he flirted with her, but if he really knew how inexperienced she was, he'd laugh. Or feel sorry for her. She hadn't forgotten the pity on his face the day he'd first asked her out. Telling him the whole sad story about her father and his disease would only make that worse. She'd rather not put him in the position of making him stammer pointless platitudes. They changed nothing.

"Well, that just proves you're the angel I'm always calling you." He turned a heartthrob smile her way.

Heavenly felt half a second from swooning. "You're funny. And you're sweet."

"Sweet? That's something I haven't been called in a long time." He winked. "You need a ride home?"

"No!" She bit out, then dialed back the panic. Since he always looked like he was determined to figure her out, Heavenly had to get it together or he would know something was off. "I need to hit the grocery store to grab a few things for dinner."

And she would...if she had the money. Looked like she and Dad would be eating ramen again tonight.

"I saw one right around the corner. How about if I take you?"

If he dropped her off, that would be great. It was a couple of blocks closer to the bus stop, which meant less time on her feet. "Sure."

Wrapping an arm around her waist, he led her to the passenger door and helped her inside with an exaggerated sweep of his hand. "Your chariot, my lady."

She giggled. Yes, she probably sounded silly, but he made her feel like a star-struck girl. "Thanks."

As Seth closed her door, she glanced through the windshield and inside the lobby. Dr. Beckman still stood, staring. He looked something. Sad? Troubled? Upset?

No. He was mad.

Deciding she probably shouldn't invade his personal space or kiss him again, she sent him an apologetic smile.

On his way around the vehicle, Seth raised a hand toward the doctor. He must have waved; she couldn't see for sure. She only knew that when Seth stepped into the car, his grin was even wider.

"Good day?" she asked as he started the engine.

"It is now." He dropped his hand to her knee. "I've been thinking about you."

Heavenly's breath caught. She'd heard the cliché about butterflies in her stomach, but she seriously had them. He'd actually thought about her? And he was touching her, too. Her whole thigh sizzled as if he'd heated her up with his rough, hot hands. Breathing wasn't easy, either.

Oh, mercy...

When they'd first met, she had thought Seth so blindingly gorgeous. But when he'd used *that* voice on her at Raine's party? She'd melted. Now, she had no doubt what he was thinking when he ate her up with his gaze. There was no nighttime to shroud them, no champagne to sway her. Just the two of them in broad daylight, in public, sober as church mice.

And she still couldn't drag her stare from him.

Her breath caught when his fingers tightened on her leg. "I've been thinking about you, too."

"Yeah? All good things, I hope."

"Yes." Sexy things. Totally new and different things. Exciting things. "But I'm sure you hear that a lot."

"I'd rather hear it from you." He squeezed her knee again, then put the car in drive and headed for the street. "What did you think of our conversation the other night? I was really honest with you."

She swallowed. "I...liked it. A lot."

"Any part in particular?"

Heavenly turned to find his mouth curled up in a playful grin. His long fingers tightened on the steering wheel as he turned onto the road when the traffic parted. His shoulders and chest filled out his black T-shirt. She could see the ridges of his abs through the soft cotton and...yes, their conversation excited him, too, if the huge bulge in his well-worn jeans was any indication.

Oh, gosh... She swallowed. "I liked all of it."

"That's what I wanted to hear, angel."

"I've never met anyone who could make me feel what you did with a few words."

He braked at the stoplight and glanced at her, his smile a seduction. "I'd like to do more than talk to you, Heavenly. How would you feel about that?"

His husky words hit her in the chest, then dropped between her legs, where they tightened and burned. "Happy. Um...excited."

"Yeah?" He pulled into the parking lot of the grocery store and dropped his hand to her leg again, higher on her thigh. "How excited? Enough to make you wet?"

"Yes. Even enough to make me"—she bit her lip—"touch myself."

He braked in the middle of the row and crooked a finger under her chin, lifting it. His green eyes had gone dark. "Excellent. Do you have to study tonight?"

Was he asking her if she was free? "No more school until January fourteenth."

"This day just keeps getting better." He diverted his attention long enough to pull the car into an empty spot. "Then let's get you into the store so you can grab your groceries. Unless you'd like to go out to dinner. I'd love to take you somewhere."

Heavenly wished she could say yes. But duty—and reality—called. "I'd love to go out, but I've got to, um...get some stuff done around the house and look in on the older man who fell. I'm also exhausted after a long week of work and finals. I'm not sure I'd be great company right now."

"How about a rain check?"

She felt a goofy smile spread across her face. "That would be great."

"Tell me when you're free, angel."

"I'm starting a new waitressing job tomorrow night. But I'd love to see you in the afternoon."

"Where are you working? I could hang out and keep you company."

Heavenly tried not to flinch. "No place you'd want to go. Loud, crazy restaurant with unruly brats. Besides, I'd die if you saw me in that ridiculous getup."

"I'm sure you'll look adorable, but I won't make your job harder. How about if I call you in the morning and we make plans?"

"Perfect." She had to be beaming—and she didn't care. She was going on a second date with Seth Cooper, whose charm and swagger made her flutter and tingle. "Thanks for the ride here. I'll see you tomorrow."

As she reached for the handle of the door, Seth wrapped his fingers around her arm. "How about some company while you shop?"

Heavenly froze. What could she possibly buy without breaking the bank except a few more packages of ramen? Maybe eggs and some generic oatmeal. But that wouldn't look like dinner to Seth.

"You don't have to. I'm sure you have better things to do with your time."

"I came to be with you. Why don't you let me keep you company? Hell, I'll even push the cart."

How could she say no to that? Impossible, so she'd just have to grab a few things, make excuses, and scurry home. "Sure. Thanks."

With numb fingers, she pushed her way out of the vehicle and stood. Instantly, her feet protested. At least her sandals were more comfortable than her work shoes. But it still seemed crazy that she was wearing flip-flops days before Christmas.

Suddenly, Seth was beside her, locking the car with the fob in one hand and tangling their fingers together with the other. She looked down at their clasped hands, then up to his confident grin. For a moment, she could almost pretend she was like any woman spending time with a guy who liked her, free to see where the attraction led them…

She really liked the feeling.

Inside the store, Seth grabbed a cart. Grocery shopping with him felt weirdly domestic. She'd done this chore alone for so long, usually clutching the store's flyer and a handful of coupons. In fact, she almost never came here because the prices were higher, so she didn't know where anything was. Maybe if she kept him talking he wouldn't realize she was lost.

"So...when are you going back to New York for the holidays?"

He shrugged. "I'm actually thinking about staying."

Could that possibly have anything to do with her?

Don't be ridiculous...

"Well, you can't beat the weather," she remarked.

He slid his arm around her, anchoring it on her hip. "I can't beat the company, either."

Heavenly floated up the first aisle. "There you go, flirting again."

"With you? Always."

Their conversations were easy—unlike her intense exchanges with Dr. Beckman. And sometimes, she got the feeling the brilliant surgeon was saying one thing to her but meant something else entirely. He fascinated her...and she didn't know what to do about the potent, one-sided attraction.

"Have you talked to Raine since the party?" Heavenly asked.

"I had breakfast with the three of them this morning. She's doing great."

Heavenly was relieved but not surprised. After all, sassy Raine lived with two loving men. Come to think of it, a similar relationship might solve her own problems. Then she'd never have to choose between the two men who flipped all her switches. She could wake up beside them every morning with smiles and kisses, spoil them rotten all day, then crawl into bed with them each night and crook her finger when she wanted them to touch her...

It was official; she'd lost her mind.

"I'm glad to hear it. She's so kind and strong and funny." And secure—both in herself and her place in her men's lives. Raine was someone Heavenly aspired to be like. "I think she's great."

"It's mutual. So, when you figured out they're a threesome, how much did it shock you?"

"A lot," she admitted. "I've never seen anything like that. Have you?"

He shrugged. "Ménage relationships? Sure."

"Oh. Of course. You've been a cop."

"Something like that."

Mischief danced in his vivid eyes. He wasn't telling her something, but the secret obviously made him smile. Gosh, she'd love to know the thoughts running through his head now.

"What does that mean?"

Seth laughed. "We've been up and down half the aisles in this store. You still haven't put anything in your cart, angel."

He was right. Goodness, she must look like a stumbling goofball. "Oops. I got distracted."

Her blushing admission only made him laugh more. "How about if I help you out?"

Before she could answer, he tossed a bag of pasta in the cart, then a couple of jars of sauce. She gaped at the splurges she hadn't been able to afford in years. But he was already tugging the cart around the corner, balancing it on two wheels, and heading for the produce.

"What are you doing?"

"Grabbing you some stuff for dinner." He tossed a few peppers into the basket, followed by an onion, garlic, and some tomatoes. "Do you prefer parmesan, Romano, or a blend?"

"Um…" She couldn't afford any of it. "I don't—"

"Know? Care? How about I surprise you?" He pushed the cart to the specialty cheeses, picked up a few containers of grated stuff that nearly choked her with the price, then tossed them in the cart. "That's the thing about growing up in New York. I know lots of Italians. They showed me the good stuff. You'll love this."

She'd probably melt the instant it hit her taste buds. Cheese was a weakness. Hazard of growing up in Wisconsin. But those few sprinkles almost cost more than she spent on groceries in a week.

How could she tell him she couldn't buy any of this stuff without the evening becoming utterly mortifying?

"And you'll need some of this…" He zipped farther across the store, to the meat counter, bypassing anything on sale. He picked up a few packages, then discarded them until he found the biggest slab of beef in the case. "Perfect. You like meat, right? You're not one of those vegan girls who will only eat something if it never had two eyes and a mother?"

"No. I'm not. But I—"

"Great. Know what to make with everything in the cart?"

Heavenly had no clue. "I don't."

"Garlic steak pasta is magic." He grinned as he scanned the basket. "Do you need anything else while you're here?"

Staples she couldn't afford for a month if she bought all this. "Um…I'll never be able to eat this much food. And since I don't know how to cook the dish you're talking about, I think I should stick with the basics."

When she reached into the basket to pluck things out, he pulled her closer and pushed the cart to the front of the store. "Angel, since you won't let me take you out, I want to cook for you. All you have to do is invite me over and show me to your kitchen. I'll do everything else. And after dinner…we'll see if you feel like acting on some of that conversation we had. What do you say?"

Her first thought was a knee-jerk no. But she was really tempted to say yes. She didn't want her time with Seth to end. Still, if she invited him over, she'd have to explain her situation, her father's health, her complicated life—all the things she'd been avoiding.

Would it matter to him? Maybe not. He seemed determined to get to know her. Or get her into bed. Maybe…she should let him. She was hopelessly attracted to him, and sex would probably be the most amazing thing ever. And she wasn't hanging on to her virginity for any particular reason. When it happened, she just wanted to be with someone who would treat her well and make her feel good. Seth would. Sure, some silly part of her wanted her first time to be special, but she wasn't sixteen anymore, hoping to be plucked by the prom king on a bed of roses. She wanted it to mean *something*, but she wasn't ready for happily ever after. Being happy for a moment would be okay…

As he maneuvered the cart into a checkout lane, she stood on tiptoe and whispered in his ear. "I don't need a lot but…is this anything more than sex?"

He reared back and stared, a furrow between his brows. "Oh, angel. I'm dying to make love to you, but I'm interested in more than your beautiful body. You have a beautiful heart, too. If I didn't like spending time with you, I wouldn't be trying this hard."

Right. Because he didn't have to. That was enough for her. He only had to like her some. When they got back to her place, she'd figure out what to say to him...and how to explain him to her father.

She was being impulsive. After all, she and Seth had only been on one date. They'd seen each other a handful of times. Trusting someone with all her baggage was a big step. A scary one. She'd never done it and she hoped he didn't scurry off once he got an eyeful of her reality. But just once, she wanted to live in the moment. And the truth was, if she kept waiting to start her life, she'd never experience anything.

Finally, the woman bagged the groceries. Seth paid, and it shocked her to think he hadn't blinked at spending nearly fifty bucks for a single meal. But he grabbed the bags and dropped them into the cart, then put a hand at the small of her back and hustled her to the door.

Before they went any further, though, she needed to make a couple of things clear. Heavenly pulled on his sleeve. "Wait."

"What's wrong? Don't change your mind now, angel..."

"I'm not," she murmured as people bustled in and out of the store around them. "I need to be honest with you about something. Well, two things. First, we may not be able to have sex tonight. You'll see why when we get to my place. But I want you to know it's not because I don't want to. I really do."

"Hey, I'm not in a hurry. I don't want you to feel rushed. Is it your first time?"

She winced. "Is it that obvious?"

"Only because I'm so fascinated by you that I watch every move." He smiled and tucked a strand of hair behind her ear. "We have time. It will happen when it happens. I can be patient. I just want to be with you."

Heavenly let out a sigh of relief. "Thank you. That means a lot to me. Since I've never done this—dated or hooked up or whatever we're doing—I don't know if I'm saying this wrong. Or if I should say anything at all." She sucked in a deep breath. "The thing is, I like you. You make me laugh and you make me feel special. I've needed that for a long time. But it seems only fair for me to be honest. I like Dr. Beckman very much, too."

She bit her lip and waited for his reaction. His face remained carefully blank.

"You said he was your friend." He didn't sound pleased.

Should she have kept her mouth shut? But how would that be fair to Seth? If he was going to navigate around all the difficulties in her life, he had a right to know that she had feelings she couldn't seem to help for someone else.

"He is, but I like him as a man. I've thought of him…as a lover."

Seth jerked and sucked in a breath as if she'd punched him in the stomach. "That's honest."

Heavenly grimaced. "Was I not supposed to be?"

"No. You absolutely were." He gave her a sharp nod. The air between them turned brittle. "On second thought, I should go. Do you need a ride home?"

What? Panic screamed that she'd screwed up. Seth hadn't wanted honesty, just a quick tumble. She sighed. Why was trying to be with a man she liked so complicated?

"I can take the bus, but… Don't leave. I didn't mean to upset you. I'm sorry."

He pulled his keys from his pocket. "Maybe this is for the best."

As much as she hated it, maybe he was right. It wasn't fair to expect Seth to want her when she also wanted Dr. Beckman so much. "Please don't be angry."

Seth shrugged like it was no big deal, but she knew better. "I'm the one who came on strong. My apologies." He tossed his keys in the air and they landed in his palm. "Enjoy your dinner."

He didn't kiss her or touch her. Heck, he barely looked at her as he turned, headed for his rental with that long-legged stride, and disappeared. She already knew she wouldn't see him tomorrow for that date they'd planned. In fact, she wondered if this was the last time she'd ever see him.

Gosh, even that thought hurt.

Fighting tears, she grabbed the grocery sacks and huddled against a sudden chill as she made her way to the bus stop.

THIRTY MINUTES LATER, Liam drawled a question that instantly got Seth's back up. "So that's it? A little competition made you decide to piss off back to New York?"

On the trio's sun-soaked patio, Seth pushed away from the table and stood so abruptly the iron chair clattered to the flagstone. Was the big Irish bastard listening to a word he said? He'd wasted ten damn minutes explaining what had happened between himself and Heavenly and why he should leave LA. He wasn't jealous of her feelings for Beck; he simply had no reason to stay.

Liam had a very different opinion.

Seth ran his stiff fingers through his hair in frustration. Coming here after leaving Heavenly at the grocery store to spill his guts to his old friend had clearly been a mistake.

On his way, he'd stopped at the club to pick up his bag. When he'd arrived at the trio's house, he'd found Liam alone. He was sorry to have missed Hammer and Raine, but he was ready to get the hell out of this sunshine-laden, earthquake-riddled shithole. Familiarity, sanity, work, family during a white Christmas—that's what he needed. Not doe-eyed blondes torqueing him up and turning him inside out.

"I'm taking the red-eye home tonight."

Liam shook his head. "You realize if you go home now, mate, you'll be leaving the door wide open for Beck to sweep in and claim Heavenly for himself."

"Yeah." Impossible to miss that part. But by her own admission, she wanted Beck as a lover.

Fuck, hearing that she had feelings for the shitsack stung. The fact he even cared pissed him off more. After all the things he'd whispered to her at Raine's party... He bristled. Had she used his words to get herself hot for that fucking sadist?

Liam still sat, peering up at him with a considering expression. Christ, the guy was doing that quiet thing again, like his clairvoyant mother. That worried Seth.

"And what about the girl?" Liam demanded. "What about what *she* needs?"

"Well, I guess Beck will give it to her." That made him want to punch the doctor stupid.

"I'm sure he'll try. But I've seen you with Heavenly. Like I said, I think you belong with her."

"I thought so, too, but apparently not. I'm done letting a woman who fucking wants someone else yank my chain."

He dragged in a breath to find calm. The nagging pain in his chest made that impossible.

"Didn't you learn anything from watching what Hammer and I went through with Raine? You and Beck don't need to brawl. And you don't need to reinvent the wheel. You both saw firsthand how it was made. Macen and I will even tell you how to drive the bus."

Liam had lost his mind.

"Ménage is totally out of the question."

The man's skeptical brow and patience-of-Job sigh grated on Seth's last nerve. "Because?"

"Don't play dumb. Heavenly is nothing like Raine. Your girl finished growing up in a BDSM club. She knew exactly what to expect. Heavenly might be a grown-ass woman, but she's naive and unworldly and… She's Bambi, for fuck's sake."

"Why is that a problem?"

"I already told you. Heavenly. Is. A. Virgin."

"All you and Beck have to do when you take her together is be gentle. The real problem is you two wankers. Figure your shit out and find out what *she* wants. What *she* needs. The answers might surprise you both."

Liam's lilting voice usually soothed him. Tonight, the tone irritated him like fingernails on a blackboard.

"That threesome you and I had was enough to scratch any itch I might have had for ménage. Besides, you know I don't take on subs for more than a night or two. I'm not even sure why I've been lingering here. And I refuse to share air—much less a woman—with that snarky sadist. The two of us helping you and Hammer with Raine was one thing. That came easily."

"My point exactly."

What point was that? "But Heavenly? Not happening. In case

you've missed the obvious, Beck and I fucking hate each other." With every word he spewed, Seth felt his blood pressure shooting through the roof. Liam was one of his closest friends. Hell, like a brother. So why wasn't he listening—or at least trying to understand? "You and Hammer worked it out because you had ten years of friendship and shared history to fall back on. Beck and I? Nothing but mutual loathing."

"You say that now, but it's amazing how close two men can become when someone they care about more than themselves needs what they both have to give her." The almost patronizing smirk on the man's face made Seth itch to slap it off. "Despite what Raine went through with her father, surely you've seen she's much happier now."

No denying that, but... "Not everyone is built for your kind of domestic bliss. Besides, I just wanted to fuck Heavenly, not get involved with her."

Liam's mocking smile widened. "You're a liar... You were far more interested in Heavenly than you've been in anyone since—"

"Don't go there. It doesn't matter. Besides, Heavenly isn't into BDSM. She probably doesn't even know what it is."

"I'm confident you gentlemen are capable of showing her the ropes, so to speak." Liam smirked. "And Raine will be around for advice if or when Heavenly needs it."

The tone and inflection of his words—even and deliberate, as though they spoke of nothing more mundane than the weather—only made Seth angrier.

"You're not listening to me, goddamn it!"

"I've heard every word you said," Liam assured.

Seth was done. He'd helped Liam when his friend had asked. Now that the Irishman had his life in order, Seth was out of here. He'd been hanging around for one reason, and she didn't want him. She wanted the wolf in sheep's clothing. Fine. Fuck it.

He was gone.

But Liam kept on yapping, like he was the guru with all the answers. "Now you listen to me. Get your shit together. You and Beck can both teach her as your relationship grows. The first thing you two have to do is figure out how to get on the same page. That can be tough. Believe me, I know. But it's got to happen—"

"Like fuck it does. I don't want to slap balls with Beck. And I won't let Heavenly twist me up anymore."

Finally, Liam's dark eyes gleamed with some empathy. "You're hurt and mad because she means something to you and you want to be enough for her. But you may have to accept that she needs you both."

Never in a million fucking years. "You know how to reach me if something else comes up or you want to shoot the shit, but that woman won't be leading me around by the dick anymore."

Now the big man stood, advancing until they were toe to toe. Good, Seth was itching for a fight. He dragged in a breath and rolled his shoulders. He was mad at himself—and at the world in general. If Liam pushed him one more time, Seth would happily plant his fist in the man's pretty pearly whites.

"Let me get this straight…" Liam's voice dropped to an incredulous growl. "That woman you're accusing of intentionally leading you around by your cock is…how did you put it? Naive and unworldly. Yet she has enough wiles to manipulate an experienced Dominant like you? Please. I've watched you maneuver cunning subs for years and come out unscathed. So how in the ever-loving hell could a little virgin possibly wrap you around her finger? Is she an innocent babe or a manipulative bitch? You can't have it both ways."

"You don't get it," Seth growled back.

"Oh, I understand completely. The part I'm stuck on is why you'd blame her for your shit. When she gave you her honesty, you tucked your tail and ran. After all you've been through, I never thought you'd give up on someone you obviously have feelings for. If you ever want to be happy, I suggest getting over yourself, shelving your ego, and most of all, making peace with your past."

That was a low blow. "Back the fuck off, Liam. I mean it."

"Oh, I see. You expected me to empathize with poor you. You wanted me to pity your dilemma and validate your feelings." He scoffed. "How about you grow a pair instead? When I called a few weeks ago to tell you about my troubles with Raine, isn't that what you told me?"

Yeah, he had. "You're enjoying this, aren't you?"

"On the contrary. I'm saddened that the man I've always respected is behaving like a coward. You're scared shitless to admit you want

Heavenly in your life. That's the biggest problem of all."

Red mist hazed his sight. It annoyed him even more that Liam wasn't wrong. One more word and they'd come to blows. "Fuck you and fuck this bullshit. You don't know—"

"Of course I do. I was there, remember?" Silence enveloped both men for a heartbeat. "I know exactly what happened, why you're the man—and the Dominant—you are now. Isn't it time you stopped—"

"Isn't it time *you* stopped tossing my tough love back in my face?"

"You didn't die that day. Why don't you start embracing the fact you're still alive?"

But Seth had heard more than enough. He shoved Liam back hard enough to send him crashing against the table. Without another word, he turned his back and headed for the front door.

Liam still managed to cut him with his parting shot. "Nothing that happened was your fault, Seth. You're wasting your second chance. Wake up and realize that before it's too late."

CHAPTER EIGHT

B ECK GRIPPED A fresh mug of coffee, wishing for something stronger. It was almost five o'clock here in Vegas, and he was on vacation. He should be relaxing, damn it. Instead, he was fixated on Heavenly. What was she doing right now? He hoped like fuck she wasn't naked and spreading her legs for Seth while he rutted on top of her. Would he come back from Christmas break and find out that Heavenly was no longer quite so innocent? If that happened, he'd have no one to blame but himself. He had chosen to keep his distance. Yes, for her own good, but now he was paying a steep price for tucking away his inner Dom and being a gentleman.

Jesus, maybe he *should* find some booze…

Beck stood, paced. Cursed. If Seth fucked and ran, he'd help Heavenly pick up the pieces—after he buried the bastard's body.

If Seth hadn't yet touched her… Well, Beck was already wondering how much longer he could resist temptation when he craved her so desperately.

Faint footsteps padding across the hardwood floors jerked him around to face Gloria. She stood in the doorway, looking sleepy and disheveled, her short red hair spiked in every direction. She squinted against the setting sun spilling through her west-facing windows. She had faint lines around her eyes that hadn't been there a few years ago, but she didn't look anywhere near fourteen years his senior. Then again, she never had. Gloria paid the best plastic surgeons to stay young. In her line of work, it was imperative. And she was a beautiful force to be reckoned with.

"What time did you pull in? Why didn't you wake me when you got here?" Gloria asked in a husky tone.

Beck ate up the distance between them in two strides and wrapped his arms around the tiny dynamo. "About two hours ago."

"It's really good to see you." With a contented sigh, she brushed her lips across his cheek, then headed straight for the coffeepot. "I fucking hate mornings."

Thank god Gloria was still as saucy as ever.

He laughed. "The sun is about to set."

"Well, it's morning for me."

"Which is why I didn't wake you when I let myself in. I figured you'd be working tonight. Merry Christmas, sweetheart."

"Merry Christmas back, you big, handsome stud. I'm glad you're here."

"Me, too." He pulled her close again and lowered his chin to the top of her head, inhaling her familiar scent. She felt like comfort and home, and he drank in the much-needed peace. "Grab a chair and I'll pour you a cup of coffee."

"Spoiling me already?"

"You spoiled me for years," he pointed out with an arched brow as he filled her mug with steaming brew and handed it to her.

As he sat across the table from her, she took a sip and moaned. The caffeine hit her system, and she pinned him with a dissecting stare. "So what's going on in LA.? Out with it."

"Oh, the usual… Bloody arteries all day and bloody asses all night."

"Any bloody ass in particular caught your eye recently?"

He had no idea how to explain a grown-ass sadist falling for a virgin. "Yes…and no. It's complicated."

She took another drink from her mug. "Obviously. Or you would have talked to me when whoever she is started getting under your skin a few weeks back."

Of course Gloria knew. She'd always been able to read him.

As Beck tried to figure out what to say, he was interrupted by a knock at the door. Gloria turned to the sound of keys jingling and hinges squeaking.

"You up, baby?" a man called out.

"In the kitchen." Gloria's eyes lit up as she stood.

When Beck had met the man in her life last Christmas, he'd known immediately she might actually fall for this one.

Buddy entered the kitchen, and she wrapped her arms around the fifty-something guy in jeans whose hair sported more salt than pepper. His beard matched. Gloria had always preferred men suave and flashy. Funny that she'd finally lost her heart to a quiet, modest plumber. But they fit together perfectly.

An almost teenage delight crossed her face before he kissed her lovingly. Beck found himself envying their closeness.

Buddy lifted his head, arm still wrapped around Gloria. "Hey, Ken. How are you?"

"Good, man." Beck stood and extended his hand. "So you're still dating my wife?"

"Yep. Hope you're all right with that."

"If you make Gloria happy, then hell yes."

"Which reminds me, *Kenneth*..." Gloria mocked, making Beck grimace. She only called him that when she was busting his balls. "Our eighteenth wedding anniversary was last month and what did I get? No flowers, no card. Not even a phone call. And never mind sex. You haven't fucked my brains out in years."

He rolled his eyes. "If you want to start celebrating now, I'll go pick some dandelions from the front yard while you bend over the kitchen table. That sound romantic?"

She snorted. "No wonder you've been unattached for so long."

"Eighteen years?" Buddy sounded awed. "That's longer than either of my marriages lasted."

"Because you kept marrying the wrong kind of whore, sugar." Gloria winked. "Sit down. Want some coffee?"

"As much as I'd like to stay, I can't." Buddy frowned. "A pipe at one of the restaurants inside Caesars burst. I just came by to tell you to have a good night at work. Be careful, baby."

"Always am." Gloria hugged him tight and gave him another lingering kiss.

With a crooked grin, Beck refilled his mug, damn glad to see Gloria happy. She'd had a hard life on the streets and on her back. She'd definitely earned some joy.

Suddenly, Buddy's phone rang, and he broke the kiss. "Gotta go. I love you."

"Love you, too. Call me later."

With a nod, he was gone. Gloria was still glowing when she sat at the table again.

Beck reached across the surface and wrapped his hand around hers. "He's a good man."

"Almost as good as you."

"You deserve happiness with a man who loves you to the moon and back. Why don't you marry him? For real." Beck sat back. "You and I never had a normal marriage, and you don't need a 'husband' to keep you safe from overzealous customers anymore."

"I don't," she admitted. "I haven't turned a trick in years. It's nice being the madam. Saves some wear and tear on my pussy, too."

"Gee, thanks for sharing that tidbit."

"You know me…" She shrugged. "I appreciate the security blanket having a 'husband' gave me."

"But you don't need it anymore." The security had once benefitted him, too, but their union had long ago served its purpose. They'd certainly never been in love, but neither had found any reason to pursue a divorce…until now. "I can have my lawyer draw up the papers. Just say the word."

"Are *you* ready?"

"I'll be fine."

Gloria studied him. "Tell me about this woman who's distracting you."

Beck would rather not confess everything like some sappy, lovesick teen, but no one knew him better.

He blew out a breath. "Her name is Heavenly."

"Sweet scene name."

"She's not from the club. Hell, she doesn't even know it exists, much less that I'm a member. Heavenly is her real name. I met her at work."

Gloria's brow took on a disapproving arch. "Work?"

"I know you taught me never shit where I eat, but she…" He groped for the words. "Well, she's a volunteer and… Fuck!"

"She's got you by the balls?"

"I wish she'd put her hands on my balls," he grumbled. "But I haven't even kissed her."

Coffee caught in Gloria's throat, and she nearly choked. "Excuse me?"

"Want to hear the even-more-shocking part? Since I met her, I've tried to take a couple of subs to my room, but…" He shook his head. "I'm not interested in anyone else."

That took Gloria aback. "You're serious?"

"Yeah. I'm not acting like myself. At all. I feel stupidly off balance."

"The last few times we talked, I knew something was up. What are you going to do?"

"Nothing." Beck tossed his hands in the air. "What do I know about vanilla dating?"

"Your knowledge would probably fit in a thimble," she acknowledged. "When did you meet her?"

"Almost a month ago."

Gloria gaped at him, slack-jawed. "Holy shit, Ken. You haven't gone a month without sex since you were sixteen."

"Nope. But Heavenly is a virgin. You know how I feel about that."

"Yeah." Gloria scowled. "How old is this girl, anyway? Thirteen?"

"Ha! No. That's the gap between our ages."

She tsked. "Honey, that's basically the same gap in our ages."

"You and I are different."

She laughed so hard she cackled. "Is that what you're telling yourself?"

Beck glared. "Why don't you ask me the obvious question? I know you're dying to. C'mon… How the hell does a pervert fall for an innocent young thing?"

"You're not a pervert. Well, not the criminal kind."

"Thanks," he returned tartly. "If Heavenly knew the truth, she'd probably think I was."

"Did you ever think I was?"

He'd been sixteen and homeless when she'd taken him off the streets and given him a new life. "Hell no."

"So why wouldn't Heavenly count her lucky stars that she'd found a protector and a provider? And be grateful for your big heart?" It was her turn to squeeze his hand. "The look on your face says you don't think so."

"We have nothing in common, except a passion for medicine."

"Yes, you do." She gave him a knowing smile. "You simply haven't figured out what yet. Tell me about her."

"She's sweet. Sassy. Shy." He sighed. "Submissive."

A big smile spread across her face. "She sounds perfect."

"I doubt she's ever heard of an erotic spanking, so how is she going to react when I whip out the single-tail?"

"Please… That kind of progress takes time. You suddenly lack patience?"

When it came to Heavenly, yes. He wanted all of her—her body, her soul, her submission—right now. And for the first time in a long time, he couldn't simply take what he wanted.

"Even if I gave her a hundred years, I'm not sure she'd get there."

Gloria frowned at him, and he could hear her now. *You're not giving yourself enough credit. You're quitting before you've even started.* He needed to make her understand. And if a picture was worth a thousand words, this one ought to do it.

Gut tensing, he pulled out his phone and scrolled through his pictures until he found the one of Heavenly he'd secretly snapped at lunch while pretending to read a text. Sun from the skylights lit her hair, illuminating it like a halo. She really did look like an angelic little girl. At a glance, heat flooded his veins. His pulse kicked up. His cock stirred.

"Here." He flashed Gloria the photo he stared at every night while punishing his dick.

"Oh, my god." She shot him a look of pity—as she repressed a grin. "She's incredible. You really are screwed."

"Glad you're finding humor in this."

"I'm laughing *with* you."

"Do you see a fucking smile on my face?" He tossed the phone aside. Stood. Paced. "I have no control over how I feel and I hate it. What the hell is wrong with me?"

Understanding softened her eyes. "I think you're falling in love."

His stomach took a rolling plunge to his toes. "That's not possible. It isn't logical."

"The heart never is."

He plopped into his chair. "Shit."

"Heavenly looks very fuckable. And if she's stealing into your heart, she must be a good person. Why should any of that be a problem?

Forget the age thing." She waved his protest away. "I doubt she's given it two thoughts."

He let out a harsh breath. "She's hung up on Seth."

"Who the hell is Seth?"

"A friend of Liam's who's visiting from New York. He takes her on fucking picnics and sticks his nose up her ass like a damn dog. She's too trusting to realize he's a player looking to put another notch in his bedpost. She deserves more. Knowing he might be, even now, sweet-talking her out of her panties—and into her heart—is fucking crushing me."

"Then why are you here? Get back to LA."

"I always spend Christmas with you. I just wish that asswipe would go back to New York—and fucking stay there. God, what if I come home and he's used her? Hurt her?" He gnashed his teeth. "I swear I will cut off his dick, throw him in a fucking ditch, and let him bleed out."

"So much for your Hippocratic oath…" She was laughing at him.

"Some assholes don't deserve to live."

"That's true enough. So what happens if he pops Heavenly's cherry over the holidays? Would that change how you feel about her?"

Was Gloria really asking if he liked her for her hymen? "No."

Though he'd be jealous as hell.

"This is fascinating, you know. She really has you unhinged."

"She does," he admitted. "And I don't know why. The moment I looked at her, she did something to me. I'd write it off as simple lust, but every minute I'm with her, my feelings grow."

"So let me get this straight… You're worried Seth will seduce the woman you're falling for but you've refused to touch since you're a 'pervert?'" Gloria shook her head like he was a dumbass. "Stop playing head games with yourself!"

"What would I do with a twenty-two-year-old virgin? Knit?" He threw his hands in the air. "I can see it now, me sitting beside Heavenly as we make scarves for people in…fucking Siberia. While she's swatching colors and showing me the perfect stitch, I'll be harder than hell and dreaming about tying her up in yarn, then sliding my fat cock somewhere—anywhere—inside her. Sounds like buckets of fun, doesn't it?"

Gloria burst out laughing. "Oh, my god. You should hear your-self."

"Shut up. I'm vomiting up my emotions here. I don't know what to do."

"Is she attracted to you, too?"

"Yeah. She flirts. She asked if I was single. I catch her looking at me like she's thinking something hot enough to make her blush. But Friday after her shift ended, we talked about school and the holi-day…and Seth. Then the motherfucking prick pulled up, and she kissed me *on the cheek* like some dirty uncle. Then she bopped out to his car and blew me off with a smile, while he saluted me with one finger."

"Poor baby." Gloria tilted her head—never a good sign. That meant she was about to dig deeper. "What's she supposed to think? This guy is pursuing her, and you've never given her any indication how you feel."

Beck rubbed at the back of his neck. "Maybe you've got a point. But I'm a hardcore sadist. I doubt Heavenly dreamed her Prince Charming would get hard by spanking her ass red. She needs a patient lover with a tender, compassionate touch, not…me."

"Oh, Ken. You *can* be tender and compassionate. It might have been a while since you've done the vanilla thing, but—"

"Try fifteen years."

"It's probably like riding a bicycle."

"I'm not sure I'd even enjoy the bicycle anymore."

"You, not like sex?" She scoffed.

"You're missing the point. I'm seriously asking myself if I could give up kink for her and stay sane."

Gloria squeezed his hand. "When we met, you were an angry man in a teenager's body, needing a way to process everything, and there's nothing more emotionally cleansing than sex. You helping subs purge their pain helped you to purge your own. But you're not that kid anymore."

Not only had Gloria saved him from life on the streets, she'd changed him from a boy to a man with patience and dignity. After sex, she'd refused to allow him to retreat behind walls of shame or pointless guilt. Instead, she'd merely lain beside him, warm and naked, and coaxed him to talk about his feelings. When she'd realized he craved control during sex, she'd introduced him to a Dominant who'd taught him what to do with submissives and pain sluts. Then nature had taken its course.

The woman understood him, always had. From her, he'd learned about closeness and trust. Never once had she let him wallow in uncertainty or self-defeat. Instead, she'd constantly assured him that nothing could hold him back but himself. Ultimately, she'd helped him mesh a new life with a new identity so he could become the man he was today.

Could that man possibly make Heavenly happy?

"I know you help masochists back in LA," Gloria went on. "But do you *need* to? More than you need her?"

Fuck. "Thanks for not asking the hard questions."

"You don't come to me for easy. I pointed you down a sadist's path to help you then, but I've always suspected that someday you'd take a different one. Maybe that day is here. Did you think you'd need that outlet forever?"

"Um...yeah." It was ingrained in his habits, his psyche, his cock. "How do I make the sadist in me stop wielding a paddle or a whip? That's like the surgeon in me cutting off my hand."

She sent him a quelling stare. "Being a surgeon is a calling. Being a sadist is a choice."

"Oh, then I'll just find my local twelve-step program and quit beating asses cold turkey. No problem."

"I didn't say it would be easy or happen overnight. If Heavenly becomes your priority, your needs will probably change. And you never know, she might meet you halfway."

Beck scoffed. "Do I need to show you her picture again?"

"How do you know she won't surprise you? I did. The first time you saw me, you saw a hooker working a street corner. Did you think then I'd become your parental figure, lover, and wife-of-convenience?"

She had him there.

"When are you supposed to see her again?" Gloria asked.

"Next Monday."

"That gives you a little over a week to figure out whether you're going to remain just her friend...or be her everything."

"I would love to be her everything. I just don't know…" If he was the man for her. If Heavenly could accept him—flaws, kinks, and cravings. If he could fulfill her.

"Oh, honey. I understand. Your ghosts are haunting you. But it's time to move forward."

He froze. "Ghosts?"

"Come on. You're too self-aware to play dumb. Heavenly sounds an awful lot like Blessing."

The moment her memory whispered through his brain, Beck broke out in a sweat. The air thickened, choking him with regret.

He tried hard never to allow that.

"No. Heavenly is self-sufficient and determined. And so damn proud. She's broke but chose to *starve* rather than ask for my fucking help. She pushes back…but now I buy her lunch every day. Trust me, she's the last woman who'd ever let a man run her life. She's *not* Blessing."

"Okay, calm down. Just…if you decide to pursue Heavenly, make sure it's not because you're trying to atone."

He fell deadly cold. "I can never atone."

She tangled her fingers in his. "Ken, you have to forgive yourself someday."

He jerked away.

"Try. Please." Gloria sighed. "For me."

Beck didn't want to dig through the rubble of his past, pick open his years-old scars, and bleed. What would it change? But she never asked him for anything, goddamn it. And he respected her too much to refuse.

"Fine."

"You know, if you want to talk, I'm always here for you." She stood and dropped a hand on his shoulder. "And now I've got to get gorgeous for work."

He watched as she hurried out of the kitchen. As she disappeared, he strode to the refrigerator and studied its contents. While Gloria showered and readied for work, he prepared pork fried rice, steamed vegetables, and a fresh fruit salad. Usually, he found cooking therapeutic, but tonight there was no joy as he sliced, diced, and stirred. His mind raced.

What was he going to do about Heavenly?

When dinner and small talk ended, Beck cleaned the kitchen. By the time he dried the last dish, he felt as if he'd engaged in a mental masturbation marathon. Worse, he was no closer to an answer. God, his friends would laugh their asses off if they had any clue how utterly an innocent blue-eyed blonde had long ago annihilated Shadows' big, bad sadist. And how close a second one was to doing it again.

He slammed the dishwasher shut, then yanked his phone from his pocket, staring at his photo of the crux of his discontent.

If you decide to pursue Heavenly, make sure it's not because you're trying to atone.

Beck shoved his phone back in his pocket with a disgruntled curse. Fuck, was he subconsciously trying to repeat history so he could rewrite it? That couldn't be his fascination with Heavenly…right? These feelings he couldn't fight must be a sign she was something more.

"I'm ready," Gloria called. "I'll be back about nine tomorrow. Try to keep the overnight party to a dull roar. My neighbors think I'm respectable."

He did his best to smile, but his head was too crowded. The walls were closing in. He had to get out of here and think. "Why don't you let me drop you off?"

"You don't have to, honey. I don't work downtown or the slums anymore. I'm renting a bank of posh new condos with lovely views of the Strip. Each of the girls has her own apartment. It's all very discreet and upscale. I have an office down the hall, along with security…"

"I want to drive around, catch up a little. My car is low on gas, and I'd rather take yours."

Gloria shrugged. "Here are my keys. Don't do anything I wouldn't enjoy."

Beck took the ring and headed to the garage, Gloria in tow. After climbing behind the wheel, he fired up her new Cadillac and left the subdivision in silence. Sagely, she didn't speak and add to the noise in his head.

He'd dropped her off in a matter of minutes with a promise to return for her after sunrise. She waved him off after a compassionate brush of her lips on his cheek. "You'll figure this thing with Heavenly out. You're too smart not to."

Right now, Beck wasn't sure that was true.

Once she'd disappeared into the swanky building, he steered toward the highway. He fought the urge to rush home to Heavenly. Instead, he zipped in the opposite direction, up the ramp to Interstate 15, heading north toward the desert. There were no people or chatter out here. He could think.

Turning on both the heat and the stereo, Beck sped down the long, flat highway, not even sure where he was going. Was he running from his future…or facing his past?

As he sailed through the tiny town of Mesquite and zoomed over the border into Arizona, Beck had his answer. Past it was.

What could he possibly hope to find in the shithole he'd abandoned long ago? Closure? Forgiveness?

Answers.

Gloria was right. If he ever wanted more out of his relationships than pain and meaningless sex—if he wanted to figure out if he had any future with Heavenly—he had to come to terms with the nightmare he'd left behind.

Ninety minutes later, the mountain peaks reached toward the stars. Dread gnawed at him. But he'd come this far; he wasn't stopping now. So Beck stomped on the gas pedal. It didn't take long before familiar signs lured him off the interstate and onto another highway. His gut clenched as he traveled the last long minutes to hell.

Finally, he slowed, pulling into the all-too-familiar gas station and cutting the engine. The place looked older.

He stepped from the car. It was colder here, the air thinner, the wind more brutal.

Quickly, he pulled out his wallet and slid his credit card into the slot. He'd rather not be here, but after a couple of hours on the road, Gloria's tank was empty, and this was the only game in town. He didn't have a choice.

Didn't that sum up his entire childhood?

As he stood pumping gas, he gritted his teeth against the wind and stared inside the run-down convenience store. Déjà vu slammed his system. He'd been here a hundred fucking times, holding his mother's hand and eyeing candy he hadn't been allowed to buy. Was the woman even alive anymore? Did she ever think of him?

He shoved those questions back, along with the memories. But more rushed in to take their place, snippets of the past he'd buried under rage, resentment, and regret. And all of it had culminated in this one place...

His gaze slid to the side of the building, where his old life had ended and his new one had begun. The image of that damn rusted green pickup parked just outside the restrooms, along with the body slumped in the driver's seat, flashed through his brain. The jagged slice along the man's throat had gushed, splashing his pristine white shirt. Beck swore he could still smell the bitter copper scent filling the cab as blood dripped to the floorboard.

He jerked back to the present to find sweat sliding down his face. Hands shaking, he focused on the gas pump, reminding himself that was a lifetime ago. But he couldn't seem to snap himself back to the present. One memory—the only one he cherished from his years here—lay waiting like a mental landmine. It had the power to blow his mind.

Easing down to the dirt behind the barn, he lifted his chin toward the sky. The summer sun warmed his skin while the scents of hay and horses melding with the dry desert filled his lungs. Usually, he found serenity in this secret place, but today anticipation buzzed under his skin.

Peering around the corner, he watched the house across the road and waited. Several nerve-racking minutes passed before he saw the girl lugging a basket of laundry toward the clothesline.

Rising slowly, he drank in the sight of her budding feminine curves. A thick blond braid lay draped over her shoulder, caressing one breast.

Mentally counting to ten, he made sure the coast was clear before sprinting her way. He darted between two hanging white sheets billowing in the wind and skidded to a stop. "Psst. Blessing! Hide in here with me."

As he stuck his hand through the opening between the edges where the fabric met, she cast him a worried frown. "Are you sure it's safe?"

"It will be like our own private fort. C'mon."

Long seconds passed. He feared she'd chickened out, but then she side-stepped between the rustling sheets. A goofy smile stretched across his face. Until he stared his way up her body. Then his blood chugged fast and hard. Their stares locked. Her lips parted in the silence. She was so close...

He swallowed. "See? It's private in here."

She darted a furtive glance over her shoulder. "I can't stay. I shouldn't even be talking to you. If they look out the window and find me..."

"Whatever time we have together is a blessing, Blessing."

They both softly smiled at his stumbling words.

Then he couldn't stand not touching her anymore and pulled her into his arms. As she gazed up at him, trust brimmed in her blue eyes. Their smiles faded, replaced by rough breaths.

"I think about you," he confessed as he stroked a finger down her soft, milky-white cheek. "A lot."

"Same for me."

Her words sent a rush of heat far warmer than the sun sizzling beneath his skin.

"I have to know," he whispered.

"What?"

"How your lips taste."

"W-we can't," she gasped. "I-it's a—"

"Shh," he soothed. "No one will ever know."

She stared up at him, fear filling her eyes.

Dang it. He hadn't meant to scare her. "If you don't want me to, I won't."

Blessing hesitated. "I-I want to. It's just..."

"You're afraid?"

"Yeah."

"I won't let anyone hurt you," he promised.

Before he lost his nerve, he cupped the back of her neck with shaking fingers and slanted his mouth over hers. Blessing's warm, soft lips made his whole body tingle and his cock stretch to life. Pressing his mouth to hers more firmly, he cinched a hand in her hair. Her tiny moan tickled his lips. He couldn't believe that, for this forbidden moment, she was his.

Guided by some innate instinct, he slid his tongue over the seam of her lips. When she opened for him, he plunged inside her warm, slick mouth. Blessing welcomed him, acting on the same primal impulse. Then—

Beck aborted the memory with an ugly curse. He had to get the fuck out of this place.

Clenching his jaw, he slammed the nozzle into the pump and jumped back in Gloria's gray Caddy. With trembling hands, he fastened his seat belt, started the engine, and floored it, wishing he could outrun the memories.

Pointing the car back toward Vegas, he dragged in ragged breaths. Thankfully, the anger and guilt eased with each mile. Then snippets of his conversation with Gloria began pinging through his brain.

Though Heavenly and Blessing were both young, innocent, and shy, the parallels ended there. While Blessing had been rooted in place, Heavenly had mustered the courage to leave behind everything familiar and chart her own future. She soldiered on every day to further her ambitions because she wanted more from life. Blessing had done only what she was told. Heavenly warily questioned people and situations. Blessing had merely accepted authority with a placid smile. Under Heavenly's quiet disposition, she was smart, brave, intriguing, steadfast, and dedicated—everything Blessing had been too timid to be.

Now that he'd settled Gloria's nagging question, Beck slammed the door on his past.

No denying the need to protect Heavenly burned inside him. It had nothing to do with the failures of his youth and everything to do with the unshakable feeling that she needed him. That sheltering her was his privilege and his right.

God help her, he was going to break all his own rules, even the one he'd held most sacred. Virgin or not, she was going to belong to him. Hell, in his mind…she already did. There was just one problem… How did he convince Heavenly that she was his?

"Stop behaving like her 'professional daddy' and tell her you want to be more than her *friend*, dipshit," he grumbled out loud.

If he didn't, he was going to lose out. Seth was running circles around him—with his pearly whites and one-fingered waves. Beck couldn't effectively compete if he only ever spent an hour a day with Heavenly in a crowded cafeteria talking about term papers, diseases, and hospital BS. He needed to take her out—and not on some prissy-assed picnic. No, on an honest-to-god date where they could peel off their professional skins and get to know one another as man and woman.

If that went well, *then* he'd find out if he could coax her over to the kinky side. In the event that was a no-go… Well, he'd have to ask himself hard questions about how much of his sadistic side he could give up. Honestly, he didn't know. But no matter what, Beck's heart—and his cock—were determined to find a way to make it work...and make Heavenly his for good.

SITTING BESIDE HEAVENLY in the hospital cafeteria hadn't been smart. They'd only been apart for ten days, but it felt like ten fucking years. All he wanted to do was drop his hand beneath the table—and onto her thigh. And he couldn't...yet.

Beck had nailed down a plan to introduce her to the man behind the lab coat. He'd fail if he caved to the impatient beast inside him and felt her up at work.

"Have any big plans to celebrate New Year's Eve tonight?" One thing he did know? She wouldn't be spending it with Seth.

Thank fuck.

While in Vegas, Beck had called Hammer to wish the throuple a Merry Christmas. Imagine his thrill at learning the girl-poaching PI was back in New York. It had been Beck's second-best Christmas present. His first was an unexpected seasons greetings text from Heavenly. Her message that she'd been thinking of him had been a thrill, almost as exciting as if she'd asked him to fuck her.

The next morning, he'd left Gloria's place—halfway through his stay. He'd had grand visions of having her on a date by Friday, in his bed by Saturday, and wearing his collar by Sunday.

Stupid, optimistic fucker.

It was Monday, and he was finally laying eyes on her.

When he'd asked if she wanted to kick off the weekend with him and catch a movie, she'd turned him down because she had to wait tables. Same for dinner Saturday night. Ditto Sunday. Not seeing her frustrated the shit out of him...but it made him more determined to come up with a plan C she couldn't refuse.

"I've always wanted to get dressed up and go to a fancy New Year's Eve party." Then she slumped glumly. "But I'm low woman on the totem pole, so I'm waiting tables. Again."

At a kids' pizza place on a night of adult revelry? Weren't the curtain climbers in bed by ten? "I was hoping we might ring in the New Year together."

"I would have loved that. I'm sorry I'm always working. When they hired me, I asked for all the hours I could get between now and the start of my next semester. I got them."

Beck swallowed a curse. She was putting herself through college and doing her best. He had to dial back on the impatience—and the horniness. But he was going to lose his shit if he couldn't persuade her to go out with him soon.

"Understood. But fair warning: I'll keep asking. I can be a very patient man, given the right motivation." *And you, little girl, are all the motivation I need.*

"I don't mind you asking. I just feel terrible. It shouldn't be this hard to spend time with a friend."

You'll figure out we're more than friends when I'm filling you with my cock, and your pretty little pussy is clutching me in orgasm.

Beck stifled a growl as he picked up his fork. They ate in tight silence, Heavenly nibbling on her pork chop and casting searching glances his way.

After washing down the last bite, Beck pushed his plate away and changed tactics. "How did you do on your finals?"

Heavenly wrapped her rosy lips around the opening of her water bottle. He tried to ignore the way her throat worked. Impossible. His mind filled with images of her on her knees, mouth wrapped around his cock, big blue eyes staring up at him as his wide crest nudged the back of her throat.

"My tests were much harder than waiting tables, but I did good."

"I won't lie and tell you they'll get easier. But every exam you pass means you're closer to making sure you don't spend the rest of your life schlepping food."

"Oh, thank goodness," she muttered. "At the end of the night, my feet hurt so bad, despite the new shoes you sent me for Christmas—thank you; they fit perfectly, by the way. But waitressing is a lot of peopling for me."

Beck fought a smile. "So when you get off work, do you shut yourself in your room?"

"No. The first thing I do is take a long shower so I can be blissfully alone. It's weird because I love coming to the hospital and helping people who genuinely need care and comfort. But after waiting tables, I ignore the rest of the world until I have to go back."

"While dreading every moment until your next shift?"

"Oh, so you've waited tables, too?"

"No. I guessed, based on your...enthusiasm." When she giggled, Beck sipped his water. "How was your Christmas?"

"Fine." She paused. "Quiet."

"No family?"

"Some, but other than work it was almost too peaceful with you and Seth both gone."

Beck was still celebrating the fact the asshat wasn't around to cock-block him.

"When are you going to let me add some excitement to your life?" His words teemed with innuendo.

"When Seth tried that, I didn't do so good. I barely spent an hour with him, and he just...left." She pushed her plate away as if she'd suddenly lost her appetite. "I'll probably never see him again."

The hair on the back of Beck's neck stood on end. Had that motherfucker stolen her virginity before jetting back to New York?

Rage, white and hot, surged through him. He locked stares with Heavenly. "Tell me everything he did to you."

His snarl had her inching back. She opened her mouth to say something, but snapped it shut.

You weren't supposed to scare her, asshole!

Beck groped for his control. "I warned you Seth was nothing but a bad decision waiting to happen, little girl."

"You did, but—"

"Did he hurt you?"

Heavenly shot him a quizzical frown. "What do you mean?"

"When he took you to bed."

Her cheeks turned bright red as she shook her head. "Oh, he didn't... I mean, we never... That didn't happen."

Relief poured through him, so profound he shook. "I'm glad you were too smart to fall for his bullshit."

"He didn't feed me any. He didn't do anything at all, not even kiss me."

While that overjoyed Beck, Heavenly's disappointment shredded him like a thousand knives. "Then why are you convinced he'll never want to see you again?"

"I-I said something I probably shouldn't have. He was gone before I could explain or tell him I was sorry. I feel terrible that I upset him. I miss the fun we shared."

Hearing that she actually mourned the prick's departure felt worse than chewing on glass. Beck had no idea what she'd said to hurt Seth's fragile little feelings. But the important takeaway was, if she hadn't, the time Beck had spent sitting on the sidelines with his dick in his hand would have cost him everything.

If Heavenly missed the "fun" she'd had with Seth, he'd do his damndest to show her a better time. In fact, Plan C had just presented itself—and he'd give her the best fucking day of her life. And maybe the best night of his would follow...

"Well, I have some fun in mind. How would you feel about coming with me to the happiest place on earth?"

"I don't... Where's that?"

She didn't know? Oh, he couldn't wait to see the look on her face.

"One of my patients is a bigwig at Disney. He gave me a couple of passes to Disneyland. What do you say? Want to spend Saturday with me, having fun?"

Like a kid on Christmas morning, her eyes grew huge and excited. "*This* Saturday? You're asking *me* to go?"

"Yeah. Have you ever been?"

"No. Never. Oh, wow! I've always wanted to go." She bit her lip, looking so adorably thrilled. "You're serious?"

He basked in her delight. "There's no one I'd rather go with."

"Then yes!"

"Don't you have to work?"

"It doesn't matter. For the chance to go to Disneyland, I'll call in sick."

A deep laugh rumbled up from his chest. "So I'm already corrupting you, is that it?"

"Yes. And I'll happily let you."

His cock stood up and wept. "Be careful, little girl, I might make that a habit."

"Would that be such a bad thing?" she ventured in shy flirtation.

Oh, dear god. How long before he could have her naked and panting and begging? It couldn't come soon enough. "Not at all."

CHAPTER NINE

FIVE DAYS LATER, Heavenly was convinced that Kenneth Beckman knew magic. From the moment they drove onto Disney property and he parked his red Mercedes near the entrance, the VIP treatment began. He looped a distinctive colored lanyard around her neck with a smile, then put a matching one around his own. "These are Extra Special Double Secret VIP Golden Fastpasses."

"That's a very long name. What do they do?"

"Okay, so I'm making that up. I don't know what they're actually called, but these golden cards allow us in the Fastpass lane of any attraction. We can walk past the line anytime we want."

Her mouth fell open. Coming to Disneyland had been a girlhood dream. But to skip most of the waiting and just experience everything? "Oh, my gosh. Really?"

He gave her an indulgent nod. "Really."

Heavenly squealed as he led her to their guide, who ushered them through a private park entrance. Soon, they stood in front of the colorful flowers grown onto the hillside in the shape of Mickey Mouse. Kids jumped, parents pushed strollers, and people everywhere took selfies. She drank in the experience, anticipation buzzing in her belly.

Today, she could pretend to be a princess. And the gorgeous man by her side could definitely play her Prince Charming.

"This train"—he pointed to the big red steam locomotive—"circles the park with stops throughout. We can get off or on at any of them. Want to ride it?"

Eventually, yes, but the Disneyland of her imagination came from TV specials, pictures on the Internet, and YouTube videos that always started with one thing. "Can we walk up Main Street first? I'm dying to see it in person."

"Whatever you want to do. This day is for you, little girl."

Joy bubbled up. She felt like a shaken bottle of soda pop that might explode at any moment. "I still can't believe I'm actually here."

With you.

"I remember feeling blown away during my first visit, too."

The morning sun was quickly warming into one of those picture-perfect California days as they made their way under the arched bridge, past colorful posters of the park's most famous attractions, then emerged near City Hall. And she got her first glimpse inside the park.

Heavenly had to gasp; she'd never seen so many people at once. Dr. Beckman didn't seem at all fazed by the crowd. Everyone from toddlers to great-grandparents looked eager for the adventure ahead.

"Take this park map." He plucked a pamphlet from the slot beside him and put it in her hands. "You'll need it. This is a big place."

Heavenly tucked it into her pocket as he led her past the fire station and the town square. When she rounded the corner at the Emporium and got her first glimpse of the long stretch of Main Street USA, she froze, hardly noticing when someone bumped her from behind.

At the end of the road stood the most magical structure of all: Sleeping Beauty Castle.

"Oh, my gosh. It's…" The castle of Disney movies. The icon people instantly associated with Disneyland. The place she'd been most longing to see. "Everything."

"Then we'll be sure to check it out, but there are lots of other things to see. Did you know"—he drawled, his deep voice caressing the shell of her ear—"Main Street was inspired by Walt Disney's hometown?"

"The charm is so turn-of-the-century."

"Want to explore?"

Everything around her looked so quaint and interesting. "Can we go in there?"

When she pointed to the Emporium, he ushered her in that direction, smiling as she oohed at vignettes in the windows depicting scenes from their movies and aahed at cute plush characters.

Slowly, they wound their way along the busy street, moving from store to store, tempted by bright lights, shiny toys, and the scent of fresh popcorn. They ducked into the cinema to watch *Steamboat*

Willie, the first distributed debut of Mickey and Minnie Mouse.

Ten minutes later, she emerged into the sunlight, all smiles. She stepped off the curb to dash through the crowd, lured by the scrumptious smells of sugar and vanilla. Suddenly, a protesting horn startled her. Dr. Beckman wrapped his arm around her middle and yanked her back against him—and out of the path of an oncoming trolley filled with parkgoers.

Heavenly pressed a hand to her chest and dragged in a calming breath.

"Careful," he whispered against her ear, still holding her tightly.

She gave him a shaky nod…then realized her backside was plastered against his hard abs and muscled thighs.

Her heart began thumping in an all-out gallop that had little to do with fright. Heat rushed over her. Everything in her panties began to ache.

He often had that effect on her. And he was probably thinking she was an idiot for not watching where she was going.

"Sorry. I was looking around and…" she blurted. "Thank you."

"It's all right. I've got you."

His low-voiced assurance made her shiver. Her nipples stiffened. Through her T-shirt, they pressed hard against his bare forearm. Was there any way he could fail to notice?

"I'm okay now." She tried to wriggle free. Of course she'd rather stay in his arms, but he'd soon know she didn't think of him as a mere friend if she did.

"You sure?"

Heavenly gave him a shaky nod.

"Is that a yes?"

How was it possible he sounded even closer? His voice lower? That he held her even tighter?

"Yes."

But he still didn't let go. She glanced over her shoulder at him. His dark eyes pierced her, hooded, narrowed, focused. And she felt his penis swell, thick and as hard as a lead pipe.

A silent gasp parted her lips. Their gazes fused. Then his hips seemed to press and roll against her backside. She hadn't imagined that, right? Heavenly didn't think so. And well…she could tell with

Dr. Beckman that it wasn't a small world, after all.

In that moment, he imprinted his body on hers. She answered in kind, turning wet, her breathing unsteady. Awareness flared in his eyes.

He knows I like him.

The urge to babble and cover her embarrassment was too much to resist. She pushed out of his arms. "Gosh, I've been here five minutes, and I almost got myself killed."

Slowly, he stepped back. "I'll try to keep you alive a bit longer. What would you like to do next?"

Heavenly couldn't stop thinking about Dr. Beckman as a man. Her stirring desire messed with her ability to talk like a normal human. Had he been hard simply because he was male…or because he wanted her?

She must seem totally unsophisticated to him. She always did bumbling, inept things. And yet, she would have sworn he was looking at her like a grown-up, sexy woman.

A gaggle of children, their voices shrill with excitement, ended the moment. Heavenly watched as they flocked, parents in close pursuit, toward a living, breathing Cinderella, all dressed for the ball. Yes, she knew it wasn't *real*, but she could barely muffle her thrilled gasp behind her hand. "Sorry. I don't mean to get excited."

"I like it when you do." His tone was thick.

That delicious tingle of arousal slid through her again. Six little words—and yet Dr. Beckman's suggestive voice turned her inside out.

"Be yourself," he clarified. "Not who you have to be at the hospital. I'm going to enjoy experiencing today through your eyes since they're less cynical than mine."

"Okay."

Pleasure and approval suffused his handsome face, along with something that seemed like more than friendship.

Was that wishful thinking? After all, look what had happened with Seth. One minute she'd thought they might get much closer. Then she'd opened her mouth…and ended up alone. Of course, that didn't stop her from thinking about him. Nothing did. He was like a ghost, out of sight but always haunting her.

Pushing away the thought, she turned her focus back on Dr. Beckman, determined to enjoy today. "So how many times have you been here?"

"Maybe more than a few. I would have sworn I was too jaded to really enjoy it again, but I might change my mind." He gave her a slow smile. "Tell me what you want to do."

The castle was still ahead, begging exploration, but… "I've always wanted to ride a roller coaster. Can we?"

"You never have?"

"There weren't many opportunities in Wisconsin. When I was eight, I went with a friend's family to this place in Wisconsin Dells." She grinned wryly. "But I was an inch too short to ride."

"You'll never lack inches when you're with me."

"Huh? Are you laughing at me?"

"I'm not." He cleared his throat. "Um, you're tall enough now."

"I am, so no short jokes. I'm sensitive."

He grinned. "I'll bet you are."

There was something behind that smirk she didn't quite grasp, but it made her warm all over.

By the time they ambled to the top of Main Street, they reached a hub of sorts. Slowly, she turned in a circle, trying to decide which "land" to conquer first. But her stare was drawn again to that magical castle sharp against the bright blue sky. She remembered being fascinated by videos showing amazing pyrotechnics exploding behind it, in sync with the wistful strains of "When You Wish Upon a Star."

She grabbed his arm. "Do they really have fireworks?"

"Every night, weather permitting."

"Wow. I wish we could stay for them."

"We can stay as long as you'd like, Heavenly."

She bit her lip. "When do they start?"

"Look on your map. The big show of the night is usually the last thing before the park closes—"

"Oh," she grumbled in disappointment.

Her father was much too sick to cope all day and half the night without her. Thank goodness one of the fellow vets who volunteered at the VA had agreed to visit him this afternoon. Still, she'd worry, so whenever she went to the bathroom, she'd text him to make sure he was all right. No need to dump her woes on Dr. Beckman.

When she'd told Dad about the trip to Disneyland with a friend, he'd insisted she go. "Have fun on your day off. Lord knows, there has been precious little of that these past miserable years."

She'd tried to reassure him that she was happy and had everything she could ever need in life.

They both knew it wasn't true.

"We can watch the fireworks earlier. I think the first show is at nine thirty." Beck sent her a frown filled with concern. "You okay?"

She snapped back to the present and pasted on a smile. "Let's see how we feel after being on our feet all day. Now where is that roller-coaster?"

"This way." He gestured to the right and ushered her toward To-morrowland, where they soon found Space Mountain. "I'll be right beside you if you get scared. I'm a doctor, so you can trust me." He winked.

She burst into a fit of giggles. "Ha! If I didn't trust you, I wouldn't be getting in a little car that jets around on a track too dark to see."

"It's fun. I promise."

"I'm sure, but...I've had so many new experiences today, you know?"

He raised a brow at her. "I'm hoping we experience lots of firsts together."

With one innuendo-laden sentence, he made her flare hot again. Was she reading too much into his words? After all, he'd mentored her, protected her, befriended her. None of that meant he wanted her. Then again, would he have invited her today if he didn't feel *something* for her? There was that buttery voice of his, not to mention his erection, too...

Mentally chewing on the possibilities, Heavenly followed him through the shadowy, blue-lit passages inside the building. A surreal techno voice followed them along the path that seemed to get darker with every step. Before she knew it, they were boarding the gleaming silvery-white cars with yellow stripes.

Apprehension bit at her belly as she began to climb in. "I'm so nervous."

He stayed her with a touch to her arm. "I understand, but don't forget to look around and get the full experience. Some firsts are worth savoring."

"You're right. Sometimes I get caught up and forget everything else."

So Heavenly stole a long glance around the loading zone, felt the cool air in her face, and soaked in the excitement hanging in the air.

When Dr. Beckman gave her an approving nod, she stepped toward the waiting car—and would have stumbled if he hadn't been right behind her. Instantly, his hand wrapped around her elbow. "I've got you."

"Sorry. I can be so clumsy."

"No, I've watched you. You're graceful," he assured as he helped her settle into the car.

Only then did he release her.

Heavenly sighed. No wonder half the female staff at the hospital were gaga for him. "You've always been so sweet to me."

"You make it easy."

She wasn't sure what to say, but park employees distracted her by instructing riders how to fasten the safety belt. Beside her, the doctor made certain she was secured snugly before the ride operators double-checked. Then with a lurch, they were off.

Nerves gnawing a hole in her stomach, Heavenly grabbed Dr. Beckman's thigh.

"It's okay." He settled his hand over hers, tangling their fingers together. "Breathe. Enjoy it. You're going to have fun."

"Uh-huh," she agreed—but she didn't let go. As they ascended a flashing red tunnel, she turned to him. "In case I forget to tell you later, I really had a great time."

By the time they emerged into the sunshine, she was still grinning and her throat felt slightly scratchy from screaming. Dr. Beckman squinted, holding a finger to his ear.

"Oh, my goodness. I'm sorry."

"It's fine. Really. I've got another ear."

Rolling her eyes, she swatted him playfully. "I'll try to restrain myself next time. There will be a next time, right?"

"If you want one, yes. And don't you restrain anything on my account—ever. That's my job." He sent her an ironic grin she didn't understand.

"You're sure?"

"Nearly everyone who walks through the front gates leaves their adult self behind and turns into a kid at heart. I won't even tell you how embarrassing I was on my first visit."

Her heart did somersaults at his wide grin. "How old were you?"

"Twenty-eight, I think. I even have a pair of ears from that trip embroidered with my name. I wore them all day. Not kidding."

She laughed. "Did you eat cotton candy and sing Disney songs?"

"I might have. Are you judging?"

"Of course not." But a giggle slipped free.

"It's fine. We'll see how mature you are as the day goes on."

Heavenly pressed her lips together, fearing she would fail miserably at adulting, but she didn't care.

The morning passed quickly as they raced each other in the cars at Autopia. Heavenly laughed when she won, then pleaded for a ride on the Matterhorn Bobsleds. She managed to scream less this time, earning her a smile from Dr. Beckman, before she dragged him to Fantasyland for a ride on King Arthur Carousel. She climbed on a white horse with bells, while the doctor stood beside her and held her steady. After riding Snow White's Scary Adventures and Peter Pan's Flight, they made their way to Frontierland.

"Hey, Disney Princess. It's one o'clock. How about some lunch?"

She'd eaten a hearty breakfast at home so she didn't have to spend money on an expensive theme park meal. "Sure. I'll keep you company while you eat."

"Nope. You're eating, too."

Before she could argue, he pointed to an empty table. Feeling oddly compelled to do as he instructed, she sat. Ten minutes later, he returned with burgers, fries, and fizzy sodas. She dug in, nearly finishing every bite.

Afterward, she cleared the table. "Thank you, Dr. Beckman."

"When we're not at work, call me Beck."

A smile lit up her whole body since only his friends called him that. "Sure...Beck."

"Ready for more rides? Or do you need a few minutes to let your food settle?"

She raised a brow at him. "Why? Do you?"

"I might."

"You look at blood and guts all day but you have a delicate stomach?"

"I do not have a delicate stomach. Just…a more sensitive equilibrium."

"Maybe I should call you princess."

"Be careful, little girl."

"Or?" She raised a brow at him.

"You might find out."

"I think you're all bark and no bite."

His grin told her she was terribly wrong. "You keep thinking that. You'll find out differently. Now, come with me so I can prove how manly I am by shooting something."

As they headed toward the shooting gallery, Heavenly couldn't remember the last time she'd felt this happy. But when Beck reached for her hand and tucked it in his own, her euphoria swelled into wide-eyed surprise.

He liked her. As a boy liked a girl. No, as a man liked a woman.

The day couldn't possibly get more perfect.

She swore she was walking on clouds as they rode the *Mark Twain* around Tom Sawyer Island, caught Big Thunder Mountain Railroad, then got soaking wet on Splash Mountain. She probably wore him out with the three trips she *needed* on Haunted Mansion, but it was so clever and full of details. Maybe he didn't mind too much, because when he slid beside her in their "doom buggy," he held her close and smiled indulgently.

After that, they stumbled up to Pirates of the Caribbean.

When the ride ended, she was still singing "Yo ho, yo ho, a pirate's life for me…" He escorted her to Blue Bayou, which overlooked the ride's gently lapping waters. They were shown to a table that ringed the perimeter of the swampy darkness, complete with fireflies. It was…romantic.

"What are you hungry for?" He glanced up from the menu, brow raised.

He meant food—maybe—but her heart still skipped a few beats. "I-I don't need—"

"To eat? Yes, you do. Let me rephrase my question. Is there anything on the menu you're allergic to or don't like?"

"I'm not fond of lamb."

"We'll avoid that then."

Beck ordered surf and turf for them both. Heavenly tried not to choke or object. He wouldn't appreciate it, but it was so expensive... She could feed herself and her father both for weeks on the cost of this one meal.

After delicious gumbo, the waitress delivered filet mignon and lobster with potatoes au gratin, along with a bottle of earthy red wine. Every tasty bite was exquisitely perfect.

"We talk during lunch at the hospital, but there are a lot of things I don't know about you, Heavenly."

She wrinkled her nose. "I'm boring."

His stare chastised her. "I doubt that. Tell me everything..."

What could she tell him without bringing the mood down? "You know I'm from Wisconsin. I grew up loving *Rugrats* and—"

"What the hell is a rug rat?"

"It's a cartoon. Well, it was. They don't make it anymore."

"I'm sorry?" He looked as if he wasn't sure whether to apologize or laugh.

"It's fine. As an adult, I'm no longer entertained by animated shows about kids in diapers."

He almost choked on his wine. "I'm glad to hear that."

"Oh, come on. You must have liked a cartoon or two as a kid. Fess up."

Beck hesitated. "I was far more interested in being outdoors. If there was a ball involved, even better."

"That sounds so incredibly...male."

"I'm glad you've noticed," he quipped. "Okay, favorite ice cream."

"What's yours?" she countered. "I'm going to make fun of you first."

That had him laughing. "Raine might have corrupted me lately with her love of caramel caribou."

"I can't fault you for that, though I prefer mint chip. When I was a kid, there was this place that used to make it with chunks of Andes Creme de Menthe and...oh. It was"—she snickered—"orgasm in a cone."

"Really? And you'd know that how?"

She closed her eyes, mortification rolling through her. "Figure of speech."

"So I have to be better than an ice cream cone?"

Did he mean if he ever gave her an orgasm? "What?"

Beck cleared his throat. "Favorite season?"

"Um…when I lived in Wisconsin, it was summer, for sure. But LA is like summer all year round, so… What about you?"

"Fall."

"You like crisp leaves and autumn breezes?"

He smirked. "And football. That's way more important."

"Of course. Definitely a man."

"You need me to prove it?"

"You really have to stop teasing me…"

"Who says I'm teasing?" He gave her a disreputable grin.

She rolled her eyes at him. "Favorite band?"

"I'm an old-school grunge guy. Give me Nirvana, Pearl Jam, Stone Temple Pilots…that kind of thing. But I listen to all kinds of music. Who do you like?"

"Maroon 5. Adam Levine—"

"Sings like a girl?"

She swatted his arm across the table. "Is incredibly talented and sexy."

Beck scoffed. "You think?"

"He has some really amazing ink."

Beck pulled the sleeve of his shirt over his elbow to reveal something tribal around his bulging bicep. "Like this?"

"You…" Heavenly stared, trying to string her words together. Never in a thousand years had she imagined the good doctor would have tattoos. "I'm surprised."

"A lot of things about me might surprise you." That grin of his nearly combusted her. Sly, brimming with knowledge, slightly dirty.

"Like what?"

"I've shocked you enough for one day." He leaned closer, over his forgotten dessert. "But let's just say my arms aren't the only place I'm inked."

She opened her mouth, but the waiter came by with a refill of his coffee.

Beck glanced at his watch. "It's a little before nine. If we don't leave this joint, we won't catch the fireworks."

After he paid the bill, she followed him through the darkness as they finally explored the castle. She squealed with delight when he bought her a pair of princess mouse ears, embroidered with her name. They made it just in time to slide into a VIP area to view the fireworks near the castle before the first song cued and the first bright bursts of color lit the sky. They stood close, and she was absolutely spellbound as the pyrotechnics show exceeded her wildest dreams.

With her stare riveted to every dazzling explosion across the sky, tears of happiness slid down her cheeks. Beck traced a finger across her face, capturing a stray tear and tasting it. She shivered, suddenly unable to look at anything but him. He said nothing. No words were necessary. Something magical was happening that terrified her yet lured her even closer.

"A-are you going to kiss me?" she finally whispered.

"When we're alone." He caressed her face with his warm palm. "But not now. It's worth waiting and doing right."

Then the last of the fireworks burst with a sweeping crescendo of music, and the moment passed.

It was time to head home.

Beck took her hand in his again and led her to his car. He wasn't terribly happy when she asked him to drop her off at the mall where he'd picked her up, but thankfully he didn't argue.

Today had truly been the best day of her life…so far. If she could believe him, the best might be yet to come.

THE FOLLOWING SATURDAY evening, Beck pulled up to the art gallery, took a deep breath, and headed in to find Heavenly. Their date at Disneyland had been strictly vanilla, but she'd loved every minute— and he'd loved every one of her squeals and smiles.

Now that he knew they were compatible away from the hospital, he was anxious to test their chemistry on a *much* different level.

Tonight was make or break.

Unfortunately, it hadn't started well. He'd planned to pick her up, wine and dine her while he asked her questions and dropped hints. Then together, they'd view the show. But she'd insisted on meeting him at the art gallery. Errands or some shit. Her promise to wait for him in the adjacent bar hadn't eased his gnawing anxiety. If she'd already peeked at the exhibit…he'd have a lot of explaining to do.

Thankfully, he spied her sitting on a stool, as promised, her cascade of golden hair and feminine grace unmistakable. Black strappy sandals adorned her feet, now delicately crossed at the ankle. Visually, he caressed his way up her slender legs, settling long moments later on the sensual curve of her ass, hugged by a classic black sheath.

She was always beautiful, but tonight? *Fuck me.*

A hundred times Beck had asked himself if he should skip this risky experiment and simply get her alone. A hundred times he'd told himself no. This wasn't about a quick lay; it would tell him what kind of future he and Heavenly might share. If tonight didn't go as he hoped… Well, they could still be friends.

Fuck, that sounded horrible.

Easing closer, he stole a clandestine moment to inhale her sultry, hint-of-berry scent and fought the urge to bury his nose in her silky hair. "Why are you sitting alone, little girl? Did some jerk stand you up? Come with me instead. There are things I could show you…"

Heavenly turned, a smirk playing at her lips. "I can't. I'm waiting for a handsome doctor. If I'm not where he asked me to meet him, I might be in trouble."

Submissiveness *and* role play? *Hell yes.*

He motioned to the bartender to replace her water with a smooth, imported Sauvignon Blanc. Moments later, the man set a slender stem on a fresh napkin directly in front of her.

Beck paid and tried to cool himself with a swallow of beer. "Well, the doctor is one lucky son of a bitch. He's also an idiot for making you wait. If I had the chance to spend the evening with such a gorgeous little girl, I wouldn't leave you alone for a second."

"Oh, he's not late. I'm a bit early." Heavenly leaned around him, scanning the room. "I expect him any minute."

"Well, until he shows, I insist you join me. For your safety."

"My safety?" She blinked at him.

"We wouldn't want some lowlife off the street snatching you from that barstool, right?"

"Of course not."

"Then let me take care of you." About that, he wasn't joking.

"All right." As Heavenly eased to her feet, she plucked a tiny black clutch off the bar, lifted her wineglass, and flashed him a mysterious glance. "I've never had a bodyguard before."

If I had my way, you'd need more than a bodyguard to keep me from stripping you bare and ravishing you in a million wicked ways.

Somehow, Beck managed to simply smile and palm the small of her back. He guided her across the marble floors, where they joined the waiting crowd. Palpable excitement churned the air.

Heavenly clung to his side with an eager smile. She wouldn't appreciate everything she saw, but he'd watch her, cataloging even her subtlest reactions until he knew how—or if—he should proceed.

"I've never been to an art gallery," she whispered with a nervous hitch.

"Then we're both in for a special treat."

"You've never been to one, either?"

He shook his head, chuckling softly. "I have, but I'm especially looking forward to tonight's show. A private buyer loaned his rare collection of Joshua Lars's sculptures for this exhibit."

"I've never heard of Joshua Lars."

"He's amazing. Seeing his work in person will be a real treat. Shame he hasn't unveiled any new works for years."

"What does he sculpt?"

"People, mostly women. Tonight's theme is, um…alternative lifestyle art."

He didn't say more; she had to experience the show for herself. And he needed her unvarnished reactions.

"What does that mean?"

Sighing, he pulled her into a secluded corner and cupped her shoulders. "What you see tonight may confuse, shock, or excite you. Any of those reactions is valid. Just…approach everything with an open mind. Give me your opinions. Ask questions. I'll explain if I can. Will you do that for me?"

"Of course."

Naturally, she wanted to please, and it was easy to give her assent now. Keeping her promise would be much harder once she got inside.

He guided her back to the entrance and handed over their tickets. Anticipation and disquiet thrummed through his veins as they stepped into the wide space of concrete floors, industrial ceilings, and white walls.

A surgically stacked brunette in form-hugging red latex welcomed them, balancing a tray of champagne flutes on her palm. Black leather cuffs hugged each wrist. A thick collar squeezed her neck with an engraved plate that proclaimed her PROPERTY.

Beside him, Heavenly cocked her head, looking puzzled. Damn, he'd pay money to hear her thoughts. But he couldn't push her. He had to let her process.

Beck thanked the submissive greeter, who deferentially dipped her gaze before ushering Heavenly farther into the room. Now, everything would get real. His nerves buzzed as the soft chatter around them hummed.

He stepped in front of the first painting, guiding her toward the unframed canvas of a naked woman lying on her side facing forward, hands tied behind her back, head lolling to the ground in tormented anticipation. Ropes framed her breasts and looped around her neck. Her legs were spread and trussed to remain bent, binds encircling thigh and shin.

The piece was stunning. Picturing Heavenly waiting for him in this pose revved his libido hard.

Clearing his throat, Beck studied her as she glimpsed the light-and-shadow masterpiece. The startled blink of her lashes preceded the wide flare of her eyes. An instant later, color rosied her cheeks. Then her lips parted, and her berry-pink tongue flicked against her upper lip. Thoughts clearly raced through her brain as she dragged her gaze toward him, as if reluctant to take her eyes off the erotic piece.

"Wow."

"Yes. What else?"

"I, um… It's striking. She's anatomically correct and really flexible."

Beck repressed a grin. "How does the painting make you *feel*?"

She squirmed as she gathered her words. His cock jerked.

"Will this exhibit be all about naked people?"

"Answer my question. Then I'll answer yours."

Turning back to the canvas, she stared, a little furrow between her brows. "Helpless. But not in a bad way. She looks at peace. It's oddly...pretty. Does that make sense?"

Absolutely. And he'd bet Heavenly was at least vaguely aroused and didn't understand why.

Beck did—and his blood roared. "Of course. Art is not only beautiful, it's designed to make you feel something, to stir the imagination. It's a personal journey for whomever views it."

She nodded absently, still staring at the painting as if trying to understand her reaction. "Now you'll answer my question?"

She'd soon discover he always kept his word. "Because it's an exhibit of erotic works that focus primarily on alternative sexual lifestyle, I'm expecting a lot of nudity, yes."

"Oh. Okay." Her blush deepened. "Do you, um...think she posed like this for the artist or did he paint her from his imagination?"

Beck slid a finger beneath her chin. "Good question. As lifelike as that is—look at the sweat beading her brow and the quiver of her thighs—I'd guess she posed."

She gave him a shaky nod, biting her lower lip as she stared again at the piece in fascination, nervously sipping her vino.

So that was a yes to attempting bondage.

Somehow, he managed not to seize her lips and rip off her dress. "Ready to move on?"

She nodded, and together they wandered to the next piece, this one a photograph of a pale woman standing alone against a dark wall, wearing stilettos, a collar—and nothing else. Her limbs were chained at wrists and ankles, stretched wide apart toward the edges of the frame. She'd tossed her head back as her body gave way to her bindings.

Beck turned to find Heavenly studying the photo. He could all but hear her wheels turning. "What's going on in that gorgeous head, little girl?"

She glanced at him, worrying her lip. "I don't get it. Why is she wearing a dog collar? And why is she strung up like that? I would think she's a victim of something terrible, except..."

"Go on. Except what?"

"She seems to like it."

Of course. She was floating blissfully in subspace. "She's euphoric."

"That doesn't make sense to me. How could she enjoy someone degrading her?"

"Why do you assume someone is degrading her?"

Heavenly was slower to answer this time. "Well, first, someone tied her up and left her."

"How do you know she doesn't find pleasure or comfort in being bound?"

"You mean like being tightly swaddled soothes a baby?"

"That's a good analogy, yes. It may not make sense to us, but to her the chains may provide serenity."

"Okay, but he left her exposed, almost like…"

"He wanted to stare at her as if she were a work of art?"

Heavenly chewed on her lip, but Beck noticed she didn't question why a woman would want her lover to enjoy the view of her body.

"Why the dog collar?" she asked instead.

"Why do most owners put a collar on their pet?"

"To decorate them. To signify ownership."

"Exactly. And in her case, someone who holds her dear understands her desire to be owned, bound, and visually worshipped." Beck gave her something else to consider. "Sex is no different than any other primal need. Everyone has varying taste. This exhibit is merely an expression of each artist's individual preference. Do you like this image?"

"It's unusual."

"It's not something most people see every day."

"Or ever. I-I mean, I've never seen anything like this."

She must not Google much. Beck kept the smartass observation to himself.

"Understood, but art challenges us to consider, maybe even tackle our preconceived notions. Sometimes, it disarms us with unexpected reactions." He tried to shrug casually. "Some might view this and find themselves repulsed. Others might wish they were in her place."

She nodded, still mulling as she imbibed more wine. "What do you think?"

"The peace in her posture is beautiful. Tell me what seeing this makes you feel."

It took her a moment to answer. "I don't know how I'd feel about being so...on display."

"Being naked makes you self-conscious?"

She pondered that question with a cock of her head. "I'm not ashamed of my body, but...no one has ever seen me naked."

Her answer gave him hope. "So you're apprehensive but not repulsed."

"Something like that."

He'd get her damn used to being naked around him, but he'd also assure her she'd never have to be "on display" for anyone else.

She shot him a suspicious frown. "How do you know so much about this stuff?"

Beck had wondered how long it would take her to ask. "Well, as a medical professional, I've encountered some interesting things over the years."

"I want to experience life." She sighed and shook her head. "I mean *really* experience it."

"And you should."

Together, they moved to the next piece. The oil painting was a close-up of a woman's profile, lips red, a blurred hint of her arms strung up above her head in the background. Her Dom had attached a clothespin to her wayward tongue.

Beck bit back a chuckle. He'd used this punishment on a few unruly subs.

On his left, Heavenly's brows slashed down in confusion. "I guess someone really doesn't want her talking."

"Clearly, she's said enough."

Heavenly wrinkled her nose. "I don't think I'd like this at all."

"I doubt that woman does, either."

"So some people like to be bound but none want to be silenced. If that's true, why do this?" She gestured to the painting. "It seems like a punishment a parent might have given their child for swearing or lying once upon a time."

"You're not far off. Think about it... Sometimes, even adults have to be corrected. Granted, this may seem like an extreme way to get one's point across, but do you think she'll forget the lesson anytime soon?"

Heavenly shook her head. "If someone ever did that to me, I'd want a warning that I was saying too much before he felt compelled to hunt up a clothespin."

Duly noted, little girl. I'll be more than happy to keep your sexy ass in line.

He reached for her hand, leading her around the freestanding wall to the feature on the other side. Front and center, a bright splash of a photo greeted them—this one of a sub's freshly whipped ass. Some blows on her hip were deep enough to have drawn blood. A red drop ran down her pale thigh, contrasting artistically with the almost innocent yellow-flowered shirt that brushed the edges of her welts.

Imagining his marks on Heavenly's untouched ass roused the sadist in Beck and pushed his desire nearly to the edge of his control.

Beside him, she gasped and recoiled, burying her face in his shoulder. "Why would anyone do that to her? It's savage and cruel."

How did he explain that this Dom had lined his sub methodically, giving her a beautiful endorphin high while pushing her to her pain threshold?

"Several of the mediums on display depict various aspects of the BDSM lifestyle. Do you know what that is?"

Heavenly shook her head. "I've heard the term before but…"

"Bondage, Dominance, submission, masochism. It contains elements of discipline and sadism, among other things."

She dragged in a breath. "Did you bring me here because you like this stuff?"

He should have known she was too clever not to catch on. "I brought you here to view the art, to open your mind. I find it intriguing."

"You're not turned off by…that?" She pointed to the photo.

Right now, whipping was clearly a hard no for her, and that made him want to howl. On the other hand, a good Dom's job was to push his sub's limits to help her find her truest submission. Maybe in time…

But maybe not. If he wanted her for his own, he might have to live without wielding a whip.

"I find a unique beauty in it. But remember, I'm a physician, so I know she'll heal up fine in a few days."

"But whoever did this to her is abusing her."

Beck gave a sharp shake of his head. "My understanding of the lifestyle is that the people who practice it do so willingly. She always has the power to say no."

"Really?" She sounded almost skeptical. Understandable, given her innocence.

When the time was right, he'd provide her a thorough explanation of safe words and boundaries. But for now, Beck let her wander around the next corner. "Ready to see what's over there?"

"Please." She finished the last of her liquid courage and set the empty glass on the tray held by a passing waiter.

Since he'd worried she would demand they leave the gallery altogether, her acquiescence filled him with relief. Maybe the wine had done its job.

As he cupped her elbow, he led her into the next open space. It held more photos and paintings, as well as several pedestals displaying bronze statues. Instead of methodically perusing each piece, Heavenly skimmed a discriminating eye over them, showing neither aversion nor excitement.

Finally, one particular photo caught her eye. She strode straight to it, transfixed. When Beck saw the image, he wanted to cheer. He'd brought her here hoping some of the pieces would call to her. One finally had.

A blindfolded woman wearing a black demi-bra, panties, and a garter straddled a chair with her stockinged thighs. Her hands had been tied helplessly behind her back. She listened raptly, head cocked to one side, while her fully dressed Master whispered in her ear.

"Oh…" Her murmur was so soft he almost missed it.

"Do you like it?"

"It's powerful. Evocative. There's a sense of…anticipation."

Fuck yes! Beck's head filled with all the wicked things he could say to Heavenly once he had her bound for his mercy. Clandestinely, he adjusted his aching fly.

As they continued through the gallery, Heavenly steered clear of the hardcore fetish or masochistic pieces, but works containing bondage almost always made her linger, a soft yearning filling her face.

Winding their way deeper into the exhibit, they found a narrow rectangular board mounted to a door frame with a protruding vertical line of a half-dozen penis sculptures, each in various stages of arousal.

When Heavenly caught sight of the protrusions, she giggled. "Really?"

"Any of those, um…stand out for you?"

She rolled her eyes. "You're incorrigible. I'm not answering that."

"C'mon. The limp one at the top is pretty pointless, but this one…" He pointed to the most sizable erection, complete with copious veins raised along the shaft. It resembled the one now throbbing against his zipper. "Have any thoughts on it?"

Heavenly darted a curious gaze at the particular cock and lowered her lashes. "That one looks capable of…whatever." She glanced into the next room. "So what's over there?"

Holding in a laugh at her abrupt change of subject, he followed her as she moved to investigate a particular bronze sculpture illuminated by a spotlight in an otherwise shadowy room. A naked woman lay across a pedestal with her dangling legs spread wide, breasts thrust up in ecstasy. She cupped one, thumbing the nipple, as a man gripped her hips and knelt between her thighs, burying his face in between.

Heavenly froze, stared, lips parted, not breathing for long moments. Finally, she let out a shuddering breath. The musky scent of her arousal rose in the air.

Saliva pooled in Beck's mouth. He closed his eyes to savor her for a guilty moment. Then he bit back the promise that he'd eat her pretty pussy until she came hard and often. It would be so easy to whisper that against her ear and let the chips fall…

But he said nothing. Not in public, not before he'd had time to analyze tonight's findings. Not until he was certain they could be as compatible in bed as the date at Disney had convinced him they were out of it.

Another shiver rippled through her. His blood pumped hotter and harder, further testing his control. His brain burned with images of tumbling her into his bed, sliding his tongue up her thighs, and teasing every slick fold. Then he'd suckle her swollen nub for the sheer pleasure of hearing her keen his name just before he latched his mouth over her untouched pussy and drank in all her hot virgin cream.

Beck opened his mouth to break the tension between them—no

idea what to say since his hunger to claim this girl was quickly approaching desperate. Instead, Heavenly's stare remained riveted on the statue and she let out a soft, wistful sigh.

Tamping down another frustrated growl, he glanced around the room for a distraction—and found Pike standing in the doorway. The cocky, tattooed DM from Shadows wore a mocking grin as he all but undressed Heavenly with his stare.

Beck's temper flared. Rolling his shoulders back, he curled his hands into fists, drew in a deep breath, and shot the prick a glare. Pike merely smirked, gave him a mocking salute, then strolled away.

"Who was that?" Heavenly asked. "He looks familiar."

He couldn't out Pike—or himself. "Nobody you want to know. You want to talk about that?"

When he gestured to the bronze couple, she shook her head, a rosy flush still hueing her cheeks. "Let's move on."

He fisted his shaking hands as they ambled into an adjoining, well-lit room filled with Joshua Lars's stunning collection of statues.

They both stood silently awed at the elaborate detail and lifelike expressions of each piece. The snow-white sculpture of a sub kneeling on a pillow, bound in ropes, and wearing a bright red blindfold especially captured Heavenly's interest. Her breathing fell shallow. From this angle, he noticed her nipples draw tight as she fidgeted restlessly.

Beck almost lost his composure and restraint.

Her reaction was much the same when she spied a sculpture depicting a sub lying across an ornately set dinner table, arms bound above her head as if she was the meal. Above her, someone dripped fresh drops of red wax across her breasts.

To the right of that piece, they found a two-toned statue of a sun-kissed man behind a pale woman who bent forward on her knees, arms bound behind her back. He clutched her hips, thumbs sinking into her round ass as he buried himself balls deep inside her, head forever tossed back in ecstasy.

The kitten-soft moan that slid past Heavenly's lips almost undid Beck. Somehow, he managed not to reach for her, but sweat beaded his brow as the fantasy of taking Heavenly the same way spooled through his head. He'd barely absorbed the fact that she seemed all too open to being dominated and fucked when she tore her gaze to the right and stared slack-jawed at another piece hanging on the wall.

The stark black-and-white photo held a gut-punch far more visceral than any image he'd seen all night.

A naked woman stood against a post, hands tied above her head. Behind her, a fully dressed man reached around her body. The fingers of one hand sank into her breast. The palm of the other silenced her by pressing tightly against her mouth. A startled mixture of pain, fear, and ecstasy filled the woman's eyes.

The image screamed that she was helpless at her Master's mercy.

Beck scrutinized Heavenly's slightly dilated pupils. She seemed transfixed, the pulse point at her neck thrumming wildly.

"Will he hurt her?" she asked softly.

"He might, temporarily. Do you think she's afraid?"

"No. Her body is…almost relaxed. She wants this."

For him to play rough. To surprise, startle, and maybe even scare her. "Very observant, little girl. Everything they'll do is consensual." He mulled his next move and took a calculated risk. "You like this one."

"I-it's intriguing."

She whispered the words as if afraid of her own desires. All the while, her nipples pebbled even more, jutting beneath the fabric of her dark dress as her chest rose and fell raggedly. The pungent scent of her arousal strengthened, nearly knocking him to his knees.

Heavenly had wicked fantasies of being taken and used and made to perform at a Dominant's command.

Jesus, they needed to skip the fucking dessert he'd planned so he could take her home, tie her up in pretty shibari knots, and awaken this innocent virgin.

But it was far too soon. None of what he wanted from her—and what she seemingly wanted from a man—would work without trust. He had to know how much she would extend to him before they went any further.

As they left the gallery and walked to his car, Beck held her close to his side. "What did you think of your first art exhibit?"

"It was…amazing. And surprisingly educational," she said with a laugh. "Some of the pieces icked me out, but most were…I don't know. Sensual. Intense. Provocative."

I'd love the chance to make you feel all of that under me, little girl.

The invitation burned the tip of his tongue as he held the car door open. She slid in, lowering her lashes shyly.

Wishing the January night were cold enough to soften his erection, Beck jogged around the vehicle and hopped behind the wheel. "Where would you like to go next? There's a great bistro that serves a mean crème brûlée down the street. We could—"

"I'd love to, but I need to get back to the hospital by ten."

"Why?"

"A classmate who volunteers every other weekend promised to meet me so she could return one of my textbooks. I need it for class on Monday."

"Okay. We can head over there now, then decide if you want to go someplace else or—"

"Actually, she's going to give me a ride home. We live pretty close." A painful smile tugged her lips. "I hope you don't mind."

He stifled his disappointment. "If that's what you need..."

It hadn't escaped him that on both of their dates, she'd refused to let him pick her up or take her home.

"I really had a great time tonight." She brushed warm fingers across his forearm. "Thank you for inviting me."

"No need to thank me. I like being with you." That was true, and if he was only going to have her for another few minutes, he needed to bank his surly mood and enjoy her. He threaded his fingers through hers. "Now that you've experienced Disneyland and your first art gallery, I have another adventure I'd like to share with you."

Sex. Lots and lots of sex!

Beck shoved a ball gag in his pubescent subconscious.

"Adventure?"

He nodded. "You game next weekend? Or do you have to work?"

She smiled shyly. "I'm off Saturday."

"Excellent."

Scoring a third date filled him with hope...not enough to bank his frustration at having their time together cut short. But on their next date, he'd find out exactly how much she trusted him and start building from there.

And if Heavenly put herself in his care? Oh, he'd make her his a hundred times over.

Beck pulled into the familiar circle drive in front of the hospital and killed the engine. "I'll walk you up."

"Thank you."

Beck took her hand. At this point, he didn't give a fuck if everyone saw their public display. When they reached the door, he drew her to face him. "I had a wonderful time with you, Heavenly."

"I enjoyed tonight."

He felt her warm breath close to his lips and gripped her tighter. The inviting bow of her mouth was just under his. She nestled closer to him, her eyes big and blue and filled with invitation. Fuck it, he wasn't waiting another second to taste her.

As he took her face in his hands and leaned in, the door beside him slid open.

"Well, isn't this the coziest little picture?" Kathryn drawled. "What happened to your rule about dating co-workers, Dr. Beckman?"

Heavenly blanched and jerked back. Beck cursed the bitch for interrupting. And when Heavenly scrambled away, wrapping her arms around her middle, he cursed Kathryn again for making his little girl self-conscious.

Sliding her behind him, he turned to the interloping shrew. "The rule only applied to you. Next time, take a hint."

With a pinched mouth and a vengeful glare, she stomped away. Beck refused to waste another moment on her. He turned his attention back to Heavenly.

"What was that abo—"

He pressed his fingers to her lips. Damn it, he should have been kissing them instead. "Nothing important. If, for any reason, your classmate can't give you a ride home, call me."

At his commanding tone, Heavenly's eyes widened. A tremor shook her as he reluctantly lifted his finger from her mouth. She licked her lips and darted a self-conscious glance around as other employees filed out the door.

"I will."

Well aware of their audience, he sent her a tender smile. "I'll talk to you soon."

"Good night, Beck."

He kissed her forehead softly. "Good night, little girl."

It was a quick drive home, one he wished he didn't have to make alone. The more time he spent with Heavenly, the stronger his attraction to her grew.

After parking in his garage, he strolled through the kitchen, tossed his keys, and climbed the stairs to his bedroom. He peeled off his clothes, flopped into bed, and stared at the ceiling. His date with Heavenly flooded his brain. And his cock stirred, as it did every time he thought of her. But now he *knew* the heady scent of her arousal—and he'd fantasize about it. Obsess over it. Though he was miles away from her, it still lingered in his nostrils, permeating his senses and engorging his cock.

The night had also given Beck hope. The images at the gallery had touched Heavenly on a deeper level than he'd imagined. Beneath her surface lay a sleeping submissive; of that he had no doubt. Thankfully, he knew how to awaken her. He'd have to go slow, of course. But the idea of corrupting her innocent soul with his wicked urges…

Groaning, he wrapped a fist around his shaft and slowly stroked the all-too-familiar ache, imagining how good it would feel to have her on her knees before him as he gripped her pale curls in his big hands and slid his cock in and out of her slick mouth. In his imagination, she'd stare at him with big eyes filled with the longing to please.

Fuck.

Thinking of her draped over his lap while he spanked her sweet backside didn't cool his libido any, especially when he thought about squeezing the supple orbs and feeling the warm sting of her flesh heating his palm.

Now fisting himself faster, he imagined the heat pouring from between her legs as he worked his fingers deep inside her dripping, clutching core before teasing her clit until she spilled onto his pants, breathless, writhing, and clutching at him as if she sought a savior. He'd only fill her with more lust and sin.

Sweat beaded Beck's forehead as he continued to punish his cock. The image of Heavenly tied and spread across his bed, all lovely and helpless, ramped him up even more. She'd be drenched and puddling on his sheets as he whispered every dirty thing he intended to do to her before he proceeded to part her pretty pink folds with his thumbs and feast on her cunt without mercy. Then, when he'd explored her every curve and crevice, when she was begging him to fuck her, he'd finally align his fat crest to her tiny, innocent opening.

His balls were churning, his cock a rod of blazing fire as Beck continued to stroke his fist up and down in a hard, jerky rhythm. His limbs grew numb, and he squeezed his eyes closed, picturing himself hovering over Heavenly.

"Do you want me to fuck you, little girl? Make you *mine?*"

"Please!" Her voice would ring with desperation while she stared up at him, eyes brimming with trust as he aligned his crest with her untouched center and his cock nudged her virgin barrier. He'd slide a hand between them and stroke her clit, prepare her as well as he could, all while damning himself for ruining her simply because he couldn't stop himself any longer.

An instant later, he imagined baring his teeth, pressing his lips to hers, and swallowing her cries…and shredding her innocence as he claimed Heavenly for himself.

Every muscle in his body tensed. His hand was a blur now as he pounded his flesh. Tingles burned up his shaft. His balls drew up tight. Then, with a feral roar, thick ropes of semen splattered his chest and belly as he pumped and growled to oblivion.

Slowly riding his orgasm back down, Beck gasped in ragged breaths and continued to milk himself dry. Once he'd stopped, he opened his eyes. Disappointment dashed any hint of satisfaction.

He was alone. No Heavenly to hold against him. To touch, to command, to cherish. Just him—and his fist.

With a curse, he grabbed his shirt and mopped up, then jackknifed to his feet. Jesus, soon he hoped he could stop jacking off like a kid, earn her trust, and finally be her man.

"Then, little girl, I *will* drink in every one of your whimpers and cries…"

SIX O'CLOCK CAME way too early for Heavenly, who'd waitressed until two a.m. But across their little studio apartment, she heard her father stirring. He'd need a trip to the bathroom soon, then breakfast so he could take his morning medicine. She'd have to settle him comfortably so she could study for her first exam of the semester, which had to be completed online by noon. Then hopefully, she could sneak in a nap before Beck took her on another date—for the third Saturday in a row.

He liked her. He was going to kiss her; he'd promised. And the art exhibit he'd taken her to had opened her eyes to both a whole new world and a whole new side of the man who fascinated her. Fantasies of him tying her down so he could admire her, blindfolding her to whisper in her ear, tasting between her legs, or taking her from behind—just like the images from the gallery—had been running unchecked through her head for days. She'd worked herself into a hot frenzy a few times late at night. Orgasm was still elusive...but getting closer. The thought he might finally be the man to give her one put a smile on her face.

Once or twice, she'd imagined Seth doing such things to her, too. Foolish, wishful thinking. The man was gone. But that didn't stop her from wanting him, from getting so intoxicatingly aroused by the thought of him...

"Boo?" her father croaked from his bed, barely audible over the rustling of sheets.

"Coming, Dad." Biting back a groan, she rolled out of bed.

When she stood, the sound slipped out. Crap, her feet still hurt from last night's double shift at Bazookas. At least the tips had been good. Unfortunately, the customers had been extra handsy. They were mostly rich frat boys and single young suits, all looking for an easy lay. She was getting better at smiling and flirting and making them feel important while keeping her distance. Best of all, she should have a little money left after paying the rent if she remained careful with other expenses. That meant no indulgences, like the kind Seth had bought her that terrible day at the grocery store.

But if he'd given her a choice between scrumptious food and him...she would definitely have chosen Seth.

Instead, she'd opened her mouth, been too honest, and chased him away. Raine said he'd gone back to New York that same night. Heavenly was saddened more than surprised.

Her apology text to him had garnered a minimal reply, a politer version of *whatever*. It stung, but worse, she felt somehow incomplete without his charm, his easy manner, his way of making her feel like a woman. Maybe, like he'd said, it was for the best. But it didn't feel that way, even after weeks had passed. Even though she loved spending time with Beck.

That confused her, too.

Her father's low moan of pain snapped her out of her reverie. She knew his sounds, and this wasn't his usual morning, full-bladder moan. Something was wrong.

She dashed across the room, flipping on the kitchen light, which illuminated the apartment, then took her father's shaky outstretched hand. "Where does it hurt?"

"My stomach. My head. It's hard to move my legs. And I'm having trouble breathing," he wheezed.

Her heart nearly stopped. "Do you want your breakfast and your pills? Or do we need to go to the hospital?"

"No. No… Give me my morning pills. I'm sure they'll help."

Maybe, but she wasn't convinced. "I'll get your walker and help you to the bathroom, then get your food going. You dizzy?"

He nodded, and as she sat him up, he wobbled. "A little."

Dread hit her. Was he having another relapse? *Please, no.* She feared his frail system couldn't withstand that and she was nowhere near ready to lose him. Forty-six was way too young to die.

But is he really living now?

She shoved the awful question from her head, then hustled to his walker and helped him to his feet. The trip to the bathroom was a mere six feet—and an excruciating five minutes. When she finally got him inside and turned on the light, she helped him to the toilet, turning her head as he pushed his pajama shirt aside and settled on the commode.

"Goddamn it, I hate this for you, Heavenly," he croaked out. "I'm sorry."

How could he worry about her at a time like this? "Don't apologize. I hate this for you way more. Tell me what I can get you. I brought home the paper someone left behind last night."

"That would be good." As she dashed off to find it, he called after her. "I don't like you working at that hospital until the middle of the night."

He'd like her working at the smoky bar in a skimpy crop top and a short skirt even less, so she spared him that detail. "I'm only doing it twice a week now that school is back in session. The money is too good to pass up."

As she entered the bathroom again, he was shaking his head. "Be careful out there, sweetheart. I worry about you on the bus so late at night."

She handed him the paper, trying not to show him that her heart was breaking. Just a few months ago, he'd been able to help himself to the bathroom most days. Now it was rare he could reach the toilet without her assistance.

"I'm a big girl. Did you manage a bowel movement yesterday?"

He closed his eyes. "We shouldn't have to talk about this."

"Well, we do. Your condition and the pain meds together constipate you, I know. You need to be honest with me and—"

"No. I didn't."

She pursed her lips together. "When was the last—"

"Three days ago."

"Dad!"

"I'll work on it. Maybe…get me one of those laxatives with my breakfast."

The over-the-counter meds didn't do much, but she had to try. If she could stabilize him, maybe he wouldn't need a visit to the hospital…

"I'll head to the kitchen and get everything ready." She bustled over to the table beside his bed, then grabbed his phone, setting it on the counter beside him. "Text me when you're done."

He looked humiliated and frail and ready to give up. "Yeah. Go."

With a fretful sigh, Heavenly ducked out, shutting the door behind her. She needed to pee, but that was the least of her problems now. Absently, she collected his pills and started peeling his hard-boiled eggs, all the while gnawing her lip.

If he had to go to the hospital, it would eat up every bit of her extra funds. And how would she get him there? If she had to pay for an ambulance, it might bankrupt her. The volunteer who had sat with him when she'd gone to Disneyland was out of town. Beck? No. She wasn't his responsibility, and she didn't want his pity. Heavenly thought of calling Raine. But the woman was pregnant and still dealing with the trauma of her father's attack. During their last conversion, she'd sounded down and admitted that Hammer wasn't dealing with the situation well. The last thing her friend needed was more problems.

She was boiling water for some oatmeal when she heard a groan and an ominous thud from the bathroom. "Dad?"

No answer.

After shoving the measuring cup and cardboard canister on the counter, she turned off the stove and raced to the closed door. "Dad? Are you okay?"

Still nothing.

Dread biting her composure, she gripped the knob. Her fingers shook as she cracked the door open. The creaking hinges shredded her nerves, but she didn't want to violate his privacy or dignity any more than she had to.

When she poked her head in, she found him sprawled out across the floor. "Dad!"

Shaking him frantically elicited a low groan. "Boo."

He was barely conscious.

"What happened?"

"Dizzy." His body twitched, and he gave a pained moan. "Fell."

His blood pressure must be way off. His pain was becoming unmanageable. Her father hated to admit these things, but she knew the signs.

"We need to go to the hospital."

"No." He shook his head weakly. "Help me to bed. I'll be fine."

How did he expect her to do that? She was young and healthy, but he still outweighed her. And he was practically dead weight right now.

"I'm going to need help, Dad."

"Sure. I can—" Suddenly, he doubled over, clutched his stomach, and let out a terrible wail.

Heavenly felt utterly useless. "I'll get help." She had no idea from where. "I'll get you to the hospital."

He couldn't even answer; he was writhing on the floor, too caught up in agony.

Panicked, she rushed into the main room and rifled through the plastic chest that contained the few clothes she owned. When she flung open one of the drawers, her mom's old sewing machine, which she'd propped on top, nearly wobbled over. After steadying it, she dragged on a pair of yoga pants, an oversized T-shirt, and some sandals. She shoved her bra in her purse and set it on the sofa beside the door. She'd slip it on as soon as she delivered her dad into safe hands. Then she let herself outside, shivering at the predawn chill, as she scanned her neighbors' windows. She didn't know any of these people, but maybe one of them would feel sorry enough for her dad to help them...

The only light on belonged to their landlord, Mr. Sanchez. He was at least ten years her senior and the way he looked at her made her vaguely uncomfortable. But none of that mattered now. He had a car.

Dashing through the dark morning, she crossed the courtyard and began to pound on his door. "Help! Please..."

A long minute later, he wrenched it open with a disgruntled scowl...that he quickly righted when he caught sight of her.

They weren't particularly friendly. She'd only seen him a few times since they moved in, but if he was willing to help right now, she didn't care.

"Hi, Mr. Sanchez. I'm sorry to—"

"What is it?"

"I need to borrow your car or ask if you could drive my father and me to the hospital."

"I just made coffee."

"I'm sorry. I know it's early. But it's an emergency and—"

"All right." He sighed. "I'll take you."

"Thank you." She grabbed the man's arm in a thankful gesture.

He sidled closer. His eyes turned dark. His stare dipped and lingered. "I'm happy to help you. Let me pull the car around."

"Actually, I need help lifting him off the floor. Can you..."

He set his coffee on a table near the door. "Show me where he is."

With a bobbing nod of relief, she rushed back across the courtyard, making a vague mental note to grab a coat to protect her from the stiff wind. Suddenly, she realized the cold had hardened her nipples.

Normally, she would have been embarrassed. She had been at the art gallery. Beck had been too polite to stare...but she had a feeling he'd noticed. Seth, on the other hand, would probably have given her a knowing smile, maybe "accidentally" brushed his hand against them. He seemed like the sort of guy who would seek forgiveness way before he asked for permission.

Not that it mattered now. Nothing did except her dad.

As she reached the door to her apartment, she flung it open. "Dad!"

Please be alive. Please be conscious. Please hold on.

"Here," he managed to choke.

She turned to find Mr. Sanchez behind her, his stare raking her. Was he really staring at her butt at a time like this?

"Follow me." She directed him to the bathroom.

Her landlord wasn't a terribly tall guy, but he was bulky, maybe had even been brawny once. He'd still have a much better chance of getting her dad off the floor and into his car.

Mr. Sanchez recoiled. "Ugh. You didn't tell me he'd be half-naked. Don't you have any pants, old man?"

"He was worried about relieving himself, not going to a fashion show," she snapped.

The guy flipped her a surprised glance. "Uh, yeah. Okay. Where am I taking him?"

"The VA."

Her landlord didn't look thrilled but he lifted her dad to his feet and propped him up with the walker while Heavenly fetched him a robe and slippers. It would cover the essentials.

Within a few minutes, she helped her father to the curb. Mr. Sanchez waited inside, revving the engine, until she eased her father into the front seat and folded up his walker. As soon as she chucked it into the backseat and climbed in behind her dad, her landlord sped off.

They reached the hospital blessedly fast since rush hour was still relatively thin. They took him back surprisingly quickly. As soon as Heavenly filled out a few forms and talked to one of the nurses, she had nothing to do but wait. She found the bathroom, finally relieved herself, put on her bra, then went to find Mr. Sanchez.

In the waiting area, he lounged out, ankles crossed and hand clasped over his bloated belly, staring at the morning news he couldn't hear because the sound had been muted in favor of closed captioning.

He looked up when she entered, stare intent.

They were alone.

Heavenly sank gingerly to the chair beside him. He made her more than a little nervous. "Thank you for bringing us here. You don't have to wait around. It will be hours before—"

"What's he got?"

"A rare autoimmune disease." She didn't go into details. He already seemed bored by the short answer.

"Huh." He shrugged. "So that's why he doesn't work and you do?"

She nodded, though she didn't see why he cared as long as she paid the rent. "Yes. Look, I'm sorry to have disturbed you so early in the morning. But I really, really appreciate your help. I'm so grateful."

He sat up, leaned across the thin wooden arm separating their chairs, and raised a brow. "How grateful?"

Heavenly shrank back, putting some distance between them. She knew where this conversation was going. "More than you know. And I can give you fifty dollars for your trouble."

It almost killed her to part with what little reserve she'd tucked away in the sofa cushion back home after last night's shifts. But it was damn cheaper than an ambulance. She prayed Mr. Sanchez took it.

"Fifty bucks?" He scoffed. "Keep it. If it will help you, *chica*…"

"That's generous. Thank you again." Maybe she'd figure out how to get a taxi back home. Every warning instinct she possessed told her to steer clear of this man.

"I can be very generous." He edged closer, skimming his knuckles across her cheek.

She shuddered. It wasn't the first time a man had touched her face—Beck and Seth both had—but it was the first time she'd been afraid.

"Mr. Sanchez…" With her back already plastered to the chair that was flush with the wall, she really didn't have anywhere to escape except to her feet.

When she would have leapt up, he grabbed her shoulder and held her down. "Extremely generous, in fact. You ever have trouble paying the rent? I can let it slide for a month or two." He grinned.

"Really?" Was he kidding? That would be a godsend. "You'd do that?"

"Absolutely, *chica*. For you, yes. All you have to do is swing by and spend some…quality time with me."

Heavenly narrowed her eyes. Was she understanding him correctly? "Doing what?"

He gave her an ambivalent shrug she didn't believe for a second. "You know… You're a pretty thing. You'd look fine in my bed."

"I'm a virgin," she blurted, shaking her head.

His smile widened. "Even better. It's been a few years since I've had a cherry pie, and I'll bet I've never had one as sweet as yours."

She gasped and recoiled, mentally berating herself for thinking this man might have the decency to respect her innocence. "I, um…have a boyfriend."

It wasn't totally untrue. She hoped.

"Then he's either gay or blind, because if you're a virgin, he's not getting the job done. I will, *chica*. I'll get you done good." He moaned and flexed his hips, sending her what he must think was a smoldering stare.

She nearly choked.

Never. Ever. She'd live on the streets before she let this man touch her.

You might, but what about Dad?

She shoved down the question. "Well, as it happens, I have the rent money early this month so…thanks very much for the offer. I'm going to go check on my father." She dodged his next attempt to grab her and stood. "We appreciate the ride. I'll find us a way home. Bye."

As she charged for the exit, she nearly hit the door face first in her haste to escape. On the other side, she dragged in a calming breath and pressed a shaking hand to her chest. She wasn't sure what was wrong with her dad, how she was going to get home, or how she'd continue to make rent every month with their bank balance running lower and lower. She'd have to skip the fall semester of school. Work more, save more, then maybe go back the following spring. She hated to keep putting off her future, but he was her father. She'd always been able to count on him. He needed to be able to count on her now.

"Ms. Young?"

She snapped around to find a familiar doctor coming her way, a resident who'd assisted Dad's neurologist before. "Yes."

"Come this way. You father is asking to see you."

"How is he? What's going on with him? What can you tell me?"

He took her elbow. Regret crossed his face before he even opened his mouth. "He's had a relapse. I'm afraid it's not good."

Eight hours later, he was stable enough to come home with her. Heavenly suspected that was mostly because they didn't want to waste a bed on someone who would never get well. The nursing staff wheeled him to the hospital door. She clutched new prescriptions in her hand she feared would cost a fortune. Then slowly, they walked to the bus. She knew it took all his energy and hoped he could muster a bit more when they reached the closest stop to home. If not, she didn't know what she'd do.

"The landlord couldn't bring us home?" he asked, looking pale and spent.

Guilt assailed Heavenly. He should be resting in bed, and she was making him walk. But even if she chose to use her small cash reserve on a taxi, the money did her no good when it was at home.

"He was busy this afternoon. I'll make macaroni and cheese tonight to make it up to you."

"Don't you have someplace to be with that friend from the hospital? What's his name?"

"Dr. Beckman." She shook her head. "He had to cancel. Emergency."

More like the other way around, since she'd texted him an hour before they'd been due to meet and told him that the old man in her apartment building needed her help and she was so sorry to bail. Beck had sounded supportive, if disappointed. But if she admitted any of that to her father, he'd only feel worse.

"I'm sorry, sweetheart."

She shrugged. "I have an exam to finish." Thank goodness she'd emailed her instructor, who had been both empathetic and accommodating. She had until Monday to take the test now. "Besides, I'd always rather spend the evening with you."

For the first time in her life, that wasn't true. She itched to be with Beck, anticipated seeing him like a kid looking forward to a favorite movie. And if she were honest, she craved the chance to see Seth again, at least long enough to explain what she'd meant that fateful day. Since neither of those things were going to happen, she pasted on a smile, patted her father's hand as the bus lumbered its way closer to their stop, and held in her tears.

CHAPTER TEN

A LMOST A WEEK later, Beck paced the small waiting room at the
University Medical Center in Las Vegas. It was the best level-one
trauma hospital in the city. He should know; he'd interned at the
facility.

He slanted a worried glance over at Buddy. "Tell me again what
happened. Exactly."

Just as he'd finished his shift at the hospital earlier this evening,
Buddy had called, sounding shocked and frantic, blurting that Gloria
had been attacked. Beck had tossed a few necessities into a duffel, then
jockeyed through the last of rush hour to speed across the desert and
reach Gloria's side. She was still in surgery. It had been hours, and he
was doing his best not to crawl out of his skin.

The older man swallowed. "She was coming home from the grocery store. When she unlocked her front door, two men jumped out
from the bushes, then shoved her inside and tied her up. They
demanded to know where she kept her cash and papers. They threatened to kill her if she didn't hand them over."

Son of a bitch. These fuckers had probably known who she was,
what she did for a living. Were they disgruntled clients? Henchmen for
some neighboring low-life pimp?

"I know Gloria too well. She didn't give them shit."

"She's a stubborn broad," Buddy confirmed. "But I don't think
they gave her a choice. They beat the crap out of her and knocked her
out with the butt of a gun. When she came to, they were gone. At
some point, they had ransacked the whole place and taken all the cash
they could find." He scratched his head. "But they left behind her
electronics and jewelry."

And since the woman adored both, that meant her attackers had
walked away from a small fortune. Why?

"What did the police say?"

"They don't have a clue. They're calling it a robbery, but..."

Yeah, that didn't make sense to Beck, either.

He paced. How much fucking longer before the surgeon was done so he could ask questions and see her? Fear sliced him deeper with each excruciating minute that ticked by.

"I should have been beside her instead of watching TV." Buddy's guilt-ridden tone broke the brittle silence. "I was tired and wanted to relax with a beer and..."

Beck scrubbed a hand over his face and dropped into the seat beside Gloria's boyfriend. "It's not your fault. Obviously the pricks who did this thought a woman carrying in groceries at dusk was an easy target."

"They'd have thought differently if I'd been there with my Smith & Wesson." Buddy gritted his teeth, looking all too ready to commit violence. "What's taking so damn long, Ken?"

Had the surgeon found Gloria's injuries more extensive than expected? It happened... But he kept that information to himself. Still, the longer she remained on the operating table, the harder it was to force down his panic. "Could be anything, man. Stay calm."

Beck had no idea how to follow his own advice.

Excruciating minutes later, an older doctor wearing mint green scrubs and a shock of white hair entered the room. He and Buddy immediately launched to their feet.

"I'm Dr. Evans. Are you the Beckman family?"

"Yes," the two men replied at once.

Beck extended his hand, anxious for a peer-to-peer conversation. "I'm Dr. Kenneth Beckman, RPVI."

The surgeon's expression lightened. "Vascular, huh?" At Beck's nod, he continued on, "Ms. Beckman is your...?"

"Wife."

The other doctor quickly banked his surprise—because of their age gap?—and took a seat. He and Buddy each claimed one as well.

"She was worked over pretty badly, but we've done our best to put her back together. I performed a splenectomy. I'm sure you know that she'll need to schedule regular follow-ups with her primary doctor."

Beck nodded. "She sustained a broken ulna, so I called in our orthopedic surgeon. He did an open reduction internal fixation and inserted a couple of screws into the bone. The X-rays of her ankle didn't show any fractures, but she's got a sizable hematoma and will need to stay off it for a few weeks. Ribs eight, nine, and ten were fractured, but the pulmonologist assured me none perforated her lung. He stabilized her rib cage since he was there as well."

The litany of Gloria's injuries sucked the air out of the room. Rage roared through Beck's system.

"She had a substantial laceration across her forehead—"

"Please tell me you brought in a plastic surgeon." Because if Gloria woke up and discovered her face had been sewn up by someone without an ounce of finesse, Beck knew there'd be hell to pay.

"We did." The doctor dropped his voice. "I know who your wife is."

That gave Beck pause. "Client?"

"No, but...we have mutual friends."

Thank god. "Anything else?"

"Edema of her numerous contusions, especially on her face. Several teeth were avulsed, but when the swelling goes down and her gums heal, a prosthodontist can fit her with a partial or full set of false teeth."

"Jesus," he breathed out.

The surgeon nodded grimly. "I suspect she's concussed. When the anesthesia wears off, we'll be keeping a close eye on her. They're getting her set up in ICU now. I don't foresee any complications, but we'll keep her there for a few days before letting her go to the step-down unit. If all goes well, she'll be home soon after that."

After Beck thanked Evans, the surgeon left. He collapsed against the back of his chair, both seething and heartbroken.

"I don't understand much of what that man said." Buddy cut into his thoughts. "Will Gloria be okay?"

"She'll be all right...eventually. But those bastards beat the fuck out of her." Imagining her helpless while someone took delight in damn near killing her infuriated him.

As he and Buddy made their way to the ICU waiting room, Beck used layman's terms to relay the extent and repairs of Gloria's injuries. Buddy had already looked overwhelmed, but now he seemed in danger of crumbling.

"When was the last time you ate?"

"I don't know." Buddy shrugged. "I had a late lunch. Maybe two."

Over fifteen hours ago? "The cafeteria opens for breakfast at six thirty. It will take you ten minutes to walk over there, so they'll be open by then. Grab something to eat. We could be waiting awhile to see her."

Buddy looked reluctant, but before Beck could give him the canned speech about eating to stay strong for her, the man nodded and left.

To his surprise, he received permission to see Gloria about twenty minutes later. Recovery must have gone well.

He dragged in a bracing breath, but nothing could have prepared him for the needles, tubes, and electrodes feeding air, fluids, and pain meds into her beaten and broken body. The bandages and mangled flesh of her face made her nearly unrecognizable. His gut twisted. His heart splintered. The strong, tenacious fighter who had saved his life and taught him love, fortitude, self-esteem, and a million other life lessons looked half-dead.

Beck buried his forehead into the corner of Gloria's pillow, but he couldn't seem to keep his shit together. Hot tears stung his eyes, falling into her starched linens. What the fuck was he going to do if she didn't pull through?

No. Dr. Evans had her listed in stable condition. She was going to be fine. He had to believe that. Just like he had to pull himself together. If Buddy came back and saw him break down, the guy would freak out.

"I'll make those gutless pricks suffer tenfold for what they did to you," Beck vowed.

Gloria's lashes fluttered. A low moan rose from her throat before she lifted her puffy, purple lids and peered at him. "Ken?"

Beck kissed her forehead. "Shh. It's me, sweetheart. You're safe now and you're going to be fine. I'm so sorry I wasn't there to protect you."

"You already know you can't protect every woman you care about," she slurred from between split lips. "I'm alive. The bastards didn't win."

"They didn't," he assured as he watched her slide back into a drug-induced oblivion.

A few minutes later, Gloria woke again. "Christ, I hurt. Do I look as bad as I feel?"

"No," he lied. "You look like a million."

"Oh, god," she groaned. "It must be worse than I thought if you're feeding me that bullshit."

"At least you still have your sense of humor." Then he sobered. "When you feel up to it, the police will want to question you. Do you know who did this? Customers maybe?"

"No. I've never seen either of these guys."

"How much do you remember?"

"Unfortunately, all of it—until they knocked me out. Whatever they wanted, they wanted it bad. And I don't think it was cash. They seemed almost disappointed when I finally gave them the previous night's take, which was fat. The tall, ugly asshole kept asking me for papers. When I told him I didn't know what he meant and that I kept most everything important in a safety deposit box, he got pissed and slammed the butt of his gun to my head."

Papers? Title to her car? Deed to her house? Beck had no idea what they meant. "Good god."

"When I finally came to, my place was a wreck and the two clowns were gone. I managed to work my hands free, crawl to the phone, and call Buddy before I passed out again."

If not disgruntled clients or competitors, who the hell would have done this to her? Who had an axe to grind? Beck had to find out if he intended to make them pay.

Days bled into one another before Gloria was finally released from the hospital. Once home, frustration and anger left her perpetually irritated. Beck couldn't really blame her. Helpless wasn't in her vocabulary, but she was trapped in her broken body. She even needed help to walk to the bathroom. Buddy hovered protectively. He meant well…but it didn't improve Gloria's mood.

The only thing that kept him sane was daily texts with Heavenly.

During Gloria's second week of recovery, he sat in the living room while she napped, thanking god her disposition had finally taken a brighter turn. The chime he'd assigned on his cell phone to Heavenly pealed. Fuck, he missed the girl fiercely. He wouldn't leave Gloria while she needed him, but he was counting the days until he could return to LA—and Heavenly.

Just wanted to say hi, her message read.

A goofy grin tugged one corner of his mouth as he tapped a reply. Hi back. How's it going there?

The usual. Work, work, work.

"Not good, little girl." He tsked as his fingers flew across the keys. You need to balance yourself with plenty of rest, too.

How is your friend doing today?

He noticed she didn't acknowledge his command. A bit better.

Coming back soon?

She wanted him there. Because she missed him as much as he missed her? He hoped so because it would really suck if he were the only one mentally replaying each minute they'd spent together.

I'm hoping to be back in no more than a week. I still have another surprise for you.

What?

He'd love to text back dirty details of all the "fun" they could have if she were naked and splayed out on his bed. Instead, he told her, You'll have to wait and see. It's a date when I get back, right?

Absolutely. Oops. Gotta go. Incoming patients. Talk soon. She ended with a winking emoji.

Too bad there wasn't an emoji for horny doctor giving his girl hours of pleasure. He'd send her that one. Since there wasn't, he simply tucked his phone away, unable to wipe the grin off his face.

"How is Heavenly?" Gloria asked without even opening her eyes.

"Good."

She smiled. "This is hardly the right time, but I'd love to meet her someday."

Beck pulled at the back of his neck, trying not to grimace. "Someday, maybe. But, um…"

"You haven't told her we're married?"

The woman knew him too well. Guilt crawled up his spine.

"Of course you haven't." She gave an absent wave of her hand. "What was once so logical and simple is now so complicated."

"Exactly. I don't know where this thing with Heavenly is going but…"

Gloria grimaced as she struggled upright and patted the cushion beside her. She wanted to talk. More accurately, she had something to say and wanted him to listen. With a sigh, he crossed the room and eased down beside her.

She took his hand and threaded her fingers through his. "Ken, call your lawyer and have him draw up the papers. It's time. Neither of us needs to hide behind the smokescreen anymore."

Life was a series of changes. Beck knew that, just like he knew she was right. Besides, even when Gloria was no longer his wife, they'd stay close, talk often…be friends. "All right."

"It makes sense. Our lives have been going in different directions for years. I have Buddy. And you have Heavenly."

Not yet, but he hoped so soon. That meant he had to divorce Gloria. Having two wives was out of the question.

"I'll call next week and tell him to give you half of my—"

"I don't want your money," she snapped. "I have more lucrative investments than I'll ever need. All I want is for you to be happy. If Heavenly can help with that, then sweep that little virgin off her feet and march her down the aisle."

The image of her walking toward him in a flowing white gown, a huge smile spreading across her face as her eyes misted with joy bombarded his brain. Lost in the visual, he progressed them, saw her beside him every morning, saw her belly round with his babies. He didn't hate the idea. At all.

"We've only had two dates," he pointed out.

"And you never called me back after either to give me the juicy details."

"I'm glad we have such clear personal boundaries." Beck chuckled.

"Fuck that. Tell me everything!"

"It's a little weird talking to my wife about my feelings for another woman."

"Please." She rolled her eyes. "I talk to you about Buddy, so stop stalling. Where did you go on your first date?"

"Disneyland. She'd never been."

"And she loved it?"

A fond smile curled Beck's lips. "She really did."

"And the second date?"

"I took her to an art gallery."

"Oh, god," Gloria groaned. "I did you a disservice. Since you were sixteen, you've had all the sex you could want and you never had to woo a woman to get it. You even took one of my girls to prom."

He shrugged. "I got a date without any effort, and she was guaranteed to put out."

"A mistake. Clearly, I forgot to teach you that women need to be charmed. If you want to keep one, the quality time you share out of bed is important, Ken. An art gallery? Really? Watching a round of golf would be more entertaining."

"It was a BDSM exhibit." He paused. "I had to know her reaction. I had to know if there was any chance…"

"Ah. And what did Heavenly think about kinky art?"

"Mixed bag, but mostly positive. She's got a few surprisingly edgier fantasies buried deep down." Those kept niggling at him.

"Don't we all?" Gloria chuckled. "Be specific."

"Either being helpless at the mercy of a Master or being forced into that position flips her switch. I need more information to know for sure."

"Intriguing. So what's next?"

"Well, the Disney date proved we have chemistry and made her more comfortable with me outside the hospital. The art exhibit told me exactly what she'd respond to sexually…and probably gave her more than an inkling about what I want from her."

"Inkling?" Gloria snorted. "Unless she's stupid, you beating her ass with a paddle that reads I'M A SADIST would have been more subtle."

"Funny. Now I just have to know how much she trusts me, so I'll know how far and how fast I can take her."

"How do you plan to do that?"

"Something unexpected," he replied cryptically.

"Do I need to warn her?"

"Nope. It'll be a surprise."

"You're being awfully cautious…and you're overanalyzing the situation. Heavenly is the one. You know that, don't you?"

"I want her to be." He sighed and stared at the rug between his feet, gathering his thoughts. "I think she is…but I can't say for sure yet. She's got a lot of secrets. Then again, so do I. It's too soon to spring everything on her. Hell, I still haven't kissed her yet."

Gloria's mouth dropped open. "Even after two dates? Do we need to talk about the birds and the bees, Ken?"

"Hey, I'm wading through uncharted territory here. Like you said, I've never had to romance a woman," he grumbled. "My gut tells me if I screw up with Heavenly, I may not get a second chance. At least Seth is back in New York, and I have all the time in the world. Patience...not as much. But I'm digging deep. She's worth it."

She gave him a sleepy smile. "It's good to see you finally in love."

Beck opened his mouth to argue, but it was pointless. First, because Gloria had already dozed off again. Second, because she was probably right.

Fuck.

As the sun set, he was still mentally gnawing on the L word. Buddy staggered out of the bedroom and headed straight to the coffeepot.

"Morning." Beck chuckled.

"I don't know how Gloria keeps these vampire hours." Buddy shook his head, obviously trying to clear it. "Maybe she should retire."

"Good luck convincing her of that."

"I think I know how." He took a long sip of coffee and even longer to swallow it down. Finally, Buddy raised his head. "I'd like to marry your wife."

"Well, she'll need to be my ex-wife first, but...we're going to work on that. Have you asked her yet?"

"No. I figured I should talk to you first since..."

"I'm technically her husband?" Beck couldn't help but grin. "We sound fucked up."

"Yeah."

He clapped Buddy on the shoulder. "Go get her, man. But you better make her happy or I'll have to hurt you."

Gloria's boyfriend laughed. "I got it. Thanks."

Twenty minutes later, the groom-to-be helped Gloria into a kitchen chair. She thanked him with a smile and a kiss. Beck sat across from the lovebirds.

"Ken, I really appreciate you dropping everything to take care of me. But you've been here for two weeks, and I'm feeling much better."

"It's no problem. I'd do anything for you."

"I know. And you mean the world to me, but...Buddy and I want some alone time. And, well, you're cramping our style."

Beck raised a brow. "You're kicking me out?"

"Think of it as me letting you get back to your life. To Heavenly."

"Uh-huh. You just want to fuck Buddy's brains out."

"Yep." She grinned.

Buddy choked on his steak, then tried to recover. "I'll take good care of her, now that she'll let me. I popped the question a few minutes ago and she said yes."

Gloria flashed a modest engagement solitaire and a beaming smile.

"Congratulations!" Beck hugged Gloria, then clapped Buddy on the shoulder.

"Thanks," the other man continued. "I'll be moving in with Gloria. And I'm going to take her to the 'office' with me tomorrow night. Her girls are missing her something fierce."

"Don't scowl at me, Ken." Gloria shook her finger. "There's a bed in my apartment. I can convalesce there as easily as I can here. But you need to worry about your own problems. I've kept you from your job, your life, and your girl long enough."

"I wanted to ensure you got the best medical care. And I knew I'd have to stand over you to make your stubborn ass follow doctor's orders."

"Stubborn?"

"I know you too well."

"True. I'm glad we got everything straightened out. After dinner, you can pack your shit and go back to LA so Buddy and I can get naked."

Beck pinned the other man with a pointed stare. "You sure you know what you're getting yourself into with her?"

Buddy settled a delighted smile on Gloria. "I do."

After dinner, Beck packed, then paused in the doorway, duffel in hand. "I'm leaving. No going to the grocery store alone anymore, all right?"

"You got it," she promised.

"I'll make sure of that." A beaming Buddy slung his arm around Gloria's shoulder. "Now go home and get your own girl."

December 22
Seven weeks earlier

SETH FLEW ALL night to reach home, getting zero rest on the plane. Every time he shut his eyes, he saw Heavenly's last forlorn glance.

He'd begun yesterday full of hope that he would finally have her. Today, he was three thousand miles away, greeted by a New York sunrise shrouded in gray drizzle.

When he stepped off the plane, festive wreaths, lights, and bells filled the terminal, assaulting him with holiday cheer. Sighing tiredly, he made his way to baggage claim, expecting to find his brother waiting to chauffeur him to the Cooper family house for a big, loud, probably white Christmas. Instead, he saw his mother...but not as he remembered her.

The gray streaks were gone from her dark hair. So was her usual messy bun. Suddenly, it was shoulder length and styled into loose feminine curls. Even her clothes looked more fashionable and flattering. The change startled him. Then again, at fifty-three, his mother was still a beautiful woman.

"Hi, Mom. Wow, you look great." Seth hugged her as she rushed to greet him.

"Thanks. I decided to spruce up a bit for the holidays."

It was more than a mere sprucing. She looked ten years younger. "Um, I thought Danny was picking me up. Is everything all right with Maggie and the baby?"

"Fine. The baby hasn't come yet. I thought you'd be happy to see me. We haven't been apart this long since I sent you away to that summer camp you hated when you were thirteen. But if you didn't miss me, I can turn around and go home."

"Sorry. Of course I missed you. It was just a long, sleepless flight." He frowned. "You shouldn't be driving in this crappy weather."

"Pfft. I drove you boys to every sport in creation on slick streets for years. You have any other luggage?" She frowned at his duffel.

"Nope."

"Then let's go. Traffic is going to be terrible." She threaded her arm through his. "It's good to have you home."

Seth wanted to say it was good to be home. Right now, it felt like hell.

No, it felt like defeat.

Emerging from the airport to a telltale overcast gray and the scent of snow after so many balmy blue Los Angeles days was a rude awakening. Seth hadn't packed a winter coat. He'd worn a hoodie, which had been more than warm enough out west. Now, he was fucking freezing. He blew on his hands and rubbed them together vigorously.

"How's everyone else?" he asked as they reached her car.

The West Coast sliding into the ocean had been only one of Seth's fears before jetting out to LA. The other had been leaving his family. Since his father's death, Seth had been head of the household. For fifteen years, he'd helped his mother cope, pay bills, maintain the house, and keep his four younger brothers in line. In the grand scheme of life, his three weeks' absence equaled three minutes. But he also knew from experience things could go horribly wrong in the blink of an eye.

"Fine. Anxious to see you." She cast him a curious glance. "We expected you home weeks ago."

Yeah, he'd expected to be home much sooner, too. Seth didn't have an excuse, other than his dick—and his heart—had been stupid. And he was fucking furious that he'd let himself be led around by either. But he kept that to himself.

"How's Maggie feeling?" he asked as he climbed into the passenger's seat and turned on the heater. "She's getting really close to her due date."

"The poor girl looks ready to burst, and last night was rough," Mom answered as she pulled out of the lot.

"Danny handling that all right?"

Seth remembered the night Danny had shown up at his door and shoved a six-pack in his hands, apprehension blazing in his eyes. After shooting the shit and draining three beers, his brother had finally confessed that Maggie was pregnant. Seth had put on a big show of being happy for them and banked the rest, especially since his mother was thrilled. There hadn't been a baby in the house for years.

"I think so. Matthew, Jack, and Conner are all good. And Matty has a surprise for you. He finished up the cradle you'd been making for Christmas."

Seth scowled. "It was my gift. Why did he do that?"

"Oh, honey. He was only trying to help."

He probably had been, but Seth had been looking forward to getting lost in the project. Carving something beautiful from a simple block of wood had brought him peace, especially in recent years. Matt finishing the cradle had robbed Seth of some much-needed serenity. Of course, Matt had done a great job. Their father had painstakingly taught them both to work wood. But having the ability to finish the cradle didn't give Matt the right.

"Well, I'm here now, so I'll put the beeswax on it before Christmas Day…or the baby's birth, whichever comes first."

"Matty did that, too."

Seth stared. So basically, he was useless?

"Don't scowl. The warm honey color looks amazing." His mom patted his hand. "They're going to be thrilled and touched by your gift. That's what's important."

Since Mom was right, he let his irritation go. "Did the mattress arrive yet?"

"Yes. I tucked it away before anyone saw it."

"Thanks, Mom."

"You're welcome." She sighed wistfully. "I wish your father was here to see our family now. But then, I tend to believe he's only a whisper away, watching over us all…"

Seth had been sixteen when his father had been killed in the line of duty. That miserable day and the aftermath were still imprinted on his soul. The crushing shock. The parade of somber strangers who'd converged on their house. The funeral procession that had wound down the streets like an ocean of officers dressed in blue. The eerie wail of the bagpipes crying out "Amazing Grace" still haunted him. Despite the devastation, their mother had been a force of nature and seen the family through.

Years later, tragedy had struck again. Though his family had rallied together with all their strength and love, it had taken years to heal.

Sometimes Seth wondered if he ever really had.

He and his mom each slipped into silence. Snow flurries began to sweep across the landscape as she navigated the busy roads brimming with both rush-hour and holiday traffic. His thoughts drifted.

Echoes of another Christmas slid through him. Then, like now, the city had been decorated in festive lights and snow blanketed the ground. As always, ghosts of guilt and remorse raked him. What-ifs echoed down the years, which would linger long after he and his mother had lit candles in remembrance.

Shelving his gloom, he turned and caught the knowing sadness on her face. "Try not to dwell on it, sweetheart. We'll get through the holidays. We always do. Tell me about Los Angeles."

The change of subject was a welcome reprieve, but the mention of LA launched images of Heavenly through his brain, huge blue eyes gazing up at him above her gorgeous smile. Her little laugh lingered between his ears. He could all but smell the intoxicating scent of her, something so unique that he'd recognize it—even blindfolded—in a crowded room.

Every moment he'd spent with her only made him crave her more.

But she'd chosen Beck.

Seth still couldn't process that without his blood boiling. Hell, he couldn't even remember the last time a woman had turned him down. He'd certainly never had one dump his ass.

It was done. He refused to be hung up on her. Heavenly wasn't the only gorgeous woman in the world.

"The West Coast is an acquired taste." He forced a smile. "Damn place is perpetually sunny and has a million palm trees. Did I mention the earthquakes, fires, and weirdos? And their traffic can be even snarlier than ours."

"Oh, dear." Grace cringed. "And Liam? How is he doing?"

"Better now." Dancing through a minefield might be easier than explaining his friend's unorthodox relationship to his very traditional Catholic mother, but he didn't keep many secrets from her. "He's in a serious relationship. Actually, he and Hammer both are—with the same girl. Raine is a little dark-haired spitfire."

"She's with them both? At the same time?" Grace gaped, eyes wide.

This conversation wasn't awkward at all. "Yeah, Mom. It's called polyamory."

"Goodness," she tsked. "How would you know that? Never mind. Don't answer."

He laughed, this time for real. His mother might suspect he had an interesting sex life, but she never asked. "Liam and Hammer are really happy with Raine. They've even got a baby on the way."

"Oh. My. Well…babies are always a blessing."

Seth knew what his mother was thinking. "You don't have to worry. That kind of relationship isn't for me."

"Whew! I've always tried to be open-minded. Remember when you mooned over that grunge girl—"

"Mom," he groaned. "I was fifteen."

"But I don't think I'm ready to handle something as unconventional as a threesome…"

"Put your fears to rest. Tell me, has Matt had any problems with the agency while I've been gone?"

"None." She seemed happy with the change of subject. "In fact, he's even started contacting the clients on your waiting list."

First the crib, and now his business? Matt was taking care of every fucking thing these days.

Some part of Seth realized he should be thrilled and impressed. Instead, it just pissed him off that his younger brother had stepped into his shoes so easily. First, Heavenly hadn't wanted him. Now, Matt seemed determined to usurp him.

"Well, good for him."

Grace didn't miss his sarcasm. "I thought you'd be happy that everything is going smooth as silk. Well, almost everything. The twins have been driving me batty—all the girls and booze and…I don't even want to know what else. I'm sure the good Lord put Jack and Conner on this Earth to test my patience."

"I'll talk to them tonight."

"Matt already did. They've been better since."

Of course.

"In a few weeks, they'll head back to college and the rest of you boys will go back to your lives," she went on. "Then I'll have the house to myself again, and I'll miss the chaos. Maybe."

He felt like snarling too much to share her laughter.

As his mother stopped at a red light, she turned to him, grin fading. "What's wrong?"

Honestly, he couldn't explain it. He should be happy he wasn't coming home to a Christmas present unfinished, a business in shambles, and a family at each other's throats. Instead, he was annoyed that the Cooper family didn't seem to need him. If that was the case, why the hell was he here?

"Okay. Enough is enough." Grace darted a concerned glance his way. "What happened in LA? You're not melancholy about coping through Christmas. You're pissy. Start talking."

Though she'd been a wonderful wife and a terrific mom, the woman would have made a kick-ass shrink. Grace was intuitive and tenacious, especially when it came to her boys. Seth knew better than to feed her a string of platitudes. She'd only dig until she unearthed the truth.

He sighed. "I met someone…"

"Really?" She sounded shocked—with good reason. "That's great. Why are you here, instead of with her?"

"Because it's Christmas, and I'd never live to tell about it if I missed the holidays at the Cooper household. Plus, I have an agency to run. I can't blow off my responsibilities indefinitely."

"I'd miss you terribly if you weren't here, but you deserve to spend your life with someone special. You've taken such good care of your brothers and me over the years. But your duty to us is done."

Those words felt like a kick in the balls. Even his own mother didn't need him anymore?

"Don't look dumbfounded. I'm not trying to make you feel unappreciated. You'll always be important to us, and of course we're glad you're home—"

"It's fine, Mom." It wasn't, but nothing she said was going to change the fact she'd spoken about him like he was dead. Shit, he'd been gone three weeks, not three fucking years.

"I just don't want you to feel like your obligations to the family or your job take precedence over your happiness." She darted a firmer look. "Why didn't you bring this girl home with you for the holidays?"

"Because she'd rather be with another guy."

"Oh." Finally, his mother looked as bewildered as he felt.

"Yeah. I only saw her a handful of times. We had one date. After all these years, my gut told me I'd met someone, but…"

In his mind's eye, he could still see Heavenly, fingers clutching plastic grocery sacks and plodding toward a bus stop, head bowed. A part of him had itched to pull to the curb, drag her into the car, and kiss her until she forgot about Beck. The other part had been too shocked—and pissed—to do anything but drive away. No matter how many times he replayed their conversation, what he heard above everything else was that she didn't want him. Oh, she'd been willing to have sex with him…but her heart belonged to Beck.

Fuck that. And fuck her, too.

"I understand. Your father and I took one look at each other and fell in love, but our relationship wasn't without its trials. If you thought this girl was special—"

"I was wrong. End of story."

"So that's the reason for the long face. Who is this other guy?"

"Beck. He's a pal of Hammer's, a surgeon—and an asshole—way beyond Heavenly's speed. I knew he was her friend," he drawled. "I just didn't know she wanted him to be more."

And didn't he feel like a fucking fool?

"Heavenly… Is she as beautiful as her name?"

He'd given her the whole speech, and that's what she wanted to know? "Mom…"

"Is she?"

He groaned. "And then some. But it doesn't matter now."

"Seth James Cooper, if you thought she was important, it does. You're letting stupid male pride overrule your heart and backing down from a challenge. It's unlike you." She tsked. "What would your father say?"

He glared at her. "Don't bring Dad into this."

"I'm not trying to upset you. But when you find someone, you stay and fight. You know that."

Seth was over this conversation. He was still shocked, not to mention bone-tired, disgruntled at all the changes, and fucking furious that everything had gone so wrong. "There was no reason to stay and nothing to fight for. Heavenly chose Beck. Game over."

Grace pursed her lips together. "Tell me about her."

"Why?"

"Because I'm your mother and I asked you to, young man."

Great, now she was going to get stubborn. Since disrespecting her wasn't in his genes, he sighed. "She's a tiny little thing with blond hair. I've never met a woman so innocent. I enjoyed making her blush with just a few words."

"Innocent and blushing?" She raised a brow. "That's a departure from the women you've spent time with these last few years."

How the hell did his mother know who he dated? Well, screwed. He never brought women home or talked about them. One of his brothers had obviously turned snitch. He held in a resentful sigh. Probably Matt.

"Heavenly is only twenty-two. She's a baby inside a thoroughly gorgeous woman's body. She cares about people. She's studying to be a nurse. She's kind and funny, and she has this pure heart..."

Just listing out her qualities crushed him again. Should he have tried harder? Done more? Said something else? Thrown caution to the wind and kissed her? Or just taken her to bed, despite her feelings for Beck?

"Oh, honey. She sounds wonderful, and the fact she made you feel hopeful and alive again is..." Pity lined his mother's face. "Is there any chance you left too soon?"

"No, Mom." He scrubbed a hand through his hair as his mom pulled the car into the driveway. "Let's drop it, okay?"

The glow of the Christmas lights strung around his childhood home brought a bittersweet smile to his lips. Then a scowl replaced it. The snow had been cleared, not only from the driveway but from the front steps as well—a job Seth had always been responsible for. No doubt, Matty Poppins had taken care of that, too.

Your duty to us is done.

Shoving aside his mother's words, he stepped out of the car. The front door opened, and the whole family rushed out to greet him. Danny grabbed Seth first, clutching him in a bear hug before he'd even left the driveway. He stared over his brother's shoulder, smiling at sweet Maggie, who waited patiently with one hand at the small of her back and the other cradling her heavy belly. She really did look ready to burst. How was it possible her pregnancy had progressed so much in a few short weeks? Seth wrapped her in a gentle hug, then carefully released her before the twins, Conner and Jack, latched onto him in a boisterous hug that nearly tumbled him to the snow.

As they wandered inside, Matt stepped in beside him, clapped him on the shoulder, and began catching him up on his caseload at the office.

"Thanks." Seth tried not to sound resentful. Matt had done him one hell of a favor. Many, in fact. "I'll head in soon to handle the paperwork and return phone calls."

"Oh, you don't have to. I've already taken care of it so you can kick back and enjoy your holiday. You know...I think I have a knack for this shit."

It sounded like he did. Not surprising. Matt had always been both strong-willed and snoopy.

"Good for you." The words popped out, then he winced. "I appreciate everything you've done."

Forcing a smile, Seth hurried up to his old bedroom, tossing his duffel on the mattress. He scrubbed a hand over his face. He'd been here three flipping minutes and already he wanted to be alone. It was going to be a long two weeks under one roof during the holidays... Not that he wasn't happy to see his mom and his brothers, but the usual joy had been obscured by a dark cloud. How long could it possibly take to get over a woman he barely knew?

Maybe he was off-kilter for a different reason. Jet lag. Lack of sleep. Weather change. Or...being rejected by the hottest girl on the planet. He sighed. For whatever reason, his body was in New York, but his mangled heart was still in LA, bleeding and in pieces.

After he rejoined the others, they finished decorating the tree as a family, hung stockings, and sampled some of his mom's holiday cookies. As afternoon waned into evening, they caught up over chips and beer before sitting down to a big, home-cooked dinner. The raucous mealtime was familiar, but he felt oddly removed, as if he merely watched his brothers laughing and ribbing one another from a distance.

His mother leaned over to him. "You're quiet."

"I'm tired." It was true...but that wasn't the only reason.

Tomorrow would be better, right?

Shortly after dessert, Seth bid everyone good-night, then wandered back up to his room and stretched out on his bed. Despite his exhaustion, he only managed to stare at the ceiling.

Had Heavenly been interested in Beck all along? Had she used him to make the prick jealous? No. Anger aside, she didn't have a manipulative bone in her body. She'd simply been honest about her feelings—more honest than he could take.

With a grunt, Seth closed his eyes, resolved to get over her, then fell into a fitful sleep.

But the next day wasn't better. He found himself measuring every hour by how long it had been since the last time he'd seen Heavenly's face. The bigger the number, the blacker his mood got.

By evening, he'd decided that enough was enough...and went through a couple of six-packs with his brothers, laughing about old times. He was feeling all right—until he received a text from her.

`I'm sorry about the other day. I upset you and I never meant to. I just talked to Raine. She said you've gone back to New York. I'll miss seeing you. Happy holidays.`

Translation: *Sorry, but I like Beck more than you. Merry fucking Christmas.*

He gripped the phone and counted to ten. But no, resentment still simmered. He had things to say, questions to ask. But none of them mattered. He refused to give her more of his energy. And no way would he wish her luck with the sadist who'd break her spirit, her body, and her heart. Seth just wished he'd been smart enough to fuck her out of his system before he left.

Instead, he replied with, `It's fine. Same to you.`

Grumbling, he deleted the text, darkened his phone, and shoved it in his pocket.

Was it possible he'd misread her? He was admittedly out of practice actually getting to know a woman.

He didn't want to care...but he couldn't stop wondering if he would ever talk to her again. If he did, would it change anything?

Matt leaned in, his expression concerned. "You okay?"

Seth forced a smile. "Oh, don't act concerned about me and forget to fess up about that time you put an air horn under Sister Mary Rose's chair in Sunday school."

The rest of his brothers howled with laughter.

Matt gave him a sly grin. "You're just mad because you got blamed."

That made them laugh even harder.

And thankfully no one gave his mood a second thought.

The next morning, he tried to enjoy Christmas Eve with his family. He plastered on a cheerful mask and skated through the long, frustrating day as if he didn't have a care in the world.

The Cooper family celebrated Christmas Day with a new dusting of snow and a lavish, chaotic, all-too-familiar shit storm of crazy. Presents were waiting to be unwrapped beneath the massive tree in the living room. The fire that never went out crackled and filled the whole house with fragrant pine. Mom had cooked a huge meal. As usual, the overindulgence of feasting, family, and festivities lasted throughout the day and well into the night.

After the winter sky had gone dark, Seth, Matt, and Danny sat outside around a roaring fire pit, sipping whiskey, smoking cigars, and talking smack. It was one of his favorite Christmas traditions...but the shitty movie where the pretty girl chose the villain kept pelting his brain.

Suddenly, Conner rushed out of the house. "Danny, hurry! Maggie... It's time! Mom's helping her put on a coat."

His brother stood and spit his whiskey into the fire, looking wide-eyed and terrified. "I-I'm not ready to be a dad."

Grace approached, a smile tugging at her lips as she pressed her forehead to Danny's. "You're going to be an amazing father. You had the best role models on the planet."

Seth swallowed down a lump of emotion. She meant their father...and him.

Danny gathered his mental shit and nodded. "Let's do this."

Seth was really proud of him—until Danny dashed to the edge of the patio and spewed his guts all over the pristine snow.

"Way to suck it up, bro." Seth clapped him on the back. "Don't worry. We've got your back."

Danny wiped the back of his hand across his mouth. "I'm good."

Piling into two cars, they caravanned to the hospital. Anna Mae Cooper was born an hour later, making her the highlight of their

Christmas. Mother and daughter had come through with flying colors, while the loud Cooper clan had cheered, earning disapproving frowns from the nurses.

Over the following days, the new baby filled the house with joy. It was bittersweet for Seth. He remained annoyingly unbalanced. Everyone gave him a wide berth. The extra bit of breathing room was nice, but he couldn't shake the oppressive need for something...somewhere...or someone. Seth would have written it off since this time of year always messed with his head. But it felt as if he'd outgrown his own skin.

Things would get better after the holidays. They had to.

Finally, New Year's Day arrived—along with a bitch of a hangover. At least his brothers hadn't fared any better.

He packed up his belongings and prepared to head back to the city and his normal life, relieved the holiday confinement with his well-meaning family was at an end. Then he spent the weekend righting his brownstone and trying to lose himself in work. But continued emptiness rode him hard. Where was the warmth and cheer? He'd left them in LA. With Heavenly, who kept intruding into his thoughts.

How had she spent Christmas? Rung in the New Year? Had she celebrated in Beck's bed?

As he stood in the shower on Monday morning, his thoughts once again gravitated to the blue-eyed beauty. Even before he'd reached down to wash his balls, his cock stood at attention. Refusing to jack off yet again, Seth cranked the hot water off and let the icy spray pelt his body until, teeth chattering, his eager appendage finally gave up. When he stepped out and stared at his reflection in the mirror, an unfamiliar face with hollow eyes stared back.

"What the fuck is wrong with you?"

Nothing mindless, uncomplicated sex won't cure.

That had to be it. Between Liam's woes, Heavenly's wiles, and all the family closeness, he hadn't gotten laid in weeks. Time to fix that shit.

He walked through his workday, his mind already on the evening and what he'd do to shake this malaise. After a frozen dinner in front of some cable news, he checked his watch. Nearly nine. Time to find his leather pants, head to Graffiti—his kinky home away from home—

and take control of his life again.

Twenty minutes later, he sat on a stool, absorbing the palpable hum emanating from the Doms and subs scening in the dungeon as he breathed in the heady scent of sex.

Gemma, a sub with whiskey-brown hair and pale green eyes, sidled up to him. "I was beginning to think you'd left us for good, Seth Sir."

While he hadn't had the chance to work her over, she'd definitely been on his radar before Liam's distress call had taken him out west. Gemma was his type—a few years older, experienced, and not interested in a full-time Master. A few weeks ago, he'd itched to have her under his control and in his bed. His impatient cock had scraped his zipper the instant he'd set eyes on her trim, scantily clad body. Now, it didn't even twitch.

Too bad. That fucker between his legs was going to get happy.

He nodded Gemma's way. "Good to be here."

"If you're looking for someone to play with, I'll happily volunteer, Sir."

Yeah, he was going to move the hell on and stop giving his mental power to Heavenly. He would find the goddamn will to bend Gemma—or someone like her—to his.

"Then kneel, girl."

The smug smile Gemma sent him from beneath her dark lashes and her graceful slide to the floor was all the consent he needed.

So how was it that, less than forty-five minutes later with Gemma still tied to his bed, looking rosy-assed and well fucked, he itched to free her, forego his usual lavish aftercare, and go home?

Because the only woman he wanted naked and at his mercy was thousands of miles away.

Right on cue, the dreaded movie in his head starring Heavenly played in its entirety again.

Clearly, settling back into his apartment, his routine, and his sex life hadn't cured him.

What the fuck was he supposed to do now? He could pick up the phone. Hell, he could catch the next plane. But no matter how strong his feelings for Heavenly were, they didn't change hers for Beck. He was going to have to give himself time. Suck it up and move forward.

After a seemingly endless stream of pointless days, January crept to a close. Seth avoided Graffiti and picked up a compulsive gym habit, morning and night. In between, he drowned in work, eschewing cheating spouse cases for pursuing bounties and criminals. Between the endorphin and adrenaline highs, he managed to get through each day and reach exhaustion every night.

But it didn't take long before his cheap escape stopped working. His steady-paying business dropped off, and he couldn't bring himself to give a shit. Instead, he began looking for some other way to fill the time and emptiness. Insomnia set in. Since he hated infomercials, he figured he had two choices: climb the walls or indulge in pointless fantasies about Heavenly.

A busy but hollow self-sex life won out.

A craptastic blizzard ushered February in. Finally, Seth's yearning trumped his pride. He almost didn't care that Liam would give him a ration of shit for dodging his calls since Christmas. He couldn't stand not hearing about Heavenly anymore.

With a sigh, he dialed Liam and apologized for being "busy." His old pal tormented him for twenty minutes with the happenings in the Hammerman/O'Neill/Kendall household, Raine's pregnancy, and their first holiday in their new home. All the while, Seth burned with wanting news of his angel…

His old friend finally paused, letting the silence between them stretch uncomfortably. Then Liam sighed. "Go on, then. Ask me."

Seth didn't bother playing coy. "How is she? Tell me now or I'll throat-punch you next time I see you."

"You can try." Liam gave a hearty laugh, then sobered. "Are you sure you want to know?"

"Christ, what do you want? I've been an idiot. A jerk. I was wrong. Just tell me."

"Say you're sorry," Hammer taunted in the background.

"Fuck off," he groused. "I need to know."

He imagined a million reasons Liam was stalling, everything from yanking his chain for fun to Heavenly eloping with Beck.

"She's fine. Better than fine, actually. I did warn you what would happen if you pissed off and left the gate open, didn't I?"

Seth's heart stopped. "Are she and Beck really together?"

"They're dating."

He gripped the phone tighter. The two-ton weight on his chest got heavier. "And?"

"She seems happy. So does Beck. You, my friend, might have been, too, if you'd stayed."

So there was no hope at all. He wasn't surprised. But it still hurt like a bitch.

"She gave me no reason to—"

"She gave you no reason to leave, either," Liam insisted. "If you want to be a part of Heavenly's life, you have to earn your place in her heart."

Liam's cutting observation hit a painful, perfect bull's-eye. "You just told me she's taken. I don't poach."

And I can't make her want me.

His friend's platitudes about not giving up went in one ear and out the other. Seth hung up minutes later, feeling more discouraged than ever.

Early February was full of frenetic, meaningless shit, except now he saw hearts, flowers, and lovers everywhere as Valentine's Day approached. Seth tried not to lose his damn mind. Each monotonous day bled into a long, miserable night in which he'd fall into a fitful sleep, only to gasp awake with his fist clutched around his cock and Heavenly's name on his lips.

After skipping out on Mass and family dinner the previous Sunday, Seth tried to shelve his surliness and visit his mom before heading to the office. He'd been avoiding her because he didn't want her grilling…but maybe it was time for her sage advice.

As he entered the front door, he heard a feminine groan from the kitchen. Shit. Had she fallen? Burned herself? Or gotten hurt trying to move the damn refrigerator to clean behind it again?

Seth rushed through the family room, only to come to a violent halt when he caught sight of his mom in the breakfast nook bent over their family kitchen table with her flushed cheek pressed to the surface. He stood unmoving, unblinking, struggling to process the sight of her eyes closed and holding the hem of her skirt around her waist. Her panties lay bunched between her knees as a bear of a man Seth had never seen stood behind her, his big hands gripping her hips, plowed into her from behind. His mother's moan filled the air again. The man threw back his head and groaned with her. Christ, he hadn't even dropped his trousers, merely unzipped his fly, and—

Seth lurched. Shit, he was going to puke.

Suddenly, his mom jerked her head up and saw him.

Grace gasped, but the man fucking her mistook it for passion, because he clutched her tighter and bellowed in a feral, hoarse roar.

Finally, Seth's body unfroze and he stumbled into the living room.

"Seth!" his mom called in a trembling voice.

"I'm on the couch. I'll give you a minute." *Or however long it takes to pull up your panties and lower your dress.* "In fact, I'll come by tonight."

Grace appeared in the doorway, hand across her mouth and tears streaming down her cheeks. "No. Wait. I-I'm so sorry you walked in—"

"Don't be."

Sure, no child wanted to think about, let alone witness, his mother sexually, but she'd never remarried. She'd never even dated when they were kids.

Embarrassment tightened her face. The last thing Seth wanted was to see her beat herself up for being human.

As he hurried toward her, she broke down in sobs. He wrapped her in his arms. "It's okay."

"Please understand… I loved your dad. He was my whole world and I was devastated when… We all were."

"Mom, don't—"

"After he was gone, I concentrated on raising you boys. I didn't have time to dwell on my own needs. But…things change."

Yeah, they did. That truth had been slapping him in the face all winter.

"Don't cry. I just came to talk. I didn't know you were…" *fucking a stranger on our kitchen table.* "You're a single woman entitled to…" *fuck a stranger on our kitchen table.*

The man peered around the corner, regret thick on his face, before he stepped into the family room, shoulders thrust back, head held high. He leveled a worried stare on Grace, then stuck out his hand. "Carl Mahoney."

"Seth Cooper." He accepted the man's shake.

Grace grimaced. "Someone please shoot me."

Despite the situation being awkward as hell, they all laughed. Seth would have stayed to calm his mom, but Carl took over, folding her in his arms. She glanced up at the man with love in her eyes. He met her stare with devotion. It was strange to witness his mother's affection for another man, but Seth was glad she'd found happiness again.

After vowing to call before dropping by again, he kissed her cheek and headed to work.

Hours later, he was seated at his desk, shuffling papers while trying to forget the morning's debacle, when his phone rang. He picked it up, expecting his mother. Instead, he was shocked to hear the sweet Irish lilt of Liam's mom.

"It's good to hear your voice, Bryn. How have you been?"

"Fine, but you've had a day of it, haven't you?"

"As a matter of fact…" She had some wicked psychic abilities. He'd never believed in that shit—until her. So Seth wasn't surprised she knew the sight he'd encountered that morning.

"Send your mother some flowers. She needs reassurance." Bryn paused. "They're in love, you know? She doesn't need you watching over her anymore."

Yeah, he'd gotten that message. And after all these years, she deserved to move on.

"If you give them your blessing, they'll make each other deliriously happy for the rest of their lives."

Had Bryn called him just to say that? "Thanks."

"You're welcome. Now I have a lot to tell you, and we'll get through this quicker if you listen."

Bryn called him occasionally without warning. She'd steer him in this direction or that. Though skeptical at first, he'd eventually accepted her words as well-meaning gifts. In fact, he'd thought about calling her a time or two over the past few weeks to ask about Heavenly…but he hadn't wanted her to confirm the situation was hopeless.

"What's going on?"

"I'm concerned about you."

The hair on the back of his neck prickled. "Me?"

"Of course. You haven't stopped thinking about your girl for weeks. Honestly, dear…" She sounded exasperated.

As always, the woman was spot-on. "Go on. I'm listening."

"The minute we hang up, order those flowers for your mother and tell her you love her. Then pack your bags."

He froze. "Where am I going?"

"Don't be daft. It's time you headed back to LA. In fact, you're almost too late."

Seth didn't pretend to misunderstand. "You mean I still have a chance with her?"

"You do—if you hurry. And if you don't give up this time."

His stubborn feelings for Heavenly weren't ridiculous and hopeless?

Maybe it wasn't logical, but hope lit the dark corners inside him for the first time in almost two months.

"Am I coming back here?" But his gut already told him the answer. He would put his business and his life here behind him if it meant having a future with Heavenly.

"Do you feel as if you belong in New York anymore?"

"No." He'd been an outsider looking in from the moment he'd returned.

"You've come to that conclusion time and again. Why are you asking me what you already know?"

No sense arguing the truth. "I'll be on a plane this weekend."

"I'm afraid it has to be today. Right now, in fact. Time is not only critical for you, but…Raine, Liam, and Hammer are about to face their most difficult hurdle yet. Your expertise and support are imperative. Give your family that excuse if you must, but grab a bag and meet us at LaGuardia when our flight from Dublin lands at two. I've already arranged a plane ticket out west for you. It's at the counter. And while you're waiting for us, you might want to replay the last conversation you had with your wee angel."

He didn't need to replay it; it was hardwired into his brain.

"And when you see her, this time find out how she feels about *you*," Bryn suggested.

Seth froze. Damn, the woman had a point; he'd never asked.

"She needs you, more than you know," Bryn went on. "The sooner you look deep enough, the sooner you'll understand."

"So you're saying…I'll end up with Heavenly?"

"Nothing is preordained. The future is always fluid. What I see are paths. If you stay in New York... Well, that would be a shame. Such misery. On the West Coast, you stand a chance of being happier than you've ever imagined. But it's up to you. I have to go now. Our flight to New York is boarding. I hope we'll see you at the airport."

"Wait! I—"

But Liam's mom had already hung up.

Despite her stunning bombshell, Seth saw light at the end of this dark, miserable tunnel. Screw how Heavenly felt about Beck.

Looking around the office he'd been content to work from for the last two years, he realized it was nothing but a skeleton of a room cluttered with a large desk, chairs, a pair of filing cabinets, and an aging copier—none of which he gave a shit about. This had been a place to pass time while he sought direction. Now it seemed cold and dingy, like the gray day outside. After snagging his keys off his desk, Seth locked the door, then hauled ass to his apartment, rambling absently on the phone to a florist along the way.

Ten minutes later, he'd packed his bags, squarely focused on the future. He couldn't wait to see Heavenly. To fill his nose with her scent, to finally fucking kiss her—and let her know he was in her life for good.

CHAPTER ELEVEN

Thursday, February 14
Valentine's Day

SETH HAD BEEN back in LA for less than twenty-four hours and he was already mired in a giant clusterfuck. Bryn hadn't been wrong about Hammer, Raine, and Liam needing his help ASAP. Raine's long-lost dipshit of a brother, River, had sworn to the police that Hammer committed statutory rape with an underage Raine years ago and had been pimping her out ever since. The lies would be comical if the possible prison time wasn't so horrific.

Hammer had been taken in for questioning, as had Liam and Raine. Their situation didn't look promising. Almost immediately, Seth had begun using his police and PI skills to keep Hammer out of the slammer—making phone calls about River, digging through the police's evidence, and piecing together their mounting case…but so far he hadn't been able to unearth anything useful.

The other part of this clusterfuck? He hadn't seen Heavenly. He didn't want to call her in case she refused to see him because she was dating Beck. Seth intended to surprise her, look her in the eyes…see for himself exactly what she felt for him.

Unfortunately, he'd been forced to spend most of the day with Beck. For a good cause, yeah. They'd escorted Raine to confront her brother. The face-to-face had served a couple of purposes. First, they had made damn sure Raine had protection while she set her brother straight about her relationship with Hammer. Second, Seth had gotten a read on this guy…and he had a feeling River was mistaken, not malicious.

Afterward, they'd brought River back to officially meet Hammer and Liam. The peace summit had nearly ended in war. He and Beck had been forced to bodyguard River in order to prevent bloodshed on

Raine's pale beige carpet. Thankfully, River had seen the error of his idiocy, so Seth hoped all would end well now.

And he could get back to finding Heavenly.

"You good here, princess?" Beck asked Raine.

She hugged the sadist and sent him a dry smile. "I think we'll be okay. I don't know what the world is coming to when I'm the coolest head in the room, but we'll make do."

Smiling, Seth pressed a kiss to her forehead. "Go get 'em once more, tiger. You can do it. We'll check in with you soon."

"Go take Heavenly to dinner." She gestured to them both.

He glanced at his watch. Late afternoon. By the time he fought traffic and headed to the hospital, Heavenly would probably be gone. Hell, she might even have left early. It was Valentine's Day, after all. And who would she be planning to spend the evening with except the guy she was—gag—dating?

As much as it chafed, he'd have to follow Beck some more.

"I plan to." Seth flashed a cocky grin. "Before I have her for dessert."

The doctor looked dead furious. "No, you fucking won't."

Seth ribbed Beck again—just for fun—and they argued all the way out the door.

He exited into the California sunshine, grinning at the temperate, blue-skied day. His family had complained about another Arctic blast of cold when he'd checked on them last night. It sucked to be them. And he had barely thought about the possibility of a catastrophic earthquake since arriving. Maybe he was getting used to the idea of dropping off into the ocean. Or he just didn't give a shit anymore. The perks of living here just might outweigh the fiery, eventual end.

"The only date you're going to have, pal, is with Rosy Palm and her four sisters," Beck taunted. "I'm taking Heavenly to dinner tonight. Get lost."

With a one-fingered salute, the doctor hopped into his flashy red Mercedes convertible that screamed midlife crisis and revved the engine. The good news about his nondescript gray midsize rental? He'd blend in with the rest of the traffic on the highway...and Beck would never know he was being tailed.

It paid to have skills.

Seth slid behind the wheel and followed at a discreet distance as Beck made his way out of the neighborhood and zoomed toward the freeway. Sure enough, once they both got on Wilshire near rush hour, the doctor stopped looking in the rearview mirror and started laying impatiently on his horn.

A few miles later, Seth followed him into another residential neighborhood. It was a hodgepodge of different architectural styles. He wasn't surprised when Beck pulled into his garage and shut the door behind him. Of course the SOB had the sleekest, most modern house on the whole fucking block.

With a sigh, Seth pulled to the curb a few houses down and waited. It shouldn't take long for him to change clothes, throw on some expensive cologne he hoped would get him lucky, and pick up his extra-small Trojans. And whaddaya know, Beck backed his German phallic symbol out of the garage fifteen minutes later, looking all refreshed and smug.

Twenty bucks said he'd just polished his knob in the hopes of controlling himself tonight.

Chuckling, Seth pulled slowly away from the curb and followed at a safe distance. He couldn't wait to get an eyeful of Heavenly.

Before she got into Beck's car, Seth hoped to intervene, say the right thing—whatever that was—then sweep her off her feet and take her someplace both fantastic and private.

Shit, he should have brought flowers or candy—or both. Right now, he couldn't stop, but he vowed he'd give her something much better later.

To his surprise, Beck didn't pull up at another house, apartment, condo, RV, shack by the river, or even a freeway underpass. The fidiot drove straight to a swanky restaurant on the beach. What the fuck? Did he think he was too important to pick Heavenly up himself?

The doctor valeted his red motorized penis. Seth pulled into a spot at the back of the parking lot and watched as Beck emerged with a spring in his step, box of candy in hand, and paced the fancy restaurant's portico. Seth frowned. Didn't he know Heavenly took the bus? Suddenly, Seth doubted it...just like he doubted his rival had learned where she lived.

He whipped out his phone. Yeah, doctors could save lives, and that was nifty. But PIs could dig up secrets. Shouldn't take him more than a few minutes to figure out where Heavenly called home. Then, he'd go get her himself and take her someplace less country-club pretentious and more romantic.

After a few taps on his screen, he glanced up to find Beck talking into his device, fingers clenched around a box of Godiva. He looked frustrated as he marched, argued, and gestured to the restaurant—not that whomever he talked to could see.

Oh, my god. Was Heavenly cancelling their big date?

How fucking priceless!

Holding in a good belly laugh, Seth pocketed his phone and strolled across the parking lot. This was going to be fun...

As he sauntered just under the portico's light, the doctor looked up, jaw clenched. "You again? Are you following me? Fuck off back to New York."

"Not gonna happen. Hammer needs my help, and Heavenly needs my...skills. What's the matter, cupcake? Did she stand you up?"

Beck ground his teeth. "She has to work."

"Understandable. I'd rather clean bedpans than go out with you, too."

"Ha ha. She's not cleaning bedpans, fucker. She's waiting tables. She got called in at the last minute, not that it's any of your business. How long are you staying this time?"

"As long as it takes." He smiled. Let the fucker make of that what he would.

Behind them, a young, fresh-faced hostess stuck her head out the door. "Beckman, table for two is ready."

The doctor sighed and shook his head. "Fuck."

"I'm sorry, sir?" The young woman frowned.

"Not you."

Her gaze lit on Seth. "I see your party is here. Right this way."

Before either of them could object, the hostess disappeared into the restaurant once more, the door swinging closed behind her.

Beck snapped a stare in his direction.

Seth raised a brow back. "You going to buy me dinner?"

"If that's what it takes for us to get a few things straight and for you to leave my girlfriend alone, why the hell not?"

"Girlfriend? Well, Heavenly is a girl. And last time I heard, she was your friend. How sweet."

Beck snorted. "Since you and your wounded pride went home for the holidays, Heavenly is definitely more than a friend now."

"So you've kissed her?" Seth taunted because he already knew better. Heavenly was confiding in Raine…who'd been more than happy to share her insider secrets.

The doctor's eyes narrowed. "You want a free meal? Get your ass inside."

Without looking back, Beck stomped into the restaurant. Chuckling, Seth followed, taking in the muted candlelight barely illuminating the intimate shadows around the room. The hostess led them to a table against the window, overlooking the Pacific. The poor woman was a little unsure whose chair to hold out and who to hand the wine menu to.

"I'll take that," Beck grumbled as he grabbed the wine list and sat himself with a glower.

Seth nodded at the hostess and settled into the seat directly across from Beck. "So, darling, how do the wines look?"

The doctor glanced up with a distinct *fuck you* on his face as a busboy poured them each a glass of water. Then Beck leaned in to whisper, "I'd only buy a bottle of wine for someone I want to blow me. Looks like you're stuck with H2O."

Seth smirked. "If you want oral for vino, man, I'd absolutely rather have water."

"Hi," chirped a perky waitress. "Welcome. Happy Valentine's Day! Free roses for all our couples." She reached into the basket dangling from her arm, looked between the two of them, then laid the stem across the middle of the table. "Enjoy! Now what can I get you lovebirds to drink?"

"Grey Goose martini, straight up. Make it a double."

"Iced tea." Seth picked up the rose and sniffed it. "You relax with your cocktail, honey. I'll drive home."

Beck looked ready to come across the table and punch him, but the waitress chimed in. "Great. I'll get your drinks, come back with some bread, and take your order."

When she walked away, her utilitarian braid swaying across her back, Beck turned to him with a scowl. "What the hell are you doing? Honey?"

"Would you prefer baby?"

"I prefer you to shut the fuck up and go away. I get why you came back from New York. Hammer needs you. Hell, Raine could clearly use your help, too. We have to figure out if River has an agenda and keep her out of danger."

Yes, especially since River had already once tried to kidnap her in the name of "saving" her from Hammer and Liam. "But?"

"Heavenly is off-limits."

"I'll see what she says. I don't take direction from you."

"You blew your chance with your late-night vanishing act. You're not getting the chance to upset her again. Don't visit her at the hospital. Don't follow us on our dates. Don't call, text, or stalk her. She's moved on."

"Nice speech." Seth braced his elbow on the table. "But you're out of luck. See, at Christmas, she texted me and told me that she was going to miss me. I'm rolling with that."

Surprise widened Beck's eyes for a split second before he banked it. "And have you talked to her since?" When Seth hesitated, Beck smiled. "I didn't think so. Look, that was then, and I'm keeping her more than occupied now."

"We'll see. You know, Raine has a very different opinion of this situation."

Beck scoffed. "Well, Raine is wrong. And don't think I'm sharing Heavenly with you, either. So if you're into that—"

"No. God no. I don't want to get that close to you. The swinging junk thing with Liam once awhile back cured me. What about you? You like knocking nuts with another guy when you have a woman between you?"

"I don't share, period."

"Well, there's one thing we have in common. A first." He lifted his water glass in a mocking salute. "And I guess we have Heavenly in common...for now."

Apparently, Beck wasn't in the mood to raise his glass. "You're wrong. You had your chance and you ran away when she hurt your little feewings."

Before Seth could reply, the waitress brought their drinks, took their dinner order, and left with a cheery smile. He wasn't keen about sitting across from the taciturn doctor for another hour, but if he wanted Heavenly, he had to deal. At least until he could figure out how to make Beck go away.

"Let's get real." Seth leaned in. "How can a sadist who's…what, fifteen years older be good for Heavenly?"

"Shy of fourteen," Beck ground out. "You don't know me or have any idea how I treat her. You certainly don't know my intentions."

"I know you'd ruin her."

"That's your opinion. While we're on the subject of who's bad for her, have you looked in a mirror? You don't even live here, so—"

"Who says I can't move?"

"But you're not. Right?"

Seth shrugged. Let the bastard wonder…

Beck crossed his arms over his chest. "You don't even have a job out here."

"I'm self-employed, asshole. I can go anywhere. And by the way, putting bloody stripes on her ass won't get me hard. You can't say the same."

"I'd never fucking hurt her. I've been taking my time and learning her, so when she's ready, I'll know exactly what she needs and how far I can take her."

"What a fidiot."

"You're not perfect, Casanova. I doubt you can keep your pants zipped long enough to be faithful. In fact, it wouldn't surprise me to find out you got some action back while you were back in New York."

Seth felt a guilty flush crawl up his face. "Is your sex life so lacking that you have to ask about mine?"

"Get serious. Heavenly won't be able to handle you playing musical beds."

"The truth might actually shock you."

"Oh? You don't know anything about commitment."

"I know it isn't doing the same club sub two nights in a row. It takes caring, compromise, understanding—"

"Don't lecture me. I'm not the one with the revolving-pussy policy."

Seth didn't owe Beck any information about his personal life. "For the right woman, I'd be very monogamous."

"Really? Earlier today, Hammer mentioned a woman you loved who scared the shit out of you. Were you faithful to her?"

Seth clutched the butter knife and fought the urge to eviscerate the bastard. "Every fucking day, so why don't you shut up? I listened to you. Now hear me: I'm not leaving Heavenly until she realizes I'm the one for her. So we can squabble about it like boys. No, like Hammer and Liam—"

"I wouldn't waste the energy to punch you in the snow."

"You're not worth freezing my ass off, either. So we can spend dinner talking about weather, sports, and Hammer's situation or eat in silence; I don't care which. After that, I'm bringing my A-game and letting Heavenly decide who she wants."

"That's fine by me." Beck lifted his martini. "I know the best man will win."

"Hɪ!" Rᴀɪɴᴇ ᴏᴘᴇɴᴇᴅ her front door the following afternoon. "Come in. I'm glad you had time to hang out today."

With a smile, Heavenly stepped inside her friend's big house. The place always awed her. It was somehow opulent and cozy at once.

As she entered, the scents of vanilla and cinnamon hit her, along with baking nuts and something yeasty. "Me, too. Thanks for inviting me. Gosh, something smells divine."

Raine shut the door and led her inside. "After the morning I had, I needed to bake."

"What happened?"

"Several things. Hammer's got a lot going on. It's"—the brunette waved her away with a sniffle—"hopefully fine now. Everything is emotional. I visited my mother's and sister's graves for the first time today, too. I had to do it."

Sympathy twisted Heavenly's heart. Dr. Beckman had given her sketchy information about the sad fate of Raine's family. Raine herself had filled in with detail. "I'm glad you went. Do you feel better? Did you get closure?"

The other woman gave a shaky nod and pasted on a smile. "Yeah. But after coming home, I needed to make snickerdoodles and banana bread, so now I'm feeling a lot calmer. Want some?"

Heavenly's mouth watered. She wasn't skipping lunch anymore, thanks to Dr. Beckman, but she still had an occasional sweet tooth. "Please."

"Be right back."

Before Raine could disappear into the kitchen, a big hulk with vivid blue eyes that matched Raine's pushed out the kitchen door, offering them goodies from their plastic containers. Who the heck was this guy?

"Thanks." Raine turned to Heavenly. "This is my brother. River, this is Heavenly. She took great care of me at the hospital after…well, after Bill."

"I remember seeing her while I blended in the waiting room. Hey." The big guy stuck his hand in her direction. "Nice to meet you."

Heavenly didn't remember seeing him at all that morning. As she stared at his outstretched palm, his size alone made her wary. But the sharpness of his stare unsettled her more… Clearly, this guy didn't miss much.

"Same to you." She finally shook his hand, then glanced Raine's way. "This is the brother you've been looking for all this time?"

"Yep. Though his grand reentrance in my life wasn't exactly the way I pictured it."

River winced. "Okay, so I misunderstood your relationship with Liam and Hammer. Can you blame an older brother?"

"Misunderstood?" Raine shot him a quelling glare. "That's a vast understatement."

River snorted. "On that note, I'm leaving to resume my job search. I'll see you soon, storm cloud."

When he kissed her cheek, she smiled. "Sounds good. Call me."

He nodded, then turned Heavenly's way. "Have a good one."

"You, too." She waved.

When the big guy let himself out of the house, Raine faced her again and reached for a cookie, wearing a genuine smile. "He's a good guy. Hardheaded and misguided at times but…he's a man."

That made Heavenly laugh. "Well, since your big brother is back, maybe Beck will pester you less. Or not. I think he enjoys it."

Raine rolled her eyes. "Keep him busy, will you? I have my hands full with Liam and Hammer. Oh, speaking of Beck, you never did tell me how your date at the art gallery was?" Raine's sideways glance seemed both searching and knowing. "I wanted to see the exhibit myself but we never found the time."

The works of art floated through Heavenly's thoughts again, as did the memory of the doctor standing beside her, asking questions, explaining patiently, and watching her as some of the pieces elicited instant, deep arousal.

Heavenly cleared her throat. "It was…interesting. Did you know the subject of the show?"

"I heard." And she didn't sound shocked. Then again, the woman had two lovers… "Did you find it entertaining or educational?"

"Both." In fact, part of Heavenly itched to try some of the things she'd seen depicted, things she'd never even imagined until Beck had opened her eyes.

"But you haven't spent much time with him since that date?"

"Except during lunch at the hospital, none."

And that troubled Heavenly. They were still friends, but they hadn't had the chance to explore something more. Of course, some of that was her own fault. She'd had to cancel on him twice since their date at the gallery. She was beginning to hate Bazookas, but she needed the money too much to quit. Still, if he had more than friendship on his mind, he certainly wasn't in a rush to get there…

Raine looked shocked. "Seriously?"

"Well, he was out of town for a couple of weeks. Friend of the family had a medical emergency in Vegas, he said."

"Hammer told me Beck went to medical school there," Raine offered.

Heavenly hadn't known that.

"What about Valentine's Day?" Raine leaned in, grinning. "Didn't Beck finally lay a big ol' kiss on you then?"

No. He'd promised her one at Disneyland. So far, he hadn't delivered. She was dying for it. Him…not so much.

"My jerk of a boss said if I didn't cover a shift, he'd fire me. I never work on Thursdays, but someone broke an ankle and I was the first waitress to answer his distress call." She shrugged. "It sucked, but at least the tips were decent."

"Sorry." Raine sighed. "I know you're busy, so I appreciate you coming by. I was feeling a little down after the visit to the cemetery. The men in my life try to cheer me up. But every so often, I need girl time."

"I'm happy to cheer you up. Especially if you baked cookies."

When she plucked one from the container and nibbled with a groan, Raine laughed. "So…do you still think about Seth?"

The question caught her off guard. Heavenly bit her lip. "I've tried not to. But, yeah. A lot."

More than she should. It wasn't that she didn't enjoy her time with Beck, especially away from the hospital. He was handsome, witty, fascinating. He made her feel important and special…just not always romantically. Sometimes she was convinced he wanted their friendship to be more. Other times, he seemed content with the status quo. He confused her.

Seth, on the other hand, had made her feel beautiful and desirable from the moment they'd met. He'd constantly undressed her with his stare. He'd said things that made her blush in a voice that made her wet…until he'd gone.

Raine grinned and picked up her phone, dashed off a quick text, then set her device upside down on the table between them. "I wouldn't be surprised if he still thinks of you, too."

Excitement bounced in her belly—until reality dashed it. "The last time I texted him, he barely replied."

"Hmm." Raine shrugged. "What exactly did you say to Seth before he left? Liam didn't tell me."

Heavenly pressed her lips together and felt her face flame. "It probably sounds stupid now, but I was trying to be honest. I told Seth that I, um…had feelings for Beck. He left not two minutes later."

Raine rolled her eyes. "Oh, spare me wounded male pride. I mean, it's not like you didn't have feelings for Seth, too."

"Right." After all, she'd been prepared to take him into her home and into her body that night. Walking away had looked embarrassingly easy for him. She cringed just thinking about it.

"And you told him that, didn't you?"

Hadn't she? "I think so. But I'm not sure it would have mattered to him." Not the way he had mattered to her. "We only had one date."

But Seth had planned the most romantic afternoon she could have imagined. The wine, the bread, the dessert…the company. Even the weather had been perfect. The memory still made her sigh.

"Oh, it mattered," Raine assured. "The question is, do you want to see him again?"

"If he ever comes to town again, sure. But I'm not holding my breath."

"Maybe you should." Raine gave her a too-innocent smile. "Tell me about school. How are your classes?"

They fell into an easy conversation, Heavenly chatting about her semester, followed by Raine lamenting about the early symptoms of her pregnancy. As they giggled over old wives' tales meant to end morning sickness, someone knocked on her door.

Instantly, Raine jumped up, seeming more excited than surprised by the interruption. "Stay right there."

Footsteps resounded through the big room. On the other side of the wall, Heavenly heard the door open. Raine didn't greet anyone or speak at all. Maybe it had been the postman. Heavenly eyed the cookies. Maybe she could steal one more…

As she lifted the contraband to her lips, Raine ran—literally—through the living room and headed for the kitchen. "I totally forgot to offer you coffee. Want some?"

"Sure."

"I'll be back. It may take a while," she said as she disappeared into the kitchen and the door shut behind her.

The coffee wasn't a big deal. Heavenly would be happy with her company—and cookies.

She took another bite, closed her eyes, and moaned as the sinful cinnamon and brown sugar mixture melted on her tongue.

"Hi, angel."

Heavenly swallowed, then froze. She knew that voice.

Seth?

She turned slowly. It couldn't be real.

But there he stood in the doorway. Tall. Wearing jeans that hugged him in all the right places. Green eyes intent, body still, everything about him so sharp—especially his stare, which he focused solely on her.

Feeling like she was in a dream, Heavenly set her cookie aside and rose. "Is that really you?"

He took confident strides into the room. "Damn, I forgot how beautiful you are."

Five seconds, and he already had her blushing. She smiled, unable to do anything but float in his direction.

"You look..." *Gorgeous. Masculine. Way more edible than Raine's cookies.* "Good. I didn't think I'd ever see you again. What are you doing here? When did you arrive?"

"A couple of days ago. I've been busy helping Hammer, but all I've wanted to do is lay eyes on you." A little smile lifted the corners of his lips. "Your last text said you were going to miss me. Did you?"

Seth's stare drilled down into her eyes as he took her fingers between his. Her blush spread. Arousal darkened his face. Her body flashed hot in response as he surveyed her every curve and swell, drinking her in with barely a touch. She felt as if she stood before him stark-naked.

The hunger on his face had her heart skipping beats. She suddenly forgot how to breathe. Would he kiss her? Did he want to?

She was almost disappointed when Seth lifted her hand and pressed his lips to her palm instead. Then he dragged the tip of his tongue up her sensitive flesh in a deliberate stroke. She shivered, her skin burning when he touched her. Before she could help herself, her fingers cupped his face, brushing his sexy, sandy five o'clock shadow as if they had a mind of their own. He looked so vital and virile, almost dangerous. Her heart rate picked up. Her nipples peaked.

"E-every day."

His smile widened and something like thrill lit his eyes as he brushed the hair from her cheek and tucked it behind her ear. "Yeah? I missed you, too, angel."

Gosh, he was so handsome he made her insides gooey. Made her lips ache with wanting to feel them covering her own.

Heavenly imagined him kissing her breathless. Her brain sputtered. Her words evaporated. All she could do was blink at him and get lost in his expression that silently promised pleasure beyond anything her innocent fantasies had conjured.

"Can we talk?" He threaded his fingers through hers and led her to the sofa before lifting the last of her snickerdoodle back to her lips. "Want to finish your cookie first?"

Taking a bite from his hand was incredibly intimate. She chewed, still dumbstruck, unable and unwilling to look at anything but him. The way he watched her spread goose bumps all over her body.

"Thanks." The word fell from her lips, mostly because she wasn't sure what else to say.

The rapport they'd shared before he had gone to New York had been flirty and light. In its place lay a deeper awareness. A new focus. Something she couldn't put her finger on.

He swiped his thumb across her lip, gathering leftover crumbs and taking them back to her tongue. Without thought, she licked them away. Then she froze, stared, hearing nothing but her own breathing and the wild beat of her heart. Gosh, why had she put her tongue on him? He wasn't a spoon or an ice cream cone. Was he annoyed? Disgusted? Perturbed?

A wide, slow smile broke out across his face. His eyes flared hot. And Heavenly had her answer. He'd liked it. She knew that when he pushed his thumb farther into her mouth. It seemed like the most natural thing to wrap her lips around the digit and gently suck as he slowly pulled free with a groan.

The air between them felt too thick to breathe and crackled with something she barely understood. All Heavenly knew was that she was afraid to blink because she didn't want him to go away again.

"Oh, angel… You make me remember exactly why I couldn't stop thinking about you while I was gone."

Heavenly understood. If anything, Seth was more potent to her than he had been last December. At least then, she'd been able to manage a little witty conversation. Right now, she barely remembered her own name.

"Seth…"

"Don't tempt me. I already want to kiss you so badly I can't stand it." He squeezed her shoulder, then eased back. "You have no idea how hard being away from you has been. I'm sorry about December, the way things ended. It was my fault. I misunderstood everything you said and I didn't accept your honesty the way I should have. I didn't even ask questions. But I'm asking now. Do you have feelings for me, Heavenly?"

His words punched through her besotted haze. "Of course. I had no idea…" *that it mattered.* "I thought you saw me as a…" How could she put this? Heavenly frowned, her thoughts gathering slowly. "A vacation fling. I knew you weren't staying and I didn't think you'd ever be interested in me for more than quick sex. I had fun with you on the picnic but…" She sighed and wished she could get unflustered and stop talking in circles. "I'd made up my mind to spend that, um…evening with you, but I thought I owed it to you to be honest first. You have to know, I would never have decided to, you know, be with you if I didn't like you, too."

"You weren't just sex to me, angel. Don't you remember me telling you that I was interested in more than your beautiful body? That was my clumsy way of saying I wanted more. I was willing to give you the patience and attention you deserve because you needed to be sure." He fell quiet, then penetrated her with another fierce stare. "Because I'm definitely interested in all of you."

Heavenly couldn't keep the surprise off her face. "Oh, gosh. I never thought… I mean, most of our conversation was about… Everything you said to me at Raine's party was… So I assumed you wanted…"

"Sex. I see that now. Damn, I told you that day at the grocery store I wanted to make love to you. I thought you understood the difference between…" He shook his head and raked a hand down his face.

"I didn't. I'm sorry. And I didn't believe—couldn't imagine—that I meant more to you than just easy pleasure. I mean, you could have anyone…" *An experienced woman who knows how to please you.* "Why would you think I didn't like you? In my mind, you wanted sex, and I was willing to give it to you simply to be with you because that was the only way I thought you'd have me."

"What a freaking mess." He sighed. "We both made assumptions and didn't communicate clearly. I'm going to fix that, and I need you to work with me. Okay?"

She bobbed her head. "I'll do my best."

"Good." He took her hands. "Look, I admit you stung my pride that evening at the grocery store. Suddenly, you didn't want Beck as merely a friend, and hearing you actually wanted to sleep with him was a shock."

That made her feel terrible. "I knew immediately I'd upset you. But truthfully, I didn't think you'd care how I felt as long as I was willing to be with you, but I needed to be honest."

"I admire honesty, Heavenly. I do. But imagine how you would have taken it if I'd told you that evening that I was interested in sleeping with someone else, too."

Wretched. Awful. Confused. "You're right. I'm sorry." She bit her lip against the sting of tears. "I messed up everything."

"No. Come here, angel." He pulled her into his big arms and held her to his solid chest, against his beating heart.

Suddenly, she felt warm and comforted. Safe. Desired. Almost whole.

Seth stroked her back, nuzzled her neck, inhaled her as he seemingly lost himself in the moment. "Don't cry."

"I'm mad at myself. I spent weeks at a loss to understand what happened, and now to hear that if I had chosen my words better—"

"If I had asked questions. If I had pressed you to explain. If I had thought before I reacted. If I had remembered you're a virgin who maybe didn't understand what I was trying to say." He cupped her cheek and shook his head. "Don't put all this on your own shoulders. What's important is that we're talking now."

Nodding, she sniffled and backed away. "And I'm glad but..."

Heavenly feared finishing that sentence. The last time she'd been honest about her feelings for Beck, he'd ended everything between them. Granted, he said he understood now. But did he? Really?

"You're dating Beck and you still have feelings for him? I know. But angel, I'm back and I want you more than ever."

She met his stare, knowing he would see the apology all over her face for something she couldn't help. "I'm getting that. And I'm shocked. In a good way..."

Clearly, she was going to have to choose between them. But...Seth and Beck were incredibly different men who made her feel very different things. Her Viking PI from the East made her melty and hot. He whispered words that made her head spin, even as he talked to her, bantered with her, not like the girl she often felt, but like the woman she wanted to be.

The witty doctor challenged her to think and to live, to be brave, even as he protected her, seemingly always hovering, a snarl ready to keep the beasts of reality away. One minute, he tried to grow her mind so she thought like his equal. The next she felt cosseted and nurtured.

They both made her yearn and crave them more than she knew how to resist. They both had a grip on her she didn't know how to cure. How was she supposed to walk away from one?

"But you don't know who you want," he finished for her. "And you need time to make a choice."

"Yes."

"You need to know me better, because we haven't spent enough time together for you to be sure we're a fit."

"That would help."

"Take your time. You see, I've been around the block enough to realize we're something special. But you haven't, and me rushing you isn't going to help anything. I came here to help Hammer…but I want to be with you. I want to see you. Date you. Kiss you. Take you to bed and fucking never let you go. And we can do all that while you figure out how you feel about Beck. I only ask you to focus on me when we're together. He doesn't belong between us. Understood?"

Heavenly blew out a breath. Wow, she hadn't expected such a huge concession.

Could she even date two men? Heck, she'd never dated one. Both of these men were so self-assured, interesting, and obviously experienced. She was probably in over her head. Was she crazy to try? Maybe, but how was she ever supposed to get experience if she never got brave enough to put herself out there? YOLO and all that… Besides, it was dating, having fun…fooling around. They were just asking her to choose a boyfriend. It shouldn't be this dramatic.

"You're okay with that?" she asked.

"I've had seven weeks to come to this conclusion. You've had fifteen minutes. So I want you to think about it and let me know if you want to see me again."

"I don't have to think about that. I'm so happy you're back. Of course I want to see you. I want to know what could happen between us."

He leaned in, kissed her nose, and stood. "Then I'm here for you. Call me when you're ready for the next step and we'll take it together."

TWO DAYS LATER, Beck pulled off the paved highway and onto the gravel road, sliding another lingering glance at Heavenly as she sat in the passenger's seat of his Mercedes and peered out the window at the looming San Gabriel Mountains. "I love getting out of the city and coming up here."

"It's beautiful."

"Not as beautiful as you."

She dipped her head, gaze falling to her lap, but that didn't hide the sweet blush rushing up her cheeks. He grinned, loving that a few whispered words always got to her—and that he always had a hint how she felt.

She'd worn exactly what he'd asked her to—yoga pants, a soft, comfortable T-shirt, and athletic shoes. She always looked gorgeous, but seeing her in clothes that hugged her curves shredded his libido. The second he laid eyes on her, dirty fantasies started unraveling in his brain and continued to wreak havoc the entire forty-five-minute drive. But it was her compliance and attention to his detail that stroked his Dominant beast.

"You come here a lot?"

"As often as I can." He reached for her hand and twined their fingers together. "But I'm enjoying this trip so much more because you're with me."

She peered at him from beneath her lashes. "Then I'm glad you invited me today. We haven't spent any time together in a while. Seeing you away from the hospital is nice."

"I've been looking forward to this day for a long time." Hell, he would have brought her here a month ago. He'd planned to shortly after their outing to the gallery. Then life had gone to hell.

"Why's that?"

Because today, he would finally find out how much she trusted him. Today, if all went well, they'd take a big step forward. "You'll see."

Just being near her brought a big smile to his face, but he wanted more. He wanted to slam on the brakes and pull her onto his lap, crush her mouth beneath his, and swallow every kitten-soft moan. He wanted to imprint his mouth on hers. He wanted to kiss her so senseless she forgot Seth Cooper existed.

He knew the shithead had come back for Hammer's sake, but Beck worried Seth intended to stay. Damn it, he was on the cusp of making Heavenly his. He didn't need the PI returning like a bad case of herpes.

"But I have to admit I've been looking forward to staring at your sexy ass while we hike up the mountain."

She looked surprised for a moment, then sent him a flirty smile. "Have you?"

"Oh, yeah."

"So you're taking me hiking? That's the surprise? I've never been."

"I've got something even more fun planned. We're just hiking until we get there." And Beck would bet she'd never done what he had in store for her.

"What is it?"

Because he couldn't stop himself, he leaned in and inhaled her scent. "I'm not telling. Patience, little girl."

"I haven't asked in ten whole minutes."

"And that's five minutes longer than the time before, but anticipation is still rolling off you. By the way, you're flirting with me."

She sent him a ball-churning glance from beneath her lashes. "Do you mind?"

"Not one bit."

Had she flirted with Seth, too? Wondering drove him batshit crazy.

Gripping the wheel tighter, Beck tried not to dwell on the competition, but he knew Heavenly had seen the bastard yesterday. He'd pulled Raine aside this morning when everyone gathered to figure out how the hell to keep Hammer out of prison now that he'd been arrested...and gotten some scoop about Heavenly's reunion with Seth. When the raven-haired vixen admitted she'd actually invited the East Coast cock-hole over to see Heavenly, he'd called her a Judas. Not surprisingly, she'd rolled her eyes and assured him that she was an equal-opportunity matchmaker. *Sneaky little wench...*

Beck still wasn't sure if Heavenly had welcomed the silver-tongued bastard back into her life or told him to go pound sand. He had only one way to find out...

"So I guess Seth is back in town."

She nodded. "We talked yesterday."

"You were pretty upset when he left last December. Did you..." *fucking kiss and make up?* "Work everything out?"

She withdrew her hand and looked away. "Yes."

Beck gnashed his teeth as he pulled into the parking lot, came to a stop, and killed the engine. "Will you date him again?"

"He wants me to."

Of course he does. *Horny fucker...* "What do *you* want?"

Heavenly didn't answer him for what felt like a year. "I said yes. He's promised me time to figure out how I feel and..."

When she bit her lip anxiously, Beck knew what she hesitated to say. "Who you want?"

She nodded. "Are you mad? Maybe you're not. I know you consider us friends—"

"We're more than friends, little girl. Let's get that straight right now."

"Oh." The soft flush stole across her cheeks again. "I wasn't sure. I thought I'd been too forward when I asked you to kiss me—"

"I only said no because I wanted our first kiss to be special. If I'd touched you then, I would have tossed you to the ground, climbed on top of you, and not given two shits about the hordes of kids watching."

Heavenly jerked her stare to him, all wide-eyed. "You would not."

"Wanna bet?"

"I haven't been sure what to think since you said no. Then our date at the gallery seemed so sexual, but you didn't touch me. And I haven't seen you much since, so I wasn't sure if..."

"I wanted you? I do. More than air."

"Oh." A smile crept slowly up her face. "Oh."

"I've tried to hold back so I didn't scare you."

She tilted her chin and frowned. "I don't think you could."

His deep laugh filled the car. "Oh, I'm the man your mother warned you about."

Her face closed up. "My mother never warned me about anything. I haven't seen her in eight years."

That might be the most personal thing she'd ever shared with him. Beck wanted to ask a thousand questions, but he'd probably have to answer a thousand in turn. Besides, talking family got them off topic.

"I'm sorry. Mine wasn't around much, either. My point is, I tried to move at your pace, but if I've misjudged it, I'll be more than happy to speed things up." He flashed her a devilish grin.

"M-maybe a little." Then that furrow appeared between her brows again. "But if I want to date him, too, will you stop seeing me?"

Was that why Seth had taken off, because he couldn't handle the competition? Yeah. Why else would he promise her time now to figure it out?

Heavenly's question had exposed her insecurity. On one hand, it helped because a Dom couldn't guide a sub without knowing her strengths and weaknesses. On the other hand, it pissed him off that Seth had wounded her when he'd disappeared. So he squelched the jealous urge to make her choose and focused on implementing the last phase of his plan. If today went well, he'd hopefully leave Seth in the dust.

"Not a chance in hell. I won't like it, but I won't rush you to make up your mind."

"Thanks." She squeezed his hand and sent him a relieved smile. "I appreciate your patience."

"Sure." Beck wanted to growl that he'd been fucking patient, but he'd once told her he could be a patient man. Now he had to show her. "You ready for an adventure?"

"Yeah."

The excited smile spreading over her face rivaled the sun. She was beauty, grace, and light. And for today, she was all his.

"Then let's do this."

When they climbed from the car, Beck grabbed his backpack and slid it over his shoulders, then wrapped an arm around Heavenly's waist. As he led her up the uneven trail, they talked and laughed, stopping to rest in the shade and share the water and snacks he'd stashed.

Standing against a sturdy alder tree, Beck lifted a plump red grape to her lips. Their eyes locked. His heart revved and roared when Heavenly parted for him, biting the grape between her teeth. Barely containing a feral growl, he dragged his fingers over the soft texture of her lips as she bit down into the juicy morsel. He'd give anything to sink his teeth into the other half and devour her until they were a spent, sweating, panting tangle of arms and legs.

Not yet. Once he knew she trusted him, it was on. But until then, he had to dial it back. Maybe he'd already said too much, but instinct told him she would come through. That she belonged to him.

If she didn't, it would gut him.

After the brief respite, he tucked the snacks away, tried not to wince at his pulsing erection, and hoisted the pack back over his shoulders.

As they continued their trek up the mountain, he pointed out a pair of whitetail deer.

"They're so graceful and beautiful," she whispered, her voice awe-filled. "Do you think we'll see more?"

"Maybe. Keep your eyes open."

As they got closer to their destination, they didn't encounter more wildlife, just raucous laughter and high-pitched screams. Beck's gut knotted with tension. In less than thirty minutes, he'd finally know if he had been pointlessly pining over Heavenly for the past three months…or whether they had a future.

"What's going on over that hill? Sounds like a party."

Beck squeezed her waist and drew her to a halt. "This is the other part of my surprise. You'll find out over the rise." He plucked a black satin blindfold from his pocket and dangled it from his finger. "How brave are you, little girl?"

Heavenly stared at the shiny scrap of fabric with wide eyes. "Y-you want to blindfold me?"

"I do." *For starters…*

Heavenly swallowed tightly. "What if I trip or stumble over something?"

"I'll be right beside you, holding on, just like I've been since we started up this trail." He dragged a knuckle down her cheek. "I won't let you fall."

"I've never…"

"Worn a blindfold or let someone lead you through the wilderness?"

"Either."

"Do you trust me?" he asked in a low, hoarse tone.

"Yes."

She didn't hesitate, and Beck felt a surge of something more potent than hope and stronger than lust. It wrapped around his heart and squeezed until he almost couldn't breathe.

"Then show me."

With trembling fingers, Heavenly took the blindfold from him and positioned it over her eyes. As soon as she settled it in place, she wobbled at the loss of sight and reached for him, instantly putting herself in his hands, seeking his guidance.

Electric thrill pinged inside him.

"Oh, wow… I'm disoriented," she murmured.

Gently, he turned her to ensure the elastic at the back of her head was secure, then he bent close to her ear. "I've got you. Ready?"

Heavenly nodded, but her breath came at an uneven, nervous pace. Beck wrapped her tightly against his side. She gripped him and held on for dear life as he carefully directed her up the incline. As they crested the slope, he guided her onto the flat concrete surface. The people gathered turned and grinned as he led her forward. Some gave him a thumbs-up.

Hearing the commotion, Heavenly tensed and slowed, as if unsure.

"Easy," he murmured. "You're safe with me. I promise."

"Where are we, Beck? The wind is really blowing."

He dialed back the urge to pump his fist in the air. Like a well-seasoned submissive, she was relying on sound, scent, sensation—and him. Toying with a sweet sub's senses was one of the many reasons he loved blindfolds.

Before he could answer, a woman let out an ear-piercing scream. The assembled group erupted in a collective cheer. Heavenly tensed and reached for the blindfold.

Beck gripped her wrists to stop her. "Trust me, just a minute more."

"But that woman sounds terrified. What's happening?"

He skimmed a soothing palm down her back. "She's excited, but she's fine. Everyone is. Do you still trust me?"

"I-I…"

The pulse point at the base of her neck thundered like a jackhammer. Adrenaline must be careening through every cell in her body.

"Heavenly?"

"Yes." She finally nodded. "I'm nervous, but I trust you."

In moments, he'd find out if that was true.

"I'll take the blindfold off soon," he promised. "But let's get you some water first."

Beck reached into his pack for fresh *agua*. She jumped slightly when he pressed the bottle to her lips, but he was pleased she didn't try to hold it herself. Instead, she tipped her chin back and drank from his hand.

"Better?"

"Yes," she said as she finished. "Thank you."

"It's time to get you set up for your surprise. Just relax. I promised to keep you safe, and I never break a promise. I'll be right beside you the whole time."

"What is it?"

"Just a little more patience…"

He led her under a massive beige awning and pulled her to a stop, then nodded to Chet, a familiar twenty-something guy wearing a logoed tank and carrying a clipboard. "We're ready."

"Excellent." Chet smiled, and Beck raised a brow when his gaze lingered for a moment too long on Heavenly.

Then the guy was all business, and Beck spoke to her in gentle, soothing tones while Chet secured the full-body harness. Heavenly didn't protest or ask questions. She simply jerked a few nervous nods in response to Beck's queries. As he was strapped into a matching contraption, he caressed her arm and maintained the nonstop verbal reassurance.

After Chet snapped the last buckle in place and turned away, Beck pulled Heavenly to his chest. "When we were at the art gallery, you said you wanted to really experience life. Remember that?"

"Yes."

"There aren't many better ways than what we're about to do…"

He removed the blindfold, watching as she blinked against the bright rays of sunlight. "Welcome to the Bridge to Nowhere."

She slapped a hand to her mouth. Her eyes flared saucer-wide as a teenage boy not three feet from them let out a war cry and leapt off the bridge. With a strangled gasp, Heavenly peered over the edge at the crinkled bungee cord and the tethered jumper.

Beck tugged her closer to the railing as the recoil lifted the teen back into the air before gravity slammed him down once more. Everyone on the bridge cheered at his successful leap.

Beck looked away from the jumper and focused on Heavenly. She looked afraid…and more than slightly curious.

"Ever bungee-jumped before?"

"No! Never. And you have?"

"All the time." He gestured to the guy in the tank. "Chet, here, knows me well."

"Oh."

As if suddenly aware they were perched a hundred feet above the San Gabriel River, Heavenly tore herself from his grasp and stumbled away from the railing. Her face went ghostly white as she pressed a palm to her stomach. "I should have mentioned sooner that I'm afraid of heights."

Beck mentally kicked himself in the ass. He eased in front of her and brushed the wisps of hair from her face. "If this is too much for you, we don't have to jump. We can head back down the mountain and get some—"

"No." She shook her head slowly at first, then with more conviction. "I think…I want to do it. I mean, when will I ever have another chance?"

Even as she said the words, she looked ready to pass out.

"Anytime. We can do it whenever you want." He skimmed his knuckles down her pale cheek, half expecting to see her eyes roll back in her head before she crumpled toward the pavement. "I didn't bring you here to scare you."

"I know." A tiny giggle rolled from her lips. "When you said you had a surprise, you weren't kidding."

He grinned as a peach hue slowly returned to her cheeks. "So you're up for it?"

"Nothing will happen to me, right?"

"You'll be fine. I wouldn't promise you that if it wasn't true."

"Let's…do it." She darted a nervous tongue over her lips. "I'll warn you now, you might have to push me off the edge."

He laughed. "How about I just drag you with me?"

"You mean we can jump together?"

"Or you can go by yourself."

"No!" She grabbed his arm and clung. "I'd rather do it with you."

"Good. Doing it alone isn't nearly as much fun." He smirked.

"You've done it alone before?"

"More than I care to admit," he confessed with a laugh.

"You two ready, Beckman?" Chet asked.

Heavenly blanched. "We're doing this now?"

Beck nodded. "Why wait? If you hang out up here, you'll only talk yourself out of it."

"You're right." Heavenly swallowed tightly as Chet fastened a bungee cord to their harnesses. "I'm as ready as I'll ever be. Just…hold on tight and don't let go."

"I was hoping you'd say that." Beck grinned.

She was trembling like a leaf as he helped her onto the edge of the bridge. She peeked down before jerking her head up, fear and excitement all over her face. "Oh, my gosh. Oh, my gosh. Oh, my gosh."

Her quivering mantra made him smile. He lifted her stare to his and stroked her cheek. "Trust me, little girl."

She dragged in a breath and sent him a resolute nod.

"Tell me you do," he commanded in a low, Dominant voice.

"Yes," she assured. "I trust you."

"Good girl."

Wrapping her in his arms with a hold that promised he'd never let her go, Beck listed to the side…and together, they took the plunge, tumbling off the bridge and freefalling into the craggy jaws of the canyon.

Heavenly's eyes were as huge as saucers as she screamed at the top of her lungs all the way down. But by the time the cord grew taut and yanked them back into the air, she was laughing spontaneously, the sound full of joy.

It echoed inside him. "You really do trust me."

"What do you think?" She let go of her death grip on his torso and cupped his face. "Of course."

A loopy grin curled his mouth up. Fuck Seth. Heavenly was going to be his—no hesitation, no questions, no doubt—starting now.

As she dangled in the air, her blond hair fanned out around her face like a halo of pure golden sunshine. Her blue eyes sparkled, and Beck couldn't wait another second to claim her plump, perfect lips.

He cupped her nape, leaning in for the kiss he'd been dreaming about for endless weeks. Heavenly moaned. Oh, yeah… He'd be happy to make her moan all night, every night.

Before he could move in, a look of panic flashed across her face. Jerking from his grasp, she twisted her head to the side, body bucking, as she promptly vomited into the canyon.

"Oh, baby." He quickly gathered her hair up into his fist and held her close as she retched. "You're okay. It's an adrenaline crash. Let it out. You'll feel better."

"No…" she groaned, refusing to look at him. "I can't believe I did that. I'm so embarrassed."

Beck cupped her cheek and forced her gaze his way. "Don't feel bad. It's not the first time I've seen someone vomit, you know. I shouldn't have pushed you so quickly past your…" *limits.* "Comfort zone. I'm sorry."

"Don't apologize. I agreed to jump. It was fun…until I got sick."

The bungee cord jerked and they began rising toward the bridge.

At the top, the crowd patted her on the back and doled out congratulations. Beck smiled as she softly thanked them, then hid her red face in Beck's chest.

"Don't worry about it. Puke happens more than you can imagine. Congratulations on your first jump." Chet grinned as he removed the harnesses.

Beck led her away from the edge, under the canopy, and pointed to a bench. Once she sat, he plied her with water, a granola bar, and more grapes. He felt her forehead and checked her eyes until she swatted his hand away.

"I'm fine. Just humiliated."

"Don't be."

"I almost threw up all over you."

"But you didn't. Besides, how many men out there can say they made their girl throw up on their third date?"

She scowled. "I'm not sure that's something you should brag about."

"Then I'll brag about you. Having you jump with me meant more than you'll ever know."

No, he couldn't tell her that, in his eyes, she'd proven they were suited for each other. They had great chemistry, she was open to kink, and she was willing to put herself in his hands. He wished like hell he'd claimed her very first kiss today. But he would taste her. Soon.

Once he was certain she was stable enough to hike back down the mountain, Beck tucked her against his side. When they reached the car, he opened the passenger door.

Heavenly paused and sent him a weak smile. "You might not believe this, but I had an awesome time today. Now I know what a bird feels like when it's soaring through the air. It's so…"

"Freeing?"

"Yes." She nodded enthusiastically. "Freeing and totally amazing."

Beck just smiled. She had no clue yet, but one day soon he would send her soaring in so many amazingly freeing ways.

CHAPTER TWELVE

THE FOLLOWING WEDNESDAY, Beck waited for Heavenly outside the hospital cafeteria. He hadn't stopped thinking about their bungee date, hadn't stopped wishing he'd had the chance to kiss her. He'd been looking forward to it, counting on it. Hell, craving it.

But he *would* taste her lips—and the rest of her body—soon. Already, he was planning another opportunity to get her alone.

The ding of the elevator snagged his attention. As the doors parted, he turned and watched people crowd into the hallway. Heavenly wasn't among them. Beck glanced at his watch, scowling.

"Are you lost, Dr. Beckman?" Kathryn invaded his personal space.

"Nope."

"If you're waiting for your usual lunch date, you should know I'd never make you wait." She flashed him what she meant to be a sultry smile. "For anything."

Jesus, he'd all but told her to go fuck a doorknob the night he'd nearly kissed Heavenly in front of the hospital. And still, the woman wouldn't let up.

"You've made yourself clear. Thing is, I thought I had, too. I'm not interested."

She gave him a frustrated huff. "Why are you wasting your time and energy on a girl when you could have a real woman?"

"Who'd you have in mind? You don't mean...you, I hope." He laughed.

"You're only saying that because you don't know what you're missing. When you're done babysitting, call me. You won't regret it."

Yeah, he would. He already regretted the last two minutes he'd wasted with her.

Kathryn blew him a kiss before she turned away and sauntered into the cafeteria. He felt as if he needed a second shower.

Behind him, the *whoosh* of the elevator doors opening again snagged his attention. He turned to find Heavenly stepping out. Head bent, she sniffled, then raised her gaze just enough to meet his. Her eyes were rimmed red, her nose a matching shade. Her cheeks were damp.

She'd been crying. What the hell?

Pushing off the wall, he ate up the distance between them and cupped her shoulder. Jesus, she was trembling. Then she blinked up at him with big tear-filled eyes. He didn't know what had happened or who had hurt her, but obviously someone had to die.

"Talk to me. What happened?"

Heavenly scanned the cafeteria, then bowed her head and leaned into him as if needing his support. "Not here."

Immediately, he slid an arm around her waist and led her around the corner to a small alcove near the janitor's postage-stamp office. He maneuvered her into the corner, then positioned himself in front, blocking any passersby or nosy bitches from seeing her.

"We're alone now. Talk to me."

She looked up at him, looking ready to spill fresh tears. "I don't know if I can stay here anymore. They hate me, and this is the worst thing they've done so far. It's just…awful."

They? Had Kathryn and her slut squad been up to their asshole antics?

"Who did what to you?"

"I don't know exactly who, but I have a suspicion. I went to my locker to get my purse so I could meet you, but I found a"—she closed her eyes and shook her head—"a death threat."

"What?" Shock doused him.

That was low, even for Kathryn.

"When I opened my locker, I f-found a Barbie doll dangling from a noose knotted around its neck. A note saying 'Die Bitch' hung from its leg."

Rage flared, hot and unrelenting. It took all his self-control not to sprint into the cafeteria, slam Kathryn against the wall by her throat, and threaten her in return. If she were a man, his fist would already be planted in her face.

"Tell me you reported the incident."

She gave him a shaky nod. "That's why I'm late. I called Nurse Lewis. She came right away, removed the doll, and told me she would handle everything. But I can't get that image out of my head."

"Bridget will figure it out. Whoever did this won't get away with it." Beck intended to make sure of that. He scrubbed a hand through his hair and made a mental note to call the nurse administrator the second he returned to his office. "Tell me who you think planted the doll."

"I don't have any proof...but I have a feeling it's Kathryn. For whatever reason, she hates me. I don't know why. I haven't done anything to her—"

"I have," he cut in. "And she's taking it out on you."

"What?" Heavenly frowned. "Oh, she's interested in you, and she saw us together the night after the gallery."

Beck gave her a sharp nod. "She's been hounding me to take her to bed. I've flatly refused. I'm sorry she's making your life hell." He gently brushed the hair from Heavenly's face. "You said this was the worst incident so far. What else has happened?"

After a pained frown, she told him all the same pranks Bridget Lewis had apprised him of two months ago. Apparently, Kathryn had been quiet for a while. But her boss's threats must have worn off, and he'd bet seeing him nearly kiss Heavenly had reignited Kathryn's jealousy.

Still, Beck had to look at the silver lining. By opening up and divulging every devious trick the slut squad had pulled, Heavenly was giving him more of her trust. But he refused to tolerate Kathryn—or anyone—threatening his girl.

When Heavenly finished the litany of crap she'd endured, Beck wrapped her in his arms. "I'll talk to Bridget. This shit will end, I promise."

"Oh, you don't have to worry. It's not your problem." She winced. "I didn't mean to drag you into it."

Despite the anger searing him, he managed a tender smile. "You didn't. It will be my pleasure to deal with her, little girl. Right now, why don't we leave and grab a quick burger? I'm not in the mood to sit in the cafeteria with the bitches of east wing."

She laughed through her tears. "That sounds great. Thank you."

He took her hand and led her toward the parking garage.

"That's a terrible name for them." Heavenly bit her lip. "But it's true."

He was glad he could get Heavenly away from the hospital and make her smile. She needed it. Hell, Beck wished he could erase their vindictive shit from her memory, too. The fact he couldn't chafed.

After a lunch spent resolutely not talking about anyone or anything related to the hospital, he escorted her back to the ER. As soon as he stepped into the unit, Kathryn's stare all but singed him. The rebel in him wanted to pull Heavenly to his chest and kiss her in front of God and the entire staff, professionalism be damned. But that would only be detrimental to Heavenly's career and encourage more retaliation at her expense.

"Text me if you find any more...surprises," he whispered in her ear, tenderly cupping her elbow.

"I will. Thank you again for everything."

"No thanks needed. Whenever I'm with you, the pleasure is all mine."

With a sharp nod at the rest of the nurses, he glanced past Kathryn and pushed out the double doors.

Once in his office, Beck set up a meeting with Bridget Lewis that afternoon, who was all too eager to speak with him. Then he leaned back in his chair and tried to figure out how to keep his promise to Heavenly and stop Kathryn's reign of terror. He had to bust that cunning whore before his girl shed another tear.

She's not your girl yet, a voice in the back of his head poked.

No. He had to let her date that pompous prick of a PI until she could choose between them.

PI.

P. Fucking I.

"That's it!" Beck slammed his fist on his desk.

Then he realized the implications.

Enlisting Seth's help would be as much fun as swallowing acid. But no matter how much he hated it, she needed the prick right now. And Beck had to believe that if Seth was willing to cross the country to throw down a gauntlet, then he'd do whatever it took to help Heavenly.

Wearing a snarl, Beck snatched up his phone and forced himself to dial.

Seth answered on the first ring, not even bothering to say hello. "If you're calling to yank my chain—"

"I'm calling for Heavenly. She needs your help."

"What's happened?" All hint of animosity left Seth's voice. "Is she all right?"

"Physically, yes. But one of the nurses at work is terrorizing her, and the situation escalated to a death threat today."

"What the fuck? I want details!" Seth's voice assured Beck that he wouldn't let anything happen to her, either.

After clearing his throat, Beck explained everything, from the minor pranks to today's threat. By the time he was done, the PI was equally livid.

"You knew all this time that she was being harassed and did nothing to stop it?"

"Heavenly didn't tell me shit herself until today, and I didn't get involved because nothing had occurred that the hospital's HR channels couldn't handle. Until today." He hated that he'd underestimated Kathryn. He hated even more how much Heavenly had suffered. "But now that Heavenly has been threatened, I suggest we step in to fix this shit."

Seth got straight to business. "Got anything in mind?"

"Catching Kathryn red-handed. But that will require a video recording device."

"I'll get you one. Where do you plan to put it?"

Beck sighed and came to one conclusion. "In the nurse's storage room. Their lockers are in there. I'm not exactly sure where to put it."

"Every stunt this nurse has pulled happened inside Heavenly's locker, right?"

"Yes."

"Can you get me access without anyone in her unit finding out?"

"I think so." He'd do whatever it took to get Bridget Lewis on board. "You're willing to rig up a camera for me?"

"Not for you. For Heavenly."

Beck rolled his eyes. If the prick needed to play her knight in shining armor to feel big and strong, whatever. All he wanted was to nail

Heavenly's tormenter so she could work in peace. "Fine."

"I'll swing by your office in a couple of hours. I need to stop at a store or two to grab a few things first."

"Excellent. I'll be here."

ON SATURDAY NIGHT, Heavenly eased onto the back patio at Raine's house, a smile breaking across her face. She didn't love everything about living in Los Angeles, but if she still lived in Wisconsin, she'd never be attending an outdoor party in late February. And this one, with its floating candles in the pool and the fairy lights strung through the trees, was magical. The surprise gathering to celebrate Hammer's birthday and the thankful end of his legal troubles had dovetailed together perfectly.

Though she'd been helping Raine set up most of the day, she hadn't been sure she'd be able to stay for the festivities. The bubbly brunette had insisted. Since Dad was feeling stable after his last lapse and her boss at Bazookas had given her tonight off to make up for Valentine's Day, she'd agreed…but not without trepidation.

Beck and Seth would both be here. How would she juggle her time between them?

As she tried to imagine, Raine appeared in a gorgeous red dress that made her cool, pale complexion absolutely glow. By comparison, Heavenly felt dowdy in the hodgepodge dress she'd stitched together from a bolt of floral fabric she'd been saving for a rainy day, the lace she'd torn off a second-hand dress, and a pattern her mother had left behind years ago.

"I'm so excited!" Raine squealed, then clapped her hands. "And Hammer has no idea! Liam kept him busy all day, with a little help from Pike. Creating an emergency fire at his, um…office was a stroke of genius."

Heavenly was amazed the woman had pulled off a party of this size with one of her lovers none the wiser. "He'll be thrilled."

Suddenly, River sidled up and raised a friendly hand to Heavenly. "Hi. Good to see you again."

"You, too."

Raine grinned his way. "There's the porn star of the hour."

"Okay, don't remind me how low I stooped to help you, storm cloud. Every time I think of that woman, I throw up a little in my mouth."

Heavenly frowned. If she didn't know the whole story already, she'd be thoroughly confused. But she'd been hearing about his exploits all day.

River pulled at the back of his neck. "But just for you, I took one for the team and cozied up to Hammer's nemesis until she admitted all her accusations were bullshit. You're welcome."

"Thank you." Raine wrinkled her nose. "Now make me feel better and tell me she was a lousy lay."

"Well, after years in Afghanistan, any sex is better than no sex, but if I had to rate her? Terrible," he confirmed. "I don't know how Hammer ever voluntarily fucked her."

"Me, either." Raine shuddered. "Watching Dean arrest her was one of the best things ever."

"No doubt."

"We're never this mean," Raine assured Heavenly, placing gentle fingers on her arm. "But this bitch deserves it for lying in an attempt to put Hammer in prison for the next few decades."

Heavenly couldn't disagree. "Yes, and everything ended well."

"Perfectly," Raine chimed. "And we'll have a great time celebrating Hammer's birthday, too. I'll enjoy ribbing him about being an old man."

"How old?" It was a nosy question, but it hadn't escaped Heavenly's notice that at least a decade gaped between Hammer and Raine. They made it work. She sometimes wondered if Beck's hesitation with her had been their age difference.

"He's thirty-five."

And she already knew Raine would be twenty-four in June. Heavenly herself would be twenty-three in a month…

She bit her lip. "Do you know how old Beck is?"

Raine cocked her head. "He didn't tell you?"

"We've never talked about it."

"He turned thirty-six in November."

Older than she'd imagined, but still young enough that she didn't care. She loved every moment she spent with the charismatic doctor.

"And in case you're wondering, Seth will be thirty-two in July."

Heavenly shrugged. "Age doesn't matter. I was just curious."

"Good." Raine took her hand and gave it a squeeze. "If Beck is dating you, he's decided it doesn't matter to him, either. And Seth… Well, if you weren't around, I suspect he'd be on a plane back to New York tomorrow. But he hasn't mentioned leaving. In fact, when he flew in this time, he brought a couple of suitcases, like he's intending to stay for a while."

Heavenly put a palm over her tummy, trying to calm the rioting butterflies inside. "They'll both be here tonight."

"Yep. And they'll both be on you like white on rice." River grinned. "This is going to be interesting."

She glanced Raine's way, slightly panicked. "What do I do?"

"You really want my advice?"

"Think twice about listening to her," River quipped. "She's a shit-stirrer."

Raine elbowed him in the gut. "I am not. I just want Heavenly to enjoy the party…and be happy."

"Is that why you left me alone to 'make coffee' when Seth dropped in the other day?" Heavenly returned.

The smile on Raine's face only widened. "It worked, didn't it?"

Heavenly couldn't dispute that.

"You want to drive them insane?" River asked.

Did she? On the one hand, she didn't want strife, especially at Hammer's party. On the other, the woman in her shivered at the thought of being sexy enough to command their focus. "Maybe. I don't know."

"That's a yes," River corrected, then looked at Raine. "She needs to show more skin."

"Agreed." The brunette looked her over critically. "Are you wearing any makeup?"

"Just mascara and lip gloss." The truth was, Heavenly couldn't afford more.

Raine glanced at her phone. "We've got about thirty minutes before everyone starts arriving. Can you run interference for me until then, big brother?"

A wide smile transformed River's mouth. "You got it."

Raine took Heavenly's hand and tugged. "Come with me."

Thirty minutes later, Heavenly stood in front of Raine's full-length mirror, gaping at the changes. The expert makeup applied with a light hand made her eyes a vivid blue. Loose curls bounced in her hair. But those weren't the only changes. She now wore a taupe-colored shift. It was simple enough—spaghetti straps that gave way to a V between her breasts, accentuated by matching satin trim that exposed a hint of cleavage. The nearly transparent fabric flowed with the curve of her waist and hips, then ended with a simple hem mid-thigh. No lace. No embellishments. Not even a bra. The garment was barely darker than her skin. Strappy sandals aside, she looked—and felt—almost naked.

"Wow."

"Oh, yeah." Raine nodded vigorously. "Beck and Seth are going to lose their minds."

She more than liked the sound of that, and this dress definitely made her feel like a woman. Sexual. Daring. And it was a thrill. The church frock she'd worn here would never have done that.

"And keep that dress," Raine said. "It looks *way* better on you."

"I can't take your—"

"You're not," Raine assured. "I'm giving it to you for a good cause. Trust me… You'll definitely have their attention tonight."

"Thank you." At least Heavenly hoped she would end up grateful.

"You're welcome. Now, let's find a test subject." Raine tugged on her hand again.

"What?"

The woman didn't answer, merely led her down the stairs to where River waited at the bottom.

He let out a long whistle. "Damn. I hope that dress absorbs drool, because they will definitely be salivating tonight."

Heavenly felt a familiar telltale blush steal across her face.

Behind them, the front door opened, and guests started tiptoeing in quietly, careful not to alert Hammer. Raine motioned with a finger over her red lips, then pointed to the backyard. Heavenly recognized almost no one, not the older couple, nor the fifty-something man with the salt-and-pepper beard who looked like a shark in a suit. She vaguely recognized the guy with the pitch-black hair and the brow stud from her date with Beck at the gallery. He gave her a long once-over and a leering grin, not making any attempt to hide the fact he was adjusting whatever was behind his zipper.

River punched him in the arm. "Don't be a pig, Pike. She looks pretty."

"She looks fuckable," the new guy corrected, then slanted a come-on her way. "So if you'd like to get fucked, I'm your guy."

No. Not with him. Never.

Raine rolled her eyes. "She's already got takers."

Pike scoffed. "I'm not worried about Beck. I can run circles around him, sweet cheeks."

"Scram." Raine shooed him toward the back door.

Reluctantly, he went, and Heavenly blinked after him. "How do you know him?"

Suddenly, Raine wouldn't meet her gaze. "He, um…works with Hammer. The older guy with the beard is Sterling, Macen's lawyer, and…"

Over the next few minutes, the woman slipped into hostess mode, introducing her to whomever came through the door. Then an older, elegant woman trekked down the stairs. Heavenly knew Liam's parents had been staying with them, and she saw the resemblance between the Irishman and his mom immediately.

"Heavenly, this is Bryn O' Neill."

"Hi." She stuck her hand in their direction. "Nice to meet you."

"Ah, so you're Heavenly. Lovely to meet you, too." Liam's mother shook her hand, her gentle Irish lilt soft in the air, then turned to Raine with a smile. "No wonder Kenneth and Seth are tied up in knots."

"Oh, I don't think—"

"Of course they are, dear. You'll need to make the choice sooner than you're prepared for…and it won't be precisely as you imagined."

River leaned in. "Bryn always talks in riddles. You get used to it, and I'm told it will make sense…eventually."

"It will," Raine assured. "Liam's mom is psychic."

Were they serious? They must be. No one was laughing.

Bryn wagged a finger at River. "Don't think your time isn't coming. 'Twould be best if you made friends with Pike now."

River scowled. "That asshole? I'd rather dig my way to China with a toothpick."

"Men. Always so determined to do everything the hard way." Bryn tsked, then turned back to Heavenly. "Dear, you needn't be worried. Everything will come out in the wash, even the bits you'd rather not air. But so many around you care deeply. Don't be afraid to take help when you need it. And one more thing…"

Heavenly breathed, almost worried what the older woman would say next.

"Follow your heart. If you do, you'll be happier than you can possibly imagine." Then Bryn patted her shoulder and moved on.

Heavenly turned to Raine, who was obviously trying hard not to burst out laughing. "She really does mean what she says…if you can figure it out. Remind me one day to tell you how she and I first met. By comparison, your introduction is way less embarrassing."

"Okay." Heavenly wondered if she had suddenly fallen into an alternate dimension. "Um, I think I need some wine."

"Come with me. Beck and Seth should both be here any minute."

As if on cue, Beck strolled through the door, a bag of ice in each hand and a wide smile on his face. The moment he caught sight of her, his jaw dropped and the ice slid from his suddenly slack grip. "Holy shit."

"See?" Raine giggled in her ear.

Heavenly couldn't take her eyes off Beck, either. He was dressed in charcoal slacks and a crisp white shirt, rolled up at the sleeves to expose strong, hair-dusted forearms. He looked so big, so virile, so male. When their eyes met, her heart raced. A wave of heat tingled through her body, and he made her think thoughts totally worthy of her blush.

She sighed. "Hi."

A gawking Pike strolled up to Beck. "Looks like you dropped something besides your man card. Having trouble holding on to the ice because your arthritis flared up, gramps?"

Just like that, the moment was broken. Beck turned to the interloper with a scathing glare. "Why don't you fuck off?"

"And miss seeing you looking like a pussy-whipped bitch? Nah." He picked up the bags of ice and slung them over his shoulders, then sauntered past Heavenly with a wink.

Beck leveled a killing stare at his back. "It will be hard to eat without teeth if you don't shut up."

Pike laughed all the way into the kitchen. Beck followed, grabbing the bags of ice from his hands and pouring one into an elegant bucket on the island.

Raine directed him to take the other outside, then swept everyone toward the patio. "Liam will be leading Hammer out here in less than five minutes. I need everyone in place." She checked her phone. "Seth will be here in less than two minutes. Good."

Heavenly was amazed to watch the woman sprint across the back patio in stilettos yet still look graceful.

"Shall we?" River gestured her outside.

"Sure. I didn't get a chance to ask if there was anything else I could do to help. Your sister just…started helping me."

"She wants you to enjoy the party. And okay, she wants to mess with Beck and Seth. Which gives me an idea." He held out his hand with a grin. "Follow me."

Heavenly had no idea what he was up to. "What do you have in mind?"

"All bears need a little baiting once in a while."

"Oh, I'm not sure that's a good idea…"

But River wasn't listening. He'd already grabbed her hand and was tugging her out of the house and down the patio steps. He paused to put a glass of wine in her free hand.

The revving of an engine on the far side of the yard had heads turning. Heavenly swiveled to see Raine holding the wide back gate open and someone driving a sleek gray sports car inside. She couldn't figure out why, but as soon as the engine fell silent and the headlights dimmed, Seth stepped from the car—and she stopped caring why he'd parked on the grass. Instead, she stared. Even from a distance, the wave of attraction nearly pulled her under.

"They're coming," someone hissed across the patio. "Hurry!"

"Shit!" Raine dashed for the back door, Seth right behind her. They crowded onto the patio with everyone else just in time for Liam and Duncan to lead Hammer outside so everyone could yell, "Surprise!"

Cheering and laughter ensued.

"Happy birthday!" Raine shouted as she made another trek down to the car and tossed a big red bow over the hood.

The car was a gift? Heavenly couldn't imagine having the money to buy any vehicle that ran, much less enough to give someone the gift of a German precision driving machine.

How charmed their lives would seem...if she didn't know how much struggle and agony they'd all been through.

After the group lifted a glass to Hammer, the party began in earnest. Beck and Seth both made a beeline toward her, but River was closer. He took her hand again and dragged her toward a pair of guys at the base of the patio, laughing and chasing back brews.

Heavenly cast a frown his way. "I recognize Pike." And she didn't like him so far. "Who's the other man?"

He shrugged. "Does it matter? They'll appreciate the view and ogle you enough to drive Beck and Seth insane. Play along."

"But I—"

"Hey, Pike. Dean, this is Heavenly. Sweetheart, this is Officer Gorman of the LAPD."

"Just Dean." The cop's smile was full of instant charm as he moved closer. "You're Heavenly, huh? It fits. Great to meet you. You're not here with this jerk, are you?" He thumbed River's way.

"Oh, I'm just a friend of Raine's and—"

"She's here with me." Seth suddenly sidled up to her and slipped his arm around her waist. "Hi, angel. You look...amazing."

Heavenly met his infectious grin. Gosh, every time she got near the man, her heart thrummed and fluttered. And when he focused all his male attention on her, she felt so very female. The attraction scared her senseless, but that didn't stop her from wanting more.

"You wish," Beck said as he eased up on her other side and tossed his arm around her shoulders. "She's here with me."

The instant Beck touched her, another sizzle slammed through her body. Beside him, she felt delicate and precious and utterly protected. He wore a mysterious aura of power she didn't comprehend. And, like Seth, he made her embarrassingly glad she was a woman.

Her face flamed. She'd gone almost twenty-three years without sex, and suddenly she could hardly think of anything else.

"Funny…" River shrugged. "Raine told me she invited Heavenly, who came here alone." He turned to Dean. "She was one of the nurse volunteers in the ER the day they brought my sister in after she offed my shithole of a father."

"I was there that day, too," Dean said, nodding. "I'm sorry we didn't meet then. You're studying to become a nurse?"

She did her best to focus on the conversation, not the pair of men flanking her. "I'm in my first year, but yes."

"Tell me about your classes."

Heavenly did, acutely aware that she had five pairs of eyes on her. Dean listened intently. Beck looked indulgent, while Seth seemed proud. River was too busy watching their reactions to notice that Pike looked at her as if he'd like to strip her down in the middle of the party and have at her.

She backed away from his dark stare, situating herself more solidly between Beck and Seth. As the conversation turned, they all seemed interested in her recent instruction on trauma.

"Well, I'm not really sure…" She winced, remembering a recent lab. "I'm just a volunteer. I made the mistake of asking about his scar—"

"Well, shit. Who hasn't got scars?" Pike leered at her, twitching the metal stud in his brow.

"I got shot once." Dean lifted his shirt a bit higher than necessary. She got an eyeful of wide, muscled chest and his ridged abdomen, along with the circular scar in the shape of a bullet hole between his ribs.

"Put that shit away." Beck rolled his eyes.

"Oh, that's nothing." River tugged up his shirt to reveal a whole collection of muscles—and scars that made her gasp. "I've been tagged and have so many holes and repairs from back-to-back tours…"

He clearly had. The chance to study a body with so many assorted injuries excited her. She peered closer. "Oh."

"Stand down, soldier boy," Beck growled.

"She doesn't need to see your"—Seth waved at his abs—"stuff."

River and Dean shared a glance, then cracked up.

"Just making conversation." River winked.

Or so he claimed. He'd accused his sister of stirring the pot, but

River seemed awfully pleased with his mischief.

"How about you fuck off, too?" Beck suggested.

Heavenly blinked. She probably shouldn't like how possessive he sounded…but she did.

Suddenly, Liam was behind her, fresh drink in each hand. When she turned to him, he held one out to her, which was lovely. She'd lost her other somewhere along the way.

"You all right?" he asked, leading her a few steps from the group.

"Um, yes. Fine. Thank you. Your home is really lovely. I appreciate you inviting me."

Liam studied her, and she couldn't escape the feeling he saw straight through her. That he knew her secrets. Her heart stuttered.

That must be her nerves talking. Everyone saw what they expected to see—a young nursing student, busy juggling studies, volunteering, and work. Right? Her problems were hers to bear alone, and none of these people, even the perceptive Irishman, had any reason to suspect otherwise.

She hoped.

Finally, he nodded. "It's our pleasure. We're glad you could join us."

Heavenly was relieved when Beck sidled over and took her hand, tenderly folding her against his side as he thanked Liam, who moved on to circulate around the growing party.

"Stay close to me," Beck murmured in her ear, then glared Seth's way. "Lots of riffraff here tonight."

Across the yard, a band filed out onto the patio. As they set up, someone shouted that it was time to get this party started. Then tunes filled the air.

The moment the upbeat notes lit up the crowd, Seth grabbed her hand and tugged her away from Beck. "Let's dance."

She'd love to and she'd always wanted to, but… "I don't know how."

He frowned as if that didn't compute. "Not much to it, angel."

"Everyone will be watching."

"I'll guide you. Just take my hand."

Anticipation tugged her one way, anxiety the other. But how could she live life if she never tried?

Heavenly smiled Seth's way and nodded. When he wrapped his arm around her waist, the jolt of his touch reverberated through her. But she didn't have time to dwell on her spontaneous reaction to him. Seth twirled her under his arm, curled a hand around her waist, and led her through a familiar song about a girl asking a guy to call her maybe. They danced through the next catchy song about everyone getting together for a good time. Soon, she was laughing—and probably stumbling more than dancing, but gosh, she was having a blast.

As soon as the up-tempo tune ended, a Jason Mraz ballad sounded through the speakers and covered the patio. Some left the floor. Seth merely pulled her closer and pressed himself against her.

"Have you been thinking about our conversation the other day?"

"Almost nonstop," she admitted.

"I've been waiting for you to call."

And she'd thought every day about picking up the phone. "I waitressed and studied most of the weekend with an…outing on Sunday."

His clenched jaw said he guessed she'd been with Beck and he wasn't pleased. "Glad you got a day off."

Even when she'd unwittingly upset him, he was kind. "This week, the hospital has been busy and school has been tough. Now…we're here."

"And now, you're mine."

They moved together to the music. The burn of his fingers seared her everywhere his hands touched, yet she felt ethereal as he led her across the dance floor so effortlessly she would have sworn she floated. Everyone else faded into the background until she saw only Seth, until she got lost in his eyes. Just him and this moment that belonged to only them existed.

She wasn't even aware when they left the dance floor. One moment they were swaying together under the lights. The next he backed her against the wall and closed in, pressing palms flat on either side of her, his mouth mere inches away.

"Christ, I can't stand it anymore. I have to kiss you, angel. You going to let me?"

She didn't have to think. Couldn't, really, except about how badly she wanted him to and had since he'd appeared in Raine's living room last week. "Yes."

Heavenly barely had time to worry that she didn't know the first thing about kissing before he cupped her nape, cradled her jaw in his wide hands, and swooped down to capture her mouth.

Somehow, the kiss was soft—his lips, his touch—but his invasion was breath-stealingly direct. He didn't bother flirting or teasing. He took. He conquered, doing it so gently and skillfully she surrendered without a second thought and opened willingly when he nudged her lips apart.

He pressed in, sinking deep. His demand filled her head. If he hadn't pinned her to the wall with his sinewy body, she would have crumpled to her knees before him. *Oh, my goodness…*

Because she couldn't stand not to, Heavenly clutched his shoulders and gasped. He swallowed the sound and moaned in turn. His fingers tightened, burning her through the thin fabric of her dress. He shuddered. The intimacy of his lips sliding against hers, of their audible breaths melding, made her head go hazy with pleasure. Hot need rolled like a thick drug through every artery and vein.

Then Heavenly felt the urgent press of his tongue as it stroked, hot and thick, into her mouth. It felt like he was stealing into her soul, too. And still she couldn't stop him. She didn't want to. Each new sweep of his lips promised her the kind of ecstasy she'd only imagined—until now. She just wanted to stay suspended in this moment forever, where her troubles melted away, where she felt beautiful, where he shook her very existence.

Between one kiss and the next, she inhaled him and pressed against his body restlessly, needing more. She wrapped her leg around one of his thighs until no space remained between them and whimpered.

"Oh, angel…" He ground himself against her.

His name rose on her lips, but Heavenly swallowed it when his kiss had her drowning in sensation once more.

Seth's touch skated down her body, then finally trailed down the small of her back. As he caressed his way even farther south, he enveloped nearly all of her derrière in one big hand. That shock was still rolling though her system when he growled, dragged her closer, and fit his edges against her curves. She felt overwhelmed, overpowered, overjoyed as he devoured her mouth with an urgency that was like catching fire. Something equally explosive rose within her.

A split second later, he cupped her ass with both hands and tore his lips from hers to nuzzle her neck. The heady, dizzying, wild sensation was undoing her… Then he hoisted her against his body, notching his erection—definitely not an involuntary male response—onto her weeping sex, where she ached most.

Heavenly curled her arms and legs around him, pressing closer as she labored for breath. "Seth… Please."

Suddenly, he groaned, then ripped himself away and set her on her feet, gripping the wall with taut fingers and breathing hard. His face was twisted with agony and self-restraint. "If I don't let you go now, I will stop caring about anything except getting inside you."

His words detonated a bomb of need between her legs. "Oh."

Then he fisted her hair, his stare penetrating. "I want that. I want you. So bad you have no idea, but not against a goddamn wall with everyone around."

The night came rushing back to her. The lights, the music, the people. Suddenly, she was aware of them once more. She and Seth had never been alone. Anyone could have seen them…

"That was hot," Pike quipped as he stood a few feet away, clapping for their performance. "Don't stop on my account."

River stood nearby, watching. He said nothing. He didn't have to. That hint of a grin said it all.

Embarrassment washed over her. She was so grateful when Seth tucked her behind him, blocking her from Pike's view. As he faced the jerk, she gripped his arms, laid her hot cheek on his back, and absorbed his strength.

"Why don't you get fucked?" Seth snarled.

"There's no one else interesting here, and you two were putting on a hell of a show. You know I like to watch…"

Ugh, why wouldn't Pike just go away? He seemed like the kind of bully who enjoyed her discomfort.

Heavenly opened her eyes to give the butthead a piece of her mind. Instead, she found Beck mere feet away, his stare glued to her. Their gazes tangled, then locked. His expression had gone dark and ferocious.

She didn't have to ask; he'd seen everything.

Heavenly closed her eyes. Would the earth please open up and swallow her whole? What had possessed her to lose her head so utterly in front of him? Yes, Seth had kissed her. Well, it had been way more than a kiss. He'd taken her, body and soul, without removing a stitch of her clothes.

But Beck… What was he thinking now? That she didn't care enough about him to not shove her attraction for Seth in his face? He'd promised her he wouldn't interfere while she made her choice…but she hadn't shown him the courtesy of keeping her feelings for another man to herself. Seth had even asked her if he could kiss her and she hadn't hesitated. She'd just said yes and fallen into his arms.

Was Beck angry? Did he hate her now? Probably.

Tears stung her eyes. How could she have been so thoughtless?

She sent him a look of apology, then squeezed Seth's shoulders. "It's okay. You don't have to protect me. I think I'll just go."

He turned to her, grabbing her hands in his. "No, not like this. You didn't do anything wrong, angel."

How did she make him understand so he didn't think she regretted their kiss? "I wish we'd had less of an audience."

Seth rolled his eyes. "Pike should have been named prick. Ignore him."

"I gathered, but…" She risked a glance over her shoulder. Beck still stared. "He's not the only one."

Seth's gaze followed hers and cursed. "I see. Come inside with me. We'll talk—alone—for a minute or two. If you still want to go home after that, I'll take you."

It wouldn't be fair to kiss him and run away, and in all honesty, she didn't want to let him go tonight. Her head might be telling her that she'd done something cringe-worthy. Her body panted that she should forget everyone and throw herself in Seth's arms.

Well, everyone except Beck. She already knew forgetting him was impossible.

"All right," she murmured.

Soon, she'd talk to Beck and make it clear that she hadn't meant to hurt him, that her feelings for Seth had nothing to do with her feelings for him and that…she was utterly confused.

"Let's go." Seth tucked her under his arm and headed toward the house—until Beck stepped directly in their path.

Her gaze skittered up to him again, face flaming, eyes filled with another silent apology as they approached.

"Hold up a second." Beck glared at Seth, teeth gritted.

At her side, Seth tensed. "Make it quick."

Heavenly held her breath. Were they going to exchange words? Barbs? Punches? Tonight was supposed to be a celebration, not a brawl… "Don't be angry. Please. I—"

"I'm not, little girl." Beck took her hand. "Don't you beat yourself up. I told you last weekend that I'd give you the time and space to make your choice. You haven't done anything wrong. We'll talk more if you need to. All right?"

She let out a huge breath of relief she hadn't realized she'd been holding. Her heart lightened. A thousand things she wanted to say flitted through her head, but not here. Not in front of Seth. They had each promised to allow her to keep her romances with them separate, and she had to honor her part of the bargain until she made her decision. Saying more now would be compounding her error with another mistake.

"Thank you." She squeezed his hand. He could probably read every one of her feelings. For once, that didn't make her uncomfortable.

"I'm here if you need me," Beck assured, then stepped out of her path.

Heavenly felt his eyes on her every step of the way until Seth ushered her into a study and shut the door firmly behind them.

FROM PARADISE TO clusterfuck in two-point-two seconds.

As Seth led Heavenly away from the shit show and into Hammer's study, he shut the door and tried to put a lid on his worries. He'd left her once for a misunderstanding. He wasn't about to make the same mistake twice. But damn if her crushing guilt about Beck seeing their kiss wasn't like a knife to the chest.

She sat on the far edge of the sofa, head bowed, hands folded in her lap. He knew her laugh, her smile, her smell, her kiss. But he had no idea what she was thinking right now and that was fucking him up.

"Heavenly, look at me."

For a long moment, she hesitated, and he wondered if she'd comply or just bolt out the door. He waited, breath held, until her gaze finally climbed up to his. She bit her lip, looking so unsure and nervous it tore at him. Goddamn it. He'd been a cop. He'd learned how to interrogate early and from the best. Getting inside her head shouldn't be much different—if he could keep his own in check.

"Good." He tucked a strand of hair behind her ear. "Talk to me, angel. Tell me how you feel."

A furrow appeared between her brows. "Confused. Overwhelmed. I don't…" She shook her head as tears pooled in her eyes again. "I don't know how to answer you."

"You don't know how you feel?"

She shook her head. "I'm just not sure how to explain. I've never had anyone to talk to about my feelings. Sorry if I'm not doing it right. I'm learning as I go."

"Never?" No parents? No giggling girlfriends? He already knew she'd never had a boyfriend, which still shocked the hell out of him. She lived in a new city and hadn't made many friends…

Her words hit him with a TKO of reality. He'd never been involved with a woman who had so little experience, not only in bed but in life. Emotionally, Heavenly wasn't a woman yet. She didn't know how to please—or even understand—herself, much less a man. She knew nothing about the subtleties of relationships or communication. On some level, he'd understood that, but tonight… Huge wake-up call. He didn't need to simply calm her now; he needed to understand her. Coax her into opening up. If he didn't do that, if he didn't take control and assure her he was committed to whatever they could have, it might be over—not because she didn't want it. Because she had no idea how to work with him to make that a reality.

"No," she breathed. "So when you want me to tell you how I feel, I don't know if you want to hear how the kiss affected me…or all the stuff after. Do you need to hear how I felt when you touched me or should I explain why I'm embarrassed? I really don't get what you want."

"Let's separate what happened outside into two categories. We'll work backward. You're embarrassed. Because a few people saw me kiss you? Or simply because Beck saw?"

That had her looking down again. "Mostly because Beck saw. Pike is annoying—"

"I'll deal with him."

"But I never want to hurt anyone, especially someone who's been as wonderful to me as Beck. I also don't want you to think I regret kissing you. I wish the time and place had been different." Surprisingly, she lifted her chin and locked stares with him. "But you gave me a first kiss that surpassed *anything* I'd imagined."

He cupped her crown and tangled his fingers in her hair, tugging just enough to ensure she kept eye contact. "Did Beck's reassurance make you feel better?"

"Somewhat." She sighed. "I know that can't have been easy for him. I wish I'd known something better to say."

Beck had looked as if he'd rather chew glass than swallow down his own jealousy so soon after watching someone else kiss the hell out of Heavenly. But he actually respected the doctor for putting her well-being above his own. In Beck's shoes, he would have tried to do the same.

"It's entirely possible I'll have to see him kiss you someday. Will I like it? No. But we're big boys. We'll deal with our feelings. They aren't your responsibility. Don't guilt yourself over them."

As much as it sucked, he'd spoken the truth. Until she made up her mind, he and Beck would simply have to deal. But her reaction to the doctor made it blatantly clear she carried a torch for him. The kiss proved to Seth that she definitely had feelings for him, too. Where the fuck did that leave them?

What would it take for her to finally make a choice?

"So you understand Beck will handle his own feelings?"

She nodded.

"You understand River's opinion doesn't matter? And Pike can pound sand?"

A little smile crept across her face. "I hope he does."

"Your responsibility going forward is to focus on your feelings about you and me and to share them with me. I need you to do that."

"Okay." She nodded softly. "I will."

"Good." He nodded. "Now that we've talked about what happened afterward, let's talk about the kiss itself. You said you don't regret it."

"Not for an instant." A pretty pink blush flared across her cheeks. "I loved it."

He couldn't keep the satisfied male grin off his face as he sat beside her and scooped her into his lap. "I have to tell you, that was the best first kiss ever."

Surprise transformed her face. "Really?"

Did she think all first kisses were hot enough to set the house on fire? Maybe. It wasn't as if she had anything to measure it against... "Really. Maybe you felt how hard I was for you?"

The pink on her face turned utterly red. "It was...um, difficult to miss."

He laughed. "Definitely hard, all right."

Heavenly pressed her lips together. "Sometimes I don't know whether you mean to embarrass me or just tease me."

"Never embarrass you. But tease you... Yeah, I'm guilty. I love to see you blush." He skimmed his lips over the shell of her ear. "You're beautiful, and I enjoy getting to you. When I'm with you, I feel more alive than I have in years."

She blinked at him. "I haven't done anything."

"You've been yourself. That's all I need."

Seth cupped her jaw, swept his thumb across her cheek, then leaned in. She met him halfway, eyes closed, breath held, lips soft. Christ, she was picture-perfect innocence, so sweet and trusting. He couldn't help himself.

He took her mouth tenderly, opening her, feeling her responses unfurl like petals in the sun. When he sank past her lips, he heard the soft rush of breath as she sighed across his tongue. Passion flared. Unlike last time, he braced for the heady need, holding himself back so she had time to examine the heat, taste the fire, explore the sensations of his lips savoring hers. He reveled in her tightening fingers, her catches of breath. Fuck, if he let it, this kiss could blaze into a full-on inferno.

Seth stopped it while he still could and eased back. She sat looking flushed everywhere—cheeks, lips, upper swells of her chest—almost as if she'd melted in his arms. He ached to dive in again. But he'd given

Heavenly enough to process tonight. Her responses to him had proven his doubts this past week had been pointless, so the next step between them belonged to him—and it was a big one.

Because after tonight, he had no doubts at all. Heavenly might be confused about choosing between him and Beck at the moment…but with a little patience and persuasion, he could make her his. The doctor was nothing more than a bump in the road.

"You still want to go home?"

She nodded. "Is that all right? I have to wait tables tomorrow and I still have a paper to finish."

He held in a curse. "Sure. How about you let me drive you home?"

"Stay. I can take the bus."

In other words, no. Seth clenched his jaw but didn't push her anymore tonight. "At least let me put you in a car. I'll pay for it. But I need to know you'll get home safely."

She hesitated. "All right. Thanks."

It didn't take long to call her a taxi and let the guy swipe his card. As he opened the door for her, she paused, turning to face him. "I'll talk to you soon."

He nodded. "I have to fly back to New York, clear up a few things."

Heavenly looked distinctly unhappy. "Again?"

"I won't be gone long, angel. Believe me, nothing is going to keep me away from you."

That made her smile. He left her with a soft kiss, then shut the door, tapped on the cabbie's roof, and watched her speed into the night.

The minute she'd disappeared from sight, Seth turned back to the party with one thing on his mind.

He tore inside the house, barreling out to the back patio, then spotted Beck and River giving Pike a snarling dressing down.

"Stand aside," he demanded of the duo holding Shadows' dungeon monitor upright. "This asswipe is mine."

As both men dropped their hold, Pike rolled his eyes. Seth shoved him against the same wall he'd devoured Heavenly against a mere twenty minutes ago. The blood roared in his brain.

Then he settled nose-to-nose with Pike. "You crossed a line. Do not ever speak to her again. Don't even look at her. If she happens to cross you in the street, you turn and run the other way. Got it?"

Pike's cocky bravado ensured the guy wasn't smart enough to shut his pie hole. "What if I don't? What the fuck are you going to do about it?"

Seth was done talking. He drew back his fist and threw all his weight into the cross punch. It landed straight across the man's jaw. Pike's head snapped back with the impact. His teeth knocked together with an audible crack. Seth saw the exact moment the blood flow to the main artery in Pike's head stuttered. Seconds later, the man crumpled, sliding down the wall, temporarily unconscious.

"Fuck," he heard someone mutter. "One punch. Did you see that? Remind me not to piss him off."

Point made, Seth turned and headed back the way he'd come. He was done here. He had every intention of wishing Hammer a happy birthday, then heading back to Shadows for some R and R. Unfortunately, Liam stepped in his path, halting him mid-stride.

"Wait," the Irishman called. Seth wasn't in any mood to linger or discuss tonight's events, but his friend's next words froze him in place. "Can you come here, Beck? This concerns you, too."

Seth tamped down his impatience as the doctor drew up alongside him. They exchanged a wary glance.

"What's up?" Beck asked.

"I've something to say, and I need you to listen. No butting in before I'm done, mind."

Seth nodded. He owed one of his oldest and dearest friends a little patience after punching a guy out cold in his backyard. "I didn't come to cause trouble."

"I don't give a shit about Pike," Liam assured. "It's Heavenly I want to talk to you about. For one so innocent, your lass is a complicated contradiction, layers upon layers. Take heed and peel her open fast. If you don't, the looming darkness shrouding her—and getting closer by the day—may tear her away for good."

"Huh? What's that mean?" Beck asked.

Liam shrugged. "The message is for you two to figure out. I just convey what I know."

Seth cocked his head. "Are you channeling your mom?"

Liam flushed a dull red. "She rubs off a bit on me, is all."

"I'll keep that in mind." In Seth's estimation, if he was half as intuitive as his mother, Liam's warning bore heeding.

"What the hell does that mean?" Beck tossed his hands in the air.

Seth didn't fill the idiot in, just walked away. Message received. He had to earn Heavenly's trust or he might lose her forever. No way would he let that happen. He would damn well save her from whatever trials lay ahead and make her his for good.

CHAPTER THIRTEEN

Aⁿᵗᵉʳ MAKING HIS morning rounds, Beck pushed through the double doors of the ER, anxious to take Heavenly away for some much-needed alone time.

As he turned the corner, Kathryn stood over Heavenly with a condescending sneer. "You're a *volunteer*. You don't know enough yet to think. Leave that to the nurses who have actually earned degrees."

Beck marched toward them, jaw clenched. He was so over this shrew's shit. Kathryn hadn't opened Heavenly's locker for a "prank" in the week since he and Seth had planted the surveillance camera. It was time to prod the viper into striking the way she was dying to and end this for good.

Heavenly held up her hands. "You told me to—"

"Hi." Beck slung his arm around her waist and stroked her downy cheek. "Ready for our date, little girl?"

Kathryn gasped, nostrils flared, then tried to bite back her outrage. But he heard.

Yeah, he had the bitch's attention…

"Um…yes." Heavenly tensed and tried to wriggle free.

Nope. Wasn't happening. He sent her an easy smile and snuggled the sweet ray of sunshine closer.

"Dr. Beckman, we have standards of professionalism here that don't include PDA." Kathryn huffed. "That should be private."

A tremor shook Heavenly, and Beck hated knowing she was afraid of this cunt.

Hopefully not for long.

"You're right. I know the perfect spot, and it's not the janitor's closet," he quipped, then nudged Heavenly. "Let's go."

Indignation filled Kathryn's face as Heavenly grabbed her backpack. "I'm more than ready."

"Change your clothes, then we'll head out."

"I didn't say you could leave early," Kathryn protested. "I need you here."

"Since I was determined to spend time with Heavenly, I cleared the schedule change with your boss. Bridget said yes. Now I have this girl to myself for the rest of the day." He dropped to whisper in Heavenly's ear, making sure Kathryn wouldn't miss a word. "And all night."

Kathryn's eyes sparked with fury. A wave of palpable hostility rolled off her.

Bull's-eye.

Heavenly gave the woman a nervous glance. "Well, um—"

"Bye, Kathryn. Don't work too hard," Beck tossed over his shoulder as he grabbed Heavenly's hand and pulled her down the hall beside him until they were out of the bitch's earshot.

"I told you I have to wait tables tonight," Heavenly whispered furiously.

"I know." Beck didn't like it, but he understood. He'd worked a few odd jobs through med school, too. "But she doesn't."

"Why are you trying to make my time here worse?"

"Change your clothes, then we'll get out of here. And I'll let you in on a secret," he promised with a squeeze of reassurance.

She sighed but complied, slipping into the ladies' room. He waited outside until she emerged again, wearing a little bohemian sundress in an easy-breezy white with a band of lace around her waist that played peekaboo with the bare skin beneath and a handkerchief hem that flirted with her thighs. His eyes almost popped from his head. His mouth watered. His erection sprang to life instantly.

Damn. How was he supposed to focus on charming her if all he could think about was commanding and fucking her? "You look great."

"Thanks. Are you going to tell me what's going on now?"

"Let's go outside." He took her hand and headed for the door.

Once they found his car, Heavenly pinned him with a disgruntled scowl. "Now, what was all that about?"

"I'm giving Kathryn enough rope to hang herself…with an extra foot or two for incentive."

She gaped. "What is wrong with you?"

Beck slid a grin her way. "Do you want the list alphabetically or chronologically?"

"This is serious. The minute your back is turned, Kathryn will shred me with her fangs and claws."

"No, she won't."

Heavenly rolled her eyes. "Yeah, she will."

"No. She. Won't." He arched his brows.

"What are you up to?"

One day, he'd teach her that questioning him would earn her a sore, red ass. For now, he humored her, as he'd been doing for three long, ball-straining months. Inside, he was eager to tear away the bindings leashing his inner Dominant and wrap them around her sinful body until she was at his mercy and moaning.

Shit, first he had to kiss her.

"What you don't know can't get you in trouble."

Her eyes grew wide. "Oh, my gosh. Please tell me what's going on."

"I thought you trusted me, little girl."

"I do. After all, I jumped off a perfectly good bridge for you."

"Because you knew I would protect you, like I'm doing now. Let's just say Kathryn will get exactly what she deserves."

"Oh, you make me nervous. You know there's no way she doesn't take the bait?" She sighed. "Of course you know that."

Beck burst out laughing. "Are you figuring out that maybe I'm scary after all?"

"Sure, but do you understand that Kathryn is really sly? You can't be with me every moment—"

"Trust me. She won't hurt you again. That's a promise." Beck cupped her cheeks and kissed her forehead.

It wasn't the heated kiss shithead Seth had planted on her at Hammer's party, but Beck wasn't about to taste her lips for the first time in the bowels of a parking structure. It was decidedly unromantic, and Heavenly deserved better. But then, she'd also deserved more than choking on Seth's tongue while he dry-humped her in front of a throng of partygoers. He'd ask what the asswipe had been thinking, but it was obvious all his blood had migrated south and shriveled his brain cells. Seth obviously hadn't bothered to learn anything about Heavenly or he would have known such a public display would only embarrass the shy, sensitive girl.

The whole thing had been a fucking nightmare. Watching Seth claim Heavenly's mouth as if he owned it—and seeing her respond so hungrily—hadn't even been the worst. Being unable to do a damn thing to stop them while they'd all but fucked with their clothes on had. Even a week later, no amount of mind bleach could disinfect the memory from Beck's brain. But the war wasn't over. The smooth, seducing prick might have kissed Heavenly first, but Beck vowed he'd be the first—and only—man to drag her beneath him and pleasure her until she shattered over and over.

Reluctantly, he released her and opened the passenger door. After she settled into her seat, he climbed behind the wheel and headed toward the freeway, determined to put everyone else from his mind. This day was for him and Heavenly alone.

Clasping his hand in hers, Beck pulled onto Coast Highway, toward Malibu. Beside him, Heavenly stared out at the ocean.

"Oh, my gosh!" She sent him a delighted grin. "The Pacific! It's so beautiful. And huge! Can we stop?"

"You've lived in LA for months. You've never seen the beach?"

She shook her head, unwilling to tear her gaze away from the vast blue water. "I haven't had time."

"Then you're in for a treat, little girl."

Beck found a place to park, looking forward to her reaction as the chilly water rolled across her bare feet for the first time. Hand in hand, they strolled through the blinding California sun along the short, tree-covered path and down the stairs to a sandy beach.

Heavenly's stare filled with wonder. "Wow, I feel so small." Then she turned in a slow circle, taking in the massive rock formations, the opulent mansions poised on the hill, the lounging sunbathers, and the water rolling onto the sun-drenched sand again. "This is amazing."

"Not as amazing as you are," he murmured in a low voice.

"You're making me blush. Then again, that's easy." She laughed at herself.

Damn, she was adorable. "Take off your shoes; feel the sand between your toes."

With a giddy giggle, she kicked off her sandals. He hooked their straps over his finger and watched her grin widen as she curled her toes in the sand. "It's softer than I expected."

He drank in her awe as he shucked his own shoes and cuffed his pant legs. Taking her hand once more, he led her to the edge of the water. The sand grew cold and firm, and he watched her face as a wave rolled in and broke around their ankles.

"It's freezing!"

Yeah, that had surprised him the first time, too. "So you don't want to go for a swim today?"

"Oh, gosh no."

He laughed, loving that, like their trip to Disneyland, he could feel the newness of this experience through her. "How about a leisurely walk, then?"

"I'd love that. I'm not ready to stop looking at the ocean. It's just…" She sighed. "Wow."

A companionable silence settled between them as they strolled down the beach. Heavenly finally stopped ping-ponging her gaze between the massive homes and the ocean waves to smile up at him. "Thank you for stopping here. It's beautiful."

"And today, I'm letting you keep both feet on the ground."

"I'm really happy about that."

"Yeah? Well, I brought a barf bag in case you need to—"

"Oh, hush," she chided, slapping at his shoulder.

Beck led her to a jutting stone rising out of the sand. "We need to talk about Hammer's party, little girl."

Her face clouded over. "I'd rather not. Besides, we've eaten lunch together this past week and you haven't said a word. Why bring it up now?"

"I respect your privacy. I wasn't going to discuss it in the cafeteria, where Kathryn or anyone else could overhear." He pinned her with a serious stare.

"Thank you."

"But I haven't said everything I need to." Beck hooked his finger under her chin and locked their gazes together. "I'm going to now."

"I swear, I wasn't trying to shove it in your face. I'd never been kissed and I-I lost my head. I stopped thinking. And I feel terrible about it."

"I told you I'm not mad at you. Of course you were caught up. It was a completely new experience for you." Cocksucking Seth, on the other hand, damn well knew better and he'd just kept coming at Heavenly with every seductive weapon in his arsenal. "After all the time we've spent together, I know you'd never intentionally hurt me."

She sent him a regretful shake of her head. "I saw the expression in your eyes, the anger on your face…"

"I'm not going to lie, watching you kiss him back stung. You've been open about your feelings. But seeing the heat between you two was…an eye-opener."

Actually, it convinced him he'd been tiptoeing around his blazing attraction to Heavenly for too long.

"I'm sorr—"

"Shh." He placed a finger over her lips, wishing his mouth covered them instead. "Don't apologize for caring about people. Your big heart is one of the reasons I find you so fascinating."

"You have a big heart, too, you know."

Beck shook his head in denial, then delved into her big blue eyes and gathered all his courage to ask the question screaming through his head. "I just need to know if your feelings for me are as strong."

Heavenly didn't hesitate. "Every bit. That's why I'm so confused."

Her answer didn't surprise him. "I'm sure you are."

"When I'm with either of you, I have the best time. Since I saw how upset you were after Seth kissed me, I've been telling myself that I have to choose. I can't keep hurting either of you. But I don't know how to do it."

At the guilt in her tone, he cupped her cheek. "I don't want you agonizing over this right now."

"I can't help it. I hate the thought that either of you might think I'm playing some sort of game."

"I don't. What you're feeling isn't right or wrong; it just is. The choice will become clear to you—in time. It might come faster if you stop trying to force yourself to decide."

"I'll try." Heavenly sounded somewhere between unconvinced and dejected.

"Do your best." He sent her a tender smile. "I need to ask one more thing: When Seth took you inside after he kissed you, did he talk to you, try to calm you down?"

"Yes."

"That's all I needed to hear." *Maybe I won't have to kill him, after all.*

Of course, after watching the PI knock Pike out with one punch, Beck wondered if he could possibly win a fistfight against his rival...

Heavenly's stomach growled, interrupting his thoughts. "Did you skip breakfast?"

She sighed. "Yes."

"Come with me. Time for lunch." He took her hand, and they headed back to his car.

Finally, he was going to kiss her. Not in the parking lot. Not with cars whizzing past them on PCH. But he had a plan—one that guaranteed no one but him would lay eyes on Heavenly when she first felt his touch.

A few blocks away, he parked in front of an Italian hole-in-the-wall he frequented. He opened the door for Heavenly, watching as she stepped inside and took in the quaint interior with its rustic chandeliers, plastered walls, and checkered tablecloths, all offset by the little white lights gleaming off the stained concrete floors. A few diners were already here, come early to beat the lunch rush. More would be filing in soon.

"It's not fancy, but the food is amazing. One day, all the ravioli and spumoni is going to catch up with me." He patted his stomach.

She smiled at him. "If you brought me here, I'm sure the food is great. But the company is even better, and that's why I'm here."

"Aw, now you're going to make me blush."

"I doubt I could. Somehow, I get the feeling you've seen it all."

And done it, too. But she didn't need to know that.

"You come here a lot?" Heavenly asked.

Before he could answer, Angelo, an older man with a big belly and thinning silver hair, hurried their way. "Good to see you again, Dr. Beckman." He shook Beck's hand enthusiastically and sent Heavenly a welcoming smile. "Your table is ready. I don't take lunch reservations, but for you, I made an exception. Now I know why you insisted."

"Angelo, this is Heavenly."

He took her hand between his, soft and spotted with age. "A lovely name for a lovely woman."

"Thank you."

"My pleasure. The doctor has been coming here for years, and I always think he should not come alone. Yet he always does. So today, we celebrate."

Shit, if that didn't make him sound lonely and desperate.

Heavenly turned to him with shock in her bright smile. "If I'm the first person you've brought here, coming here is even more special to me."

That seemed to delight Angelo. "Follow me. I will show you to your table and bring your wine while you decide what you'd like to feast on today."

Beck already knew; he wanted to feast on the gorgeous little girl at his side.

When they passed through the dining room and reached the cozy alcove tucked in a private hallway off the back of the kitchen, he motioned Heavenly into the lone booth. Beck slid in beside her as Angelo handed them each menus and left.

"We really are alone." She glanced around, seemingly surprised not to see a single soul.

Beck smiled. "Tell me what you're hungry for."

Heavenly studied the menu. "What's good?"

"Everything." When she flipped a page, then another, followed by another still and frowned, he cut in. "Do you want me to order your lunch?"

"Please."

After Angelo reappeared with a bottle of red wine and poured them each a glass, Beck ordered. Then the old man hurried away with a wink.

Finally, he and Heavenly were alone.

Beck handed her a glass of vino. As he raised his own, he studied her rosy lips. She licked them nervously.

Fuck, he'd fantasized about today a million times.

"Remember when I told you we were more than friends?" He slid a knuckle down her cheek.

Heavenly nodded shyly. "That made me happy. I thought for so long that my feelings were one-sided."

"Not at all. I don't merely like you." He leaned closer, took her hand. "You intrigue me. I want you and I can't stop thinking about you. I've pursued you more than I have any woman—ever. And somehow, someway, I intend to have you."

She swallowed, scanning his eyes, seeming to test his sincerity.

He let the gravity on his face speak his truth. "I'm telling you this because I'm not good at romance, but I want you to know that if my feelings change, it will only be because they've grown stronger."

"You can't know that—"

"I can. I know what I feel. And I'm mad about you." He ran his finger along her jawline. "I'm consumed with you."

Heavenly stared mutely, breathing, blinking, pulse pounding in her neck.

He pinned her hand between his. "Are you afraid?"

"No." Her answer was breathless and immediate.

He reined in a smug smile. "Good. I can't make apologies for who I am, but when I'm wrong, I say I'm sorry. I won't always be easy on you, but I'll do everything in my power to make you happy."

"I'm happy when I spend time with you. I don't expect more from you than that."

"You should, and I want you to. I've spent months studying you for a reason. I needed to know what you need." He kissed her hand. "I think I've figured out what you want."

She stilled. "What do you mean?"

"Your body told me your deepest fantasies without saying a word the night I took you to the art gallery."

Now she looked nervous. "I was responding to art."

"You were responding to sex. You like the idea of being adored while being made to submit, of being orally pleasured, of being controlled and overpowered and fucked. But most of all, you like bondage. You ache to be tied up and utterly helpless. At my mercy. You've thought about it since that night, haven't you?"

A flush swept up her face, not the sweet blushing pink he often saw, but a blazing, undeniable red. Her plump lips parted. No words came out, but her rapt expression told him everything.

"I want to explore a few of those things with you today, Heavenly. Are you willing to give it—and me—a chance?"

She fidgeted. "I'm nervous."

"I know. But I chose this booth for a reason. No one can see us. Angelo won't disturb us after he brings our appetizer."

"W-what did you have in mind? Are you going to kiss me?"

"Absolutely." He slanted a wolfish smile. "I've been obsessed with tasting you."

Her gaze flitted down. "I've thought about kissing you, too. A lot."

"I was hoping you'd say that. I need your honesty going forward." At her nod, he plucked the napkin from beneath her hands shook it out. "You still trust me?"

"Yes."

"Good. I'm hoping you enjoy this, but if you don't or decide it's too much, tell me to stop. Understood?"

"All right."

Beck wrapped the fabric napkin around her wrists and tied it in a loose knot. Understanding slowly rippled across her face. She squirmed in her seat, her breathing turning ragged. Yeah, he was homing straight in on one of her hot buttons—and she was reacting exactly as he'd hoped. "If you want me to slow down or you want to talk about what's happening, say 'wait.' All right?"

"O-okay."

He caressed his thumb across the soft skin of her hand. "And if you're happy with everything I'm doing, say 'more, please.'"

"I will," she breathed.

"Good girl."

As soon as he praised her, Angelo appeared at the end of the shadowy hall, making far more noise than necessary. Beck covered Heavenly's bound hands with his napkin and signaled the man over.

"Your ravioli appetizer." He slid a tray in the middle of the table, along with a basket of bread and spice-laden olive oil. "Anything else for now?"

Impatience bit at Beck. "We're good. Give us half an hour?"

Angelo sent him a sly wink. "You won't be disturbed."

The moment the restaurant owner disappeared, Beck whispered in Heavenly's ear. "Put your hands on the table and keep them there."

She hesitated a mere instant before she complied.

"Excellent." He popped a ravioli in his mouth to test it. Perfect temperature. "Stick out your tongue, little girl."

Heavenly parted her lips and presented her wet, pink tongue. His blood surged. He lost himself in imagining his stiff cock disappearing between the sweet bow of her mouth. If she only knew how badly he wanted to melt all over her tongue right now…

He inhaled an uneven breath as he lifted the appetizer to her lips. A tremor of need rippled through him as he placed the pasta in her mouth. "Take a bite; let all that meat and cheese roll over your taste buds."

Again, she obeyed. Beck both felt and saw the shiver wrack her as she closed her eyes, sank her teeth into the crispy crust, and moaned. When she swallowed, he pressed the wineglass to her lips. "Drink."

As she sipped from his hand, she blinked at him, her pupils dilated.

Beck swallowed back a growl. "Your eyes are the same deep blue they were at the gallery. You like being bound and cared for by someone you trust. Someone like me, don't you?"

She pressed her lips together and sent him a barely perceptible nod.

"Little girl? I need you to talk to me. Answer my question."

Her lips trembled and he wanted to kiss away her fears, but dredged up a little more patience.

"Yes," she whispered. "It feels so…"

"What?"

"Wrong…but not. Forbidden, I guess. I'm scared, but not in a way I've ever felt." Her words trembled. "I'm not sure what you plan to do to me."

He swept the hair off her shoulder and leaned in before dragging his tongue up the side of her throat. Berry and the subtle hint of salt on her skin flowed over his taste buds. "For now, I'm simply going to feed you. Close your eyes."

Heavenly sent him an unfocused, almost spellbound glance before her lashes fluttered onto her cheeks.

Jesus, it was all he could do to hang on to his self-control. His hand shook as he tore off a piece of bread, swiped it through the herb-infused oil, then dragged it across her lower lip.

"So pretty," he whispered. "I bet your pussy glistens like that when you're hot and wet and ready to come. I'd love to slide my tongue over every fold and crevice, drown in all that sweet, virgin cream as you come for me."

"Beck…" Her breathing had grown choppier.

The scent of her arousal teased his senses. "I can smell you, little girl. You're already wet. Aren't you?"

She bit her lip shyly.

"Answer me. Communicate. I can't give you what you're aching for if you don't. Are you wet?"

"Yes."

Her voice was almost imperceptible but he heard. "Good."

Beck dipped into the marinara sauce on their appetizer plate, then tapped his finger against her lips. Without pause, she opened, and he dragged his digit over her tongue. When she wrapped her lips around his finger and began sucking the sauce away, he couldn't hold back his low growl.

"That's it. Suck it down. One day, you'll envelop my cock like that. And when I shower your throat, you'll swallow every drop, just like you're doing now."

Heavenly whimpered and swirled her tongue around him, sucking in earnest.

His fucking heart nearly stopped. His cock jerked, all but bursting his zipper. "Fuck, your mouth feels like molten velvet."

She squirmed as she suckled his finger again, her lips sliding slowly up the length. Beck buried his face against her neck and nipped the tender flesh below her ear. "Do you ache for me?"

With a moan, she nodded. The sound vibrated up his arm and slammed south to his pulsating cock.

He gritted his teeth, then begrudgingly eased his finger from her mouth. "Tell me."

"Yes." She breathed hard.

He tugged the napkin that secured her wrists. "So pretty and helpless and at my mercy."

"Beck…"

"The fire between us is burning me," he admitted, flicking his tongue over the shell of her ear. "Every night, I think about tossing you into my bed, binding you to the frame, and teasing you until you beg me to let you come."

Her cheeks flared red anew. "Oh…"

"When it happens, you'll be saying more than 'oh.' Trust me. I'll have you sweating, throbbing, and pleading with me to say four magic words: Come hard for me. Once I do, you'll shatter on command."

She whimpered and fidgeted, writhing in her seat, more than ready for him to touch her. Beck reached beneath the table and eased his fingers under the hem of her cotton dress, skimming over her soft, silky thigh.

Holy shit. Finally...*finally*, he had his hands on her. His patience was paying off—and it was sweeter than anything he'd imagined.

Demand thrummed through his veins as sizzling heat enveloped him. Her musky feminine scent grew stronger. His mouth watered. His cock screamed, strangling beneath his harsh denim. Beck did his best to ignore it and focused on Heavenly, on providing the relief he'd made her crave.

"Then while you're writhing and screaming, I'll align my cock to your innocent, weeping cunt and slowly press inside you. Your virgin walls will still be fluttering like butterfly wings as I squeeze each thick, fat inch inside your tight pussy. I'll rub my thumb around your sensitive clit until you soften and let me in. All the while you'll be clutching and milking my cock as you take me balls deep."

"I-I can't breathe," she panted.

Beck held in a smile. "Do you want me to stop?"

"No." Her voice cracked. "But..."

"But what?"

"I'm going to...combust."

He laughed softly in her ear. "I'm here to put your fire out...after you go up in flames."

Heavenly's head fell back, exposing her throat as she sucked in a gasping breath. "How?"

God, she looked flushed and beautiful and so fucking ready.

Beck grazed his fingertips closer to the juncture of her thighs. "Open your legs for me."

To his delight, she eased her legs apart instantly, welcoming him. The heat emanating from her pussy sizzled him, making him want to howl, as he slid his fingers up, up...until he was toying with the elastic of her panties and sliding his fingertip just beneath.

She jolted. Her eyes flared wide, suddenly meeting his stare with a gasp. But she didn't shy away. Didn't say no.

Beck pulled free. "You're supposed to close your eyes."

A moment passed, a heartbeat where their gazes locked. Then Heavenly shut her lids obediently once more.

"Good girl." He flattened his tongue against the hammering pulse point at her neck.

With a sweet moan, she tilted her head and parted her thighs even more, offering him all the flesh he coveted. "So soft...so hot. Your scent makes me want to torment your pussy." He dragged his middle finger down the center of her sodden panties, watching intently as a powerful shudder tore through her. Her pure, unfiltered responses were the most erotic thing he'd ever seen. "All I have to do is slide my fingers over you, just like this..."

She held her breath as he eased his fingers beneath the elastic edge of her panties again, this time stroking her wet, downy curls. Her little gasp told him that his touch affected her as much as her response got to him. He petted her softly until she unconsciously writhed against him. Then he slid his wet finger down the seam of her folds. She clenched her fists and moaned.

"When you're in my bed, I'll get my mouth on you, lap at your tiny slit, nibble on your clit—and not let up until you're screaming my name."

A breathless moan slid past her lips. She rocked into his palm. His heart sputtered. Jesus, she was close, and he could feel her body tightening, revving up. And once she came, Beck didn't know how the fuck he'd stop himself from laying her across the table and driving deep inside her.

But he goddamn had to. Here wasn't the place, and now wasn't the time. That's why he'd planned this outing, simply to give her a taste.

"Would you like that?"

Heavenly twisted, falling back against the booth, chest rising as she whimpered. "Please..."

"Please what?"

"Please, yes. Yes!"

Begging. She's already fucking begging.

"No one's ever touched you here before, little girl," he whispered thickly. "Have they?"

"No," she choked out in desperation.

Pride charged through him in a heady rush so potent his cock jerked. "I'm going to put out your fire right now. Someday soon, when we're truly alone, I'll start it again. Then I'll make you come until you're boneless, gasping, and so spent you can't move or scream."

He dipped his finger between her slippery, swollen folds and burrowed into her impossibly tight opening. Heavenly whimpered and rolled her hips into his touch as he eased around her tightening core and found just the right spot. Seconds later, she was mewling, panting, and grinding. Her virgin cream coated his digit and pooled in his palm.

She was so close, and he was damn near ready to follow her over.

When he softly strummed her pebbled clit, Heavenly rocked her hips and bit her lip to tamp down her keening cry.

"Let me feel you come," he growled against her ear. "I want your soft, hot walls clutching my finger as you let go."

As he glided his thumb over her clit, she inhaled a startled breath and held it. Her body stiffened. She threw her hips at him. Her eyes flashed open, teeming with panic and confusion. "Something's happening. Beck. Oh, Beck…"

He cinched a hand in her hair so he could watch her. The shock and bliss warring over her face completely stole what was left of his heart.

"Come hard for me, little girl. Now," he commanded in a feral growl as he worked another finger into her gripping core.

Heavenly sucked in a deep breath. Her back bowed. Color flooded her chest, neck, and cheeks. Then she was hurtling over the edge. Beck melded his mouth over hers, swallowing her muffled orgasmic screams with their first kiss. Her pussy clenched his fingers in a crushing grip while her body shuddered as she fractured into a million tiny pieces for him.

Finally, she fell back against the booth, panting against his mouth. After the tension left her, he nudged her lips apart and plunged inside, delving deep and claiming her lips in a tender sweep meant to reassure and reward her.

The surge of electricity flowing between them shocked Beck. Awed him. He didn't want to let her go, didn't want to stop touching the sweet cunt only he had stroked. He wanted to stay, brand her thick feminine scent to memory.

It fucking sucked that she had to be at work in two hours and refused to call in sick. God, he'd spend all night making his fantasies come true while teaching her new ones she'd never dared to dream of.

One last time, he tangled his tongue with hers. She tasted like sunshine and sin. Beck couldn't deny this innocent little girl had obliterated his very soul.

Finally, with a groan, he pulled away. Heavenly gasped as she continued fluttering and quivering around his fingers. Beck kissed her cheeks, her nose, her lips softly as she glided back down, with a glassy, dazed look in her eyes.

She was stunning, ethereal. Everything he hadn't known he'd been searching for.

"Oh, my gosh," she breathed, blinking at him. "You did that. To me."

He sent her a wicked laugh. "It won't be the last time. I promise you."

Beck sipped at her swollen bottom lip before he reluctantly withdrew his fingers from her sweltering center. With the other hand, he untied the napkin and slid it from her wrists, massaging them one at a time.

"I don't…" she whispered, sounding lost. "I've never felt anything like…whatever you did to me."

Oh, fuck! She'd never even given herself an orgasm before? Beck wasn't sure how that was possible, but her words galvanized him to vow he'd sail her to the stars every chance he got.

"Did I put out the fire, like I promised?"

A sleepy, sated smile stretched across her face. "Yes, and then some."

After settling her panties back in place, he lifted his hand from beneath her dress. Her essence glistened in the muted light. Her pungent scent clung to his fingers. His mouth watered. He snagged her gaze and held it as he drew his hand to his mouth and slowly lapped at her warm, tart cream with a moan.

Heavenly sucked in a shocked gasp, her cheeks flaming.

He couldn't help but grin. "Get used to this. I won't waste a single drop you offer me, little girl."

"I think you were right."

Beck raised a brow. "About what?"

"You are the man my mother should have warned me about."

He nodded. "You'll remember that when I'm taking you hard, dirty, and often."

Her eyes grew wide and she swallowed tightly. "Oh. My…"

"You protesting?"

"No." She didn't hesitate.

"Just what I wanted to hear." He winked, then looked at his watch. "Angelo will be here with our food shortly. Why don't you take a minute to freshen up in the ladies' room? While we're eating, we'll decide what sounds good for dessert."

"Okay." She all but floated out of the booth and straightened her skirt, her cheeks still pink. "Thank you."

He stood and wrapped her in his arms, slanting his lips over hers. He kissed her, slowly and sensually, hoping he conveyed how special she was to him.

When he reluctantly pulled away, she lifted her heavy lashes and started to giggle. "You're wearing my lip gloss. I'm not sure that's the right shade for you."

As Heavenly walked away, his stare glued itself to the sexy sway of her hips while he gave himself a mental pat on the back. He might be lacking when it came to suave, seductive lines and romance, but he'd given the girl her first orgasm. His only regret? That shithead Seth hadn't been there to see Heavenly dissolve. Not that he wanted to share her pleasure with him. But after watching the bastard tongue-swab and dry-hump her, Beck wanted him to know exactly how it felt to stand on the sidelines while having his balls kicked.

But maybe he could extract a little payback through a different means…

Yanking out his cell phone, Beck snapped a selfie with Heavenly's shiny gloss smeared all over his lips. "Sweet revenge."

Chuckling softly, he tapped out a message to Seth, attached the image, and hit send.

SETH'S FLIGHT TO New York the Monday following Hammer's party was night-and-day from his trip home a mere nine weeks ago. The frustrations and questions then had been erased by happiness and hope now. His scowl was long gone, replaced by swagger.

He'd kissed Heavenly Young—been the first man to taste her lips, drink in her passion. Even forty-eight hours later, she still lingered on his tongue.

Christmas didn't assault him on this trip through the terminal. Now, he saw hints that winter was almost over. Yankees' spring training would start in a few days. It was no longer cold enough to give his balls frostbite. Most of all, he had a new outlook on life.

Because, after eight years of misery, he was finally going to embrace his future.

First, he had to say good-bye to his past—both the good and the bad. Since he still had family here, this wouldn't be his last trip, but it would be the last time he called the city home.

Not too long ago, this plunge would have messed with his head. Even when he'd impulsively hopped on a plane back to California two weeks ago, he'd been intent on nothing beyond laying eyes on Heavenly and ending his misery. The idea of moving out West had seemed farfetched, surreal. Despite Liam's cryptic warning about Heavenly, she guided him like a beacon toward a new home. He was going to spend his life with her. Every gut instinct he possessed told him so.

When he reached baggage claim, his mother stood waiting for him, just like his last trip. She looked every bit as vibrant now as she had at Christmas.

Carl must still be in the picture.

He hurried to her, swept her up in his arms, and kissed her soundly on the cheek. "It's good to see you, Mom. Thanks for picking me up. How's the family? Anna Mae growing? And how's, um…Carl?"

"We're all fine. Your niece is a good eater, just like all you boys. Carl is good." She smiled. "It's nice to have you home again. Now kindly put me down, son."

Laughing, Seth lowered her to her feet. "It's good to be here." He sobered. "But I'm not staying. I'm moving to California."

His mother blinked and set a hand over her chest. "You're serious? So things went well in Los Angeles?"

"Very well."

"Tell me everything."

"For starters, Hammer is out of the woods. The bogus case against him has been dropped and justice has prevailed. He, Raine, and Liam are free to live happily ever after. And I think they finally will."

"Then I'm happy for them." She dropped her voice. "But I meant things with Heavenly. Did you see her?"

"I definitely did." In fact, he'd more than seen the woman. He'd pressed his lips to hers, sunk his tongue into her mouth, and felt her body cling to his. He still couldn't stop thinking about it. "You were right, Mom. I left LA too soon. I want this girl. And I finally have the validation that she wants me, too...so I'm moving."

"Oh, honey. Everyone is going to be so surprised." She paused, looking uncertain. "But moving is such a big step. Are you sure?"

Liam's riddle at the party flitted through Seth's head again. Nope. No way was he letting Heavenly slip through his fingers, especially not for good.

"More sure than I've been about anything in a long time. You'll love her. Just look at her." He whipped out his phone and showed her the picture Bryn had taken of most everyone at the party the other night. "She's the pretty blonde. She's really sweet, Mom."

"She's beautiful." His mom looked a little misty-eyed. "Do *you* love her?"

"If I don't already, I'm pretty sure it's only a matter of time."

She squeezed his arm. "Liam and Hammer look very happy. Is the brunette between them..."

"That's Raine," he finished. "She's a doll."

"And the other man with the beard?" She pointed to the right of Heavenly.

"Remember that asswipe I told you about at Christmas, Beck?" At her nod, he continued. "Well, he still wants her, too. And you can bet while I'm away, packing up and arranging my move, that he'll be trying his damndest to convince Heavenly he's her best choice. Just because he's a doctor…" Seth sighed.

"What are her feelings for him?"

"I don't know." When his mother would have objected, he cut her off. "And I don't care. What matters is what she feels for me. And I don't intend to settle for anything less than making her mine." He bent to retrieve a suitcase from the turning carousel. "This is it. I left the rest back in LA. You ready to get out of here?"

She took his free arm. "Let's get you back to the house so you can tell the family."

Absolutely. He'd thought this through over the past two days. He had a timetable and an agenda.

Thirty minutes later, he sat at the dining table in his mother's house, surrounded by his family. He was holding his newborn niece on his lap and was captivated as the blue-eyed cutie stared back solemnly. She had that unforgettable baby smell, soft and fresh.

"She looks good on you."

Seth looked up at Maggie. "You did good. Here, take her before I scare her. She doesn't look too sure about me."

For a moment, he had an image of a blond-haired cutie with eyes like her mother and almost laughed aloud. *Christ, one step at a time.* He looked over at his mom, her hand in Carl's, lost in conversation. The twins wolfed down food like they hadn't eaten in days. Danny smiled at his baby girl. Matt looked back at him, like he knew something was up.

"Matt, Cooper Investigations is yours if you want it."

"What?" He reared back. "I don't understand. What are you going to do?"

That halted conversation around the table. Everyone paused to look at him.

Their mother smiled. "Go on. Tell them."

He looked at the faces of those who'd been his world for as long as he could remember. Everyone was carrying on with their lives…finding their way. The only one who'd been standing still was him. That realization no longer bred bitterness. He had a reason to move forward now. It was time to finally release the reins of caretaker and give himself permission to live his own life.

"I'm moving to LA."

Eyes grew wide. Mouths gaped open and chaos erupted.

"You're what?" Danny barked.

"Moving? You mean for good?" Shock lined Matt's face.

"What made you decide to do that?" Danny demanded.

Conner smirked. "I bet he found a woman out there and—"

"Is she hot?" Jack looked far more interested than he had moments ago.

"Definitely," Seth assured.

"I knew it! That's the reason you were so sad over Christmas, isn't it?" Maggie leapt from her chair and hugged him. "I knew you couldn't possibly be a boinking manwhore for the rest of your life! I'm so happy for you!"

"What kind of work do you plan to do out there?" Matt asked, still looking stunned.

Carl didn't say a word, simply chuckled, while his mother sent him an encouraging smile.

Seth raised his hands to ward off the barrage of questions. "If you'll give me a minute. I'll explain. Her name is Heavenly and—"

"Is she a stripper?" Conner asked with an eager grin.

"No! What the hell is wrong with you?" Seth growled as he smacked his idiot brother upside his head. "She's a very sweet nursing student."

"And she's willing to date *you*?" Jack scoffed. "Must be something wrong with her."

"Ha ha." Seth wasn't amused. "Do you want to listen to what I have to say or just bust my balls?"

Conner shrugged. "We can do both."

"Hush, you two," Grace admonished the twins with a scowl, then turned an understanding gaze Seth's way.

"As far as what I plan to do out in California, well...I've decided to open up a branch of Cooper Investigations out there."

"So, we'll be working together on opposite coasts?" Matt arched his brows.

"Absolutely. We can expand our client base and cover more territory. I'm sure there are plenty of cheating spouses, missing persons, embezzlers, and assorted troublemakers to keep us busy."

"You've thought this through, haven't you?" Matt gaped.

"Yep."

"Are you going to ask Heavenly to marry you?" Maggie asked with a wide grin.

"One thing at a time," Seth dodged. But strangely, the thought wasn't nearly as terrifying as it had been in the past.

"Hey, can we come to your place and hang out on the beach for spring break?" Jack asked.

"That would be epic!" Conner chimed in as they high-fived.

"We'll see." Seth chuckled. "I have to find a place first."

Though he had a suspicion they'd fit right in at Shadows…

"What does Heavenly look like?" Jack asked with a lurid grin.

"Curb your hormones, bro," Seth chided as he slid out his phone and passed around the photo of Heavenly he'd shared with his mom earlier. "She's the blonde."

"*Damn.* How'd you bag a babe that gorgeous?" Conner jabbed.

"He must have bought her on the Internet," Jack taunted. "No way could he ever snag a girl that fine on his own."

"Bite me," Seth growled.

"Does she have a sister?" Matt grinned hopefully. "I could move out West with you and—"

"No. She's an only child, and your ass stays here to run the business."

"While we're on the subject of good news, I have some to share as well," Grace announced at the other end of the table.

"Oh, my god. You're not pregnant, are you?" Matt choked.

"No!" She blanched. "Honestly, Matty. What goes on in that head of yours?"

"You don't want to know. Trust me." He grinned.

Grace sucked in a deep breath and darted a nervous glance toward Carl. "I'm—"

"We," the man beside her corrected, squeezing her hand for support.

"Right. We—Carl and I—are getting married. He asked, and I said yes."

A collective silence filled the room. Seth skimmed a stare over his brothers, cataloging their expressions. There wasn't a hint of anger or resentment, simply stunned surprise. Tears spilled down Maggie's cheeks as she smiled sweetly and sniffed.

Maybe his job holding them all together wasn't quite finished, after all. Seth picked up his wineglass and raised it in the air. "Congratulations. I'm truly happy for you two."

That was all the icebreaker that his siblings needed. Another barrage of questions and chatter echoed off the walls, proving once again that dinner at the Cooper household was never boring.

Grace smiled at Seth. "I expect to see you and Heavenly at our wedding, son."

"We'll be there. Who do you think is going to give you away?"

Tears filled her eyes. "You'd do that for me?"

He rose from his seat and wrapped his arms around her. "I'd be disappointed if you didn't let me."

"Then I'd be honored. Thank you, sweetheart."

"Have you set a date yet?"

"No. Everything is still in the planning stages. There's no rush, and summer is Carl's busy season, so it'll be a while yet."

Thank goodness. While he had no doubt his family would love Heavenly, he needed time to prepare her. Meeting his big, boisterous clan might be more than a tad overwhelming for her.

Later that night at his brownstone, Seth lay in bed as visions of Heavenly flashed through his brain. He pulled out his phone and started to call, but decided a text might be best. He didn't know if she was at work or, god forbid, on a date with Beck. When she replied seconds later, a satisfied grin tugged his lips.

An hour passed, then he told her to get some sleep and said good night. She answered by telling him to have sweet dreams and added a heart emoji. After tossing and turning for another hour, making a mental checklist of all the things he needed to do, Seth switched off his brain. He focused once more on Heavenly and drifted off to sleep, contentment filling his soul.

During the next four days, Seth temporarily forwarded his mail to Shadows via the post office. He'd also hired a moving company to pack up his belongings and haul both his SUV and motorcycle to LA. He'd spoken to a couple of Realtors, laying the groundwork for the sale of his apartment here and finding both a new condo and office space to rent there.

By early Friday evening, he and Matt finally had finished sorting through the file cabinets in the office. His brother had already transformed the old space with a fresh coat of paint and new furniture. It looked polished and professional. Seth couldn't help but smile.

Matt opened the bottom drawer of the massive desk and drew out a bottle of whiskey and a couple of tumblers. "I think a shot or two is in order."

Seth chuckled as he eased onto the edge of the desk. He watched his brother pour the golden-amber liquid, then each took a glass. As he raised it, a sense of melancholy slid through him. "To bittersweet endings and promising new beginnings."

"Hear. Hear." A wealth of understanding lined his brother's face.

Matt had seen Seth at his best and worst, but his brother's love and support, through good times and bad, were a constant. And Seth was grateful beyond words.

They clinked the rims and took a long gulp. As the burn slid down his throat and warmed his stomach, Seth reached into his pocket and presented his key to Matt. He swallowed the emotion lodged in his throat. "This place belongs to you now."

Matt looked both thrilled and heartbroken. "Already? I didn't think you were leaving for another week or two."

"I'm not. I've got a few more loose ends to mop up." And he wanted to spend more time with the family while he could, before detective work and winning Heavenly became a full-time job. "But I want you to feel comfortable with the fact it's now yours."

"Thanks, man."

"I'm a bit late in telling you this… I'm sorry I was a douche over Christmas. I had a lot to work through. But I'm proud to call you a partner and even prouder to call you brother."

"Ditto, man."

As they slapped each other on the back, Seth's phone dinged. He dug the device out of his pocket and scanned the screen. Beck. What did that fucker want?

He opened the unwelcome message and saw an image of the man's mouth covered in peachy-pink lip gloss—the same shade Heavenly wore. The accompanying message read: You're not the only one

who's kissed her, motherfucker. And when she comes, her
moans are so sweet…

Seth's blood boiled.

Beck. Had. Touched. Heavenly. And kissed her, too. Thoroughly
from the looks of it. Had he also fucked her?

He growled at the picture. "Oh, yeah? Game on, cocksucker."

As he typed out those exact words, Matt frowned and tried to peek
at his screen. "What's up? Who are you talking to?"

Seth darkened the device and tucked it away. "Nobody important,
just someone out west who needs his ass kicked."

"You'll do that, no sweat." Matt clapped him on the back. "The
guy doesn't stand a chance."

"You're right. But…this problem might be more pressing than I
thought. Can you…um, give me a lift? I need to grab my suitcase and
head to the airport."

"Today?" Matt blinked in total confusion. "Now?"

Normally, Seth wouldn't sweat this stuff. If some girl wanted to
mack on another guy, that was on her. But…this was Heavenly, and
Beck was the kind of shithead who wouldn't hesitate to take advantage
of her.

"Yeah." He whipped out his phone again and launched the airline's
app, relieved to see a seat on a flight to LAX in a little under four
hours. "I'd appreciate it. I'll call you when I get settled. Tell Mom I
love her and I'm sorry. But I've got to get home."

CHAPTER FOURTEEN

TWO DAYS AFTER their lunch date at Angelo's, Beck's doorbell rang—right on time.

Eagerly, he pulled the portal between them open. There Heavenly stood, a golden braid wrapped around her crown while long, loose curls flowed over her mostly bare shoulders. She wore a sunny orange dress with a teasing V neckline, held together by simple straps. Its flirty hem played peekaboo with her slender thighs.

He almost swallowed his tongue.

"Come in." Beck took her hand and pulled her into his arms.

He couldn't wait another second to touch her.

Shutting the door, Beck backed her against it, cupped her nape, and crushed her lips under his. Fuck, kissing her was like instant relief and utter torment at once. He had her on his tongue, but it wasn't enough. The way he felt right now, he wasn't sure it ever would be.

When he finally let her up for air, she was pink-cheeked, breathing hard, and looking both flushed and excited to continue where they'd left off after lunch.

This was it, the day he'd finally claim her.

Since she'd agreed to let him cook her brunch today, they were totally alone. He intended to get her into bed. He didn't want to wait anymore. Hell, he couldn't afford to.

Not with Seth breathing down his neck.

On Friday night, Beck had knocked back a beer with Hammer and Liam while Heavenly was waiting tables. He'd been sure his frenemy would stay in New York for at least a couple of weeks. It should take that long to sell his place and his car, close his business, say good-bye to friends and family...and whatever else. Or so he'd thought, until Liam mentioned that Seth was on a plane back to LAX as they spoke.

What the fuck? How did it take a mere four days to move across the country?

Maybe you shouldn't have lit a fire under Seth's ass with that picture of you wearing Heavenly's lip gloss.

The instant Liam dropped the bombshell, Beck had texted Heavenly and reaffirmed their date to have brunch at his place.

"Thanks for inviting me," she said softly, scanning the length of his tri-level contemporary pad. "Wow, your house is so interesting...striking. It's you."

"Glad you like it. Let's head to the kitchen. I hope you're hungry."

"Hmm," she moaned as he led her toward the back. "I am. Something smells amazing."

"I made you French toast casserole, eggs, bacon, fresh fruit, and"—he leaned across the island to pick up the two flutes he'd poured a few minutes ago—"mimosas. Ever had one?"

She shook her head as she accepted the glass. "Orange juice and...what?"

"Champagne." That made her smile, and he held up his drink. "Here's to a really great day."

At least he hoped so. He wanted her beyond all sanity, and his balls were so fucking blue. Gloria thought he'd been crazy doing without sex for weeks last Christmas. If she knew he'd waited months to get Heavenly in bed, his soon-to-be ex-wife would probably assume he'd developed erectile dysfunction.

Beck was thankful he'd had the foresight to wear his shirt untucked because he already knew getting hard was not going to be a problem.

"With someone special." She clinked her glass with his.

He drank and watched her wrap her lips around the flute as she took dainty sips. He saw the moment the flavor hit her tongue. Her eyes widened and, after she swallowed half the drink down, so did her smile.

"Everything is just about ready. Why don't you take a seat over there?" He pointed to the breakfast table near the wall of windows at the back of his house, overlooking the pool. It was a perfect California day, and the sun glimmered off the glasses of ice water he'd poured.

As he held out her chair, she sat. "Can I do anything to help?"

"Just sit there and look beautiful."

Heavenly rolled her eyes. "I don't know how successful I'll be, but

I'll do my best."

Beck winked at her, then pulled the hot dishes from the oven, followed by the chilled fruit from the fridge. He refilled her mimosa the instant she emptied it, then dished her up a hearty brunch.

As they ate, they talked about everything and nothing. He told her some of the stupid shit he'd done as a wet-behind-the-ears intern. She regaled him with the awesomeness of real Wisconsin cheese curds. They discussed what it was like to move suddenly and unexpectedly to LA, hospital politics, and where she might want to practice nursing after graduation.

As soon as they'd made a good dent in the food, which she'd praised repeatedly as she finished her second mimosa, he offered her a third.

"Thank you, but I can't." She sighed. "I was hoping to have the whole day off, but my boss told me last night that he needs me from three to close today."

Well, hell. He didn't want to rush this...but he also didn't think he could wait another five minutes to have her naked.

She tilted her face up toward the sun. Her hair spilled over the back of her chair. The urge to sink his fingers into those curls and drag her to his bedroom rode him hard. Maybe going caveman on her would backfire...but being direct had worked pretty fucking well last time.

"Can I ask you a question?"

"Of course." The easy answer flowed off her tongue.

Beck took her hand. "Have you thought about what happened during our last date?"

She lowered her lashes and nodded.

"That's not an answer, little girl."

She jerked her stare to his. Color crawled up her face before her gaze skittered away again. "Yes. It's almost all I think about now."

That, right there. Something in her eyes. She hadn't merely thought of the ways he'd touched her on Friday. He'd bet money she was still thinking of Seth and his kiss, too.

Goddamn it.

He stood and extended his hand. "Come with me, and I'll give you a lot more things to occupy your mind."

Heavenly hesitated for long moments, stare bouncing between his outstretched fingers and his face, which he feared was too naked with need. Had he been too unromantic? Had something he'd done made her change her mind? Or had fucking Seth somehow got to her yesterday?

Beck slid into his chair again. "Heavenly, if you're unsure or you're not interested—"

"That's not it," she assured softly, then swallowed nervously. "It's just...I'm not ready to have sex yet. I'm sure you're used to dealing with women who—"

"I'm not thinking about any woman but you. This is between us. If you're not ready, then you're not ready. I respect that."

And that was true...but his cock wanted to weep.

"I'm sorry."

"Don't apologize. I just want to be clear. Am I moving too fast now? Or does this have something to do with Seth?"

Heavenly blanched, then sighed. "Do you want me to be honest?"

"That's the only way I ever want you to be with me. Tell me anything and everything. When I said we were more than friends, I had in mind the kind of relationship where you'd feel free to share your thoughts and feelings."

"Okay..." She sighed. "Maybe I'm naive, but sex, to me, is a commitment. Not like the forever, death-do-us-part kind. But—"

"I have no problem with commitment."

She shook her head. "I'm not asking for one. I'm just saying it implies that I've made a choice. It's not hard to notice that you and Seth have...animosity. He's already left once because I told him I had feelings for you. If I have sex with you now, he'll probably take that as me choosing you over him again."

Beck tried to bite back his frustration. "You're not responsible for Seth's feelings."

"I know. And I—"

"And if he only wants you for your virginity, he's not worth the bag necessary to take out the trash. I understand you've got feelings for him, but you need to think about *you*, too."

"I am. I don't think he just wants bragging rights about being my first. It's like he took my feelings for you as a rejection, like he assumed if I wanted you, I couldn't want him, too. Even though I've told him it's more complicated than that…" She shook her head.

So basically, the dumb shit was coming between them and he wasn't even here? Peachy.

From helping him work with Raine on Liam and Hammer's behalf a few short months ago, Seth knew perfectly well that a woman could have separate but equal feelings for two different men. Why the fuck had he suddenly gone stupid?

Of course, Liam and Hammer had solved the problem by sharing the girl who'd been unable to choose between them. That wasn't happening with Heavenly. *Oh, fuck. No. Just no.* He'd hardly been able to share a meal with Seth. No way did he trust that asswipe enough to share in her care.

Beck let out a calming breath. He wasn't going to push her to give more than she wanted to…but he didn't want to let her go with a peck and a wave, either.

"Of course it's more complicated," he agreed. "Since you're not ready for sex, there are plenty of other things I can teach you, pleasures I can give you. Just say the word. And if not…" He shrugged. "We'll sit by the pool, enjoy the day, and talk."

"Thanks for understanding," she murmured, then suddenly couldn't meet his stare again. A fresh flash of red surged up her face. "Would you show me your bedroom?"

Her question made his body ping electric.

"I'd love to." He rushed to help her to her feet.

She cast a nervous glance around his messy kitchen. "Do you want help with the dishes first?"

"Fuck the dishes." He seized her mouth with his and curled his arms around her frame, cupping her ass and lifting her against his body. "Hold on to me."

Heavenly didn't hesitate to wrap her arms and legs around him. He plunged his tongue into her mouth and marched to the stairs, taking them two at a time, then all but sprinted down the hall to his bedroom.

Beside his bed, he slowly lowered her to her feet, dragging every inch of her against him, then studied her flushed face. Already, her eyes were dilated, her lips swollen, her nipples pebbled. He regretted not getting his hands—or mouth—on her breasts last Friday. He was determined to make up for lost time.

Beck skated his fingers up her waist, tracing the edge of her underwire bra, before he cupped the pert globe in his hand. Staring into her eyes, he thumbed the tight little tip back and forth in slow strokes. "What do you want, little girl?"

"So many things…" she admitted with a groan, then gave him a self-deprecating smile. "Late last night, after my shift, I laid in my bed and I replayed our lunch over in my head. And for the first time ever, I was able to give myself an orgasm."

"Good. You should know your body and what makes you hum." He pinched her nipple through her dress lightly, relishing the hitch in her breath. "What part of our lunch did you think about while you got yourself off?"

"The ways you touched me. I put my fingers everywhere you did and thought of all the things you'd said. And…" She sighed, her smile widening. "It was nice. But not as amazing as when you gave me pleasure."

Good to know. "You have other fantasies? Things you thought about when you touched yourself in the past?"

"For a long time, when I tried to, um…"

"Masturbate?" he supplied helpfully.

Right on cue, her face managed to turn even redder. "Yeah. When I did, my thoughts were mostly a curiosity. I wanted to know how my body worked. I wanted to understand the physiology. And I wanted to figure out why, if I was a woman, I wasn't interested in any of the men—or women—around me. It was almost like I didn't understand myself well enough to have fantasies. Then, you took me to the gallery." She sighed. "And everything changed."

This woman was the most interesting bundle of contradictions. It took her forever to tell him her troubles, but she readily shared her feelings and fantasies. There must be some reason. Whatever it was, her dichotomy intrigued him. Made him harder. Made him more desperate for her.

"I'm not surprised." He'd sensed what she was the moment he'd met her. Having her validate that, even unconsciously, renewed his hope. She wasn't ready for rubber paddles and whips—might never be—but she was ready for him to take control.

It was so on.

"You're not? I'm shocked."

"Still not surprised." He traced the V of her neckline, fingertip grazing the tempting swell of her breast. A wide, wicked smile crossed his face. "Show me."

"What?"

"Show me how you made yourself come."

Heat flared in her eyes. "I-I don't know if I can—"

"You can." He dragged his tongue over her collarbone, then whispered in her ear. "Strip off your clothes, lie back on the bed, and show me what you've learned."

"A-are you going to watch?"

"Absolutely." As soon as the word was out, her breathing turned uneven and she bit her lip self-consciously. He skimmed his lips along her jaw. "I want to be the first to see you naked."

Heavenly hesitated, then stepped out of her sandals, eased one of her straps off her shoulders, then looked at him for approval.

"Keep going." He flicked the other strap down and kissed the cap. "You're safe with me. Don't stop."

She gave him a jerky nod, then turned her back to him, gathering her hair and holding it up. "I-I can't reach the zipper."

His cock lurched approvingly as he sucked in a shuddering breath. Holy shit. She was undressing—for him. He would see her totally bare. That thought dive-bombed his brain and buzzed his libido.

Slowly, he reached for the tab and dragged it down her back, the quiet hiss achingly sexual as he exposed inch after inch of her milky, untouched skin.

Beck's hand shook. His control felt dangerously close to snapping, but he gritted his teeth, chained down his beast, and told himself to find his fucking patience as he pulled her zipper as low as he could.

The ivory lace skimming the small of her back and wrapping around her hips taunted him. He slipped his finger just under the band. "Next time, leave your panties at home. You don't need them with me."

Heavenly jerked a glance over her shoulder. "Wear a dress without underwear?"

Her shock made him smile. "That would please me."

"I don't know if I'm that...daring. I'll try."

He didn't love her response, but he understood he was asking her for something both new and foreign to her good-girl sensibilities. He had to let her adjust to the idea—and to his demands. Nothing with her would be simple or overnight. The fact she was open to the idea at all was a good sign.

Beck cupped her arm and dropped kisses to her neck. "Try very hard. Now push your dress over your hips. Panties, too. Leave them on the floor."

She complied, wriggling enough to have him biting back a groan as she swept the cotton, lace, and silk from her body. It pooled on the floor, leaving her clad in nothing but a strappy bra. He'd get to that in a minute; the hooks were right in front of him. But first, that luscious ass.

Dear god... He gripped her hips, knelt behind her, and dragged his mouth across each pert cheek. It wasn't enough. He had to sink his teeth in, nip and lave. In his hold, she trembled, held her breath. Shit, he needed more. He bit harder. And sucked.

She yelped. "Beck?"

"Shh." It was all he could manage to say.

Fuck, suctioning her smooth, perfect skin between his lips was already heaven, but then he took another sharp nibble and pulled her deeper into his mouth. Oh, yeah...

He stood back to admire his brand. A possessive fire he'd never felt scalded his veins, urging him to toss her down and mark every inch of her backside however she'd let him—right now.

But if he didn't stop fixating on her ass, this was going to get out of control fast. Already, he was riding a dangerous edge.

Gathering his mental shit, he flicked her bra open and let it fall to the ground.

Now she was completely naked for him. Beck couldn't fucking breathe.

As he glided his palm down her pure, peachy-pale back and cupped her gorgeous backside again, Heavenly wrapped protective arms around her chest.

Frowning, he pulled her arms to her sides. "Why are you trying to hide?"

"I'm nervous."

"About?"

"I'm naked."

"That's how I wanted you."

Heavenly let out a little huff. "What if you don't like what you see?"

"Impossible. I'm already exercising more self-control than you can imagine to stop myself from devouring you. Now turn around so I can see you, little girl. I want to watch you play with your pussy for me. I won't touch you without your permission. If, at any time, you want to end this, all you have to do is say 'stop.'"

Body tense, she nodded. Then she took in a shaky, fortifying breath and slowly turned around.

Through the windows, sunlight streamed, kissing her everywhere and making her glow golden. Beck felt his jaw drop. He nearly lost his tongue. "Goddamn, you're beautiful."

The gentle slope of her shoulders gave way to delicate collarbones, then down to lush, round breasts that seemed to defy gravity, topped off by the prettiest blushing pink nipples he'd ever seen. Beck wasn't a boob man, but he'd absolutely make an exception for Heavenly. Her torso curved into the gentle valley of her small waist, followed by the flare of her feminine hips. Between trim thighs, her pussy hid shyly behind a dusting of pale down. Hell, even her feet were petite.

She was every fantasy he'd never realized he had in one perfect package.

A tentative smile curled up her lips. "You're being kind."

"I'm being honest." He reached for her breast, then remembered his promise. "Will you let me?"

Heavenly gave him a jerky nod.

Her nipples had beaded under the gentle stir of the air conditioning, but they tightened even more the moment he cradled the weight of her breast in his hand. Then he did the same to her other, sweeping his thumbs across the hard tips, fascinated by the way she gasped and her knees buckled and a flush rose all over her body.

He had to taste them.

Beck bent and lifted a nipple to his lips. "You okay with this?"

"Uh-huh." Her voice sounded deliciously unsteady.

He smiled as he lowered his head the last inch and sucked the velvety bead into his mouth, laving her with his tongue and moaning around her flesh. Her head rolled back on her shoulders, and she curled her hands around his head, urging him closer.

After working the bud for long minutes, he drew back and popped it from between his lips, then lavished the same treatment on the other, sliding the first between his thumb and forefinger. Heavenly wriggled against him, her little moans an encouragement to lay her down, spread her out, and take everything she offered. But they'd negotiated—not that she realized it—and he'd promised her boundaries.

Beck forced himself to step back with a reluctant sigh. "Thank you. Lie on the bed."

Slowly, she eased back, sitting first, then lying down, scooting to the center, splaying out in a pose he didn't think she meant to be sexy. But hell if it wasn't—lips, arms, and thighs all parted unconsciously as if she waited for him.

"That's it. Show me how you make yourself feel good."

Heavenly shot him a nervous stare. "You're really going to stand over me and watch?"

"To start with." He gave her a wry smile. "As gorgeous as you are, I might have to join you and give myself some fucking relief."

"I'd like to see that." She smiled in spite of her tension, her expression unconsciously come-hither. "Maybe I'll help you."

Jesus, she kept surprising—and arousing—him. When he finally fucked her, Beck had a feeling she was going to wreck him.

"You're welcome to touch me anytime, anywhere, any way. Now be a good little girl and put your fingers in your pussy."

Heavenly nodded, then laid her hands on the fluttering flat of her belly before letting her right drift down unerringly into her damp curls. With her left hand, she parted her pouting folds, showing him all her prettiest, most private pink parts. Even at a distance, he could tell she was aroused.

"Are you wet?"

She gave him a shaky nod.

"Tell me. Say it."

"My pussy is wet."

Her whisper was so faint and high-pitched. He heard her nerves. He heard her need. He heard her surrender. It was killing him.

"It is. And it smells so good, sweet like cotton candy. Show me how you rub your clit."

She did, slowly at first, like she wasn't sure what to do. Or whether he would like it. *Ha!* Watching her drag her fingers across her shy little bud was mind-blowing. His mouth watered. His cock screamed. He'd give anything to dive face first into her.

Instead, he could only stare, hands clenched into fists, and subject himself to the most decadent erotic torture imaginable.

"Rub it harder. Faster." His hoarse voice came out ragged.

She complied with a beseeching stare, circling her clit with more speed and force until a desperate whimper fell from her lips.

"That's it. You're juicy and so swollen and tempting. Jesus, your velvety walls gripping my finger as you quivered and came haunts me."

Unable to resist her lure, he inched closer until his thigh met the mattress, watching her breathing turn choppy and her body go tense. She tossed her head back, arching her throat to him, and spread her legs wider. The heady scent of her sex hung thick in the air.

"Look at me while you climb that peak."

With a mewl, she did. Her blue eyes were dark, smoky. Her hips rocked as their stares fused. A rousing pink hue colored her naked flesh. "Beck…"

"You look fucking stunning." He was trying like hell to keep his hands and mouth off her.

Heavenly was close. Her keening cries echoed off the walls. The ache behind his zipper grew to a painful throb. Unable to stand the torture any longer, Beck unzipped his fly and let his cock spring into his waiting hand. He hissed in relief as he gripped his shaft and slowly stroked himself.

Instantly, her fingers stilled as she watched with wide eyes, fixated on the bunching of his biceps and the clenching of his fist. She licked her lips.

Fuck. Her innocent response was gutting him. "Don't stop. Let your fingers do the walking and we'll come together."

"But I want to see…" She eased closer to his gliding fist, looking enthralled.

"What you do to me? Every time I'm with you, I get hard. I lie in bed at night, pounding my cock, dreaming of all the ways I want to make you scream. I've been doing that for months. Did you have any idea?"

"No." She sounded both stunned and aroused. "Can I tell you what else I thought about when I touched myself at home?" She dropped her lashes, not in a demure cast, but visually sweeping his body as if she wanted to take in every hard muscle and bulging vein. "You. Exciting you. Touching you. Making you feel as good as you made me feel."

Beck groaned. She was waving a red cape in front of a goddamn raging bull. "The first time I saw you, I was dying to fuck you, little girl."

She blinked at him, her glassy eyes half-lidded and sultry and killing his self-control. "You were?"

"And the urge has only gotten stronger." He stroked his cock faster. The tip grew slicker when her hungry gaze latched onto his dick again. "If you want to touch me, I'm all yours."

Heavenly slid off the bed, giving him a little nudge with a hand to his chest...which she followed with her lips, spreading barely there kisses across his skin. He stumbled back, wondering what the hell she was up to. Not that it stopped the rapid jerk of his hand on his cock or the pounding of his heart.

Then she sighed and fell to her knees at his feet, looking up at him with pleading eyes. "You said I could touch you anytime, anywhere, and any way I wanted. What if I want to pleasure you with my mouth?"

The air in his lungs froze. His knees threatened to buckle. A hot wave charged through his blood. Beck feared he might stroke out.

One of his favorite fantasies was fucking coming true, and all he could do was look down at her, utterly awestruck and slack-jawed, and nod mutely. With a handful of words, she'd annihilated his control.

She dipped her head shyly. "But I want to do it right."

He lifted her chin with his finger, excitement nearly ripping him out of his skin. "I'll teach you. Give me your hand."

Releasing his erection, he took hold of her wrist and lifted her palm to his cock. Heavenly's touch jolted him with a nuclear thrill he almost couldn't process. He sucked in a hiss.

"Now wrap your fingers around me." He laid his own over hers, guiding her to grip his shaft snugly, and groaned. "Grip me tight, little girl. Feel the veins, the heat, and the fluid spilling off the crest. Yeah…"

"You'll tell me if I do it wrong?"

He stroked a hand over her hair. "Yes, but I doubt that's going to happen. This feels incredible."

When she emulated the motion and the rhythm perfectly, he withdrew his hand so she could explore on her own. Immediately, he clenched his teeth as her palm danced up and down his length. His cock jerked.

If she kept this up, he wouldn't fucking last.

"Is this the way you like it?" Uncertainty tinged her soft voice.

"Harder," he choked out.

She did, and he closed his eyes as his whole body melted around her touch. "Fuck, yes."

As she continued to slide her hand up and down his cock, Beck's balls churned and his body hummed. He peered down at her, watching as she gazed in awe at each smooth glide. Jesus, he'd last longer if he controlled her stroke or even looked away. But no, he couldn't tear his gaze from her firm but gentle sweeps up his length.

When had he become such a raging masochist?

"When you're ready, just open your mouth and—"

Even before he finished his sentence, Heavenly parted her lips and swiped her tongue over his leaking crest. Need rocked him like a fucking earthquake. He squeezed his hands into fists and locked his knees.

"It's salty." Her voice lilted with wonder. "I want to do it again. I just open my mouth and…"

He gritted his teeth and managed to nod.

She flicked her tongue over the tip once more, savoring his taste with a little moan. The urge to thread his fingers through her silky mane and thrust himself between her lips drove him insane. He was going to suffer a slow, agonizing death before this lesson was through…but at least he'd go with a smile on his face.

After an audible swallow, she leaned closer, opened her mouth, and wrapped her plump lips around him.

Lightning slid up his spine before slamming deep in his balls. *Jesus...*

She pulled on him once, as if he were the tastiest lollipop, then eased back to gaze at his crown. Heavenly might be inexperienced, but she didn't shy away from sliding her mouth over him again, then flicking the tip with her tongue, nearly fucking unraveling him. Then, when she began bobbing on him and sliding her hand up and down his shaft? Holy shit. His eyes rolled back in his head. Swallowing a roar, Beck sank his fingertips against her scalp and wrapped his fists in her hair, struggling to pull air into his lungs.

"Yes," he hissed. "Deeper into your mouth, little girl. Good. Yeah. Stroke down on my shaft at the same time. Hmm. Stretch the skin tight. Fuck."

She obeyed flawlessly, sucking him over and over while she squeezed him all the way to the stem.

Fighting the raging surge of orgasm headed his way was pointless. It was right there. Beck bellowed for breath and clenched his fingers into fists, desperate to shower her tongue with his seed in three, two...

His doorbell chimed. Heavenly stiffened and lifted from his cock, gazing at him with a startled expression. "Are you expecting anyone?"

"No. Ignore it. Whoever it is will go away," he assured, guiding her head back to his shaft again.

She swirled her tongue around him, then plunged him back into the molten heat of her mouth once more, growing confident and swallowing down another inch.

Their unwanted visitor gave up on the bell and pounded on his door instead.

"Fuck!" Beck released her hair and tapped the video doorbell app on his smart watch. Two impatient cops stood on his porch. "What the hell?"

"What's wrong?" Heavenly eased back on her heels, looking concerned.

"I don't know. The police are here."

"Can you think of a reason why?"

"No, but..." He sighed. "I have to answer this."

"Of course," she murmured as he helped her to her feet.

Grimacing, he tucked his screaming cock into his jeans and slowly drew up his zipper. By the time he'd done that, Heavenly had already donned her undergarments and was sliding her dress back over her head. So not only hadn't he gotten lucky today, he probably wasn't getting an orgasm he didn't give himself.

Fuck.

"Turn around. I'll zip you up."

As she presented him her back and he raised the little metal tab to the top, covering her completely, the pounding grew more urgent.

"Come on." He slid his hand in hers. Together, they hurried down the stairs.

When Beck pulled the front door open, he frowned at the cops' grim faces. "Can I help you, Officers?"

"Yes, sir. We have a report of a death at your residence. We're here to inspect the body."

Beck shook his head. "There's no body here. No death. I live alone, and my girlfriend is just visiting. You must have the wrong address."

That was the only explanation. Logically, Beck knew the cops hadn't interrupted the blow job of the century on purpose, but of all the shitty timing…

"No, this is the right place." The officer recited the address, and it was correct. "We have a report that an elderly man passed away on the premises."

"What? Who?"

"A Dr. Kenneth Beckman. Do you know anyone by that name?"

"*I'm* Dr. Kenneth Beckman, and as you can clearly see, I'm very much alive."

"I'm going to need to see some ID." The more seasoned cop frowned.

As Beck scrambled in his pocket for his wallet and whipped out his driver's license, two EMTs pushing a gurney rushed up behind the policemen.

"Have you examined the body? Need a transport to the morgue?" the younger one asked.

"There's no body," Beck bellowed. "Who the hell reported me dead?"

No one answered. The cop had a low-voiced conversation with his fellow officer, who made a discreet phone call. The EMTs simply stared. Jesus, who had started this colossal screw-up and ruined his day?

A half second later, his cell phone chimed. He yanked the device from his jeans and saw a text from Seth.

`Need the name of a good funeral home?`

Beck closed his eyes. That motherfucker. He'd planned this. He'd ruined the day with Heavenly…why? To needle him? To prove he could? To make sure he didn't have sex with her? Probably all of the above.

He'd been cop-blocked. Beck grunted. The next body in the morgue was going to be Seth's.

The officer handed him his ID back, then gave him a long stare. "We're going to need to check the premises, ask you a few questions. Can I come in?"

"Now? I'm in the middle of a date."

Heavenly laid a gentle hand on his arm. "It's okay. I'll get out of your way and let you straighten this mess out. I have to get to work anyway. I'll see you tomorrow."

Before he could object, she brushed a butterfly-soft kiss over his lips, then stepped out the door. Beck watched her go helplessly, biting back a roar, as the veteran cop trekked over his threshold.

The younger cop asked her a couple of questions. She answered so softly Beck couldn't hear.

The policeman looking to interrogate him closed the door and sent him a long, inscrutable stare. "Stand back. I'll start in the living room. This may take a while."

Now that Heavenly was gone, Beck didn't give a shit if it took all night. It just gave him time to plan how he would repay that son of a bitch, Seth. And he would—in spades.

CHAPTER FIFTEEN

A FUCKING WEEK. That's how long he'd been back from New York and he had yet to lay eyes on Heavenly. Oh, he'd called. No answer. He'd texted, asking to see her over the weekend. Hours later, she'd responded. Of course she missed him and would love to see him, too. But she was busy. She would be for *seven freaking days.*

A week to wonder if Beck was corrupting her.

Her messages explained that she'd either be volunteering at the hospital, attending online classes, waiting tables...or spending time with that goddamn thorn in his side. As soon as Seth had read that, his imagination had begun providing unhelpful images of her being penetrated and pleasured by the fucking sadist.

He'd decided then and there to make sure that didn't happen. And it hadn't taken him long to come up with a plan. A little conversation with an unwitting Raine told him the time and location of Heavenly's next date with Beck. Sending the LAPD's finest to his house for his recently deceased body had filled Seth with a perverse satisfaction. If it had prevented the jackass from making her come again, even better. Oh, to have been a fly on the wall when the cops knocked on the door...

Best of all? He'd gotten away with it. Well, Beck had sent him some blah, blah, blah text because he'd been pissed off. Whatever... But today, Seth was finally getting his chance to spend time alone with Heavenly, and there was nothing Beck could do—except pout and jack off.

Life was sweet. Sometimes Seth amazed himself with his own brilliance.

He checked the clock. Now that Friday afternoon had arrived, Heavenly was finally on her way over. He'd tossed together a little lunch, chilled a bottle of white wine, and tidied up his new apartment.

He was ready. Granted, this place wasn't much more than four walls, but he'd managed to make the one-bedroom livable, also adding passable security and camera surveillance to the front door. It would do until his apartment in Manhattan sold and he could buy in LA. Best of all, it was only a couple of blocks from his new office.

He'd spent the rest of his week opening the West Coast operations for Cooper Investigations. He'd need someone here to help him work cases, man the office when he couldn't be around. River was still looking for work. He and Seth had hit it off during Hammer, Raine, and Liam's recent trials. The dedication the man had shown to clearing Hammer's name and ensuring his sister's happiness had impressed him. So they'd met for lunch and a beer, laughed about bagging Hammer's nemesis—literally—then talked business. River had never done PI work and he'd need to get licensed. His military covert operations background sounded impressive, but Seth needed some proof River had the sleuthing skills and finesse to do the job. After all, there'd be no storming bunkers here. Raine's brother had sworn he'd prove he had what it took. No idea how he'd do that, but the ball was in River's court.

Impatiently, Seth glanced at the clock again, more than ready for this date. If he played his cards right, he might be fixing Heavenly breakfast, too.

Right on time, the doorbell rang. He checked the door cam and saw her standing on his little porch. She looked adorable, wearing a white tank with a black heart, a casual beige coat, and a wine-colored skirt that hung well above her knees. With a broad smile, he strode across the hardwoods to let her in.

She glanced up at him shyly as he framed the doorway. "Hi, Seth."

"Oh, fuck. I've missed you, angel." Two weeks apart had been two weeks too long.

Seth meant to invite her in, let her get comfortable, talk to her until she opened up. Then he'd intended to seduce her. Instead, he lost his head, plucked her off her feet, and claimed her mouth. Instantly, her flavor exploded on his taste buds, the same one he'd branded to memory the night of Hammer's party. Her familiar scent clouded his head as she clung to his neck and wrapped her thighs around his waist. Yeah, she didn't kiss him like a woman invested in another man. The meeting of their lips felt too much like their mouths making love for that.

Long moments later, she broke away, panting. They stared. Maybe for a moment; maybe for an hour. Time had no meaning as he lost himself in the bluest eyes he'd ever seen.

Then she exhaled on a shaky sigh and her stare fell to his lips. Just like that, she pulled him under her spell again.

Seth couldn't resist capturing her mouth once more and parting her lips with his insistent tongue. Groaning, he absently kicked the door shut, then slid his palms down her waist to cradle her perfectly pert ass in his hands. He took giant steps across the room and made it as far as the kitchen island before he eased her down and spread her out. Still standing between her thighs, he traced his fingers up her sensitive sides.

She giggled. "I'm ticklish."

"Yeah?" he taunted.

"Don't…"

He fingered the sides of her breasts instead.

Her laughter stopped. The palpable hunger that always surged between them roared as he seized her mouth again in an incinerating kiss. Every good intention Seth had about feeding Heavenly before he made his move gave way to unyielding urgency. He became aware of only her. Of her restless fingers digging into his shoulders. Of her hips grinding against his stiff cock. Of her sweet wetness dampening the front of her panties. Seth groaned and drank in every morsel of her answering whimper.

Oh, fuck. If he didn't find some self-control, he'd be baring and impaling her in less than thirty seconds.

Gently but insistently, he eased back. He intended to lead her to the table and offer her a drink as he removed the food warming in the oven. Instead, his stare went straight to her smooth, silky thighs and exposed panties, now visible since her skirt had bunched around her hips. The scrap barely covering her pussy was blue-and-white striped with an itty-bitty bow at the top of the little triangle. It looked well-worn, too small, and already soaked.

Seth stared, unblinking, his mouth hanging open like an idiot. *Oh, shit.* He'd probably burn in hell for the twisted, lascivious thoughts storming through his head later, but right now? He was going to enjoy being in heaven. Or rather in Heavenly.

She breathed hard and touched his shoulder. "Seth?"

"Yeah, angel. I'm here. God, you're gorgeous." He finally managed to look away. "Stay where you are, okay?"

"But…where are you going?" She grabbed the hem of her skirt self-consciously and lowered it.

"No, angel," he crooned, easing his fingers under the garment and slowly lifting it up her thighs again until he was staring at those panties straight out of his teenage fantasies. Christ, he had to form coherent words to reassure her. "I'm just going to step right over there." He pointed to his breakfast nook. "I'll be back. Then I'll make you feel so much better."

In two steps, he dragged one of the metal chairs from the table over to the island and seated himself between her legs, then pulled her pretty little ass to the edge of the counter.

She propped herself onto her elbows, her hair pooling around her as she watched him, eyes soft with desire. "What are you doing?"

"I know I promised you lunch, but I'm dying to make a meal of you first."

He didn't give her time to ask the questions he saw on her face before he lifted each of her thighs and laid them over his shoulders.

"Seth…" She sounded slightly shocked.

But she wasn't protesting. Beautiful.

Seth skated his palms up her graceful legs and cupped her thighs as he kissed all her bare skin, hungrily nipping, lapping, and eating his way straight toward her weeping center.

Her breathless pants got faster, more audible, as he outlined the edges of those snug panties with his thumbs, where her thighs met her barely covered cunt and begged him to feast.

"Remember all the dirty things I told you I'd do to you before Christmas? This is definitely one I've thought about. I want you to feel my tongue lap at your juices while I coax more from your little pussy."

She tensed and reached between her thighs with a slim hand, fingers covering the straining fabric of her panties, stained dark with her excitement. "I'm really wet."

"Thank fuck," he growled, nipping at the digits until she lifted her hand away.

Seth didn't hesitate. He simply buried his nose in the nearly sheer cotton and inhaled her potent aroma, letting it fill his nostrils. His cock turned to granite. He tongued his way straight up her center, lingering over her straining clit as it poked her panties.

With a glance up her body, he snared her gaze as the pleasure began to roll over her. Heavenly's eyes were half-closed, her jaw slack, and her cheeks flaming rosy.

Triumph roared within him. "By the time I lap up every drop of your cream, you'll be ready to explode."

"Oh…my goodness."

She was still gasping as he began eating at her through the cotton, prodding her clit and teasing her entrance with his stiff tongue before slipping beneath the elastic to coax more of her juices while he swiped at her heated flesh.

As she began to dissolve around him, he drove her higher. Heavenly writhed, spearing her fingers into his hair and lifting her hips to him in demand. He dove deeper, scraped her cotton-clad clit with his teeth, grinding his tongue against her and dragging her into his lungs. But those fucking panties were teasing him. He could smell her, almost taste her…but not enough. He needed more. He needed the goddamn barrier that kept him from savoring her out of his way.

He gripped the thin strings holding the two threadbare triangles of fabric together with his big hands and yanked. The undergarment gave way without a fight. He tossed it behind him, across the kitchen, and focused all his attention on her perfect peach of a pussy. *Oh, Christ…* It was pretty—swollen, pouting, succulent, and pungent. His mouth watered again. He adjusted his straining cock with a grimace.

"You're staring…there. Is something wrong with me?"

"Oh, Heavenly. No. Hell no. You're beautiful. And I already know you're going to taste like nothing I've ever had on my tongue."

"Why would you think that?"

"Because I'm so attuned to you, angel. I swear, when I'm with you it's like I can feel you, hear your heartbeat… I can't explain it. It just is." He sighed. "I didn't even know I was waiting for you, and now that you're here, I can't imagine me with anyone else."

"Seth…" She wore her heart in her eyes. "I've thought about you so much since I saw you last, since you kissed me."

"I've thought about you, too. I can't seem to stop, just like I can't stop wanting more of you. Open wider for me. I need to lick up all your honey. I need to hear every one of your cries. I need you to tell me what you're feeling. Then, angel, I need you to come for me."

Surprise brightened her face, mingling with the shiver of anticipation that rolled through her beautiful body. "When you say things like that, it turns me inside out."

If you think my words undo you, angel, just wait...

Slowly, Seth lowered his heated mouth to her. She watched him, unblinking and spellbound, as she gripped the edge of the counter for dear life. His stare traveled up her body and he gave her a slow, sly smile. Her whole body tensed.

With their gazes fused, he began to consume her, orally stroking his way up her soft, ripe flesh, tasting, memorizing...melding his tongue to her flesh. God, yes, he'd fantasized about this. And just like his dreams, she yielded sweetly, thighs splaying wider, allowing him to feed his ravenous hunger for her. Her catches of breath goaded him on even more. He nipped at her taut clit, straining for his attention. A teasing lick followed. That didn't satisfy him. He gave in to his Dominant need to conquer, sucking her bud into his mouth savagely, urging her—hell, demanding—she give him all her pleasure.

Heavenly went wild, shaking and shuddering as she moaned and squealed. Every noise was an unintelligible plea or praise that only drove him higher. He had to taste every bit of her, everywhere. Needed more of her dizzying response.

He dipped to her untried entrance, curling his tongue to penetrate her, and stroked deep into her soft, swollen tissue.

"Oh!" She almost jackknifed off the island. "Seth. Please... I need...something."

"I know, angel," he crooned. "I'm going to give it to you."

"But—"

Seth cut her off by ruthlessly tongue-fucking her. She surged against him, her cries bouncing off the walls. Her fingers tangled in his hair, as she pulled and tugged, making his scalp sting. He kept going, shaking his head as he licked up her slit, then filled her clenching core again—lingering, flicking, and unraveling her.

God, he hadn't known how she would react to him devouring her virginal flesh. He'd worried she would be too shy or too shocked or just too…not ready. But Heavenly's uninhibited reaction told him his gut instinct that they'd be sexually compatible had been dead right. Even better, she seemed to be as in tune with this craving to merge and become one as he was.

She almost peaked, but he eased back, danced away. Her mewl of protest had him grinning. He tormented her from a different angle, nibbling at the puffy lips of her sex and flicking a barely there swipe across her clit. Another wail of thwarted need rose from her lips. Fucking music to his ears.

He focused his control, found a dozen ways to spike her pleasure…but he never quite gave her the sustained sensation to climax. Instead, he took his sweet time learning her, figuring out how to take her apart methodically, adapting to whatever made her tense or gasp or cry out in need. Then slowly, he built her up again until her honey flowed over his lips and the involuntary thrust of her hips turned rhythmic against his mouth.

She was close again. Sweet.

Once more, he backed off and he soaked in her frustrated whimpers with a smile.

"No…" She shuddered, pleading. "I can't take it."

He looked up the curves and valleys of her body, waiting until she met his stare. "You can because I want you to. When I let you come, I want to be sure it's so hard, so devastating you won't forget it."

Then he slid his fingers through her wetness, coated them, and dipped his middle finger into her opening, sinking deep. Damn, she gripped him, beyond tight. Thank god. There was no way Beck had seduced her out of her virginity.

Seth eased up, gave her a moment to adjust, to wriggle and roll on his digit, before he slid his little finger into the soft opening of her ass. Shock and sensual torment filled her face at once, driving him harder to send her splintering into a thousand pieces under his touch. She was so fucking gorgeous, so seemingly made for him. He couldn't wait to slide every inch of his stiff, impatient cock deep inside her. To feel her clutch him as she disintegrated around his thrusts and spilled all over his dick.

As he bent his head to her swollen clit and flicked it softly, she squealed. The little bead began to flush and throb. Fuck, how heady, knowing that a mere touch or two had her in this thrall again, on the verge of begging him to pleasure her in any way he wanted simply so he'd give her the satisfaction he'd made her crave.

"Ready to explode for me, angel?" he taunted.

She clutched his hair and gyrated against his mouth. "Oh, yes. Please. Please, Seth…"

Her sweet cries, the heat and tightness of her body clutching his fingers, her scent so strong it made him drunk—all took him to the brink of his control.

With his free hand, Seth dug a condom from his jeans, then attacked his fly before he slid the denim down enough to kick his pants somewhere near her discarded underwear. Despite how frantic he'd been to free his cock, he never stopped fingering her slick openings or teasing her taut nub. Not too hard. Not too fast. No, he made her ride his touch, forcing her to stretch for the orgasm he dangled just out of her reach.

She was incoherent now, her gasps mingling with her rising wails as he lured her closer to the cataclysmic end. Climax was right there; everything about her body told him so. Another lick, another nudge, and she'd tumble over. And fuck if it wasn't going to be the sweetest thing ever. His heart chugged. His cock jerked. He was so ready…

The doorbell pealed, shattering the moment.

Heavenly stilled, stare zipping toward his door. "Someone's here?"

"It's no one. Ignore it." He wasn't stopping, damn it.

But the doorbell only rang again, strident and insistent, jarring his fucking concentration. With a curse, he swiveled his stare to his phone, sitting on the charging stand on a nearby counter, flashing a clear view of the front door.

Seth blinked, frowned, backed away from Heavenly to peer closer at the device. He couldn't possibly be seeing that right.

"What is it?" She sounded drunk and dazed.

"I'm not sure. Stay right there. I'll only be a minute."

He rose and wiped his face with a paper towel, then grabbed his gun from the holster where it hung on the nearby wall and slipped to the front door, turning the lock. He cracked it open just enough to peek around the portal.

What the hell? His camera hadn't lied. Standing on his porch was a woman in her forties dressed like a colorful gypsy and a goddamn donkey. "What the fuck is this?"

She gave him her version of a seductive smile. "Why, I am Zelda, and this is my amazing performing donkey, Clovis."

"Performing?" Did it sing or dance or bray? Seth shook his head. He probably shouldn't ask, but... "What does he perform?"

"Everything your heart desires." The crone leaned in to whisper. "Clovis is well endowed—and well trained. Though today, he is feeling frisky."

When the woman winked his way, it clicked. His mouth fell open. "He's...he's a—"

"My love slave, yes. For your viewing pleasure, he will love me long time. We do show for you now?" She peeked around the corner and caught a flash of his naked ass. "I see you are ready for him to be your love slave, as well. For two hundred more, he will also love you long time, Seth Cooper."

The gasp behind him told him that Heavenly had heard Zelda's nonsense. What the hell must she be thinking?

"Look, I don't know who you are or how you know my name, but I didn't ask you to come here. So you can take your...ass and leave. Right now."

"No." She shook her head excitedly. "We are gift. For you. Where can I lay the rubber sheet so we may begin?" She leaned in to whisper. "Clovis, he is virile...but he is messy."

"What? Oh... No. Fuck no!" Still Zelda didn't move, just blinked. He raised his gun. "Go. Get lost."

The donkey brayed loudly. The woman gasped and backed away. "Wait. Don't shoot! Clovis and I leave."

"You're damn right, you will." He slammed the door and locked it, grabbing his phone from the counter long enough to ensure the gypsy and her four-legged sex act were walking away. Thank god.

When he looked up again, he found Heavenly standing beside his kitchen island, smoothing her skirt, and looking somewhere between self-conscious and shocked. "What was that?"

He grimaced. "Don't ask."

But Heavenly wouldn't let it go. She wrapped her arms about herself and frowned. "Did that woman really mean to…"

"Yeah. Don't think about her, angel." When Seth took a step toward her, she held up a hand and backed away warily. Holy crap, did she actually think he had something to do with this? "I didn't hire her. I'm as shocked as you are. I have no idea who sent that…woman to my door."

He'd think it was a party prank gone wrong, except Zelda had known his name. It made no sense, unless…

Suddenly, the phone in his hand buzzed. He glanced down to find a text from Beck.

Enjoy, fucker. That's the only ass you'll get today.

That fucking son of a bitch. Seth gripped his phone, breathing through his fury and his urge to do violence. So the fucker wanted to play rough? Seth had no problem turning over every goddamn stone to arrange the absolute perfect revenge.

"I think I should go," she muttered.

"Not while you're upset. Sit down. Let's talk." Again, he reached for her.

She wriggled out of his hold. "I'm not upset. I'm frustrated, Seth. My last date with Beck was interrupted by the police looking for a dead body, and now our afternoon together ends before it's barely begun by a… I don't even know what to call something that sick. But it's like I have the worst luck when I'm with you two, and I don't know who would pull such awful pranks…"

Heavenly paused, then sent him a sharp stare of speculation, eyes narrowed.

Oh, shit. Had she figured out that he and Beck had been punking each other? Yep, and judging from the expression on her face, she was not happy.

"I can explain, angel. Let's sit and talk over lunch." He tried to usher her to the bistro table.

"Why? Now that I know who's responsible?" She jerked out of his hold. "I'm leaving. Get out of my way."

"Don't do this… Please. Just listen."

"No. I'm not the one who started this, but I'm the one who's going to end it." When he tried to pull her into his arms and soothe her, the glare she tossed at him was so icy he would have sworn she'd give his balls frostbite. "Don't touch me. Don't try to stop me."

Shit!

"Heavenly..." He dropped his tone to stern and Dominant. "Don't leave angry. We need to sit and talk about this."

"We don't." Her face looked frighteningly blank. "I thought you wanted me, Seth. I thought this—we—were important to you. I was obviously naive and wrong."

Then she shook her head, her face so full of regret as she brushed past him, opened the front door, and walked out.

"Angel!" He darted after her and was just about to chase her outside—when he realized he was still bare-assed. He pulled his T-shirt over his exposed junk and shouted after her. "We are important!"

She didn't even pause, just walked down the stairs and headed for the parking lot. He raced back to where he'd dropped his jeans and struggled into them. But by the time Seth had donned them and made his way outside, Heavenly had vanished completely.

CHAPTER SIXTEEN

"THEY DID WHAT?" Raine frowned, feet propped on a pair of pillows as she lay across the sofa.

Heavenly sighed. "You're not going to make me repeat all that, are you?"

"No, but..." She rolled her eyes. "What idiots. Beck and Seth are acting like candidates for the Darwin Award."

That made Heavenly laugh for the first time since running out on Seth two hours ago. "Exactly. The cops were bad enough, but a donkey that..." She shuddered. "Where did Beck even find something that sick?"

"With him, you never know. It's awful but..." Raine pressed her lips together, mirth all over her face. "I would have paid money to see Seth's face when he opened the door and saw Zelda and her ass standing there."

She found it funny now, especially since Seth hadn't been wearing pants at the time. But she didn't tell Raine that. Honestly, it was hard to focus on anything except the fact that she'd tangled herself up completely in two men who seemed more intent on playing games with each other than spending time with her.

"You'll have to ask him about it. At the moment, I'm not amused."

"Of course you're not." Raine struggled to sit up, then peered across the house and out the back doors. Liam and Hammer were still sitting outside, enjoying the temperate evening. She scooted closer. "Okay, they're not looking. Listen. I know you're upset or you wouldn't have shown up in tears."

"You're supposed to be resting, and I'm sorry to burden you with my problems. Normally, I wouldn't and—"

"Sweetie, we're friends." She took her hand. "I'm here for you. And as it happens, I know a few things about juggling two men."

Heavenly shook her head. "But Liam and Hammer are happy in the relationship. There's no squabbling or strife or—"

Raine burst out laughing. "Oh, my god. Is that what you think?"

"Are you saying they fight?"

"Not so much now, but a few months ago? All-out war. All day, every day. Ugly, ugly, ugly."

"Seriously?" Her jaw dropped. "But they're best friends."

"They were even then…until they weren't. And I was the reason everything changed. They stopped speaking unless it was to call one another names or threaten. One morning, Liam picked me up, carried me out the door, and disappeared for two days, leaving Hammer to wonder where we were and if I was all right."

She gaped at Raine. "Hammer must have been angry."

"Livid. It didn't get any better when Liam asked me to be, um…his while Hammer was away. So when he came back and I was off-limits, that didn't go over well. Of course, Liam also thought Hammer had gotten me pregnant by then. Long story. I'm rambling. But trust me, they fought. Dirty, underhanded, punching each other bloody…yeah."

If anything, Heavenly felt her eyes widen even more. She would never have guessed there'd been anything but harmony in their unusual relationship. "But that morning we met in the hospital—"

"They put it all aside because I needed them."

Because they loved her; that much was clear to Heavenly. The more time she spent around these three, the more obvious it seemed that they belonged together.

Heavenly was happy for her friend, but she wasn't in Raine's situation. "And they need you."

"I think Seth and Beck need you, too." Raine's face softened. "I've known Beck a long, long time. He's always been the big, bad…um, smartass. With you, he's really different. He's tender—and I would *never* have thought him capable of that. You're good for him. I don't know Seth as well, but he always seemed…I don't know, distant. I mean, he's there, but not really *involved*. Like he was always trying to stay slightly removed. But not with you. I saw that kiss he gave you at Hammer's party. He was all-in, and not just physically. When I first met him, he was so terrified of earthquakes that he didn't want to be here at all. Now he doesn't want to leave, and I have to think you're the reason why."

"I appreciate the perspective." Heavenly did, truly. "It's not that I think they don't care. When I'm alone with them, they make me feel special." Not to mention beautiful, sexy, womanly—all the things she'd never had the chance to be. "But I have to stop letting myself be so fascinated by them that I forget to be realistic. I don't have anything to offer them, not even time. And now it seems they're far too interested in playing pranks on one another to focus on anything else, so…"

Across the room, the clearing of a man's throat caught her attention. She and Raine both zipped their stares to the back door. Liam and Hammer stood there, arms crossed, brows raised.

Instantly, Raine scrambled to her back and plopped her feet on the stack of throw pillows. Her smile looked a bit too chipper. "Hi, guys."

"Aren't your feet supposed to *stay* up, lovely?" Liam said the words sweetly enough, but Heavenly heard the steel behind them.

Maybe he was angry. And that was her cue.

"I'm sorry. It's my fault," Heavenly said, rising. "I came to speak to Raine because…" What the heck could she say? The last thing she wanted to do was spill the details of her last two alternately wonderful and humiliating dates to Liam and Hammer. "It's been a pretty awful day. I think I'll just go."

"Because Beck and Seth are being dumbasses?" Hammer asked.

Heavenly blinked at him and nearly choked. "How much did you hear?"

"Oh, we didn't have to hear much to guess they did something stupid." Liam shook his head.

"Wait until you hear what those brainiacs did this time…" Raine began to fill her men in.

Heavenly felt herself turning twenty shades of red. "You don't have to—"

"Yeah, I do. They need to hear this," Raine assured. "Besides, rule number one around this house is we don't keep secrets."

And without waiting for a reply, the woman carried on. The men both grinned when Raine recounted the police looking for a dead body, but when she got to Zelda and Clovis, they burst out laughing.

"And I'm guessing these pranks interrupted something...important," Hammer said more than asked, his voice thick with innuendo.

Heavenly couldn't stop her face from turning even redder and wishing she had a hole to hide in. "The point is, it was supposed to be our time together, and they both promised me the space to date the other until I could make a choice. They didn't respect that. Not that—"

"I think you misunderstand, little one. Can I offer you the male perspective?" Liam sauntered into the living room and sat on the sofa beside Heavenly's chair, lifting Raine's feet into his lap.

Could this get any more mortifying? "Thank you, but I'm not sure it matters."

"Do they matter to you?" Hammer took the other end of the sofa and lifted Raine's head in his lap, stroking her hair. "If they don't, then you're right and feel free to blow them off. But if they do, then there's another point of view here, and we're willing to share."

A dozen thoughts zoomed through her head at once. Her confusion over why Beck and Seth had engaged in these stupid antics. Her embarrassment at having her love life so openly discussed with two men she barely knew. Her conflicting feelings for Beck and Seth with no end in sight. Her pressure-cooker of a life—work, school, Dad's horrifically expensive meds, and how she'd actually pay rent once she bought those. Her bewilderment about why Liam and Hammer wanted to help her. Most of all, she couldn't deny her curiosity. What other perspective could there possibly be?

She sank back to the chair. "They matter. Right now, I'm not even sure why. I'm so angry. They're behaving like children."

"They are," Liam agreed. "But while the battle may indeed seem childish to you, to them it's essential. After all, you're the prize."

"But I'm not a trophy. I'm just a woman who"—she shook her head—"who probably shouldn't have dated two men. I don't know what I'm doing. And I'm not trying to string them along."

"Of course you're not. Nor are you a trophy. That's not why I called you the prize. What they're after is your undivided attention. Your heart. Your love."

Heavenly rolled her eyes. They wanted her "love" so badly they'd staged elaborate hoaxes on each other as a means to prove it? That was the most nonsensical male logic she'd ever heard. "They have a funny way of showing it."

That made Liam laugh. "I can see where you might think that, but the truth is, they're hurting. You've told them both you have feelings for the other?"

She nodded and considered his words again. Beck had seemingly taken the news that she wanted to date Seth well. Had that been an act? Seth hadn't hidden his reaction. He'd simply left. "I've done my best to be honest...but that's been a problem in itself."

"It's a blow to the ego when a woman says she has feelings for another man."

Hammer nodded. "It's not easy for any guy to hear he's not enough."

Heavenly frowned. "I never said—"

"But that's what they heard. Right?" Hammer turned to Liam for confirmation.

"Absolutely. They may have made some ridiculous chest-beating decisions, but never doubt that, to each man, the competition is real and they are battling for their future—their lives—with you."

"What he's trying to say more eloquently than I can is that these two bozos have been busy measuring their dicks. When they figure out—if they haven't already—how fucking stupid they've been, they'll focus again on what's important: you. Trust me, all they're really thinking about is who's going to claim you." He leaned in, peered closer. "Do you know what I mean by that?"

She didn't. "Be my boyfriend? That's the choice I'm making, right?"

"Not even close," Hammer shot back. "They're done questioning their feelings. They're willing to give you their heart—if they haven't already. What they're doing now is fighting to determine who will get to spend the rest of their lives with you and father your children."

Raine patted her distending belly. "What he said. Think about wild animals. Males of the species fight to win and impregnate the female. It sounds silly in this day and age, but some things never change, I swear." She grinned. "I tried to tell these two bucks that I'm not a gazelle, but..."

The rest of their lives? And babies? She blinked. "I don't think they're *that* serious. We've only had a handful of dates and—"

"Oh, they're serious," Liam cut in.

"Very." Hammer nodded.

"They're right," Raine assured. "Beck doesn't date. Like ever."

"Seth is one of my best mates," Liam said. "He hasn't dated in years, either. If they're both taking the time to get to know you, they're definitely serious. Obviously more than you realize."

If they were, why had they wasted time pranking each other? Obviously, she didn't understand men. Heavenly wondered if she ever would. It wasn't as if she'd had a lot of opportunities to try.

"You look confused. You don't understand man logic?" Raine laughed.

"Not…really."

"Don't feel bad. I'm still trying to figure it out myself."

"We're not that complicated," Hammer spouted. "Feed us, get naked for us, and let us put a smile on your face…"

"I always do…" Raine chimed in with a grin.

"At least Seth and Beck seem to be smarter than you and me, Macen. They didn't beat the shit out of each other."

"Yet." Hammer winked.

"God, don't give them ideas," Raine groaned as her phone buzzed.

"I'm curious, little one." Liam focused his attention on her. "You seemed surprised to hear they're so devoted to claiming you. Where did you think your relationship with either—or both—of them was going? How did you see the future?"

Heavenly opened her mouth. He was looking at her expectantly. She wasn't sure what to say. "Well…I, um, don't know. Beck and I had a couple of outings as friends. After Seth kissed me, Beck declared that we were more than friends. We jumped off a bridge together, then…he kissed me, too." She blushed wildly, thinking about what else they did at the restaurant. "Then when he fed me brunch, we were interrupted by the police. And with Seth, we had a lovely picnic. Our second date was aborted because I mentioned my feelings for Beck. Then suddenly, Seth was gone, but he came back and kissed me, which was…" She sighed. *Hot. So hot.* "Lovely. He invited me for lunch, and we got interrupted by a donkey. Nowhere in the middle of that did I hear anything about commitment and love and babies."

A glance up proved that both men were shaking their heads and trying not to laugh. Raine was busy, thumbs tapping rapid-fire into her phone as it buzzed again and again.

"Maybe the better question, then, is what do you want from them?" Liam asked. "A few dates? Or more?"

This wasn't the first time Heavenly had the feeling Liam saw through her. He asked really pointed questions, ones that made her search uncomfortably for answers. "I hadn't thought of it that way. My time with them is an adventure. A fantasy. But the future? My life is so full. Every day it's just…putting one foot in front of the other—studying and turning in papers, volunteering, delivering food for tips, taking care of sick people. There's so much going on that I haven't thought about tomorrow."

"Then you must be feeling like you've been run over by a bloody great locomotive. But I'm telling you now, those two men are tied up in knots over you, girl. It's not a game to them. *You're* not a game."

"Let me ask you some questions." Raine tapped on her screen for the final time, then set her phone on the table. "Pranks aside, do you want to spend more time with Beck and Seth?"

Even if finding a few stolen hours to be with them was nearly impossible, she'd loved every moment with them. "Yes."

"Do you have feelings for them that are more than friendship?"

She thought about them all the time, even when she should be focused on far more practical things. "Yes."

"Do you see yourself falling in love with them?"

Heavenly squirmed under Raine's surprisingly wise stare. "I don't know. I've never been in love. How should I know? But I feel like maybe I'm halfway there. With both of them. And it's so confusing."

"Because you can't pick between them? Do you want one more than the other?"

"No." She swallowed. "I feel terrible about it. They want me to choose, and I've tried. But they both make me feel wonderful but different things. When I try to untangle my feelings, I just end up more lost. And miserable. And guilty. What's wrong with me?"

"I have to sit up for this one." Raine reached out to both Liam and Hammer, who helped her upright in the middle of the sofa.

"For a few minutes," Liam said. "Remember what the doctor told you."

"I'm timing you." Hammer fixed his stare on his watch.

"Guess I'll have to be quick," Raine drawled. "Look, there's nothing wrong with you, doll. I've been where you are. I know what it's like to be convinced I'd be hurting the men I love less if I could just make a damn decision. I even tried. I committed myself to Liam…but that didn't do anything to erase Hammer from my heart. At the time, I was confused and angry with myself and sure they hated me for it. Now, I think everything happened for a reason. No, not everyone in the world is suited to this sort of relationship. But I'm wondering if you three are. Maybe that's why you can't pick."

"And once again, our wee lass proves she's the smart one." Liam grinned. "The way I see it, Heavenly, is you've got two choices and neither will be easy. If you can't see yourself with just one of them, how about both?"

"They can't stand each other."

"They got along well enough before you. Did you know that?" Hammer asked, brow raised.

Really? She couldn't picture that at all. "No."

"It's not impossible they'll remember it…eventually." Liam shrugged. "We did."

Hammer nodded. "And if they don't, we'll be happy to smack their heads together for you."

Would that even matter? She might be able to steal a few more hours with Beck and Seth today or tomorrow, maybe even the day after. But realistically, she was living moment-to-moment and hand-to-mouth while dreading the inevitable fall of the shoe that terrified her every day. Did she have the time or energy to commit to even one man, much less two? Gosh, she was already drowning in responsibility. The thought of taking on more almost had her breaking. She constantly made life-and-death decisions for her father, knowing if she got it wrong it might be fatal. Adding on more responsibility, like husbands or babies… She'd been thinking first love, not a future where her heart tied her down before she ever lived even one day for herself.

"I think…it's not fair for me to be with either one." And saying that out loud was like a blade to her chest.

"Hang on," Hammer said. "I'm sure it feels that way because this is all new and overwhelming to you, but do you understand that you hold all the power? Tell those two boneheads to pull their heads out of their asses and get along. See where you three go from there."

If she didn't already have total and utter responsibility on her shoulders for another human being who needed every moment of her attention and deserved every shred of her devotion, Hammer might be right. If she didn't have dreams and yearnings to see the world and live her life to the fullest, she might agree. But she did. And staying with either was unfair to them both.

Liam leaned in and took her hand. "If you can't be all in with them, perhaps it's best to bow out."

Before she hurt Beck and Seth more. Gosh, Liam really could read her thoughts. It was eerie, but she had the feeling he alone understood.

Hammer turned to him. "What the fuck, man?"

"Liam?" Raine blinked at him as if he'd lost his mind.

"Thank you very much for listening and offering your wisdom. I should go." Heavenly stood, then reached for her friend's hand. "Don't get up on my account. Rest. I'll call you later."

Raine's phone buzzed again. She picked it up and read with great interest. A sneaking suspicion that Raine was up to something swirled in her belly. Then Raine darted a pointed glance to Hammer, obviously trying to silently convey something. When Hammer didn't get it, she turned to Liam, who rose.

Then someone started pounding on the front door.

Heavenly gasped, then turned on Raine. "Please tell me that's not Beck or Seth."

"Okay, it's not Beck *or* Seth." Raine grimaced. "It's both of them. They're worried about you, and you seem so upset. I thought if you talked it out…"

Hammer leaned closer to her. "Meddling again, precious?"

"Helping." Raine turned to Heavenly. "Sorry."

Pressing a hand to her roiling stomach, Heavenly stared. Her friend meant well, and normally Raine would be right…but now that Heavenly realized, regardless of how much she cared for them, that everything between them was impossible, she had no choice.

But she wasn't ready to face them.

Tears burned her eyes. Knowing she had to hurt them now broke her heart into a million pieces.

Liam's footsteps told her he was quickly reaching the front door. She had seconds to prepare some words, try to help Beck and Seth understand that she couldn't be anyone else's caretaker, that she wasn't ready to be anyone's wife or mother. Even asking them to slow down wouldn't alter the fact they wanted something she'd never even fathomed. If she explained all that, they'd probably shower her with more words and effort and caring and everything that wouldn't change reality.

This had to be the end.

"Come on." Hammer helped Raine to her feet. "Let's let these three talk."

Raine squeezed her hand and murmured, "Call me" before they left the room.

Behind Heavenly, Liam opened the door. Voices mumbled low questions. She felt eyes on her and froze. But her thoughts raced. Every cell in her body dreaded what had to come next.

They drew closer. She closed her eyes, tears squeezing from the corners.

Two sets of footsteps ate up the distance between the door and her side. Suddenly, warmth surrounded her. A soft hand cupped her chin, lifting gently but firmly.

"Don't cry, little girl." Beck. He thumbed away the tears that scalded her cheeks.

"We pulled a couple of stupid pranks, angel. We never meant to upset you." Seth took her hand.

"I know. They're not important anymore." And they weren't in the face of everything else. But she couldn't seem to gather the words to say good-bye. She didn't want to. The moment she did…no more flirting or kissing or adventures or first experiences. Worse, no more them.

Her chest bucked with a sob.

"Angel, damn it. Open your eyes."

"We need to see you," Beck added softly.

She bit her lip. Shivered. Their comfort was beautiful and terrible. It twisted her up inside. But those voices compelled her to comply. She couldn't put off the inevitable.

Heavenly blinked, lashes fluttering open, and managed to make it across the room on shaking legs. When they followed, she held up her hands to ward them off. "I need to know… Does what we have mean more to you than a good time? Are either of you planning a future with me?"

"Hell yes." Beck didn't hesitate. "I never meant to make you question that. The donkey didn't have anything to do with you."

Seth frowned. "I want you in my life permanently, angel. I thought I'd made that clear."

So Hammer and Liam had been right. And she'd been too damn naive to see it.

Heavenly wrapped her arms around herself and hung her head. What a fool. That buried the knife deeper in the chest. How could she tell them that she'd finally realized how much they meant to her at the same time she told them she couldn't give them what they needed?

"What future did you see?" Beck asked cautiously, watching her intently and lingering in her personal space, as if afraid to let her get too far away.

That would change soon enough, and it was breaking her heart.

"Today everything is finally clear. I…" She shook her head. "I've loved every minute I've spent with you both. You've opened my eyes, shown me things, made me feel things. Because of you, I've smiled and had something to look forward to. And I wish I had more to give you. But I…" More tears fell. "I don't. I can't. There's no future." Her chest ached, and Heavenly wondered if she'd ever be the same. When Raine had asked her a while ago if she loved them, she hadn't been sure. Now, Heavenly knew the answer. "I have to go."

She whirled for the door, but Beck wrapped his fingers around her elbow and pulled her back to face him. The shock and pain flaring in his dark eyes and across his furrowed brow stabbed her with regret. Gosh, the thought of not seeing his face every day, of not sitting across from him at lunch, of never hearing his laugh or feeling his mouth on hers…

"Wait. I don't know what you think we expect from you, but let's sit down and talk."

"Why do you think there's no future?" Seth demanded. "Talk to us."

She had no explanations left to give them. Telling them about her father, her dire circumstances, her problems, would only mire them down. They might even try to help. They were kind like that. But she didn't need meddling or good intentions. These responsibilities were all hers.

"There's nothing more to say," Heavenly choked out as Seth stuck a fist in her hair and forced her gaze to his. His image blurred through her tears, but there was no way she couldn't see his confusion and hurt. And it gutted her. "I'm sorry."

"Don't say you're sorry. Tell us what's wrong. If you're not upset about the pranks, then what?" he went on. When she didn't answer, determination stamped his face. "I won't just let you leave when you're the reason for everything good in my life. That's why I moved here, started again."

"Y-you moved?" She hadn't realized that, and guilt wracked her even harder. "I thought you'd just come back to help your friends and…"

But he'd returned again after the end of Hammer's troubles. And he had an apartment. Why hadn't she pieced that together?

"I came back this time for you," Seth reiterated. "Whatever you're thinking, I'm not expecting you to do anything to please me except be yourself."

"You can't leave." Beck gripped her shoulders and pulled her against his body. She couldn't not meet his stare. "I need you."

Her heart thudded harder toward its slow, painful death.

"Don't. Please. Just…" More tears fell before she could stop them as she shrugged free. "Let go."

As she ran for the door to leave before she fell apart, Liam stepped into her path. "I've called you a taxi, little one. It's already paid for, and he'll take you wherever you want to go."

She searched his kind face. He really could read her mind, and for once she was grateful. "Thank you."

As Heavenly opened the door, she knew she shouldn't…but she couldn't stop herself from looking over her shoulder at the two men she'd fallen hard for, who stared back at her, their faces utterly destroyed.

"I'm sorry." She choked on her words, on regret.

Then she was gone.

As THE DOOR closed behind Heavenly with a final click, all the air left the room. Beck dropped into the nearest chair and lowered his head into his hands. The guilt he'd been feeling when he'd arrived had given way to shock and devastation. The sound of her voice, cracked and filled with pain… And her fucking tears. Why?

Beside him, Seth slid onto the sofa, looking equally stunned and flattened. "What the hell just happened?"

"I have no idea." Beck shook his head. "If this had nothing to do with the pranks, what did we do?"

Seth just shook his head.

"I'm sorry. Even I didn't see this coming." Liam sauntered into the room. "We were talking, and she seemed all right, if a little perturbed. Then Raine asked her about her feelings. Heavenly loves you, more than she realizes. She said so…but something turned in her head. I don't know what. I do know she's making a mistake and my warning stands. The looming darkness is already tearing her away. If you want her back, you'll have to peel her open now."

Beck whirled on him. "How about you speak English? And how the fuck did you think we'd peel her open after you put her in a goddamn cab and let her get away?"

Seth ignored him and turned to Liam. "What is she hiding?"

"You think that has something to do with why she left us?" Beck demanded.

"Every instinct I have after eight years as a cop tells me yes."

Liam nodded. "If it helps at all, the decision tore her apart. I could feel her agony over the fact that she's not ready for the future. But I can't tell you why."

"Can't?" Seth challenged. "Or won't?"

"It's all the same." Liam gave them a regretful shrug. "I know you've been loath to work together, but I think it's time you compared notes. We'll be upstairs. Help yourself to the scotch in Hammer's office."

"There's scotch in his office, too," Macen called from the top of the stairs. "It's the good Irish shit."

"Raine all right?" Liam murmured as he walked up.

"Upset. She could use you…"

The guys disappeared, and a door in a far corner of the house shut.

Suddenly, Beck was alone with Seth, his questions, and a mountain of regret. Scotch sounded good about now. Numbly, he made his way into Hammer's study, poured a couple of stiff drinks, then returned to find Seth staring at his phone. He set a glass down in front of the PI. "I can't let her go like this, especially if she loves us."

Seth shook his head. "I can't, either. Something is definitely wrong."

Beck frowned. "A lot of things are wrong. How do we start figuring out what she might be hiding?"

Seth lifted his drink and knocked it back in one swallow. "Well, what do we know?"

Beck knew her smile. He knew her scent. He knew how much she liked adventure and new experiences. He knew whatever had caused her to leave them today had crushed her. "Not much. She'll be twenty-three in a couple of weeks. She's a nursing student. She came from Wisconsin. She likes cheese curds and mint chip ice cream."

Seth sighed. "How about something useful? Middle name? Social security number? Place of birth? Something I can search."

Right. Beck backtracked, mentally raking through every conversation he'd ever had with Heavenly. "Nothing. She almost never talked about herself."

Snorting, Seth shook his head. "Every time I asked her questions about herself, she would change the subject or leave."

"Are you shitting me?" He sipped his drink. "What *is* she hiding? What do people usually hide? Lovers? She doesn't have one."

"She doesn't," Seth agreed. "Crimes, but she seems wholly incapable of breaking the law. I don't think she's a missing person or in witness protection. Did she ever mention her parents?"

"Only that she hadn't seen her mother in years and she didn't have any siblings." Beck sighed. "Don't you know anything about her? You're a PI."

"I dated her; I didn't investigate her. And I'm coming to realize that you two talked way more."

Now wasn't the time to worry about what Seth had been doing to Heavenly if they hadn't been talking. "Do you know where she lives? She never would let me pick her up for a date."

"Same. Do you know where she's waitressing?"

"Some kids' pizza place."

"That's basically what she told me, too," Seth said. "Know which one? Must be more than a couple in LA."

Probably dozens. Fuck. She'd wanted privacy, and he'd respected that. Now he felt like an idiot. "No idea."

Seth cursed. "Does she have any friends at the hospital she might have confided in?"

"None. Raine is probably the best friend she has, and if the princess knew something important she would have told us by now."

"You're right." Seth gouged his thumb and forefinger into his eyes. "This is supposed to be my job, and I'm so fucking shell-shocked, it's like I can't move."

"Me, too." Beck sighed. "I can try talking Nurse Lewis into letting me see Heavenly's records. All volunteers have to fill out paperwork and undergo a background check."

"Do that. I'll run a few searches with the information I've got. I can also follow her, see where she leads me…" He lifted his head and speared Beck with a glance. "If we don't figure out what she's hiding, how can we ease her fears about the future? We don't know what they are."

"We can't. Obviously, we were too distracted by our dicks to ask important questions."

"She didn't just distract my dick; she distracted all of me—my head, my heart…"

Beck nodded. "I don't know about you, but for me, part of her allure was her innocence. I started with good intentions, took everything so slow. Then I was afraid I'd lose her. I got caught up in the competition. And I lost sight of how quickly her inexperience might overwhelm her."

"I didn't even consider that. I just dove in." Seth sighed. "The one thing we should have learned from helping Hammer and Liam with Raine was to put Heavenly's feelings first."

"Right. Did you know what they were until today? I sure didn't."

"No. All her feelings seemed obvious when she was with me, especially when I kissed her. At least I thought so…"

"Exactly. She feels something for us or she wouldn't have left in tears."

"People don't get upset when it doesn't matter," Seth agreed. "You know, we probably wouldn't be here if we'd acted less like jealous punks and more like Doms."

"Yeah." Beck nodded. "We need to share information going forward. If I learn anything from Bridget, I'll let you know. If you find something useful, call me. Deal?"

"Deal." He sighed, staring into his empty tumbler. "What a shitty day. It started so well, then…" He frowned and turned to Beck. "Where the fuck did you find Zelda and the sex donkey? Christ, man… Tell me she was a joke."

Despite everything, Beck had to smile. "She's for real, at least according to Pike."

"You got her number from him? Now I'm really glad I punched that asshole."

"You and me both. Actually, I wanted to high-five you for that. He deserved what you gave him."

"Thanks."

Silence fell. Beck stood. Was there anything left to say? "I guess…I'll talk to you later."

Seth set his glass aside and got to his feet, then headed for the door. "Later."

CHAPTER SEVENTEEN

I F THE WEEKEND without Beck and Seth had been miserable, coming to the hospital on Monday morning had been even worse. She was exhausted. After a double shift at Bazookas and insomnia last night, followed by her father's well-meaning questions this morning, Heavenly felt as if every ounce of energy and happiness had been wrung from her boneless body. She'd done the right thing in letting them go. But returning to her bleak, empty world after they'd shown her romance and awakened the woman inside her was annihilating her. With them, she'd crossed boundaries, been brave, felt more excitement than she'd ever dared to imagine. She'd actually had something besides duty to live for.

Now it was all gone. Everything was gray again.

Would being committed to them be so terrible? the devil on her shoulder asked.

After all, look at Raine.

Heavenly closed her eyes and sighed. Yes, the woman seemed happy and loved…but she was in charge of a house, responsible for two men…and soon twins. At the idea of adding all of that on top of her father, fear gripped Heavenly's throat. Insecurity nipped at her heels, too. Raine made managing it all look so simple. But Heavenly wasn't Raine. How would she ever please two men who had decades of experience when she had none? She'd said yes to dating them, thinking she'd have some adventure, show some gumption. What was the harm in that?

What an idiot.

And the closer the clock crept toward the lunch hour, the more dread filled her. Beck had texted minutes ago, asking if she was coming to the cafeteria. It had crushed her to send back a simple No.

Suddenly, Kathryn was beside her with prying eyes, forcing her to hold in miserable tears. "What's the matter? Did your love boat with Dr. Beckman hit an iceberg?"

Heavenly bit back a nasty retort. Her father had raised her not to say anything at all if she had nothing nice to say. "Did you need something, Nurse Hitch?"

"Deliver this note to the chaplain." The brunette shoved an envelope in her hands.

Thirty minutes later, Heavenly returned, glad to have had even a few moments away from that sow. But now that she had only busywork to do, heartbreak was setting in again.

Behind her, the double doors opened. She turned—and almost fell apart when she saw Beck coming straight toward her, tray of steaming food in hand.

Her knees buckled. Her heart stopped. Even though she'd left him with almost no explanation, he was bringing her lunch?

He handed her the plate. She took it with numb fingers, aching to touch him instead. "What's this?"

"No matter what, I'm going to make sure you eat." Beck scanned her face, gaze drilling down into her. "I see you're not sleeping."

After thinking about him for days, being so close yet so far away now was hard, but his unexpected caring ripped her chest wide open. "You're not, either."

It was obvious. His red-rimmed eyes and sunken cheeks told her he was suffering. Gosh, the guilt... She'd suspected she had hurt him, but seeing the pain she'd caused undid her.

"I can't. Every time I close my eyes, all I see is you."

She wished he'd stop talking almost as much as she wished he wouldn't. His hoarse confession was an awful, sweet agony. But she had nothing to give him, so the worst thing she could do now was leave him with hope.

"Thank you, but you don't have to worry about me anymore. Please take care of yourself." Not touching him felt foreign, and it was a good thing her hands were full or she would have been weak.

"You're welcome, but I'm not letting you walk out of my life for good unless you look me in the eye and tell me you don't love me."

His words punched through her chest and squeezed her heart. Her knees almost gave way. Silently, she pleaded with him not to make such a demand. Beck only leaned closer, his stare like a crowbar.

An orderly brushed by them, followed by one of the interns reading the tablet in her hands. Kathryn strolled past with a sniff, on her way to her locker, probably to retrieve her purse for lunch. Jennifer and Marcella followed, obviously more than a little curious.

Heavenly closed her eyes. Her voice shook. "Don't make me lie to you."

"Then don't," he growled. "Tell me what's going on."

She scrambled for something to say. Nothing came to mind, and she braced herself to endure the terrible lash of his frustration.

The phone at his side trilled, saving her. He cursed, then ripped the device from its clip and glared. As soon as he scanned the screen, his head popped up. "Wait here."

Now he was angry. She saw the fury all over his face, heard it in the warning of his tone. "All right."

With a nod, he spun around and charged for the security door between the waiting room and the unit. With a swipe of his badge and a shove against the handle, the portal flew open.

Then Seth walked in. Why was he *here*? Heavenly sucked in a breath. Their gazes met and locked. He looked a little rough, like he hadn't shaved or slept. But he also looked determined.

Her heart tilted, nearly skidding to a stop.

"Are you sure?" Beck asked beside him.

Seth held up his phone. "This look right?"

Beck grabbed the device and studied the screen, then gave Seth a decisive nod. And a dark smile. "Absolutely. Do I need to loop anyone in?"

"All done." Seth sounded supremely satisfied.

What on earth were they talking about? She watched them both stride by, blinking after them.

"Hi, angel." Seth nodded her way. "I've missed you."

She'd missed him, too. Terribly. Like there was a hole not only in her heart but her life.

"Eat something," Beck demanded.

Then they disappeared together around the corner, heading for the supply room that held the nurses' lockers.

Okay, this was just getting weirder.

Slowly, Heavenly settled the tray on the counter beside her, grabbed the apple off her plate, and followed.

To her shock, Beck appeared once more, striding back toward her with an unexpected grin. He wrapped his hand around her elbow, his eyes gleaming. "Stand here and listen. You'll like this."

Heavenly leaned around to glance into the supply room, see who was inside. She caught sight of something really unexpected and gaped. "Why are Seth and Kathryn—"

"Shh."

Jennifer and Marcella dashed into the hall, purses over their shoulders, glancing behind them as Seth, now smiling at Kathryn, sauntered her way and kicked the door half-closed.

"Well, hello there." Seth's drawl sounded surprisingly seductive.

He'd spoken in that same voice the night of Raine's holiday party, when he'd whispered all those deliciously naughty suggestions in her ear and made her shiver. Why would he talk to Kathryn that way?

"Hello yourself, hottie," Kathryn cooed. "You don't work here. I would have noticed you. Got a name?"

"Seth." He chuckled. "I'm just here for the afternoon. The hospital hired me to check the security in the unit, eliminate any vulnerabilities in the employee locker area."

"Really?" Kathryn sounded surprised. "We don't have a problem."

"They tell me one of the lockers has been tampered with."

Suddenly, Heavenly understood. She turned to Beck with a wide-eyed whisper. "He's trying to get her to confess?"

"Just wait."

"That's a rumor," Kathryn dismissed Seth's reply. "I heard it, of course. I know everything around here, but there's no proof."

"Huh. Well, if it's nothing, maybe you could help me. A sweet thing like you must be trustworthy. After all, you can't be that sexy for nothing."

"You think I'm sexy?" Kathryn purred.

Heavenly pictured the woman batting her lashes and rubbing against Seth. Her whole body tensed.

"Mmm," Seth moaned. "Absolutely, baby."

Suddenly, Heavenly felt Beck wrap his palms around her fists. She was shocked to find them clenched, her nails biting into her skin, as fury pinged through her system.

Gently, he unfurled her fingers. "Easy, kitten. Pull your claws in."

How could she? Every word Seth spoke was downright painful, even if he was manipulating Kathryn for a good cause.

Beck squeezed her hand. "Trust me, he's no more interested in that bitch than I am."

"Well, flattery will get you everywhere." Kathryn's flirty laugh set Heavenly's teeth on edge again. "How can I help you, stud?"

"That's very kind of you, Nurse… I didn't catch your name." Seth's drawl sounded low, almost intimate.

Another pang threatened to cave in Heavenly's chest. She'd let him go, so she had to accept that, someday—probably soon—he'd move on. Even if this performance was for show, it was killing her.

"Kathryn Hitch, but you can call me Kat." She dropped her voice to a throaty murmur. "I love to scratch my nails down a strong, sturdy back like yours."

Did the woman think that was flirting?

"Do you, now? Well, maybe you'll help me so I can get my work done quicker. The sooner I do, the sooner I can persuade you to show me exactly how you earned your nickname. What do you say?"

"I'd love to." There was Kathryn's grating laugh again. "What do you have to do?"

Heavenly heard the rustling of paper before Seth spoke again. "I'll check out these two lockers over here. This one is yours, right?"

"Yes."

"So, it's fine. Can you look into this one for me?"

"Heavenly's?"

"Yeah. According to this report, she indicated she's had some problems."

"Of course she's said that." Heavenly could all but hear the roll of Kathryn's eyes in her voice. "That mousy, pathetic half-wit is so desperate for attention that she's willing to make up ridiculous lies. I'm in here every day, so I know her tears about this are fake. I'm sure a smart guy like you has encountered her type. She constantly flirts with men because she's hoping one will fall for her annoying, sweet-little-girl act." Kathryn made retching noises. "Trust me, she's a helpless, hopeless hot mess."

It took all of Heavenly's self-control not to race into the locker room and slap the nasty heifer. But she wouldn't stoop to Kathryn's level. Instead, she bit back her distaste—and a scream.

Beck caressed her shoulders. "Don't let her get to you, little girl. Don't give her that power."

His reassurance nearly unraveled her. Heavenly wanted to wrap herself in his arms and melt into his safe, familiar embrace. But she couldn't take advantage of him like that.

"I know exactly the sort you mean," Seth assured. "No wonder you're not friends with her."

"I wouldn't lower myself," Kathryn spat. "She's a waste of time—mine and yours. Listen, why don't we forget about the wretch's locker? You and I can go grab some lunch. After all, a big, strong man like you should keep his strength up, especially for what I have in mind. I know someplace private we can go so I can rock your world."

Heavenly felt her jaw drop. "Is she for real?" Then she turned to Beck. "Does that actually work?"

He scoffed. "Not on me."

"Oh, baby. Do you need a real man to pay proper attention to that soft little kitty of yours?" Heavenly heard the megawatt charm in Seth's voice.

"Oh, I'm going to be sick," Heavenly muttered under her breath.

"My kitty loves to be petted." Kathryn giggled. "And I'll bet you know how to stroke me just right."

Beck grimaced. "I'm going to be sick, too."

Seth chuckled. "I think you're trying to distract me, baby."

"Why would I do that?" Kathryn asked coyly.

"You tell me." Seth's tone suddenly took on a hard edge she didn't recognize.

No one else had stepped into the room, so that must be Seth's voice...but she'd never heard him use that much force or command when he spoke.

At the sound of it, a tremor skittered through Heavenly.

"Your voice is manly," Kathryn swooned. "It makes me...wet."

"Is that right? Then let's hurry this along," Seth murmured, his voice turning inviting once again. "Open that locker."

"Technically, I can't. It's against hospital rules."

"It's all right. It's not like you're breaking in. I'm giving you permission."

"Really?" She sounded intrigued. "Did they give you the combination? I mean, I'd need that. I don't know it. Of course."

He chuckled. "Oh, you're too smart to let something as silly as a few numbers get in the way of getting into that stupid girl's locker. You're better than her, after all."

"I-I shouldn't."

"Do it," Seth whispered. "For me... Did I mention I have a really talented tongue?"

Heavenly cringed. That shouldn't hurt, but it did. "I can't listen anymore."

Beck gripped her shoulders and made her look him in the eye. "Stay strong."

She wanted to...but she remembered Seth's amazing tongue all over her most sensitive flesh. Gosh, she couldn't forget it any more than she could forget Beck's hands on her. Or either of their mouths hungrily devouring her own...

Suddenly, Bridget Lewis appeared and eased in close to Beck, who placed a finger over his lips for silence. The no-nonsense nursing administrator nodded, then sent Heavenly a reassuring smile before listening to the nauseating drama.

"Now you really have my attention..." Kathryn perked up.

"All you have to do to find out for yourself is spin three little numbers on that girl's combination and open one itty-bitty door." Now Seth sounded cocky. "You know you want to... In case you were worried, I'm told any potential triggers on the locker doors have already been disabled."

"Oh?" Kathryn giggled. "And you won't tell?"

"Why would I? Hell, I might even applaud you."

Heavenly listened intently. After a pause, she heard a soft ting of metal, indicating that she'd opened the locker door. So that bitch *had* somehow gotten her combination? A wet, squishy splash that Heavenly didn't understand followed. Then Kathryn let out an ear-piercing scream.

"Oh, my god! Oh, my... What happened? You told me the locker was disabled!"

"Oops." Seth laughed.

"You fucking liar!"

"But at least I'm a good one. I can spot a bad liar from miles away, and you're the worst." Suddenly, his voice dropped again, turning cold and unforgiving. "You've been terrorizing Heavenly."

That accusing growl peppered goose bumps all over her body.

"You're blaming *me*?" Kathryn screeched. "How dare you?"

"How dare you harass and threaten her?"

"You have no proof."

"Wanna bet?"

"I'm reporting you to security."

"Please do. In fact, call them now. I'll wait until they get here. Then I'll tell them you opened a volunteer's locker without permission."

"You can't prove that."

"Actually, I can. I have the video evidence on my phone."

Heavenly sent Beck a shocked stare. "How did he get that?"

"Seth and I planted a recording device in your locker two weeks ago, with Nurse Lewis's permission. Kathryn needed to be stopped. It was the only way we could catch her in the act."

"You and Seth?" *Worked together...for me?*

Something dangerous fluttered in her chest.

A pained expression lined Beck's face as he dragged a knuckle down her cheek. "Don't you know we'd do anything for you, little girl?"

"Are you a cop?" Kathryn gasped.

"No. I'm your worst nightmare. You played games with the wrong woman. I'm going to make sure you pay."

With an indignant howl, Kathryn ran out of the supply room, wiping away dark red liquid—was that blood?—from her eyes. Heavenly gasped and snapped a glance at Beck, who laughed at Kathryn.

"Stop right there, Nurse Hitch," Bridget Lewis barked.

"Help. Look what's happened to me!" Kathryn demanded as she sent Bridget a pleading stare. "I've given four good years to this hospital and I don't deserve to have tainted blood all over my—"

"You bullied a volunteer who did absolutely nothing to you. That's not acceptable." Nurse Lewis turned to the security guards. "Walk with me while she gathers her things, then escort her to the door."

"The door?" Kathryn screeched.

"Yes, Nurse Hitch. You're fired." Bridget dismissed her and headed toward the lockers.

Beck gave Kathryn a mocking little clap.

She turned a seething glare on him. "You're in on this?"

"You bet your ass I am. Couldn't happen to anyone more deserving."

Kathryn narrowed her eyes, glaring at Beck with malice. Heavenly almost stepped back at the pure hate in her expression.

"You set me up just because you wanted to protect your girlfriend's tender little feelings?"

"Actually, you've been miserable to almost everyone in your unit, Nurse Bitch. Or rather, Hitch. But you've been especially awful to Heavenly."

Seth stepped out of the locker area with a broad smile and twinkling eyes. "Hi again, angel." Heavenly's heart skipped as he quickly ate up the distance between them, then turned to Kathryn. "*We* set you up because *you're* a helpless, hopeless, hot mess who's desperate for attention. Well, you got it. Enjoy."

As the security guards led a sputtering Kathryn away, Beck grinned, raising his palm in the air at Seth. "Way to go, man. We got her."

Seth grinned, high-fiving him. "Hell yes, we did!"

Heavenly watched, dumbfounded. They were still taking care of her, despite…everything. Because they still cared. She had the strongest urge to rush to their arms and pepper their mouths with kisses.

She didn't.

"Thank you. Both of you," she said instead. "This means more to me than you know."

Before she gave in to her urges, she retreated to the nurses' desk alone.

HUMP DAY. MORE like humped day. It had been another awful one.

Heavenly hated being down all the flipping time. But every morning her alarm went off, her reality was still the same. Her father was weaker, her schedule was overwhelming, her wallet was empty…and her life felt beyond meaningless without Beck and Seth.

Oh, they tried to engage her every day. Beck still brought her lunch and did his best to coax her into conversation. Seth showed up at the end of her shift and walked her from the hospital to the bus, talking to her about anything and everything—how much he missed her, the fact his new business was surprisingly busy, that he still found California weather baffling. He smiled, flirted, charmed.

To be honest, they were wearing her down.

Damn it, she was trying to be noble. Why did it have to be so hard and hurt so much?

There was one bright spot in her life. It had been eight glorious workdays since Kathryn had been fired. The look on that hag's face when Nurse Lewis had escorted her to her locker for the final time, then walked her out the door had been sweet. Heavenly hated to relish in anyone's misfortune, but Kathryn had gotten what she deserved.

Since her dismissal, the ER had been blissfully peaceful. Even Marcella had been nicer. And instead of Heavenly being worried about placating Kathryn in order to get a decent recommendation after graduating from nursing school, Nurse Lewis had all but assured her that she had a job if she wanted one.

It was a relief.

Too bad graduation wasn't coming anytime soon.

With a sigh, she stepped off the bus, avoiding a twitching man who looked wild-eyed and picked at his pockmarked face as she dashed toward the pharmacy. Thankfully, the first official day of spring was tomorrow and she had a bit more sunshine to walk with every day. The trek to this discount location was necessary…but had been a little scary during the dark winter months.

Heavenly waved at the camera, and they buzzed her through the barred door without incident as she clutched her purse. It held exactly three hundred twelve dollars. Once she left here, she'd have eleven dollars and some change to feed her and her father for the week, but he would have his life-saving meds. Nothing else mattered. At least not for nine days. That's how long she'd have to come up with the rest of the rent. It was a tall order, but she'd learned to flirt better at Bazookas. Tips were slowly improving. It would be all right.

There was a line at the pharmacy, and the wait took longer than expected. Finally, she reached the counter and smiled at the tech, who nodded and reached into the bin for her father's meds.

He glanced at the invoice stapled to the cluster of bags. "That will be eight hundred four dollars and seven cents."

She froze. "There must be a mistake. It's always three hundred dollars and twelve cents."

It couldn't be more than that or she'd have to dip into her already depleted rent stash to afford it. And then where would the money to put a roof over their heads come from?

The fifty-something man shrugged and pointed. "This one isn't covered by your insurance anymore. And this one had a price increase as of March first."

He handed her the invoice. She looked down at the numbers. The bold black digits swam in her eyes. But the damning facts blared at her in black and white.

The cost of her living had just increased by twenty-five percent without warning, and she had no way to pay for it.

She tried not to cry. Where would she come up with another five hundred a month? Would she have to resort to stripping? Prostitution? She was already eating as little as possible and had whittled their living expenses down to nothing. It was impossible to find a cheaper apartment. She'd looked, especially after Mr. Sanchez had hit on her.

Heavenly swallowed. Panic encroached. The man behind the counter was staring. She didn't know what to do.

Blinking, she forced herself to look at the numbers again. "I-I'll take these two today and come back for the others tomorrow."

"Sure." He rang them up and took her money as if he wasn't completely terrifying her. As if he wasn't forcing her into an awful position.

She hadn't even managed to wrest control of her trembling hands and get her change into her wallet before the tech was leaning around her and helping the elderly gentleman just behind.

After picking up the meds, Heavenly stumbled out into the last of the March sun. She gulped in brisk air, trying to find calm, doing her best not to crumble and fall.

Why the hell was she so alone in the world? Because she had no siblings to share the responsibility. No aunts or uncles or cousins to help her carry the load. Because her own mother hadn't loved either of them enough to stay and bear the responsibility.

It had taught her a valuable lesson.

Beck and Seth care, maybe even love you. They vanquished Kathryn for you…

She bit back a sob. Yes, she could just picture going to them and begging for forgiveness one minute…and money the next. She'd look disingenuous, gold-digging, and heartless. They might have contempt. They might even hate her.

There had to be a different way. She'd figure it out, get creative. There were other opportunities to make money, right? Maybe she could talk to Nurse Lewis about cutting back her hours at the hospital for a few months…but she couldn't until May. Her nursing school gave her class credits for volunteering thirty hours a week. She'd graduate faster and spend less money on tuition by getting this valuable experience now.

The world is a hard place, and I'm not staying when it's only going to get harder. Take care, kid…

Heavenly pressed a hand to her chest and shoved back the final words her mother had uttered to her before waving good-bye and driving off for good.

Letting out a shaky breath, she reviewed her options as she made her way to the bus and slid into an empty seat on numb legs. She stared sightlessly out the window as she reviewed the facts. One, she had enough money for everything except the rent. Two, if she didn't have her father to worry about, she would go homeless until she could scrape together more funds, but she couldn't have a man as sick as him on the streets, and she wasn't naive enough to think she could show up at the VA hospital, sob story in hand, and convince them to admit her father until she found someplace else to live. Three, Mr. Sanchez had given her a way to pay the rent.

She just had to be brave enough to give him what he wanted.

Heavenly closed her eyes. Was she really going to have sex with her landlord?

Wasn't it a small price to pay to keep her father safe, warm, comfortable, and happy?

Yes.

But she'd be damned if she'd sacrifice her dignity *and* her virginity to that man. He would not be her first sexual partner. She had so little control over anything in her life, but by damned, she could control this. Beck and Seth had shown her it could be good. She didn't want her first memory of intimacy to be so bad.

Gosh, she'd give anything to choose one—or both—of them to be her first. At the thought, she laughed out loud. Several people on the bus stared at her as if they worried she'd come unhinged. Obviously, she had. What a lovely, ridiculous fantasy.

What a waste of energy to ache for something that couldn't possibly happen. She loved them too much to give them hope, only to walk away again.

So…she would have to think of someone not hideous to break her hymen. Someone she would be safe with. Someone who would be kind. Someone who would do his best to make it all right. Someone who didn't care why she was having sex with him and wouldn't ask too many questions. Her choices were limited.

Dr. Manning had given her a very wide berth since Beck had stepped in on her behalf, thank goodness. She barely knew anyone else at the hospital. She'd had a few friendly conversations with one of the new interns who was both gay and newly married. Sure, she could pick a random customer at Bazookas. At least one hit on her every shift. But she'd be a piece of ass to them. It would still feel cheap. If she was going to do something that meaningless, why not just sleep with Sanchez?

The only other people she knew in LA, she'd met through Raine. As soon as that realization streaked through her brain, the choice became obvious: River. He was still looking for a job. He had time on his hands. He liked women—a lot, from what she'd heard. He wouldn't mind doing her a favor, right?

Gosh, she hoped not. She didn't have many options, but she'd visit him tomorrow and find out.

CHAPTER EIGHTEEN

Thursday, March 30 (again)

SETH STOOD ON the back deck at Hammer, Liam, and Raine's house, sipping beer. A few friends from Shadows lurked nearby, laughing. He didn't feel like joining in. He glanced at his phone. Heavenly still wasn't here. She would come to her own birthday party, right? She wouldn't let Raine down simply to avoid him and Beck.

He hoped not.

Suddenly, the doctor strolled up beside him. "Anything new?"

Seth shook his head. "Nothing beyond what I've told you."

His search hadn't netted much information. He'd been able to uncover Heavenly's birth certificate, some high school records, and previous addresses in Wisconsin. None of that told him jack shit. After narrowing his focus to the LA area, he'd found even less. It was like tracking a ghost. She had no California driver's license, bank account, credit cards, not even a fucking address anywhere on record.

He'd know more about her if he could follow her bus in LA traffic, but that had proven to be a bitch. Sure, he knew the route, just not where Heavenly got off. If he knew the city better, he'd wait at different stops on different days. In New York, he'd have already discerned hers and gotten a feel for her neighborhood. LA didn't work the same. Still, what kind of PI couldn't follow one woman home?

"Any luck with Nurse Lewis?"

"No." Beck sighed. "I've tried three times, this last time with chocolate and charm."

Seth slanted a glance his way. "You're not charming."

"Obviously not, since she won't let me see that file."

"Damn it. Is Heavenly talking to you at all?"

"Nope. I'm still taking her lunch, but she's not saying anything more than 'thank you.'"

"I'm getting the polite routine, too." He hesitated. "Is she eating?"

"I'm not sure," Beck admitted. "I'm busying myself with post-op visits and office appointments after I take her tray. The last place I want to sit by myself is the cafeteria. But if I had to guess, not much."

"She's lost weight." It was obvious. "There's something more going on with her. I can tell. I can feel it. The last week or so, she's been…"

"Pale. Withdrawn. Jumpy. I've noticed."

"And sad." Seth shook his head. "No, more than that. She's growing more fucking despondent every day."

Hell, she wasn't even giving him a muted smile anymore. Just one unguarded moment, a stare that reminded him of their instant, jolting connection. Then she'd bow her head and look away. It fucking shredded his heart. How could she visually cling to him, then simply blink and disengage?

Beck nodded. "Exactly. I don't know why. It's not Kathryn. It's not even the rest of the slut squad. After their ringleader got canned, I hear they've been on their best behavior."

"This feels like way more than petty work shit. Do you think whatever's troubling Heavenly is the reason she suddenly left us?"

Liam had warned them over a month ago to "peel her open fast." They hadn't succeeded, hadn't even come close. He had a bad feeling that the looming darkness shrouding her with trouble had already come.

"I don't have a fucking clue and I wish I did." Beck sipped his beer, too. "Any idea what you're going to say to her tonight? This might be our last chance, you know?"

Oh, Seth was well aware of that. She was like sand slipping through his grasp, and no matter how tightly he tried to hold on, she kept falling right between the cracks of his fingers.

"I've already tried so many tactics. Small talk gets me nowhere, and she doesn't respond to confrontation. She just shuts down. What about you?"

"Same." He raked a frustrated hand through his hair. "She trusts me. I think she trusts you, too. But only to a point. She's closed off."

"Yep. And I have to wonder…" Seth sighed. "If whatever caused her to put up barriers is the reason she thinks she can't have a future with either of us, despite her obvious feelings."

"I don't know. But we can't let this party end before we figure it out."

"Amen. First, we have to find her."

A flash of golden hair caught Seth's eye through the kitchen window. He leaned left for a better view, eyes narrowing. There was Heavenly. Finally.

She and River were deep in conversation. It didn't look like party chatter. In fact, she looked decidedly uncomfortable as she sipped her wine. River pressed closer, got in her face.

What the hell?

"Are you seeing this?" Seth elbowed Beck, then pointed to the window.

The doctor turned his head and froze. Silently, they watched Heavenly's brow wrinkle as she tried to back away. River wasn't having it.

"Enough to know I'm ending that fucking conversation." Beck made a beeline for the patio door.

"Damn straight." Seth was right beside him as they filed into the kitchen, shoulder-to-shoulder.

"Sweetheart, you don't know squat about satisfaction," River began. "Here's what I think happened. You haven't so much as flirted with another man. You don't understand why 'lovely' sex is bad because you've never had it. In fact, not only did you not have sex with this mysterious 'stud,' you haven't offered the virginity you asked me to take to anyone else."

A visceral, hot rage pinged through Seth. Heavenly had asked River Kendall to take her virginity? When? And fucking why? Seth was more than willing. Beck, too.

Beside him, the doctor stiffened. "What. The fuck. Did you say?"

"Get out," Seth snapped at River. It didn't matter that Raine's brother obviously hadn't followed through on Heavenly's offer. He still wanted to strangle the bastard for not bothering to mention a word of this to either him or Beck. He and River would be having a conversation later that wouldn't require words. "Now. While you can still walk."

River held up his hands in surrender. "Hey, just so you know, I turned her down because I like my balls where they are."

At least River had been that smart.

"That's the only reason you're getting to keep them," Beck insisted. "Seth told you to get the fuck out."

Raine's brother didn't need to be told twice. After wishing Heavenly good luck, he beat a hasty retreat.

As soon as he'd gone, the silence in the kitchen turned deafening. He and Beck both leveled pointed glances at Heavenly. They wanted answers. She stepped back like she was trying to shrink into herself. Her expression held a motherlode of guilt.

That expression fucking gutted him.

Finally, Heavenly drew in a shaky breath and pasted on a too-bright smile. "Hi, guys. Can I get you a drink?"

A drink? Was she kidding? Oh, she had guts. He'd give her that, but her piss-poor attempt at redirection only made him want to light up her ass, demand answers…then fuck her senseless.

He stood, arms crossed over his chest, eyes narrowed, fury pinging. Beside him, Beck adopted a similar stance. But she was too innocent to understand the hard, uncompromising Dom in their demeanors.

"I don't want a fucking drink," Beck growled. "I want to spank your ass until I get some answers."

Seth snorted. "I was just thinking the same thing."

"What the… Why in the holy, ever-loving hell did you…" Beck sputtered, obviously too stunned—or too pissed off—to string a sentence together.

"Offer River *fucking* Kendall your virginity?" Seth couldn't keep the snarl out of his voice.

"What he said." Beck tossed a thumb his way, giving Heavenly the brunt of his displeasure.

She glanced down at her drink, the vino trembling against the glass as her hand shook. "You shouldn't care if I'm a virgin anymore."

Seth froze.

Beck grabbed her wine and slammed it on the island, then he lifted her chin and pressed his thumb in, forcing her gaze to his. "Are you saying you're not? If you didn't give it to River, who fucking took it?"

Heavenly dodged his question. Beck verbally thrust back, and they slung volleys back and forth. Every one of her evasions frustrated the hell out of Seth, but he gave Heavenly credit for moxie. She didn't turn tail and run. She simply jerked from Beck's grasp, lifted her chin, and took their fury in stride.

As much as he itched to mete out discipline that would make sure she never lied to him again, he couldn't deny that he found her breath-stealingly gorgeous.

But he'd heard enough bullshit.

"Well, as the other guy who's had his fingers—and his tongue—inside you, I think I'm entitled to know who supposedly popped your cherry."

She tried more dodging and ducking. He played along for a minute to see if she'd cough up information. But admitting his first sexual encounter had been in the men's room of a White Castle at fourteen hadn't persuaded her to be equally forthcoming. His patience was running on fumes.

Apparently, so was Beck's.

"Who did you fuck?" the doctor demanded. "We're waiting for an answer."

"No one you, um…know."

When she tried to break free from them again, Beck grabbed both wrists and anchored himself in her face, inches from her flushing cheeks. Seth struggled not to devour her where she stood. The trembling of her lower lip and the way she swiped her tongue across it had him seething and starving for her. Didn't she understand how fucking badly he needed her?

"Let's try the truth."

As Beck barked, Seth looped behind Heavenly so they surrounded her—so she couldn't escape—and grabbed her hair in his fist. He tugged until he had her attention, then bent to her ear. "If you lie again, we'll find a quiet corner and prove our threats to spank you weren't empty."

He glanced at the doctor. Yeah, he might be giving away too much, but a glance told him Beck was totally on board.

Heavenly's pale cheeks flared rosier. The pulse at her neck jerked faster. And when Beck cupped her face, she gasped. Fuck, Seth could see how wide her eyes had gone, how dilated her pupils. No missing the poke of her nipples under that thin red T-shirt she wore. Then the musk of her arousal hit his nose, and he was fucking ready to tear down the house—hell, the world—to get her into his bed. To get her back into his life.

"Spank me? I'm not a misbehaving child." Her voice sounded nervous and breathy.

"You're not, but that won't stop us from firing up your ass. Because let me tell you, little girl, no other man better be the one to make you a woman."

"That's for one of us," Seth cut in.

Seth hated to concede that, but he'd damn well rather she surrendered herself to Beck, who'd also lost his heart to Heavenly, than to River or a stranger who would make him homicidal the instant they touched her.

His mind was going ninety miles a minute, but he saw the instant Beck's anger gave way to hunger. The doctor lowered his lips toward her. Seth pulled back on his fistful of her silky blond hair until their eyes met. The moment unfolded in slow motion. She blinked up at him, pleading for mercy, though not a word spilled from her lush mouth. Holding her stare, he deliberately exposed her vulnerable throat to Beck. Her eyes darkened. Heavenly wasn't trying to go anywhere now. She liked this. She wanted them. No missing the goose bumps breaking out all over her body or the harsh pants of her aroused breaths.

Yeah… The way he felt right now with the air thickening around all three of them…he wasn't sure anyone would be singing happy birthday to her. He and Beck would be taking her to bed. And then getting some answers.

Holy fuck.

Suddenly, a god-awful air horn of racket pealed in his ears.

The sound was too close to a siren not to get his attention. He snapped upright and scanned the kitchen. "What the hell?"

Everything went downhill from there.

Like a wild thing, Heavenly struggled free from their firm grasp and wrestled to grab her phone from her back pocket. Her hands were shaking so badly she almost dropped it twice before answering it. "Dad, what's wrong? Are you all right?"

A glance confirmed to Seth that Beck was equally clueless about the fact her father was in the picture.

Within seconds, Heavenly's panic made it clear he was having some sort of medical emergency. Then Seth helped them scramble into his car and they sped to the hospital. It didn't take long to pin down that the man had an autoimmune disease Heavenly had talked to Beck about in a strictly academic way. Clearly, she'd failed mentioning all her questions about the ailment had anything to do with the man who'd given her life and raised her.

By the time they reached the hospital, it became even clearer that her father's secret illness was just the tip of his medical iceberg...

While Beck checked on Abel as he received treatment, Seth coaxed Heavenly down the hall to get some fresh coffee.

They sat together in the largely deserted cafeteria, and a sense of déjà vu played through his head. Their first conversation had taken place across an impersonal white table in the middle of a sterile environment like this. He'd been dazzled then. He was confused and mad as hell...but, damn it, still dazzled now.

He stared at Heavenly—her tear-stained face and slumped shoulders. Exhaustion pulled at her. Seth couldn't stand it any longer.

He reached out for her, so gut-wrenchingly relieved when she laid her fingers across his palm. "Angel, I can only imagine the pressure you've been under, trying to cope with all this on your own. Why didn't you say anything? Beck is a damn doctor. He could have helped. Hell, I would have—"

"None of my problems were yours." She dropped her gaze to the cup of coffee in front of her and took a deep breath. "After eight years, you get used to juggling everything alone. Maybe that sounds like an excuse to you. I don't expect anyone who hasn't been in my shoes to understand."

She was right; he didn't understand. But now wasn't the time to hound her for answers. Tonight, she needed support, especially since she looked half a breath from falling apart.

He inched his chair back and spread his arms open. "Come here, angel. You look like you could use a friend. Why don't you let me hold you?"

Tears filled her eyes as she hesitated, then bolted out of her chair and crawled onto his lap. Wrapping her up tightly, he smoothed a hand over her head.

"I'm scared." She sniffled. "Dad dying is my worst nightmare."

"I'm sure," he whispered. "But if that happens, I'll be here for you. I don't know what it's like to watch my father slowly fade away, since I lost mine suddenly. But I get the grief. I can lend you an ear and my sympathy. Think positive right now. Beck will make sure Abel gets the best medical care possible."

"Dad shouldn't be relapsing this much. Each time he does, I'm afraid he won't be coming home with me," she choked out.

Seth couldn't help her father, but he could give Heavenly something priceless: comfort.

Wrapping her arms around his neck, she pressed her face against his chest and sobbed in huge, heaving, chest-buckling gasps, like she hadn't had anyone to cry on in forever. It ripped his goddamn heart to listen to her. Seth wished he could protect her from the world and the pain and whatever happened next with her father. But he couldn't, so he let her cling, held her tight, and murmured soft assurances as he stroked her hair.

It was well after two in the morning when they pulled to the curb in the slum surrounding the dump Heavenly and her father called home. To say he was shocked was the understatement of a lifetime.

As Heavenly guided her father up the walk, Seth shared a look of disbelief with Beck.

"If you have a couple of assault rifles, pass 'em out," the doctor mumbled. "We might need them to make it inside her place."

"No shit," Seth whispered. "I can't believe she lives here."

Obviously, his angel was surviving off the nickels and dimes she made waiting tables. He'd had no idea—and he wanted to howl in regret.

"Not for much longer."

"You got that right," Seth vowed.

As he and Beck helped the old man across an uneven courtyard and up to the front door, Heavenly ripped away a bright orange overdue rent notice. Her embarrassment spoke volumes. Fuck, this night kept getting worse. Seth was kicking himself for not looking into Heavenly from the beginning, for ignoring his instincts, and for not pushing her for information. If he'd learned about her dad's health and her substandard living conditions months ago, would he be hovering over her protectively now? Would he be wondering if tonight would bring her closer or just give her another excuse to pull away?

THE WHOLE NIGHT had been an epic WTF.

When Heavenly opened the door to her tiny studio apartment and flipped on the light, Beck's stomach pitched as cockroaches scurried to find darkness. Yes, it was clean, but by the looks of the peeling paint, matted carpet, and water-stained ceiling, the place should have been condemned decades ago.

Well, he understood now why Heavenly refused to let him pick her up for any of their dates. She'd been embarrassed. He'd give her a pass for pride since he had plenty of his own, but he wouldn't absolve her for lying to him about everything else, especially her father and his deteriorating medical condition. For fuck's sake, he was a doctor. One phone call, and he'd have set Abel up with the best physicians in LA months ago. All she'd had to do was open her goddamn mouth.

Instead, tonight had felt like a game of Whac-A-Mole. Each time some new problem popped up and he thought he'd clobbered it, another took its place. She had a father. Fine. He was dying. Not so fine, but he'd spoken to Abel, who had already guessed the inevitable. Thankfully, the older man had seemed relieved when Beck had vowed to care for Heavenly after he was gone. Then they'd pulled up to this hovel. He'd been livid and heartbroken that she and Abel called this shithole in the middle of gang turf home. But her living situation could—and would—be changed. He had an empty condo complete with security, a fluffy king-size bed, thick carpet, and pristine walls. He'd get Heavenly moved in there pronto, even if he had to toss her over his shoulder and haul her out kicking and screaming. But before he could whack the mole of her living situation on the fucking head, he'd seen that rent overdue notice.

He was almost afraid to ask what would pop up next.

As he and Seth led Abel to the rented hospital bed, Beck skimmed a glance over the sparse room. A pillow and blanket lay poised on the end of a saggy, threadbare couch. The realization that he was staring at Heavenly's bed hit him like a punch to the gut. His anger and blood pressure spiked.

"Can you settle Dad on the bed? Then I'll adjust him until he's comfortable," Heavenly murmured.

"I know how to maneuver a hospital bed," Beck said as he and Seth helped Abel onto the mattress. "Relax, little girl."

"Actually, if you two don't mind staying with Dad for a few minutes, I'll pop across the courtyard and deal with last month's rent."

Beck didn't miss the quiver in her voice. Was she nervous because she knew that he and Seth would sit her down and interrogate the shit out of her the moment they could? Or exhausted because the whole damn night had been a shit show?

Granted, he and Seth were there to keep an eye on Abel, but why decide to pay the rent at two in the morning? A niggling voice in the back of his brain said something wasn't right. But he'd be goddamned if he could imagine what else could possibly be wrong.

After he and Seth helped Abel into bed, Beck bent and removed the man's shoes. "Would you like something to drink?"

"Water, thank you," he replied. "Clean glasses are in the cabinet to the left of the sink. Help yourselves."

Beck stepped across the room and opened the cabinet, grabbing three clean glasses from a shelf that otherwise held half a dozen mismatched plates, a pair of chipped bowls, and a coffee mug about nursing students always studying. Nothing else. He frowned against his mounting concern as he opened the freezer for some ice but found only a thick layer of frost. No frozen treats or vegetables. Not even a scrap of meat. Worry smacked him like a wrecking ball to the chest.

Heart thudding, he peeked inside the refrigerator. A nearly empty container of milk, two eggs, and a half-empty bottle of catsup. His alarm only grew when he pulled open the rest of the cabinets and found a few packages of Ramen, a canister of oatmeal, and some saltines tucked into one shelf. A bottle of wine lay on its side beside them. Everything else was bare.

He bit back a roar, his hands shaking with rage as he gripped the kitchen faucet and filled the glasses before striding across the room and taking a seat beside Seth. After sending the PI a sidelong glance that signaled more shit, he began mentally counting the minutes until they could talk and he could make some phone calls and start changing

Heavenly's life.

"Thank you for helping Heavenly and me tonight." Abel took a long gulp from his glass, fighting his shaking hands. "We truly appreciate it."

"We're happy to," Beck assured the man.

Seth nodded. "I wish we could do more."

"I know this place isn't fancy. It's certainly not as big or homey as our farmhouse in Wisconsin…"

Abel's uneven voice told Beck the man's strength was fading, but he rambled on with the verve of someone lonely who suddenly had an audience willing to listen. He waxed on about how cozy their house had once been, about their dairy cows, about how much it had killed him to sell the farm once his illness had progressed.

"How much has Heavenly told you?" Abel's voice quivered even more as the joy on his face dimmed.

As little as humanly possible. But Beck would love to hear whatever details the man was willing to spill since he clearly didn't know shit.

"I'd appreciate it if you filled in the gaps," Seth remarked as if he had all day to listen.

"In other words, she said nothing." Abel sighed. "That girl… She's private, a bit shy, and even more proud. You may have noticed she doesn't trust easily."

No, she didn't. Not at all. Not when it mattered most.

"We did," Beck grumbled. "Why is that?"

"Well, my wife left after I got sick, said she hadn't signed up to spend her life taking care of an invalid. Heavenly was just a teenager, in school and far too young to manage the spread by herself."

Beck's heart tripped in his chest, thundering in his ears. He forced himself to keep his expression neutral.

I'm the guy your mother warned you about.

My mother never warned me about anything. I haven't seen her in eight years.

Their conversation careened through Beck's head. Sympathy and fury mingled and crushed him in a single wave.

"Heavenly must have taken that hard," Seth murmured somberly.

"She felt so abandoned after Lisa walked out. I'm afraid the experience taught her that those who should care most often don't give two shits. Unfortunately, she's had to shoulder most of the responsibility since. But Heavenly is a good girl. She's taken good care of me all these years."

The man's words went off like a bomb in Beck's brain. In a couple of sentences, Abel had explained the reason Heavenly kept every last one of her fucking secrets to herself. She'd had no one to rely on since she'd been a child. Her own mother had crumbled the very foundation of Heavenly's life before she'd been mature enough to understand. When she should have been thinking about boyfriends, football games, and prom, she'd been a cook, caretaker, maid, and helper. She might still be a virgin, but the minute her mother had abandoned her, she'd lost her goddamn innocence.

And there was another fucking mole to whack on the head…maybe one that could never be vanquished.

He knew now why Heavenly hadn't asked him for help. But Beck still intended to take control of her situation.

Seth quickly banked his shock, then pinned him with a pointed stare. Yeah, he fully planned to stick his two cents in to help Heavenly, too.

Yippee.

"After I sold the farm, I rented a little house in town for us…" Abel went on about his illness, his doctors in Wisconsin, and the reason he and Heavenly had moved to LA. By the end of his speech, his strength had waned. His voice was cracking, his sentences trailing off.

"I promise I'll make some phone calls and set you up with the best neurologist in the city," Beck said, patting the man's shoulder.

When he pulled back, he couldn't help but notice the slew of prescription meds on the table beside the bed. After a quick scan of the labels, he closed his eyes and sighed heavily. Jesus, no wonder his little girl couldn't afford food. Every dime she made waiting tables must be paying for medicine. If she had anything left over, it couldn't be much.

The older man smiled in gratitude. "I can't thank you enough. If your medical friends can't cover all the expenses, maybe we can pay some now that Heavenly got that raise at the hospital and started working so many hours. It's the only way we've been able to afford that gawd-awfully expensive medicine my doctor recently prescribed…"

Raise? Abel's words sent Beck's warning bells ringing, his pulse racing. His mouth went dry. The old man thought she earned money volunteering at the hospital? Was that the well-meaning lie she'd been telling her father so he wouldn't worry?

Oh, little girl... You're going to have the reddest ass when I get done with you. You will learn never *to lie again.*

Beside him, Seth tensed and whipped a concerned look Beck's way. So the PI knew her "raise" was bullshit, too.

And if she barely had money to buy meds, how the hell was she paying rent?

Skin prickling, Beck glanced at the door. Heavenly had been gone a long time for someone who merely intended to drop off cash. And she hadn't actually taken money with her.

Because she didn't have any. So how exactly had she planned on keeping this roof over her head?

Goddamn it, there was another fucking mole.

A sick feeling tilted his gut as the pieces of her reality slid together. Heavenly hadn't asked River to have sex with her because she wanted the prick. She simply hadn't wanted to give her virginity to her fucking landlord.

Beside him, fear and rage warred across Seth's face before he shot out of his chair and charged for the door. So the PI had put two and two together and come up with shit, as well. Good. That saved him the time and explanation.

Beck leapt to his feet, too. Abel—nearly asleep—mumbled something Beck didn't hear.

"We're going to check on Heavenly," Seth shot over his shoulder as he ran outside.

Beck followed. Then they both skidded to a stop, eyeing the units across the courtyard.

While he was trying to remember which fucking apartment belonged to the landlord, a door on the far side of the atrium suddenly slammed against the stucco wall. A terrified, gut-churning cry followed.

Heavenly.

Beck spied the whip of pale hair in the moonlight as she raced across the concrete toward them barefoot, frantically tugging her shirt over her bare breasts. A sob tore from her throat. Tears spilled down the cheeks. Horror twisted her face.

"You still owe me, *puta*." A guy in a dirty wife-beater with a paunching beer belly chased after her, waving her bra in his fist. "You promised me that cherry pie."

A violent blast of fury filled Beck's veins. A low growl rumbled up from deep in his chest. The beast he'd kept locked away for months tore off its chain.

The son of a bitch who'd threatened his girl was going to pay.

As Heavenly neared, he felt terror and revulsion pour off of her. She shuddered, struggled to catch her breath between the panting and the tears. The sight ripped him in two.

Seth gripped her shoulders. "Get inside."

"B-but—" she sputtered, peering over her shoulder as if she expected hell to be nipping at her heels.

"Go!" Beck snarled. "We'll take care of this."

The moment Heavenly dashed to her unit and slammed the door, he and Seth stormed across the cracked cement.

"I'm going to fucking kill him."

"Not if I do it first," Beck growled right beside him.

"We could make it hurt more if we did it together."

Beck shot the man a nasty grin. "You're on."

Fury pumped through his veins. He welcomed it as he and Seth sprinted across the concrete. Beck narrowed his eyes at the cocksucker, who had the balls to flash them a smarmy smile and dangle Heavenly's bra in the air.

"She offered me her poontang. You can't do nothing about it," Sanchez spouted.

"Watch me." Seth wrapped a hand around the prick's throat, lifted him off the ground, and slammed him against the door.

Suddenly, panic replaced the dipshit's bravado. Frantically, he groped for the knob with a flailing hand.

"Touching her was your last mistake," Beck vowed before he nudged Seth aside and slammed his shoulder into Sanchez's kidney. The man's grunt morphed into a long, tortured moan. Beck didn't feel sorry for the asshole at all. Hopefully, he would be pissing blood for a week.

The next time he and Seth landed blows, the combined force splintered the door. It gave way, tumbling the cocksucker back into his apartment. The man cursed, arms flailing as he futilely tried to defend himself, legs scrambling as he struggled in vain to stand.

Seth straddled the asshole and pinned him to the cracked tile before unloading what looked like months of pent-up rage, each fist landing in a perfectly timed arc of power and bone-crushing force on his face.

Feeding off Seth's malice, Beck used the shitsack's rib cage like a soccer ball, not giving two shits about the muscles he pulverized or the bones he shattered. Oh, revenge felt sweet. And violence was even better when the fucker's high-pitched screams cut through the night.

As Seth continued pummeling the prick, blood exploded from the bastard's nose and mouth. Teeth sailed across the floor. More facial bones cracked under each brutal punch. It made what he'd done to Pike weeks ago look like a friendly pat on the back.

Moving in between the man's thrashing legs, Beck stomped his foot on the prick's crotch with a snarl, mashing his junk under his heel. Yep, he was ignoring the hell out of his Hippocratic oath and basking in the fucker's howls of pain. Then he enjoyed some gurgling pleas after slamming the landlord's kneecap beneath his loafers.

When the pig fell limp and unconscious, Beck sucked in a ragged inhalation, braced against the wall, panting to recover his breath.

Seth hadn't let up.

"Stop," Beck growled, gripping the PI's taut shoulder. "Unless you know where to hide a body and how to clean a murder scene, you need to let him go."

Seth whirled, sending him a glare filled with inhuman rage. "Why the fuck do you care? If I kill him, I'm out of your hair permanently."

"Because Heavenly cares." Acknowledging that sucked, but tonight had been too full of reality to ignore this one.

They coveted the same girl, and neither one of them were giving up. Unless he was really fucking wrong, on some level she loved them both, too.

"Son of a bitch," Seth muttered as he finally opened one fist and flexed his hand.

"Come on. Let's find Heavenly. The way that sack of shit was screaming, it's only a matter of time before the cops show up. We need to be gone."

Seth blinked and gave a jerky nod. He stood slowly and stared down at the bloodied landlord as he dragged up a wad of phlegm and spit in his face.

Beck made a mental note not to piss Seth off—ever. Thank god the guy hadn't agreed to fight that night he'd wanted to brawl at Shadows. He'd probably still be recovering in the ICU.

Both covered in blood, they hauled ass across the courtyard. Beck had to ask, "Where'd you learn to throw fists like that?"

"After I left the force, I ran with people no one should." He shrugged. "And I learned."

Beck wasn't sure what that meant or why it sounded so ominous. He dismissed it when they reached Heavenly's door. "I don't know if I want to wrap her in my arms or take her over my knee."

"Both are in order. But you're right. We have to get out of here now. What happens to Abel?"

"That man needs dedicated care. The VA had no business releasing him tonight. But I don't have admitting privileges there, so objecting wouldn't have done shit." Beck sighed. "After we get out of here, I'll make some calls and arrange a bed for him tonight. I have friends in neurology I'll call tomorrow. They can help us piece together a longer-term care plan."

"Great. And Heavenly?"

"I keep a condo near the hospital for the nights I'm on call. She can stay there."

"I'll help settle her in."

Beck arched a brow, then shrugged. Better if they didn't argue now. "Fine. Then tomorrow…"

"Tomorrow, we start making a few things clear to that stubborn woman."

"Couldn't agree more." Beck shook his head as he smirked Seth's way. "Look at us, getting along and shit."

"Will miracles never cease?" Seth countered with a crooked grin. "Now let's see how our girl is doing."

NERVES BUZZED LIKE an angry beehive in Heavenly's belly as she forced back a sniffle and grabbed the last of the clothes from the plastic chest. She shoved them into the mustard-colored suitcase her father had helped her pack when they'd left Wisconsin seven short months ago, seeking fresh hope out West.

That hope had already been snuffed out. She wasn't sure where to go next.

The doctors here hadn't cured her father. The cost of living had finally eaten away the last of their savings. And since she'd lacked the courage to pay her rent in the currency Mr. Sanchez demanded, he was going to evict them. What could she possibly tell her father? How was she going to take care of him now?

After everything she'd done to try to build a future for them, she'd failed.

A wave of defeat threatened her with a new splash of scalding tears. Heavenly sucked them back. There was no time for sorrow or self-pity, only for packing up, getting out, and trying to decide where she and Dad could go for the night. She'd heard homeless shelters were dangerous…but where else could she go?

Thankfully, her father slept, oblivious to the fact that in the ten minutes since she'd run across the courtyard like a coward, she'd managed to pack up most everything they owned. She shoved aside the memories of Mr. Sanchez's mouth crawling up her neck as he yanked her shirt over her head, of his fingers violating her skin, of the vile things he'd whispered that he'd do to her before he let her leave his bed…

A shudder wracked her. She heaved, wishing she had time to shower. But she had to focus, be practical, stay strong.

Ten seconds, she promised herself. She would give herself ten precious ticks to cry, then she'd figure out how to carry on.

Her childhood flashed through her head. It had been so easy then. She'd had clothes and toys. She'd never worried where her next meal would come from or where she'd sleep at night. Mom had worked as a cashier at the grocery store. Dad had tended the farm. Summers had been sunny and idyllic, winters full of snowy adventure. Life had been carefree.

Today, most everything she owned fit in a single suitcase. She hadn't eaten in more than twelve hours, and her stomach felt glued to her spine. She had no idea where she'd lay her head tonight.

What the hell was happening to her life?

Worse, what would happen tomorrow? No, later today. She'd still have no place to live, and her boss expected her at Bazookas or she'd lose the only job she had. Where would her father spend the hours while she waited tables? He couldn't stay on the streets.

Even though her ten seconds were over, Heavenly fell to her knees, buried her face in her hands, and sobbed. Because as terrible as all those problems were, it hurt so much more knowing that Beck and Seth now knew every single one of her woes.

How long would it take them to make their excuses and bow out of her life?

Not long, she was sure. That's how people were; she didn't blame them.

Behind her, the door opened. Heavenly scrambled to her feet and swiped at her tears, not completely sure who she'd find standing in the portal. She breathed a sigh of relief that it wasn't Sanchez.

Then she realized Seth's shirt was soaked in blood. The legs of Beck's pants and the toes of his shoes hadn't fared much better. Had they beaten Sanchez up? She let loose a shaky breath. Was he still conscious? Alive?

Do you care?

Even if that made her a horrible human being, no.

Beck took in her suitcase in a glance. "Good. You've packed. Time to go."

She nodded and stacked her lone box by the door, taking care with her mother's old sewing machine. "I-I know. I'll have my dad's things and all our papers packed up in a few minutes."

"You take care of your father's belongings. I'll get the papers," Seth insisted.

Heavenly froze, then horror set in when she thought of the past due bills for the phones, Dad's hospital bed, and her fall tuition sitting in the drawers. Beck and Seth had already glimpsed the worst of her problems, but the thought of them knowing about all those burdens too made her chest clench tight.

"I'll get them." She rushed across the room, swiping away at the hot teardrops still making their way down her face. "I need to grab my laptop for school."

Seth stepped in her path. "We don't have time to argue. Get your father's shit together. I'll get your computer and take care of the desk. Beck will get Abel up and out the door. We've got to go."

In case Sanchez came for his money.

With shaking hands, she plucked up Dad's clean pajamas and his one pair of slacks for doctor's visits, doing her best to fold them into the lovely wicker picnic basket Seth had given her. "You're right. I hate to ask, but would it be too much trouble for you to drop us off at the homeless shelter?"

Beck spun around on his heel and flashed her an incredulous stare. "Are you fucking kidding me?"

She shrank back. "I'm sorry. I'll call a cab."

Seth sent her an equally stupefied glare. "You're fucking serious?"

"Yes!" Why were they making this so hard on her? "I can't pay the rent anymore. I know you understand what happened here tonight. I already feel horrible enough that I've put my comfort over my father's well-being." Tears rushed to her eyes like acid again as she threw the rest of his clothes, his meds, and his lone pair of shoes in the basket. "Why are you trying to make me feel worse?"

"How much money do you have right now, little girl?" Beck snarled.

"Not enough, obviously." She stomped to the kitchen and grabbed the food out of the pantry. She refused to leave behind the coffee cup and wine Seth had given her. They were some of the few happy reminders she had left. Sniffling, she returned to the main room. "Do you want it in exchange for taking us somewhere safe?"

"How. Much?"

Heavenly reared back. With her, Beck had always been kind, affable, patient, wry, intellectual, and sexy enough to make her shiver. She'd never heard the hard edge in his voice. She'd never seen his temper. If he wanted to humiliate her, he wouldn't be the first person to try, but no way would she cower before him—or anyone.

She settled all the kitchen stuff in the basket, then lifted her chin. "Fifty-four dollars."

"Total? To your name?" Seth looked somewhere between horrified and heartbroken. "Damn it, angel…"

"I don't want your pity. And I'm not asking you for anything."

"Oh, you don't have to ask. Let me tell you exactly how this is going to unfold, little girl. We're loading up your things and taking your dad to the hospital tonight so our neurological team can do a full evaluation in the morning. After we leave there, Seth and I are taking you to my condo. I'm going to fix you a massive fucking plate of food and watch you eat every bite. Then we're going to tuck you into the huge, clean bed alone. And you're going to sleep until the dark circles and worry disappear. Tomorrow, you'll visit your father, shop for a whole new wardrobe with Raine, then explain how the fuck you got into this mess." Beck leaned close, nostrils flaring. "All of that is nonnegotiable, and you will do it without a word of disobedience. Is that clear?"

"No." When Beck's eyes narrowed, she shook her head. "I-I can't. I can't ask for that much. I can't pay you. I can't miss work. You're trying to help, and I appreciate it. But—"

"Don't you dare say they aren't my problems and that you're not my responsibility."

"Why not?" She tossed her hands in the air. "It's true."

"Bullshit," Seth tossed in, grabbing papers from the drawers of the old desk in the corner. "We just made you our responsibility. And we don't have time to argue. We've got a handful of minutes to get this shit in the car and leave before the police start asking questions."

Heavenly almost dropped everything. "The police?"

Seth grabbed the basket and slid her laptop and their papers inside. "Angel, do you think all this blood on our clothes came from a simple busted nose?"

Her eyes widened. "He's…really injured?"

"We beat the shit out of him, so we don't exactly have time to chat. If you're done packing, get in the car."

"Heavenly?" Abel woke, sounding disoriented. "Boo?"

"I'm right here, Dad." She speared both the men with frantic glances, then tuned them out and focused on her father. "We need to get you up and—"

"We're going to take you to a better hospital, Abel." Beck helped the man to his feet and grabbed his nearby walker, completely ignoring her blinking stare.

"I need to go back?"

"Not to the VA. We'll take you where Heavenly and I work."

The frail man frowned, bewildered. "Where is Heavenly going, then? I don't like the thought of her staying here by herself. Not the best neighborhood."

"We don't like that, either." Seth nodded. "So…"

Heavenly pleaded silently with him not to worry her dad. He'd been through enough and didn't need to fret about her virtue, too.

"So Beck knows of an empty condo near the hospital in a very secure building. The owners aren't using it right now, and Heavenly can stay there as long as she wants."

"Absolutely," Beck promised, helping the older man slide into his slippers.

"Well, that sounds wonderful. Hear that, boo?"

"Yeah, Dad. It should be great. You and Beck head for the car. Seth and I are right behind you with our stuff."

"In fact, why don't I help you, Abel?" Beck didn't wait for his reply, just lifted her father and carried him in one arm, dragging his walker behind.

Her dad gave a grunt of surprise but nodded. He must still be half asleep. His nighttime meds were meant to help him nod off, so they often left him groggy.

As soon as they were out the door, Seth lifted her box with a scowl and tucked it under one arm. "What the hell is in here?"

As he grabbed her suitcase with his free hand, Heavenly took hold of the picnic basket that included her father's clothes, the food, her computer, and their papers. "My mother's sewing machine. Sorry it's heavy."

"It's fine. Is that everything? Take a quick look around. You're not coming back."

Heavenly scanned the room, scooping up her pillow and blanket, along with the princess mouse ears Beck had bought her at Disneyland.

She clutched those to her chest. "What about the hospital bed?"

"We'll call the rental company to pick it up tomorrow. Let's go." Seth shooed her to the door.

She walked out for the last time, and she couldn't say she was sorry to see this place go. Nothing good had happened inside these four walls.

Seth gave her a nudge and slammed the door closed as she heard the first wail of sirens a few blocks over. "Go!"

"I don't have my key to lock the door."

"This place is Sanchez's problem now. We've got to move!"

Or he and Beck could get arrested. Right. Everything was happening so fast, and the shock of tonight, coupled with the exhaustion now tugging at her after all those pointless tears, was making it hard to think straight. It probably didn't matter if she didn't lock the door. After they'd beaten the crap out of Sanchez, the man wasn't going to return her five-hundred-dollar deposit.

They made a mad dash to Seth's SUV. Beck was waiting by the back with her dad. He grabbed everything from her hands, stare lingering on the embroidered ears. "Backseat. Now."

She didn't hesitate. The last thing she wanted was for either man to suffer consequences for trying to help her. And maybe she shouldn't be surprised they'd stayed and dragged her from that miserable apartment. Beck had been feeding her for months. Together, they'd slayed the Kathryn dragon for her. They'd said they both wanted a future with her. Hell, Seth had uprooted his entire life for her.

Was it possible they'd still want her now that they had seen the mess she'd made of her life? It seemed incredible they would when her own mother hadn't.

As she rushed Dad into the backseat and followed, she mentally gnawed on the fact that, despite the worst possible circumstances, sometimes people stayed. After all, she hadn't once considered leaving her father. And she saw people at the hospital every day who stuck by their loved ones, no matter what. So what made the difference? The character of the person? The strength of their love?

Heavenly didn't know.

"Give me the keys." Beck held out his hand to Seth.

"I can drive." Seth fished them from his pocket.

"I know where I'm going."

With a sigh, Seth tossed Beck the ring.

Seconds later, the capable doctor turned the engine over and shot down the street, lights dark. He was already at the stop sign at the end of the street and sliding into sparse traffic on Figueroa, heading for the freeway, when Heavenly caught sight of flashing red-and-blue lights in the rearview mirror. She turned to look out the back window. Sure enough, the police were stopping in front of her old building.

They really had gotten out just in time.

A knot of tension loosened in her belly.

The drive to the hospital passed in a blur. Beck made calls as he drove. A crew was waiting by the ambulance door. They wheeled her half-sleeping father to the neurological unit. Thankfully, the seasoned personnel barely gave Beck and Seth's bloody clothes a second glance. Once the staff wheeled him to a private room, Heavenly squeezed her dad's hand.

An unfamiliar nurse nodded their way. "Dr. Litchfield has already ordered the admitting paperwork. He'll start the tests in the morning."

"Thanks." Beck nodded.

"I'll visit you tomorrow, Dad," she promised.

He raised a tired hand and closed his eyes.

When Beck and Seth led her away, Heavenly's heart stuttered. She wrapped her arms around herself. She *was* doing the right thing. Her dad needed good care, certainly better than she could provide. But this was the first night she'd spend without him since…well, ever.

Suddenly, Beck's arms circled her shoulders. "He's fine here."

"He's where he needs to be," she acknowledged with a jerky nod.

Seth took her into his arms and cupped her face. "Yeah, he is. And now we need to get you where you need to be."

"Maybe I should stay and—"

"There's nothing you can do for him tonight, angel. The hospital is taking care of his needs. He would want us to take care of yours."

She blinked, looking down the empty hall, then turned back to the expectant men. She was so accustomed to being responsible for her father's life and well-being. Heck, for her own, too. Someone else planning everything for her, despite the fact they were far more capable, made her anxious. And totally overwhelmed her.

"Heavenly?"

Slowly, she nodded. "Yes."

Seth caressed her face, then brushed his palm down her arm before he took her hand. "Time to go."

"You're right."

As they backtracked to her familiar unit, the edges of her vision blackened and tunneled in. Her equilibrium tilted. She was so tired her legs felt like noodles. She stumbled over her own feet.

A soft curse rang in her ears. Seth. Then he wrapped an arm around her shoulders, tucked the other under her knees, and lifted her against his chest. Suddenly, she was floating.

No, he was carrying her.

"I can walk," she croaked out. Funny, what she said sounded more like slurs than words.

"You can if I put you down. But I'm not going to. End of conversation."

No missing his implacable tone. She didn't have the energy to argue anyway. Tomorrow she'd start making plans again and take all this responsibility back from them. Tonight, she needed sleep.

Heavenly closed her eyes and laid her head on Seth's shoulder, barely aware when he eased her into the car. She had no memory of the drive to the condo, only of being lifted out of the car and carried across a bright parking garage. A keycard and an elevator ride later, they emerged into an enclosed atrium. It was industrial and sleek, obviously new and pristine and very upscale.

Beck was willing to let her stay here? Ha. Even if he didn't intend to make her pay rent, she'd insist…but she could never afford it. Still, she had to admit, spending a night or two here would be absolute paradise.

He let them in the front door. Absently, she noticed he carried her suitcase. Everything else he must have left in the car. Fine. Tomorrow would be soon enough to take that off his hands.

Seth set her on her feet just inside the condo. Beck flipped on the lights.

Heavenly's jaw dropped. A gorgeous, tufted black leather sofa and a flat-screen TV took up most of the space on her left. Blinds covered the huge windows on the far side of the room where she saw a commanding yet comfy matching recliner.

"Follow me," Beck said as he walked past a bar area, then turned on more lights that illuminated a state-of-the-art kitchen and breakfast nook and pointed through a dark opening on the far side of the room. "Inside is a bedroom and bath. Go take a hot shower. I'll start making food."

She didn't have the energy to argue or even to offer help. "Thank you."

He nodded, then pointed Seth to another bathroom and offered to let him borrow some clothes. They were discussing taking shifts in the shower when Heavenly closed the door and found herself in a luxurious black and marble bathroom with hot water that felt like Shangri-La. She scrubbed vigorously, as if she could wash away not only the blood and memories of Sanchez's touch but her worries, fears, doubts, and dread.

Finally, she stepped out, wet hair in a haphazard braid, and found her suitcase on a bed that was covered in a mountain of soft pillows. Tiredly, she fished out a pair of underwear and one of her old nightshirts. On the other side of the door, she heard the sounds of bacon frying and the murmur of the men talking.

They must have a million questions. She owed them some answers. But she also had some things to say, too.

Heavenly sucked in a deep breath and tried to find the energy to face them as she opened the door.

When she padded barefoot into the kitchen and stopped beside the island, she was surprised to see they'd both showered, tossed on sweats and T-shirts, and now stood, each manning a burner on the stove, seemingly comfortable.

"Can I help?"

They swiveled their gazes in her direction. Stared. Froze. Gaped. She swallowed, nerves buzzing again. What was wrong?

Finally, Beck cleared his throat. "We're almost done. Can you get the forks out of that drawer, the napkins from the holder on the counter, and, um, set them on the table?"

She shrugged. "Sure."

Seth still hadn't blinked. "Damn."

He'd muttered the word almost under his breath, and she frowned.

Beck elbowed him, and Seth finally jerked his stare back to the stove and the rapidly cooking eggs.

They must be exhausted, too. The gratitude for all they'd done welled up as she set everything on the table. She'd been too overwrought earlier, but the magnitude of their outreach truly sank in now.

She was shocked. Humbled. More than a little confused. And she owed them big.

The day she'd told Beck and Seth there could be no future with either of them, she hadn't given any reason. She hadn't wanted to open her scars and bleed. But as much as it would hurt now, they'd earned that—and more.

As soon as she set three places, the guys hustled over with steaming food. Seth handed her orange juice. Beck helped her into her chair. Then the two of them sat. Only the clatter of dishes and the clink of forks broke the silence.

Heavenly reached for a piece of toast. "Thank you for everything tonight. I can never repay you for all you've done. And I know you have questions. I want to explain—"

"Not tonight." Beck set down his fork. "We do have questions."

"Plenty of them," Seth assured her. "But not until you've slept."

"Exactly." Beck nodded. "Right now, eat."

She let out a sigh of surprised relief. It was nice to breathe. It was also nice to be clean, have hot food, and know that both she and her father would be safe and warm.

It wasn't as if it would be hard to yield to their wishes.

"All right. We'll talk in the morning."

CHAPTER NINETEEN

Sunday, March 31

ON THE OTHER side of the shadowy living room, Beck heard Seth roll over on the inflatable mattress he'd blown up twenty minutes ago before letting out a heavy sigh.

He understood. It had been a long fucking night of blindsides and shock. The sun would be up in a couple of hours. Then he'd have to deal with all the shit, so he needed to shut his eyes and get some sleep. But his goddamn brain wouldn't stop spooling with ramifications and what-ifs.

Not everything had ended up a clusterfuck. Heavenly was safe. Abel was getting the quality care he deserved. Their scum-sucking landlord was in agony. And finally, his girl was under his roof...just not the way he'd envisioned. In his fantasies, he was in bed with her. Hell, he was inside her. But nothing about this situation was optimal. The secrets she'd harbored—no, the lies she'd told—were tough to swallow, but he'd also plowed face first into one indisputable fact:

Tonight, everything had changed.

Ten feet away, Seth rustled on the sheet again and groaned.

Beck turned over on the sofa. "Hey, if you're jacking off, take that shit to the bathroom. I don't want to hear it."

"Like I'd ever jack off in the same room with you."

"Glad to hear you've got some standards."

"Why the fuck would you think I'd jack off anywhere near you?"

"I saw your face after Heavenly pranced into the kitchen wearing that tight little kitten nightie." The word PURRFECT had stretched across her perky tits. She hadn't been wearing a bra. For a long moment, Beck had just stared. He didn't have to guess that Seth had gotten hard at a glance because, despite his fucking exhaustion, his own dick had roared to life. "I know damn well you were fixating on her kitty underneath."

"And you weren't? Please…"

"No. I'm guilty as hell. But I'm willing to admit it."

"Of course I wanted to fuck her. Is that really news?" He sighed again, the sound dripping frustration. "Now go to sleep. It's been a long damn day."

"No shit." Beck gnawed on the side of his cheek. Yeah, he should probably leave it alone, but he couldn't. "If you're so tired, why aren't you already snoring?"

Seth sat straight up. "Probably for the same reason you're not. I'm in a hundred knots because everything is so fucked up and none of this shit changes how I feel about her. You know the funny part? Heavenly isn't even my type."

Beck had to laugh. "Hell, she's not my usual, either."

"What's with that? I mean, I prefer women with a lot more experience. They're usually more adventurous and they damn sure know what they want. I don't even remember the last time I nailed one younger than me. I haven't taken a virgin since high school."

"Well, I never have."

"Never? Really? No backseat action? No prom night nookie?"

I went to prom with a hooker. "No. I always avoided them."

"Took a while, but I wised up too when I realized they always want a relationship."

Beck scoffed. "So, of course, we manage to find the one virgin who doesn't."

Seth barked out a laugh. "Karma. That bitch must be kicking our asses. Because here we are… The girl we're both desperate for is sleeping in the next room, and we're out here having a sausage party."

Beck had to chuckle. "When you put it that way, we sound stupid and we should be totally ashamed."

"You're not? Well, you have less to be humiliated about. After all, you're not the schmuck who moved across the country after kissing Heavenly once and *then* discovered that she doesn't see me in her future." He shook his head. "What's worse is that giving up again never crossed my mind. It's like I took one look at that girl and—"

"Had to have her?" Beck knew that feeling well. "Yep. I saw her and I just…knew. I told myself to stay away. She was too young, too sweet… We both know how well that worked. And I have no idea what the fuck happens next. I know what *needs* to happen." He let loose a deep breath of tension. "I'm just not sure if either of us can handle it."

Beck felt more than saw Seth go tense. "You think you know? Do I even want to ask?"

"Probably not. But I finally understand Heavenly."

"Oh, this ought to be good," Seth drawled. "Enlighten me."

"Abel told us everything important. Did you get it?"

Seth paused, like he was sorting through all the tidbits Heavenly's father had spilled and zeroed in on what mattered most. "Hard to miss her mother walking out on a sick husband and heaping the responsibility for his care on a girl who wasn't even old enough to drive. I'm against hitting a woman, but I might make an exception for that bitch."

"Exactly. The problem is, she left Heavenly with serious abandonment issues. That changes everything."

"Well, I guess it explains why she kept so much to herself. If she couldn't even trust her own mother…" Seth shook his head. "I can't fathom that. My mom and I are really close."

"Oh, her mom leaving explains a whole lot more, virtually everything we've been fighting since we met her. It's most likely the reason she thinks we have no future. Hell, it's probably even the reason she won't choose between us." Beck sat up and leaned his elbows on his knees. "You understand that we're going to have to make the choice for her, right?"

Seth stared warily. "You mean one of us is going to have to bow out?"

"No," Beck shot back. "She's too fragile for that right now. If one of us left, it would reinforce her conviction that everyone leaves. She might break."

"You're a surgeon, not a shrink. How can you be so sure that's what she'd think?"

Beck hesitated. He did not want to get into this. Not now, not ever. But Seth was sounding skeptical, and Beck needed him on board for Heavenly's sake.

"My mom abandoned me when I was a kid," Beck confessed softly.

"Oh, shit. How old were you?"

"Too young. And I've said everything I intend to on that topic," Beck bit out, slamming up walls to block the memories before they could surface.

"Is that the reason I couldn't find any record of you before you turned sixteen?"

The PI's words hit him with a blow far more powerful than any he'd unloaded on Sanchez. An icy chill froze Beck's blood before hot rage burst through his veins, sending his heart thudding wildly against his ribs. "You fucking investigated me?"

"Damn straight."

Sweat dotted Beck's brow. What else had the nosy bastard uncovered?

He stood and tossed the blanket on the sofa. "Stay the fuck out of my past."

"Why, because you're worried I'll tell Heavenly about your *wife* of eighteen years? Yeah, I found out about her. Granted, you filed for divorce a few weeks ago—finally. But give me one reason I shouldn't just tell Heavenly and let the chips fall?"

"Because it was a marriage of convenience, and the reasons for it are moot now. Because if you were any sort of PI, you'd have figured out that Gloria and I haven't lived together for almost a decade. Because Heavenly needs you and me both, and nothing else— especially not this pissing contest—matters." He sank back to the sofa. "How long have you known?"

"I found out a few weeks ago, right before Heavenly blindsided us. I couldn't wait to tell her. Oh, I was going to sleep with her first, make sure she was so into me that the news would convince her I was her obvious choice." He scrubbed a hand down his face. "But if you're right about her issues, that info could have really shaken her."

"So why didn't you blurt it all out when you had Heavenly alone at your place?"

"Besides the donkey interfering? Honestly, cheating manwhore didn't seem like your speed. I wanted to hear your side first." He shrugged. "I know you think otherwise, but I'm not a total prick."

That nearly left Beck speechless. "Thanks, man. It's not my speed. I appreciate the benefit of the doubt."

Seth shrugged. "So what do we do now? You say we can't walk

away without crushing Heavenly, but she says she doesn't see a future with either of us."

"She's testing us. She may not even be aware of it, but I know the behavior. She's pushing us to see how much we can take before we'll get fed up and leave her." Beck had been down this road, and he still shuddered when he thought of all the shit he'd heaped on Gloria until she'd verbally slapped his face and promised she was in his life to stay.

"So if we want her, we have to convince her we're not going anywhere? Christ… Then what? We have to hope she'll naturally choose one of us in time?"

"Once we help undo the damage her mother inflicted, maybe she will." But Beck wasn't holding his breath.

"Okay, I can suck it up until she's on more stable ground. Can you?"

Beck pondered that question, internally weighing options that didn't exist. "Tonight, I realized I'll do anything in the world for her. It might be a good idea for you to consider what else you're willing to do to make her happy."

Seth hesitated, and Beck suspected the PI was listening between the lines. "Maybe it would be best if we slept on it and talked again in the morning."

"Sure, but I think we both know where this is going."

"Shut up." Seth lay back again and tugged the blanket up to his neck. "And don't snore."

Yeah, Beck wasn't any happier about what likely came next…but that didn't change a damn thing.

On the far side of the unit, he heard the bedroom door open and whirled. Rustling told him that Seth turned toward the unexpected noise. The soft sounds of bare feet on the tile tiptoeing through the kitchen were unmistakable.

"Heavenly?" he asked.

"You all right?" Seth asked behind him.

She stepped into the room, at the end of the sofa. Beck saw her shift her weight, glance between them, curl her arms around her waist. "I'm really tired, but I can't sleep. I thought I heard voices and I hoped you were still awake."

Beck scooted closer and grabbed her hand. "Do you need to talk?"

"It's not that. I'm so used to sleeping with my dad breathing just a few feet away. The bed is really comfortable...but the room is too quiet."

It took less than half a second for him to grasp what she wanted. The air left his lungs. *Motherfucker...*

Behind him, he could almost feel Seth tense. "Do you need one of us to stay with you until you fall asleep?"

"Would you mind?" She sounded as if she hated to ask for the favor.

Hell, she probably did.

"No problem, angel." Seth leapt to his feet.

Beck swallowed a groan. As if the kitten nightgown hadn't been temptation enough, now she wanted them to climb in bed with her and not fuck her brains out? Yeah. And he damn well intended to cuddle up with her, too, because there was no way Seth was crawling between the sheets alone with her. "We'll both be happy to make you comfortable."

"Thanks," she said softly as he stood.

His cock seemed convinced it was going to play with her kitty, because the moment he came near her, the son of a bitch was primed and ready to go all night. He bit back a curse and told his overeager appendage to take a rest. Wasn't happening. Without any conscious thought, Beck pressed his hand to the small of her back. It only excited his dick more.

Seth seemed to have similar ideas. As soon as they reached the darkened bedroom, the big hulk lifted the covers and helped her under, then pressed a kiss to her forehead.

Beck leaned in behind him. "Clothes on. Hands to yourself."

"Yeah. Comfort, not coitus," Seth shot back as he made his way to her left and settled on top of the covers.

Ha ha. Fuck you. Beck did the same on her right.

Heavenly settled onto her stomach with a sigh and curled up with her pillow. Her breathing turned deep and even within thirty seconds.

Beck stared at the ceiling, every muscle in his body as rock-hard as his dick. If there was ever a time he needed his control...

He tried to close his eyes and empty his mind. But the luscious scent of her warm body filled his nose and teased him to the edge of sanity. All he could think about was losing his clothes, rolling her over, and sinking so deep inside her sweet pussy.

"This must be what hell feels like," Seth muttered.

Beck bit back a snarl and closed his eyes. "I don't think Satan could have thought of a torment any worse. Sweet dreams, fucker."

STILL FLOATING BETWEEN sleep and consciousness, Seth rolled over to find his face buried in the soft velvet of a woman's neck. Lifting one heavy lid, he blinked as sunlight trickled around the edges of the dark curtains and gave the room a warm glow. Heavenly, still deep in sleep, came into focus. He jerked around and stared. Unfamiliar room. Unfamiliar bed. Beck's condo.

Everything that had happened last night came rushing back.

He was still as conflicted now as he'd been then.

Thank god Heavenly was safe. And though he should probably thank Beck for stopping him from killing her landlord, Seth still wished he'd dusted the cocksucker. But Heavenly needed him far more than he needed revenge.

What else had Beck been right about?

He'd had most of a long, largely sleepless night to ponder that question.

Will you really be lost without us both, angel?

Lifting onto one elbow, he stared at Heavenly sleeping so serenely beside him. It had been a long time since he'd woken up with a woman. But waking up next to this one felt shockingly natural. It felt right.

Beneath her thin lids, her eyes darted back and forth. She was dreaming, hopefully deep in REM sleep. She needed it. He still saw dark circles under her eyes. No surprise. The poor girl had been carrying the weight of the world on her shoulders for too long.

"I'll take care of you. I'm not going anywhere," he whispered.

After placing a soft kiss on her cheek, Seth eased off the mattress.

Wearing the sweat pants he'd borrowed from Beck, he left the bed, found a spare toothbrush in the bathroom, then padded to the kitchen.

The clock told him it was just shy of eleven. A fresh pot of coffee sat in the brewer, beside two empty mugs. Seth filled one and peered out the window to see Beck sitting in a lounge chair on the balcony, sipping coffee and staring out at the Pacific.

Steeling himself for the unavoidable conversation, Seth tugged the sliding door open.

"Morning," Beck greeted. "Come on out and join me."

The ocean view shimmering under the bright Los Angeles sun was killer. Below them, the waves rolled and tumbled onto the sand. "It doesn't suck to wake up to this."

Beck smirked. "It's not so bad. Is Heavenly…"

"Still asleep." He sat down in the other empty chair, still staring out at the shimmering blue water. An awkward silence stretched between them. "Any word on Abel?"

"He's in stable condition. They're running tests now. The head of neurology has requested his records from the VA. Once Litchfield has gone over all that, I suspect we'll be making arrangements to move him to a rehab facility, but we'll wait and see what he recommends."

"Knowing her father is getting the right treatment should be a huge weight off Heavenly's shoulders. I'm sure she'll appreciate all you're doing for her and her dad."

"Maybe, but I worry she'll resist not living under the same roof with him. I already know she's going to fight the fact that we intend to take care of her."

"After everything you said last night…I'm prepared for that." He stared at the ocean some more.

When he lifted his mug of coffee, Seth accidentally bumped his hand on the edge of the table. Pain shot up his arm. He winced, sucking in a sharp breath. The battered flesh around his knuckles ripped open. Blood seeped from the wound, staining the ridges around his sore, swollen joints.

Beck tsked. "Let me see that."

"I cleaned it out last night." Seth waved him away. "It's fine."

"It's not." Beck snagged his wrist and inspected the gash. "You need a couple stitches. Sit tight. I'll get my bag."

"I don't need any damn stitches." Seth was as fond of needles as he was of California sliding into the damn ocean, but kept that to himself.

"You a doctor now?" Beck challenged.

"Shut up."

"Why don't *you*, before you accidentally wake Heavenly?"

Cursing, he watched the doctor shoot out of his seat and into the condo. When he returned with a backpack, Seth fidgeted, sending up a silent prayer not to puke.

Beck dragged his chair closer before unzipping his pack. Then he prepared antiseptic, a needle and thread, and a sterile bandage. Though the morning was cool, sweat began dripping down Seth's back. His stomach pitched like a damn Tilt-A-Whirl.

"It'll only sting a little for a minute."

"Aren't you going to numb it or something first?" Seth insisted between choppy breaths.

"If you're going to ask me that, you might as well hand me your man card. Jesus, it's only a couple of stitches."

"Yeah, in my *skin*."

"Okay, I'll give you a numbing spray." He withdrew a little bottle, and a fine mist of something sterile-smelling settled over the back of his hand. "Will that do or should I call you a wah-mulance."

"Your bedside manner sucks."

Beck laughed. "Sit back and close your eyes."

Seth dropped his lids and focused on breathing slowly, filling his mind with the most distracting visions of Heavenly he could fathom. He felt a tiny pinprick, then a tug at his knuckles, then nothing.

"How many teeth do you figure Sanchez has left now?" Beck filled the silence.

"Maybe enough to strain his oatmeal for the next few weeks." Seth smiled. "But hopefully not. I notice you beat him with your feet instead of your hands. Smart."

"Can't damage the fingers. They've earned me this amazing view." He fell quiet again as Seth felt another gentle pull on his flesh. "I still can't believe the power behind your punches. You should have been a fucking boxer."

"Nah, I don't like my brains being scrambled."

"I have to admit, I enjoyed mangling that bastard. What he expected from Heavenly was fucked up. I think that's what made mashing his dick under my heel so much fun."

Seth grunted in response. "What did you do with our bloody clothes?"

"Trashed them. I got rid of the evidence in the community dumpster this morning."

"The police won't look too hard for us. They'll probably think it was a drug deal gone bad or gang retaliation. That kind of shit goes down all the time, and Sanchez is hardly the innocent-victim type. So the cops will save their resources for someone who actually needs them."

"That's good news." Seth heard Beck snip at something, then the doctor slathered his knuckles with a thick ointment, covered it with a bandage, then sat back. "You're done."

Seth opened his eyes. "Really?"

"Really."

Already, it felt less angry.

"Thanks. You could have been a real dick about it and stabbed me." Instead, Beck had used a surprisingly gentle hand.

"I thought about it."

Seth reached for his coffee again. When Beck went inside to wash his hands, he tried to get his head together.

They needed to talk. Last night, they'd only danced around the elephant in the room. Now it was time to look the bitch in the face and tango.

Beck stepped out onto the balcony again. "She's still sleeping."

Just as well. "She needs it. And we need this time to figure things out."

"You give everything I said last night more thought?" Beck slid into his chair.

"Yeah. Kind of hard not to." Seth dragged in a shuddering breath and paused. Once he went down this path, he couldn't go back, not unless Heavenly sent him in another direction. And the more he thought about Beck's theories, the more he suspected that would never happen.

For the foreseeable future at least, she needed them both.

"And?"

Seth peered over at him, squinting against the sun. "Could you really share her, even temporarily?"

"Am I thrilled about it? No. But we're Doms. Though we may not have been acting like it lately, we both know the needs of the sub come first."

"Sure, but Heavenly doesn't even know she's a sub. Hell, I deeply suspect she is, but we have no proof—"

"Actually, I do."

Seth tensed. What had the doctor done to her? What had Heavenly let him do? "Oh?"

"Before you snarl like a damn dog, no, I didn't tie her to a spanking bench and beat her ass. I've been a good boy." He grinned. "Mostly. But I did take her to an exhibit of BDSM art."

He had to give the doctor credit; that idea was fucking brilliant. "Really?"

"She's interested."

Seth filed that information in the *oh, hell yes* drawer. But he couldn't let his dick take him off on a bunny—or rather, a kitty—trail right now. "Good to know…but even if the needs of the sub come first, you and I both know we can't force her to accept us or our help."

"Last night, she reached her breaking point. She's out of options and she knows it."

"Still, she's going to come out fighting." Seth shook his head. "She may have abandonment issues, but she's used to doing everything alone. And that girl has lots of pride."

"She does. I didn't say it would be easy to convince her to let us do the heavy lifting. I simply said we had to, for her sake."

"You know, we could—in theory—help her together, make sure she has three meals a day, a safe roof over her head, new clothes, and a secure future on the horizon… Speaking of which, I tucked this away last night." He handed the piece of paper to Beck. "Apparently, her fall tuition is past due. I'll call and take care of it in the morning. I assume no one's there on a Sunday."

Beck scanned the page. "Son of a bitch. She didn't intend to tell us about this, either."

"No. Remember, she tried to keep me out of her papers." Seth slanted a sideways glance at the doctor. "Anyway, I'm saying we could give her the encouragement and support she needs until she's feeling steady without ever laying a finger on her. After all, we did that on a smaller scale for Raine when Liam and Hammer asked for our help. That turned out all right."

Beck scoffed. "Tell me lying next to Heavenly last night wasn't absolute torture and it didn't take you right to the edge of your control. Go on," he prompted. "I'll wait while you find the balls to tell me that whopper."

"It did. I said 'in theory.'"

"Uh-huh. Realistically, there's no way we both keep our hands off her for weeks or months… And just like the care we give her, if we touch her, we have to do it together."

A couple of big objections screamed through Seth's brain. "Logically, I suppose you're right. But I still don't know how the hell I'm going to handle watching you put your hands on her."

"How about my hands on her while you've got your mouth over hers, swallowing down her moans?" Beck challenged. "Remember, last night in Raine's kitchen, you were tugging on Heavenly's hair and looking into her eyes while I damn near dragged my lips up her neck. You didn't look like you gave two shits what I was doing, just that she was engaged and aroused."

Seth froze and replayed the moment in his head. Beck was right. In fact, he'd thought even then that he and the good doctor would most likely be fucking her together soon. And that hadn't bothered him at all.

"Holy shit," he muttered.

"Exactly. If we both have her naked and screaming in pleasure, I doubt you'll be thinking about anything else." He sighed. "Think about it, man. We're too smart not to have learned something from Hammer and Liam. We have to put our petty jealousy aside."

"Of course they got on the same page. They've been friends for a decade. They'd shared a woman before. Granted, it didn't end well…but they knew each other better than anyone on the planet. You and I don't have that going for us."

"We don't, but Liam and Hammer's friendship started over a woman, right? I'm not saying we'll find it easy, but we're doing all right at the moment. The truth is, if we're serious about helping Heavenly, then we have to keep the focus on her feelings, not ours. If we can't do that, we'll lose her for good."

Yeah, Seth had been there when Raine threatened to walk forever if Liam and Hammer didn't stop snarling like a pair of dogs fighting over her as if she were a juicy bone. He still wasn't entirely sure why Heavenly thought she couldn't have a future with them, but he did know that Zelda and the dead body pranks had pissed her off enough to put on her clothes and walk out his door.

"You make valid points. But I still may end up punching you at some point."

"And I could suture your mouth closed in your sleep. It might make me feel better for a minute or two, but that won't make Heavenly happy."

Fuck. Beck was right. Again. Even so, that didn't help Seth's other major objection to this cozy plan. "All right, look. I don't know if I can do the ménage thing. Back in New York, not long after Liam separated from his ex, he and I found this sub one night…and tried it. Like I told you, I'm not a fan of swinging junk. It was awkward as hell."

"Hammer and Liam's first attempt at sharing was a disaster, and they both say it's because they had the wrong woman between them."

"Juliet was a fucking head case, definitely wrong for them both."

"Maybe…you weren't meant to sandwich a random sub between you and your Irish pal. Maybe it would be better if you had a different wingman and if we were putting Heavenly between us."

A smartass reply zipped through his brain, but it wouldn't help the conversation. The truth was, if he didn't give this a try, he already knew what would happen. Hell, Heavenly had already slammed the door on their future three weeks ago. Life had been shit since then. If he didn't want to lose her, he had to step up and complete her. He couldn't claim to love her if he refused to even try to give her what she needed.

On the other hand… "What if you're right and the sex is decent and we manage not to kill each other? And what if it takes weeks or months for her to choose between us?" Seth stared out at the endless ocean again, realizing that Heavenly's indecision could drift into infinity. "What if she never does?"

Finally, Beck fell silent, not saying anything for long minutes. "The logical part of me says we take this one day at a time. My gut tells me she might never be ready to choose, but I can't wrap my brain around that yet. One thing that occurs to me is that she won't fall in love with, much less choose, one of us if we're not being ourselves with her."

Seth scowled. "What are you saying? You've lied about something besides Gloria?"

"No, but I haven't been totally honest. I hinted that I'm in the lifestyle, but I never admitted it."

Seth pulled at the back of his neck. "Yeah, I might have failed to mention that, too. I didn't want to scare her off."

"Exactly. So…at some point we'll have to come clean about that. Because realistically, I don't know how much vanilla sex I can have without the kink creeping in. What about you?"

"Yeah, probably not a lot." He raked a hand through his hair. "So…when you took her to the art exhibit, she was into it?"

Beck leaned in. "Not just into it. She was turned the fuck on. I watched her face all evening. I catalogued her every reaction."

Seth reared back. "No shit? What did she respond to?"

"Well, she's interested in a lot of different play. More than I expected. Role play, for starters. She also wants to be commanded and made to submit. She definitely acted as if she's in favor of being orally pleasured—"

"I can vouch for the fact she's a big fan." Seth grinned.

Beck glared. "You want to gloat or listen?"

That made him laugh. "Go on."

"She likes the idea of being helpless and at her Master's mercy. But bondage, my friend, will be her gateway drug. No doubt."

Seth felt the smile creep across his face. "Yeehaw."

"I tied a damn napkin around her wrists at lunch, and she was panting and flushed in under two minutes. It was goddamn sweet."

"There are about a million ideas running through my head of all the things I'd like to do to her."

"Hang on, cowboy. We've still got two areas of concern: First, she's not into pain."

"That's not a problem for me since I can take or leave it." Seth shrugged. "But I know that's a problem for you. We'll have to deal somehow. What's the other issue?"

"I haven't exactly been able to put my finger on this. She wants to be overpowered or forced or…something in that neighborhood."

"Consensually, I hope."

"I have to think so or she would have been able to pay her rent in the way Sanchez wanted."

Seth gave him a slow nod, his thoughts turning. "You're saying our little innocent has fantasies with an edge?"

"Oh, yeah. I think under that sweet exterior is a very dirty girl. Images of subs being controlled, overpowered, and coerced had her creaming her little panties. But it would have to be with someone she trusted absolutely."

"Well, I'll be damned." He rubbed his hands together. "No problem. A sub at Graffiti often hit me up for that kind of edge play. I'm happy to accommodate."

Beck looked a little less thrilled. "You get off on consensual non-consent?"

"I'm not opposed to it. If it's what Heavenly wants and we negotiate well in advance, why not? You're not judging me, are you, sadist?"

"No." But something on Beck's face closed up. "The question that keeps turning around in my head is, she wanted nothing to do with Sanchez for obvious reasons. But River? She *offered* herself to him. Granted, to retain control of her body. But I keep wondering, would she have gone through with it if he had said yes?"

Seth paused for a pair of reasons. First, Beck's subject change was too abrupt not to notice. Second, he asked a really good question. "Maybe, since her back was against a wall. But my gut feeling…no. My sister-in-law is always telling me that most women aren't built for meaningless sex like men."

Which was why Maggie had often called him a manwhore and chastised him for never bothering with things like dating or girlfriends. He'd been about the hookup for years. Wouldn't she cheer and clap now if she could see exactly how hard he'd fallen?

"Um, I think maybe we know different women." Beck frowned.

"Well, Maggie has Heavenly's sweet sort of disposition. I think it's entirely possible our girl will only truly respond to men she loves. And somewhere in her heart, whether she wants to admit it or not, I think she does."

Beck nodded. "We've got a place to start, then."

"Yeah." An idea turned itself over in his head. It was ruthless…but it was brilliant. "Maggie also says that the more love you make to a woman, the more she loves you back."

"You're saying that if we want to pluck on her heartstrings, we need to, um, pluck her body?"

"Yep." Seth sipped his coffee, not even caring that it had gone lukewarm. "Probably a lot."

A big smile spread across Beck's face. "When the hell can we start?"

"The sooner the better. Wine and a nice dinner, kisses, a few sweet words—"

"And some rope."

Seth chuckled. "Definitely rope. But we gently seduce her and…see what happens."

A slow smile spread across Beck's face. "Count me in."

HEAVENLY HAD NO idea what time it was when she rolled over with a gasp. Her dad! He must need her. But she realized she lay in a big, fluffy bed, and she remembered that, for once, he didn't need her before her feet even hit the floor. The staff at the hospital were undoubtedly taking good care of him.

She sighed with relief, rolled over, and stared at the digital blue numbers on the nightstand clock. One in the afternoon? Oh, goodness. Granted, she hadn't fallen asleep until nearly five this morning. But she couldn't remember the last time she'd slept anything close to eight hours.

She groped the bed around her. The covers on both sides were cold. Beck and Seth were long gone now, but their deep breathing and soft snoring had lulled her to sleep almost instantly. Whenever she'd awakened, the sense of security and belonging she felt with them had tugged her toward slumber again and again.

Last night, they'd taken care of her utterly. It went against her independent streak, and she intended to get on her own two feet quickly…but she couldn't deny how much she appreciated everything they'd done for her. And how much she loved them for it.

Sliding out of bed, she listened through the door for the sounds of them in the kitchen. Silence. Frowning, she quickly brushed her teeth, washed her face, and re-braided her hair. After a swipe of lip gloss, a sweep of mascara, and a change of clothes, she was ready to face them and the day. She'd give anything to spend today with Seth and Beck. Not only did they have a lot to talk about, but she yearned to be with them. She shouldn't. It wasn't fair since they wanted a future she wasn't ready for…but that didn't stop her heart from wishing they could find common ground.

Thoughts racing, she stepped into the kitchen and stared out the sliding glass door with a gasp. The Pacific lazed in its shimmering blue perfection for as far as the eye could see. The sight was stunning, but what really caught her attention were Beck and Seth lounging in chairs on the balcony, seeming to share an easy conversation.

When had they started getting along? They had pulled terrible pranks on each other…then suddenly they'd been confronting her together about her admittedly stupid plan to use River. Heavenly felt more than vaguely ashamed about that now. Not long after that, they had raced her to the hospital, held her hand, helped her father, beat the snot out of her landlord, and brought her to safety—all without a single argument.

Because the situation had been too harrowing for squabbles? Or because something had changed?

With a mixture of anticipation and dread, she pulled the balcony door open. They both swiveled in her direction.

"Morning, guys."

"Morning." Beck stood. "Coffee?"

"Breakfast?" Seth offered.

"I can get it. Have you two eaten? I don't mind cooking. You did it last night. Then, if you don't mind, I'd like to go see my dad."

"Sure. I can take you. I need to make rounds anyway." Beck gestured her inside. "But I talked to the staff this morning. He rested comfortably last night and seems to be in good humor."

"That's a relief. Thanks."

"I'll go with you." Seth set his big palm between her shoulders. "I'd like to make sure your dad is all right, too."

That simple touch shouldn't affect her so much. But everything these two did made her fluttery and giddy and achy.

Get your mind out of your panties. There's way too much going on now to think about their kisses and caresses…and where those might lead.

"That would be great. Then, unfortunately, I have to be to work at five. I'm there until close and clean-up are done."

"We'll drop you off and pick you up," Seth said, his tone firm with steel.

That would be a problem since they didn't actually know where she waited tables. She'd never wanted the humiliation of them knowing she flashed ninety percent of her body to strangers for tips. Now…well, she had the feeling they wouldn't be pleased if they found out.

"I can take the bus."

"You're done taking the bus, Heavenly." Beck leveled a glare at her that brooked no argument.

She closed her eyes. Since she had to keep this job—none of the alternatives tipped half so well—she was going to have to lie. Dang it. She'd rather not. At least there was a kids' pizza place about half a mile from Bazookas. She'd have them drop her off there and walk down the road. They would feel better about everything, and she would be fine.

"All right. Thank you."

Quickly, Heavenly tossed together some pancakes and bacon. It was a huge treat to cook in a kitchen stocked full of food and new appliances. She hummed as she chopped cantaloupe, aware of Beck and Seth watching her intently. She could only imagine what they were thinking after everything that had happened last night.

When she set the food on the table, Seth helped her into her chair. It was second nature to grab their plates and serve them. She'd been doing it for her father for years.

When she realized her faux pas, she set Beck's plate down with a grimace. "I'm sorry. Habit."

Seth didn't mind. He was already digging in with a moan.

"Don't apologize." In fact, something in Beck's smile said he liked it a lot.

Seth nodded, almost the same little grin playing at his mouth.

Sometimes she didn't understand these men…

After putting a few bites into her belly, she sipped her orange juice and blew out a breath. "I know I owe you a lot of explanations."

Neither said a word, but their expressions were rife with silent agreement.

"I don't even know where to start. I didn't tell you anything because…"

"It wasn't our problem," Seth finished for her. "We've heard this. There's more to it."

"There is." She swallowed. "I could give you a lot of excuses, but the truth is, my mom left as soon as she found out my dad was sick and not going to get any better. She took half of their savings, the car, and everything out of her closet one Sunday afternoon. Then she left. I remember I was studying for a history test when she came into my room and…" Her throat tightened and her nose stung. Damn it, she didn't want to cry. It had happened a long time ago, and she should be over her mother's crap now. "She didn't even hug me, just said she hadn't signed up for life with an invalid. That she and Dad had taken care of me for fifteen years and I could return the favor." She bit her lip to hold in tears she didn't want to spill. "I was shocked. Then confused. Over the next few months, I became angry."

"Of course you did." Seth's face was full of pity, the same sort mirrored on Beck's.

"I never heard from her again. To this day, I have no idea where she is."

The two men exchanged a glance, then Beck took her hand. "And your mom taught you that people don't stay, so you tried to get rid of us before we could walk away from you."

"No." She shook her head as she gathered her thoughts. "Mom taught me that when you give people your problems, they disappear."

"Oh, Christ." Seth set his fork down and reached for her other hand. "That's why you kept everything to yourself? Angel, neither of us is leaving. You need us, and we're going to be here for you."

"Whatever problems you have, we're going to help you," Beck assured.

She withdrew her hands from theirs. "I appreciate the help. I really do—"

"There better not be a 'but' in that speech of yours." He raised a brow at her.

Seth looked equally displeased by the notion.

"Thanks, but I don't want a handout. I needed help with my father. I admit. His meds, coupled with the rent, got too expensive for me to keep up with and—"

"We know. I'm taking care of your fall tuition in the morning," Seth cut in. "There's no way you're not going to school come September."

"I'll pay you back."

He shook his head. "If you're able to pay for your schooling next spring, great. If not, you and I will figure something out."

That would be a huge load off her shoulders. Taking from Seth made her feel more than a little guilty, but she couldn't afford to skip school and put her future on hold indefinitely. "Thank you."

He acknowledged her with a nod, then she turned to Beck. "I'll move out of your condo as soon as I can find somewhere—"

"Stay."

"I can't do that."

"You won't be in my personal space. My house is ten miles away. This is just a place to crash when I'm too tired to make the drive home."

"It's still too much to accept." She shook her head. "I can't freeload."

"You are so infuriating." Beck gritted his teeth. "All right. I'll rent it to you for ten dollars a month. Does that make you feel better?"

Heavenly gaped at him. "If you take less than three thousand a month, you're crazy."

"It's my condo to do with as I wish. So if I want you to have it for ten bucks, that's my right. All you have to do is say yes. C'mon. Make us feel better, would you? We don't like worrying about your safety, and that shithole you lived in…"

"I'm going to be seeing it in my nightmares for a long time. You don't need another Sanchez to deal with," Seth insisted. "Say yes."

"Why are you doing this? Any of this?" She gave up on food and pushed her plate away. "I already told you that I don't know what I want my future to look like, but I'm not ready for anything serious. I'm not even ready to choose between you and—"

"You don't have to," Seth said. "We are willing to just…date you. Together."

She reared back, stared. "You mean the way Raine is with both Liam and Hammer?"

"Yes," Beck supplied. "You don't have to choose before you're ready, and we mean that this time. We're not going to fight or escalate the pranks. We just want you to keep an open mind and an open heart, to accept both of us in your life…and see where it leads."

Heavenly blinked. She wasn't sure whether shock or excitement won out. They were offering her not just a solution to most of her problems but her fantasy. "I don't know what to say."

"Say yes," Beck pressed. "You can stay here while your dad gets better. You'll be safe while you focus on school and figure out your feelings for us."

She wanted to agree so badly… "The arrangement seems awfully one-sided. You're giving me so much and—"

"You'll get what you need. We'll get what we want. Win-win for everyone," Seth added.

"All right." A tremulous smile spread across her lips. "I feel like I'm taking advantage of you when I can't give you any assurances for the future, but if you're willing to see what happens, I'm willing to try." She reached for their hands again. "It hurt me to walk away from you, and living without you both has been awful."

She glanced between them. Something told her they were inclined to pull her into their laps and kiss her. Instead, Seth pushed her plate in front of her again. "Eat. If you're going to be on your feet all evening, I want to make sure you've had enough food."

Beck gave her a considering glance. "I don't suppose you'd consider quitting so you can concentrate on school and we can spend more time with you?"

Heavenly had been employed since the day she turned sixteen. She needed the income. She certainly didn't expect Beck and Seth to support her. "I can't."

"Of course." He sighed heavily. "Dig in."

A few more silent minutes passed. She finished another pancake. Seth started the dishes. Beck took a call from the hospital about one of his patients. The scene was surprisingly domestic, almost comfortable. The fact that she liked having them so close confused Heavenly. She didn't want a future full of commitments or responsibilities…but she was loath to think of being without them.

Not sure what to make of that, she helped with the clean-up, then packed herself a sandwich for dinner tonight. Beck helped her find a cooler for her food. Then they were heading to the hospital. She was anxious to see her father. Of course, he was in good hands, but she'd feel so much better once she laid eyes on him. And he would probably feel better once she assured him she was all right.

When they walked into his room, she was surprised to find him sitting up and surprisingly alert. His color looked almost vital. He was even full of smiles.

"Hi, boo."

"Dad." She rushed to take his hands. "You look great."

"I feel strong. Dr. Litchfield and I had a long chat this morning. Nice man. He adjusted my meds. He said my condition may be up and down for a bit while he tries to stabilize my immune system, but today feels better."

"That's fantastic news!"

He looked past her and set eyes on Beck and Seth. "Dr. Beckman. Mr. Cooper."

The speculation in his stare made her squirm. Now that he wasn't half asleep, he was wondering what these two men had done to his little girl last night. Nothing, and she knew that. But that didn't mean they hadn't touched her in the past…or that they wouldn't touch her in the future. Heavenly didn't mean to, but she blushed to the roots of her hair.

"Just Seth." He shook his head as he came forward to shake her father's hand, then settled himself beside her, resting a casual arm around her shoulders.

"You can call me Beck," the doctor invited with a manufactured smile as he took her hand in his and brought it to her lips.

Heavenly froze. They were declaring themselves to her father without saying a word. They met her subtle attempt to work free from their grip with an implacable hold. Short of making a scene, she was stuck between them.

"I want to assure you, Abel, that I'm going to—"

"We," Seth cut in, motioning between him and Beck. "We're going to."

She wished she could close her eyes and escape. Or put a stop to this. What must her father be thinking?

"Yes," Beck corrected. "Seth and I have had a conversation, and *we've* decided it's in everyone's best interest if we both take care of Heavenly. We'll make sure she eats well, has a safe place to live, a quiet space to study, and can focus on her future. She'll be well looked after and well cared for."

Why hadn't they just shouted the fact they intended to take her to bed together? "Guys…"

"I see." Dad pinned the men with a knowing stare. "I'd like to speak to my daughter alone."

"Of course." Seth pressed a kiss to her temple, then he stepped out of the room.

Beck squeezed her hand. "We'll be outside if you need us."

"Shut the door." Her voice shook.

Dad might be sick and weak, but he was still her father and he was going to flex his parental muscle.

As soon as the door snicked shut, he motioned her closer.

She approached on trepidatious steps. "Dad…"

"Do you know what you're doing?"

Not really. "I'm fine."

"Do you know what they want from you?"

When her dad studied her with that shocked expression, she didn't know what to say. She didn't want to lie to him, but she didn't want to give him a heart attack. "I do."

"Baby, you don't have to…let them pervert you—"

"I'm not." Heavenly didn't want to cry. She wanted to be strong for her dad. But she couldn't stand the thought of him being ashamed of her. "I'm with them because I'm in love."

Her father was silent for a long moment, then he reached a shaking hand out to her. "Oh…boo. Are you sure? Are you ready to tie yourself to *two* men who have already lived a lot and seen the world and are ready to settle down? Because Beck and Seth are."

How had everyone seen that but her?

"You look surprised. It's all over their faces," Dad went on. "They want forever with you. You've always talked about travel and adventure and exploration. I want you to experience those things…"

And she wanted to, as well. She'd always wanted to. "I've told them I can't do forever, just right now."

"You're a sweet girl with a soft heart. You're a loyal child who's stayed with me because I needed you all these years when you should have been spreading your wings and flying away. I'm so worried you'll be the same kind of woman to them, that you'll never get to live for *you*."

"Dad…"

"Promise me you won't let that happen." His grip was surprisingly strong. "Promise me that, before you commit your future to anyone or anything, that you'll live those dreams you've always had. Meet people, experience cultures, see the world. Find out who *you* are before you have to figure out who you are with someone else. If your mother had done that, maybe she would have stayed."

What could she say when she suspected he was right? "All right. I promise." Even though he leaned back against his pillows in relief, she still felt the tension in his body, in the room, and wanted so badly to allay it. "Dad, they didn't lay a finger on me last night. In fact, they've hardly touched me at all."

That wasn't totally true. But they hadn't pressed her for sex. Her father could read between the lines. Hopefully, that would give him some peace of mind.

"It's a matter of time, boo. They want you. They intend to have you. It's going to get messy, emotional, and complicated. I hope you're ready for that."

No. It terrified the hell out of her. "I'll be all right. I promise. I have to get to work. Call me if you need anything. I'll check on you first thing in the morning, okay?"

"Take care of yourself, boo. I love you."

Heavenly bit her lip, trying to hold herself together. She'd worried and disappointed him.

She'd exchanged one set of problems for another.

At least in this scenario, Dad was getting the best medical care possible. Her feelings mattered far less.

After brushing a kiss on his cheek, she sent him the brightest smile she could manage. "I love you, too."

Tears were falling as she reached the door and opened it to find

Seth waiting inches away, stock-still. Beck paced the hall, fists clenched.

How much had they heard?

"Thanks for bringing me here to visit. I'm ready to head for work."

"Are you all right?" Seth ventured, concern all over his face.

She didn't want to talk about it, wasn't ready to deal with her conflicted feelings. "Fine."

The guys exchanged a glance. Neither believed her.

"Please. I can't be late."

Beck sighed. "We'll go. But we're going to talk about this later."

"Absolutely," Seth agreed.

The ride to Pepp-E-Roni's Pizza Palace was quiet. On the one hand, she needed the paycheck and she was happy to escape the inquisition they were obviously itching for, if only temporarily. But she would also far rather be spending the evening with Beck and Seth. Heck, the night with them. Her father was right; she wouldn't be able to put them off for long. But the way she wanted them, that thought filled her with way more heady anticipation than unease. Individually, they'd given her such pleasure. Together...she sighed. She could only imagine.

But it wasn't just the ecstasy she looked forward to. It was being with them, expressing her feelings for them, without worry that she'd be upsetting one or the other. Finally, she'd be able to show them that she loved them equally and honestly.

Hopefully, the love she made with them would be enough.

Because the future was coming, and she couldn't do a damn thing to stop it.

CHAPTER TWENTY

As River maneuvered his truck through traffic, Beck leaned up from the backseat and snagged the man's attention in the rearview mirror. "You don't need to take us out for a beer, man. What's done is done."

"Yeah, but I feel like shit for not telling you guys when Heavenly approached me. I swear, I told her to ask you two to do the, um…deed. When she refused, I should have said something. I'm sorry."

River sounded contrite, as he damn well should. His apology was enough, but if buying them a few brews would clear his conscience, fine. At least it would distract Beck from the endless mental replay of Heavenly and Abel's earlier conversation at the hospital. He and Seth had both overheard. Trouble was on that horizon. Sure, the old man was preparing their girl for the inevitable, but the prospect of Heavenly living up to her promise before settling down worried the hell out of him.

She wouldn't refuse her father's dying wish to experience life and explore the world.

Their only hope was to use every moment before her father's ravaged body gave out to surround her, devote themselves to her, drown her in pleasure, and bestow on her all the adventure she could handle. They'd give her life without monumental responsibilities, with people she could count on. They'd make sure she had a million reasons to smile. They'd show why she should reconsider her future.

Beck hoped that would be enough.

Sure, he and Seth had annihilated Heavenly's barriers last night. This morning, she'd opened up to them more than ever. But he knew that girl. They had exposed her, left her no place to hide. Necessary, of course, but she didn't like feeling vulnerable, resisted relying on anyone. If he and Seth didn't pour a sturdy foundation under her ASAP and prove she belonged with and to them, she'd be gone faster than he could blink.

Scrubbing a hand over his face, Beck tried to fight off dread.

After quick stops by Seth's apartment and his house to change into clean clothes, Beck grabbed a few essentials for later, along with a thick envelope from his attorney from the mailbox. He tore into it. His divorce settlement. About damn time. Heavenly might not see a future with him yet, but he was going to be ready, because he intended to convince her they had one.

He shoved the document in his pocket as River whipped his quad cab 4x4 into a crowded parking lot. Beck glanced out the window. A gaudy neon sign announced their destination, and he rolled his eyes. He'd never been here, but he'd heard plenty of talk.

"Why the hell did you bring us to a breastaurant?" Seth scoffed from the passenger seat.

"He's probably hoping to score with one of the babes who work here. Sorry, man. I know you get lucky a lot, but these girls are even out of your league," Beck quipped.

"They're not. Already been here and done this," River said smugly. "I thought you might enjoy the great wings and ice-cold beer. But I brought you for the scenery."

"If we wanted to drool over tits and ass, we could have gone to Shadows," Seth drawled as River pulled into a parking space and killed the engine.

"Trust me. You two want to see this."

Beck doubted that. He'd seen more naked women in his life than stars in the sky. But he played along and followed River through the front door.

The place was packed. Raucous laughter and loud music assaulted his ears. Suddenly, he regretted leaving the oasis of the quiet condo.

"Good evening, gentlemen. Welcome to Bazookas."

A striking brunette with surgically enhanced "headlights" eyed them with a smile. Her breasts nearly spilled out of her skimpy white bra. To call the pleated scrap of fabric clinging to her hips and barely covering her pussy a skirt would be damn generous. Once upon a time, Beck would have enjoyed the view. Now? Nothing.

"Well, hello yourself." River winked.

She responded with a coy smile. "Booth or table?"

"A booth would be great, sweetheart."

Beck leaned close to Seth. "Why are we here?"

Seth shrugged. "Maybe he needed a couple wingmen."

"What he needs to learn is that rejection builds character."

"I get the feeling he doesn't hear 'no' a lot."

Beck got that feeling, too.

Sure enough, River whispered something in the hostess's ear. She sent him a mischievous grin. "Follow me."

They passed tables crowded with half-drunk frat boys and single professionals on the prowl before the weekend wrapped up. One smacked a passing waitress on the ass. She paused, cocked a hip, then flashed a saucy smile over her shoulder. Yep, she knew exactly how to ply a fat tip from the idiot.

The hostess showed them to an alcove at the back of the restaurant. The two bench seats hugged the narrow walls with a giant table in between. Beck laughed when River snagged the side that afforded him a panoramic view of the waitresses, leaving him and Seth to stare at River's shit-eating grin. Beck slid into the dark corner. He didn't really care.

Seth slid in beside him, across from River, while the hostess handed them each a menu and sashayed away. As he and Seth scanned the appetizers, River craned his neck, gaze darting around the room. Clearly, what he wanted to eat wasn't on the menu.

"I can find a marker and write FREE TONGUE RIDES on your forehead if you think it'll help," Beck drawled.

"Don't be hating. It's not my fault you two are so pussy-whipped you stopped making women scream months ago."

"Your sister has a big mouth," Seth growled.

Instead of defending Raine, River suddenly snatched up his menu and buried his face.

"Hi, guys. Welcome to Bazookas. Can I—"

That voice had Beck's head snapping up from the menu and zeroing in on the all-too-familiar waitress.

Heavenly.

She stood at the end of the table, gasping, eyes suddenly wide as the moon. The red flame of embarrassment sailed up her chest and settled on her cheeks as he got a look at her getup. Just like the hostess, her breasts overflowed from her tight white bra. The smooth flesh of her bare torso was interrupted only by the gentle indentation of her belly button. The tiny strip of fabric showed off her hip bones and barely shrouded her pussy.

What. The. Fuck?

How many drunk assholes had pawed, slapped, and propositioned his girl? Probably dozens, and he wanted to kill them all.

His blood boiled.

His body tensed.

Every cell thundering in his veins turned to lava.

His inner beast jerked, fighting the urge to bend Heavenly over the table, lift that joke of a skirt, and turn her ass red. The girl fucking belonged to him, and he itched to prove it to her. But he'd be goddamned if he exposed another inch of her skin in this cesspool of overflowing testosterone.

"Oh, my gosh." Above his rage, he heard Heavenly's voice quiver. "W-what are you doing here?"

"I think the better question is, what are *you* doing here, little girl?" Beck growled.

"I-I'm working."

"Not anymore, you're not," Seth vowed as he tossed an arm around her waist and lifted her. Ignoring her yelp, he swung her over his lap and onto the bench, trapping her between them.

Beck grabbed her chin. "You've never worked at the pizza place, have you?"

"No."

Seth curled his fist in her hair and turned her toward him. "So you lied to us again?"

"Not technically. I told you I worked in a place with overgrown kids who had sticky fingers and that the uniform was embarrassing. That's all true. I never said I worked at Pepp-E-Roni. I just asked you to drop me off there."

"Are you fucking kidding me?" Beck growled, palm itching. No, it burned. "You're damn lucky there's a couple hundred people in this place."

"Amen. Have you been working here since December?" Seth demanded with a scowl.

"Yes."

It was all Beck could do to hold his shit together. "For three fucking months? Why? Why would you purposely parade your half-naked ass in front of a bunch of drunk perverts?"

Determination flickered in her eyes. "Do you honestly think I want to work here? That I like wiggling into this…costume? No! I do it because I have to. Between school and volunteering, I only have twenty-five hours a week to make money. It had to be enough to put a roof over my dad's head *and* buy food and meds and every other essential in life. I chose this over stripping or streetwalking. With my education and skill level, this was the only other job that paid enough for me to scrape by."

"We solved your problems last night. This morning, you opened up and talked about your mom. We had everything out in the open. So why the fuck did you mislead us about this job?"

"I hated to be dishonest. But I didn't want you to worry over something I can't change."

Seth huffed out a furious breath, shaking his head. "You thought sneaking behind our backs would be a great way to repay us?"

"No. I'll be forever grateful for what you've both done. You saved my dad… But I don't see how making you support me entirely is any sort of thank-you."

"Don't you get it? You don't have to scrape by anymore. Beck and I will take care of you."

"You're not going to support me, and I need this job to survive."

Her words sliced at Beck's heart. He remembered being sixteen and on his own. Being hungry and willing to scavenge for any morsel he could find from dumpsters behind restaurants simply to stay alive. Being scared to sleep for fear he'd be beaten or raped by drunks stumbling down the alleys. Then, he'd been willing to do almost anything for a clean bed and a meal. He'd been too proud to ask a damn soul for help. If Gloria hadn't intervened, Beck had no idea where he would have ended up—or if he'd even be alive.

Fuck, he understood where Heavenly was coming from. He just didn't like it.

"The hell you do." Seth looked furious enough to spit nails.

Beck held up a hand and shook his head. "I understand you need to work. Okay, but not here. We'll find you another job."

Seth sighed angrily but didn't refute him. "Fine."

"There are tons of well-paying positions at the hospital," Beck improvised. If there wasn't, he'd create one. "You don't even need to be licensed."

"Really?" Hope flashed across her face.

"Yes. I'll make some calls in the morning, but you're done strutting around this place, wearing that"—Beck plucked at the strap of her paltry uniform—"getup while every man in the room eye-fucks your goddamn brains out."

"That's fucking final!" Seth barked.

Heavenly pinched her lips together. "I'd be happy to have a job where I could keep my clothes on, but when you two helped Dad and me last night, you didn't say it came with strings."

"It doesn't," Seth insisted.

Beck scowled. "What are you talking about?"

"You don't have the right to run my life. You're not my daddy."

Beck bristled. "No, I'm not. But you need one, little girl. And I'm the closest thing you've got. Starting right now."

First order of business? Get her out of that ball-churning outfit, away from all these drooling pervs, and lay down some fucking ground rules.

When Beck locked eyes with the PI, Seth nodded. They were on the same page. "Get your things. We're taking you home."

Heavenly gaped as if they were speaking a foreign language. "I can't just walk out. I have to finish my shift."

"Your shift here—and your future as a Bazooka-Babe—are over." The PI hovered and let his displeasure show as he stood and extended his hand to her. "You hear me?"

She nibbled her lip pensively, then placed her fingers in his palm and stood. "Why are you both doing this?"

"Because we goddamn care, angel." Seth pulled her against his chest and held her tight, like he was afraid she was seconds from slipping away.

As he slid from the booth, Beck had the same fear. He moved in behind her and pressed himself tightly against her back. "We're going to prove that."

A man wearing a dirty apron, an angry scowl, and a name tag that read PETE – ASSISTANT MANAGER rushed their way. "What the hell do you two think you're doing? Get your hands off her!"

"Back off. This doesn't concern you," Seth warned.

"Heavenly is my best Bazooka-Babe. You're damn right this concerns me." Pete puffed out his chest in challenge.

"*Was* one of your best," Beck corrected. "Our girlfriend no longer works here."

"She's with both of you?" He looked skeptical. "Since when?"

"Pete..." She stepped out of their embrace and approached the man, apology softening her face. "I'm sorry to leave you in a lurch, but I never intended to stay this long. I'm quitting, effective now."

Beck heard both the guilt and the triumph in her voice. She felt empowered to be leaving this degrading job. And he loved giving her that ability.

"Heavenly, don't do this." Pete sighed in exasperation. "At least finish out this week."

"I can't. I've got school, my dad is in the hospital, and I want to spend time with my...boyfriends."

Pete's mouth curled in a snarl. "Then don't expect to get your job back."

"Fine. Don't expect to ever exploit her for a buck again," Seth gritted out through clenched teeth.

"Then leave. Clock out and get your shit! I'll hire someone who puts out," Pete growled, then stormed away.

Beck shoved down his anger and brushed a kiss onto Heavenly's temple. "I'm proud of you. Get your purse and change. We'll wait here."

"That felt good. Thanks," she murmured as Seth kissed her forehead. Then she scurried off.

"So I hope my apology has been adequate." River hopped out of the booth and slapped their backs with a grin. "I'm going to hit the head. Be right back."

As he jogged away, Seth sighed. "Our little hellion needs boundaries. She's been setting her own for too long."

"And she's in over her head." Beck scrubbed a hand through his hair. "We definitely need to put her on a short leash. And find a way to keep her from fucking lying to us all the time."

"Couldn't agree more. But first, you were right earlier. We have to be honest with her about who and what we are."

They had to out themselves.

That was fine by Beck. He'd known it was coming, and he was sick of stifling his Dominant nature behind his good-doctor façade. "Yeah. Until we do that, we can't lay out any rules or expectations. And we certainly can't spank her for this crap. That's got to change."

Time to find out just how submissive she was, and if she'd be willing to let them teach and guide her. At the thought, a whole new level of uncertainty began uncoiling inside him.

"I'm over pretending I don't need to exert control," Seth admitted. "I can't imagine the struggle you're going through. But you'll have to cage your dark side because she's nowhere near ready for that, man."

"She's not. And she might never be." He'd once told Gloria that making the sadist in him stop wielding a paddle or whip would be like the surgeon in him cutting off his hand. He'd been wrong. To his shock, the need to protect, nurture, and provide Heavenly respite had superseded his desire to inflict sweet pain.

Seth commiserated with a bob of his head. "So, we're going to tell her everything?"

"We have to."

"It's risky, especially for you."

"We'll stress the importance of anonymity."

"Yeah. And open, honest communication."

Beck chuckled. "That's the first damn thing we start with."

"If we'd been ourselves from the start, I wonder if we'd be in this clusterfuck."

"You mean if we'd spent our time helping her down her path, instead of trying to win her by peeing on her like a fire hydrant? Probably not."

"We could have saved ourselves a shitload of stress." Seth exhaled, then sent a narrow-eyed glare over Beck's shoulder. "Is he trying to piss me off?"

"Who?" Beck turned to see River, one arm slung over Heavenly's shoulders, as they approached. Thankfully, she'd donned the T-shirt and yoga pants she'd been wearing when they'd dropped her off at Pepp-E-Roni's. "You're the genius who offered him a job."

"Don't remind me," Seth groused.

When the four of them met up near the hostess stand, Beck scowled at River. "Hands off her, GI Joe."

River lifted his arms in the air. "Just trying to keep her from being accosted by a drunk coming out of the john."

Beck took Heavenly's hand. "Time to go."

She nibbled her bottom lip once more. "I know. I just feel like…I failed."

"Why would you think that? No. You've been drowning for a long time, little girl. You stayed afloat as best you could."

"Let us give you a life preserver, angel. Hang on and we'll pull you to safety, all right?" Seth cupped her shoulders.

"I'll try."

They wrapped their arms around their girl and followed River out the door. Beck and Seth climbed into the back of the massive pickup, situating Heavenly between them.

River jumped in behind the wheel, then twisted and grinned. "Hey, Seth. I got licensed, like you said. You wanted me to prove I had some PI skills. Did I pass the test tonight?"

"How did you do it, man?"

"You're the one who snitched?" Heavenly gaped.

"Twice. But I especially owe you an apology for blurting out your personal shit in my sister's kitchen last night. I didn't mean to embarrass you or air your business where anyone at the party might have overheard."

"And you have the nerve to call Raine a troublemaker," Heavenly chided. "How did you find out I was waiting tables at Bazookas?"

"Good detective work." River preened, then laughed. "And luck. When I called the guys earlier to apologize and they told me where they'd dropped you off for your shift, I was leaving the gym not far away, so I decided to swing by the pizza place and apologize in person. When I got there, I saw you walking away from Pepp-E-Roni."

"We watched you walk in," Seth pointed out.

Heavenly nodded. "I know. I stayed for about ten minutes."

"In other words, long enough for us to leave the area?" Beck raised a brow at her.

She nodded and sent him a little grimace.

"I followed you," River told her. "Imagine my surprise when you went inside Bazookas. When you didn't come back out, I peeked in and saw you in your…um, uniform. Since I'd already violated the guy code once, I called Beck and Seth back and invited them to join me for a beer." River turned an expectant stare to Seth. "Did I get the job?"

"All right. You're hired. Now drive."

"Where to?" River asked.

"My condo." Beck tried to tamp down his impatience.

Heavenly clasped her hands together and nervously worried her thumb over her finger. Long minutes of thick silence stretched through the car. She broke it with her soft voice. "I know you're both upset with me right now, and—"

"We're not happy. But we're not going anywhere." Seth threaded his fingers through hers.

Beck seized her other hand, strumming his thumb over her wrist. "Later, we'll talk about what happened tonight. Right now, there's something more important."

She tensed, trepidation crawling across her face.

"Stop," Beck admonished. "We're not leaving or kicking you out or even asking you to pay us back. Get those fears out of your sexy little head."

"We're simply going to open more lines of communication," Seth assured. "So we don't have any more…surprises."

"Okay." Heavenly lowered her lashes and nodded.

"Is there anything—big, small, or seemingly insignificant—you're still keeping from us?" Beck prodded.

She shook her head.

Oh, no. If they were going to let their kink flag fly, reinforcing rules started here and now. "We expect verbal answers, little girl."

She jerked her stare up to him. Yes, she remembered the way he'd made her speak each response at Angelo's when he'd bound her wrists.

"No. You know all my secrets."

His nerves were pinging like the signal off a cell tower. He and Seth shared a pensive stare as another uncomfortable silence filled the air.

"You two are starting to scare me. What's with the serious expressions? What's going on?"

Having this private conversation in the back of River's truck wasn't his first choice, but Raine's brother already knew about their kink. Besides, Heavenly had chosen to give him first dibs on her virginity, so he must not make her too self-conscious.

"We have to be honest, too." Seth squeezed her hand. "I know you went with Beck to a BDSM art exhibit. He said you two had a good time."

She stared at the two of them as if they were from Mars. "Yes."

"Was it educational, angel?"

A pink flush crawled up her cheeks. "I-it definitely made me think about things I never had."

"Some of those works turned you on," Beck pointed out. "Your pulse quickened, your breathing slowed, your eyes dilated, and I could smell your sweet pussy."

Heavenly's eyes widened. "You really were watching how I reacted?"

"I cataloged every shiver and gasp."

"B-but…" Suddenly, she seemed to confront the unavoidable truth and swallowed tightly. "You're into that stuff?"

"We both are," Seth confirmed, cupping her chin and turning her to face him.

"Oh, my gosh."

"We're not saying this to frighten you," Beck explained. "If we expect you to be honest with us—"

"Which will be an absolute from now on. No more lying," Seth interrupted sternly.

"Ever." Beck nodded. "That means we have to be totally honest with you."

A soft shiver wracked her body. "I'm not sure what to say."

"Then listen. There are rules. Like Seth said, one is always telling the truth," Beck began. "Another one, which is sacred, is anonymity. You always protect the identity of those in the lifestyle."

"So you can't talk about Beck's proclivities at the hospital. It could ruin his career. You understand? We're sharing our secret with you, and trusting you to keep it."

Heavenly blinked. "Raine, Liam, and Hammer. They're...in the lifestyle, too?"

The two men shared a glance. Finally, Seth shrugged. "The morning Bill attacked Raine, that fucking newscaster basically spilled it to the world."

"True," Beck bit out. "Ignorant prick."

"So, the answer is yes?" Heavenly prodded.

"Raine, Liam, and Hammer are," Beck confirmed. "Hammer owns a BDSM dungeon here in LA. Where I'm a member."

"A dungeon?" Heavenly blinked.

"Yes. And Raine has worked for him for years. He took her in off the streets and kind of...adopted her when she was seventeen, but he never touched her until a few months ago."

Seth nodded. "I met Liam and Hammer both at a BDSM club in New York years ago."

"Wow." Heavenly looked stunned. "That's... Wow. And Raine is..."

"Their submissive."

"I guess that explains why you four are so dang bossy..."

Despite the tension, Beck laughed.

"I'm not bossy." Seth looked mildly insulted.

"Oh, no. Never." She snickered, then covered her grin.

Her teasing was way closer to acceptance than Beck had expected, especially this quickly. Of course, they hadn't given her enough information yet to really comprehend what she might be getting into. Heavenly would have a million more questions, but his fear that she'd instantly run away in horror had been laid to rest.

She sobered. "What happens now?"

"Anything you want," Beck promised. "We can go back to the condo and explore the things that turn you on. Or we can grab some drinks, sit on the balcony, and listen to the ocean. Like the women in the images you saw at the gallery, ultimately you hold all the power."

"You said that but..." She grappled for words. "What does that mean? How does everything work?"

"Good questions," Seth praised. "BDSM is simply an exchange of power. The Dominant and submissive build their relationship on a foundation of honesty, trust, and communication. You, as the submissive, agree to hand over your control to us, the Dominants. Boundaries and safe words give you the ability to stop everything if you're scared or overwhelmed or…"

Beck sat back and listened to Seth explain the dynamics to their girl. He caressed her hand, watched her face, and hoped like fuck this worked.

In many ways, he would be starting at zero, too. Usually, by the time a submissive sought him, she'd traveled her path of enlightenment and grown self-aware enough to crave the wicked edge he wielded. While Heavenly might end up at that crossroads someday, Beck refused to pin his hopes on that. Instead, he'd put his whole soul into helping Heavenly grow and blossom—and enjoy the fuck out of the journey.

"It's a lot to take in," Heavenly whispered.

Beck smiled and cupped her chin. "In time, everything will make sense. For now, just let us be by your side," he murmured, leaning in low, hovering just above her lips. "We'll stay here, helping you, until you wonder why you ever worried."

He pressed his mouth to hers, reveling in the texture of her soft warmth. He glided his tongue along the seam until she parted her lips and welcomed him. Heat enveloped his body. His cock stirred, growing thick and hard. Heavenly moaned and squeezed his hand, then suddenly gasped, sucking the air from his mouth. He opened his eyes.

Seth's fist was cinched in her silky mane. "That's fucking hot."

Yes, and they were supposed to share her.

Slowly, Beck eased back, staring at her glistening, slightly swollen lips. "I still want to spank your ass."

"Why?"

"To punish you for lying."

Sadness tugged at her mouth. "I see it from your perspective. I do. But I don't need more punishment. My mom left and my dad is dying. Isn't that enough?"

Jesus, she was right; life had beaten her bloody for years. But even when she'd run out of options, Heavenly had never given up. Beck didn't love the choices she'd made, but he admired the fuck out of her moxie.

From this day on, he would protect, nurture, and adore this amazing woman…at least for as long as she let him.

"Then let us pamper you." Seth slid his hand free and cupped her nape before slanting his lips over hers.

Watching their passion evolve was erotic, but seeing them filled Beck with a strange sense of peace. He and Seth needed to ease her into womanhood beneath their capable hands gently, thoughtfully, reverently—not like she'd been shoved into adulthood as a child. Together, they would broaden her horizons…open up her mind, body, soul, and, god willing, her heart.

The smooth, soft flesh of her neck called to him. Beck leaned in and glided his tongue up the milky column, nipping and laving all the way to her ear. Under their combined onslaught, Heavenly squirmed, her muffled whimpers of delight a potent aphrodisiac.

Fuck, he wanted to feast on her day and night. "You like that, don't you, little girl?"

She moaned into Seth's kiss. He released Heavenly gradually—a nip, a brush of lips, a peck. When he pulled away, her eyes looked half-lidded in bliss. Her lips shimmered red in the shadowy night.

"This is a little bit like torture," she murmured.

"It is, angel. The sweetest, most amazing torture on the planet." Seth darted a glance up at River. "How much farther, damn it?"

"Just around the corner. Thank god," he murmured. "It was getting awfully—ahem—hard to drive with you three sucking face back there."

"Shut up and keep driving," Beck growled.

Seth cut Heavenly's laughter short when he swooped in to claim her lips again. Beck palmed her thigh. Desire hung ripe in the air. He was feeling impatient as hell.

Finally, River pulled up in front of the condo and shoved the truck into park. "Have fun, you three. Don't do anything I wouldn't enjoy."

Seth laughed and bailed out of the vehicle.

Beck shook his head as he stepped onto the pavement, too. "If you're going into battle tonight, make sure you cover your junk, soldier."

"I never let my gun get dirty," River quipped. "Heavenly?" When she paused and met his gaze in the rearview mirror, he smiled her way. "Tomorrow, you're going to thank me for turning you down, I promise."

With a blush, she left the backseat and watched him drive away.

Beck and Seth each wrapped an arm around Heavenly's waist and led her into the building. As they ascended to the top floor, they glided their lips, tongues, and mouths over every available inch of Heavenly's skin—neck, lips, and the velvety flesh above the V of her T-shirt.

By the time they reached the top floor, she was breathless and clinging.

Retrieving the keys from his already tight jeans, Beck nearly groaned as the fabric pulled tighter. He was primed and more than ready.

After he unlocked the door, they'd barely made it inside the condo before Seth pinned Heavenly against the wall. "Balcony or bedroom, angel?"

"Bedroom." She clutched his shoulders. As Beck's heart stopped, she turned to him, losing herself in his eyes. "I don't want to be unfair since I can't promise you tomorrow, but I want you both so badly right now."

Beck sauntered closer. He'd take right now. It gave them time and opportunity to show Heavenly what she was missing. It gave them the chance to finally have her. He wanted this girl more than he wanted his next breath. And tonight, he planned to claim her.

CHAPTER TWENTY-ONE

"WE WANT YOU, too, angel," Seth whispered against her mouth, his voice seemingly magnified by the dark.

Then the big PI cinched his hands in Heavenly's pale curls and plundered her mouth. Beck knew how fast and how completely Seth was falling under her spell because he knew the texture of her soft lips and the slick warmth of her tongue. He knew the feel of her lush body molding to his. He'd never forgotten, because the first time he'd kissed the girl, she'd left an indelible mark on his soul.

As she lost herself in the mind-stealing kiss, Seth swallowed Heavenly's needy moans. Beck watched, heart chugging and cock throbbing.

This was really happening.

His whole body tingled as he approached the two. The moment felt huge, and even if Heavenly thought tonight would change nothing, he knew better. It was going to change every fucking thing between them. It would answer a lot of questions.

For better or worse, what happened next would shape their future.

The first thing he and Seth were going to find out was whether they could truly keep their jealousy at bay and share her for more than a kiss or two. If they could, they'd worry about trying to make this thing work longer.

Of course, that only mattered if Heavenly stayed. When she'd told him and Seth that she didn't see a future with them and walked out the door, it had messed him up. Sure, she was with them now, locked in Seth's passionate kiss, but could they really fuck her into the kind of love that would make her want to stay?

No clue, but they were out of options.

"Seth...."

Heavenly gave a breathless little plea as she dug her nails into the

PI's wide shoulders. Then she pressed her eager mouth to his again and climbed his big body, lifting her legs and wrapping them around Seth's waist. The kiss turned feverish. Heavenly whimpered, rolling her hips against him. Seth's guttural groan hummed with low agony.

Jesus. Watching them all but fuck with their clothes on zipped arousal up Beck's spine. But he wanted some of that for himself, too.

When he sidled closer, Seth eased Heavenly's back from the wall and turned her pert ass in his direction. He was sharing her. No fight, no drama, no marking territory. It seemed like the most natural thing in the world for Beck to nod appreciatively for the gesture, then fill his hands with her soft, warm backside.

Spreading her spandex-clad cheeks, he leaned in and aligned his throbbing erection in between, then bent to her ear. "I can't wait to slide my cock deep inside you right here, little girl."

Her throaty moan made him smile. So, she liked it when he talked dirty. Good to know.

"Y-you're going to do that to me?"

"Yeah, and I'm going to look forward to hearing you scream."

Seth swallowed her gasp. Beck closed his eyes and buried his face in the crook of her neck. Sweet berries and heady feminine musk swirled in the air, making him dizzy. Every cell in his body screamed at him to claim her. Own her. He couldn't stop himself from nudging against her tiny opening one more time.

Connected to them both, Heavenly sighed and dropped her head to his shoulder, arched her back, and rocked rhythmically between them. Beck clutched her hips and guided her, dragging her against his aching cock.

Fuck, yes.

As hot as he felt, he swore the blood would boil out of his veins when he got balls deep inside her. For him, that moment couldn't come fast enough. But she wasn't ready. Double penetrating a virgin without hurting her was going to be no easy feat. They needed to take things slow, prepare her well.

Beck pressed a kiss to the pulse point at her neck before maneuvering a hand between her body meshed against Seth's. He cupped her breast and thumbed her stony peak. "But first, we're going to strip you bare, press your naked body between us, and send you soaring."

His words had her rolling her hips faster, her indrawn breath a wordless demand. An impatient rumble rose from deep in his chest.

Seth eased back and cupped her face, forcing her gaze to his. His voice rasped with need. "Bedroom. Now. Before we can't make it."

Beck related. If they didn't move, they'd end up fucking her on the carpet. Her first time—hell, *their* first time—deserved to be more special than that.

"Ready for us to make love to you?" Beck murmured in her ear.

"It's all I can think about," she gasped. "I want to feel you everywhere on my skin. I want to feel you so deep inside me."

Her confession stunned and aroused the fuck out of him. Based on Seth's expression, he was equally blown away.

"I'm all about giving you what you want. Let's go." The PI cupped Heavenly's ass, lifted her against his body, then raced from the foyer.

"I'm right behind you." Beck stayed two steps off Seth's heels as they dashed to the bedroom.

Inside, he flipped on the soft overhead light, jerked open the closet door, and dragged out his spare toy bag. He grabbed a handful of condoms and a tube of lube.

When he turned, Seth was still at Heavenly's mouth, her body inching down his wide frame until he finally set her on her feet. Then Beck locked stares with the girl and tossed the items on the nightstand. His heart jackhammered in his chest.

Another checkpoint. Another opportunity for her to change her mind. It was getting awfully real, and he couldn't help but wonder if her natural shyness or inexperience would rear its head. If it would shut them all down.

She cut her glance over to the pile of prophylactics and nondescript white tube. Her breath caught. She bit her lip.

Yeah, she knew things were getting really real, too.

"Should I take my clothes off?"

Beck couldn't speak for fully ten seconds. Seth seemed stunned equally mute as they both stared.

Their little virgin mirrored the one in his fantasies—swollen red lips, smoky eyes, chest rising and falling in uneven breaths. The only thing missing from this spank-bank vision was the pigtails. But he'd rather have Heavenly as she looked right now, because she was real.

Seth grazed his knuckles along the side of her breast, then feathered them over the sensitive tip. "How are you feeling?"

He didn't touch her anywhere else, but that one caress had her shuddering, eyes half-closed. Then the sensation seemed to roll down her spine. She tossed her head back, swaying unsteadily on her feet. Beck wrapped his arm around her for balance, but he couldn't resist trailing his palm down to cup her ass.

Heavenly worked to catch her breath. "It's like my blood is boiling and my skin is on fire. Like there's plenty of air, but I can't breathe."

"You're aroused, angel." A wide smile crossed Seth's face. "I hope you like the feeling because we're going to ramp you up a whole lot more."

"Please." The little cry slipped from her lips.

Oh, fuck. He liked to hear her beg.

Beck seethed with the need to have her writhing beneath him. "Then get naked for us, little girl."

With a nervous nod, she reached for the hem of her T-shirt and whipped the pink cotton over her head. When she dropped it onto the floor, he drank in her slender shoulders, the sweet flare of her lace-cupped breasts, and the smooth, golden skin of her torso.

Beck's cock lurched. He clenched his fingers and his jaw at once. God, help him find restraint.

"I need that bra off," Seth snapped. "Now."

Still, she hesitated, her gaze bouncing back and forth between them.

"What's wrong?" Beck tried to sound like he wasn't dying to rip the rest of the fabric from her body and get inside her now.

"I just realized, you've seen me naked...but Seth never has."

The big PI sent him a sideways glance, then opened his mouth before quickly snapping it shut. Yeah, Seth wasn't happy Beck had seen her all pretty and bare. But dwelling on it now wouldn't do any of them any good.

He'd expected they would run into a few dangerous rapids while navigating uncharted waters. They'd just have to learn to row around them.

"Don't be nervous. I already know he's in for a treat," Beck offered.

"You're damn right I am. Come on, angel…"

Seth's reply laid some of his worries to rest. Sharing hadn't been as tough as he'd feared—so far. Maybe they could cooperate, stay on common ground. But they'd have to practice absolution. Their contentious past couldn't matter tonight.

Drawing in a bracing breath, Heavenly reached behind her and unfastened her bra. The thin straps slid down her arms. The lacy fabric tumbled to the floor. Her pale, rosy-tipped breasts sprang free.

Both men exhaled with a heavy groan.

"Fuck, you're gorgeous." Seth attacked the buttons of his shirt and tossed it aside. "I can't wait to get inside you."

Heavenly's eyes flared at the sight of the man's wide chest, defined abs, and ink. With curious fingers outstretched, she brushed the tips across a Chinese symbol tattooed over most of his left pectoral. "It's beautiful. What does it mean?"

He flattened his hand over hers, near his heart. "It means Master. I've had it for years, since shortly after I found BDSM."

"And this?" She traced the design on his right shoulder with a delicate hand. "It's stunning."

The tattoo was an ornate work of black and gray, occupying all the space between the base of his neck and his elbow. The angel spilled across his shoulder, front and back, from the sword clenched in his fists to the wings unfurling behind him.

"St. Michael, the protector."

As she absorbed that, her brow furrowed. "When did you get it?"

He swallowed. "Eight years ago."

Seth seemed far less forthcoming about this tattoo. Beck understood. If Heavenly was going to ask him about all his ink…it would lead to some really tough explanations he wasn't ready to give. Hell, he might never be ready to give them.

She placed both palms on Seth's ripped chest. The guy obviously had a hell of a gym habit. The big PI sucked in a breath and closed his eyes, fighting the urge to grind her beneath him. Instead, he let her touch him at will. When she placed a kiss directly over his heart, a shudder wracked him.

"Heavenly…" He cradled her breast as if he couldn't help himself.

She covered his fingers with hers and squeezed. "You're beautiful."

He peered at her like she meant the world to him. "No. You are. So blinding I can't believe you're standing here, giving yourself to us."

Lifting his hand, she brought it to her lips and brushed a kiss across his knuckles. "Happily. And what about you, Doctor? Can I examine you?"

Her quip made him smile. "If you're inviting me to get naked with you, the answer is hell yes."

As he stripped off his shirt, Beck was surprised to find his hands shaking. Holy shit, how was a damn virgin undoing him?

Then, as she had with Seth, she let her fingertips play across his skin. Wonder crossed her face when she zeroed in on the ink splashed across his right pec. "Oh, my... This is gorgeous. A knight with a lance and a shield?"

Shit. She was going to ask questions. He didn't have answers. "A defender."

"Like you." She smiled, her eyes bright and blue and full of adoration.

If she knew the truth, would she be quite so accepting?

"What's on the inside of your bicep?"

Resolved that she was going to insist on a visual tour of his body, he held his arm out and let her read.

"I'd rather die on my feet than live on my knees." Her stare bounced from the script up to his face. "What made you get that?"

Experience. "Oh, you know. Young and stupid. I thought it sounded like a good motto to live by. There's more." With a sigh, he turned left and exposed his back.

She gasped, and he knew why. An enormous angel of vengeance consumed every inch of his skin from shoulder to shoulder, base of the neck to base of the spine. The creature's wings and arms were outstretched, muscles rippling, flames licking, fury all over his skeletal face.

"Wow," she breathed. "That must have hurt."

It had, but not as much as the reason he'd gotten it.

"I tried to stay drunk through most of it." It was true, but he hoped the humor would deflect her from more questions.

Heavenly traced some of the wings with her fingers, then caressed the angel's face. "Will you show me your shoulder?"

There was no avoiding it. He didn't say a word as he pivoted to show her the ink of a young woman, clutching flowers to her chest, wings outstretched, face scarred with tears. "Before you say anything else, little girl, we've spent a lot of time telling our ink stories and not enough time with our mouths on you."

A self-deprecating laugh fell from her lips. "I've been really curious, haven't I?'

"Uh-huh."

"And…you've been really patient, haven't you?"

"Uh-huh."

"As much as I can be," Seth added. "Now I think it's time for you to get naked and see how many times we can make you scream."

"Exactly." Beck kicked off his shoes.

Beside him, Seth shucked his pants. Beck followed suit, carefully releasing his zipper, hissing in relief when his aching cock sprang free. Seth did the same when he maneuvered his dick out of solitary confinement.

Heavenly's jaw dropped. She raked a hungry stare over them. "Wait. You're saying I don't get to explore"—her stare dropped to their cocks—"those? That's not fair."

"Like what you see?" Beck fisted his staff and stroked himself with a laugh.

"Yeah," she breathed, her stare glued to them.

"We'd like to enjoy looking at you, too. But we have to see *all* of you." Seth raised a brow. "Finish stripping."

"Oh. Right." She gave a jerky nod and toed off her shoes before dragging her pants down her slender legs and kicking them away.

She was bare, and instantly he smelled her pussy in the air.

Beck tensed. His cock stiffened. His head swam. If he didn't get his mouth on her quickly, he'd lose his fucking mind.

"Mercy…" Seth roughed out on a deep breath.

As if their thoughts were hard-wired, they began circling their girl.

Inspecting.

Appreciating.

Memorizing.

Heavenly gave a little shiver. Goose bumps peppered her skin.

Beck dragged his finger down to the swell of her breast, traced a circle around her tightly drawn areola, and pinched the tip. "Pretty."

At the same time, Seth lowered his fingers to her triangle of golden curls.

Heavenly jolted, inhaling an uneven breath that became a shudder when Beck engulfed her nipple in his mouth. She sank her fingers into his stinging scalp, clutching him tightly against her breast.

"Feel good?" Seth demanded.

"Yes." Her little hiss morphed into a groan.

She writhed under their touch, and Beck suspected the man's fingers were now doing more to her downy curls than merely exploring.

He smiled before he bit down gently on her nipple and tugged. She sucked in a tiny yelp. He soothed her sting by laving her with his tongue. When he gave the other the same treatment, she rewarded him with a shaky exhalation.

He would have happily feasted on her soft tits longer, but when Heavenly's breath began sawing in and out of her chest, Beck couldn't resist taunting her. "Is Seth rubbing your pussy, little girl?"

She responded with a dreamy moan as she writhed against the man's busy hand.

Her reply was utterly adorable…but not the verbal answer she knew he expected. Drawing his hand back, he landed a sharp spank on one of her cheeks. The feel of her soft flesh yielding beneath his hand and the satisfied tingle sliding up his arm made Beck want to roar.

Heavenly's eyes flew open, and she squealed. "What was—"

"You didn't use your words."

"No, but she just left a fucking puddle in my hand." Seth sent him a triumphant grin.

"Did she now?"

"Oh, yeah."

Beck cupped Heavenly's nape. "Would you like some more spankings, little girl?"

"I-I don't know…why—"

"Why that rush of sweet cream came pouring out of you?" Seth nipped at her shoulder.

"No." Heavenly dropped her lashes as if too embarrassed to face them.

Beck smacked her ass a little harder.

"Ouch!" She clenched against the sting.

But when he smoothed his hand over her heated flesh again, she sighed so sweetly.

"Failing to use your words is unacceptable. So is hiding your feelings," Beck chastised. "Open, honest communication. Remember?"

"Yes."

God, he was dying to spank her just to feel her under his palm and see how much having a red ass would arouse her. But now wasn't the time. When she was comfortable with the rules and their expectations, when she was secure in the knowledge she was safe between them... Then? Hell, yes.

"Now, answer the question." He dropped his voice. "Do you want me to stop?"

"I suggest you answer honestly. I feel you spilling honey like an overflowing hive," Seth added. "Even if you're not sure whether you want more, your body knows. Beck's spankings turned you on."

"And we're ecstatic they did."

"Really?"

"Hmm," Beck hummed against her neck. "You know, Cooper, it would be terrible to let all that precious cream go to waste."

"A damn shame. Get on the bed, Heavenly." Seth strode across the room and yanked off the comforter.

"I think he's anxious," Beck murmured in her ear.

Heavenly graced him with a soft, shy giggle.

As he tucked a strand of hair behind her ear, he lost himself in her eyes, hypnotized by the slashes of silver surrounding deep azure. "He's not the only one who's lost patience."

She slung her gentle palms on his shoulders. "I've wanted your touch even when I thought you'd never look twice at me."

Beck's breath caught. From the first time she'd lifted those lashes and peered up at him, she'd shocked his heart awake. Since then, she'd changed him, made him want to be a better, gentler man...the kind of man she could love. "I've never not wanted you."

Her face softened with apology. "But it happened the same for me with Seth. One look and—"

"I know." And Beck did. He didn't like or understand it, but he was done questioning it. "It's all right, Heavenly."

"We're big boys," Seth assured, circling her waist from behind.

Heavenly backed away, and for the first time since they'd crossed the threshold, she looked worried. "I know this isn't what either of you wanted, and my dad—"

"Not now," Seth insisted. "There's no one here but us. What do *you* want?"

"To please you both…and I don't know how."

After everything she'd been through, her first concern was pleasing them? That blew Beck's mind.

Understanding settled across Seth's face as he gathered the girl into his arms. "All you need to do tonight is open yourself and trust us. Can you do that?"

She nodded. "I already trust you both."

God, what sweet words.

"Then lie back." Beck helped her onto the middle of the mattress.

Impatience crawled up his spine as he stared down at their brave, beautiful girl. Innocent hunger filled her eyes. She didn't know what they intended, but she desperately wanted this…wanted them.

No matter what it took, he and Seth had to give her the most memorable night of her life.

He glanced at Cooper. The man's stoic expression told Beck they were on the same page—again.

He locked eyes with Heavenly. "Spread your legs for us, little girl. Show us your pretty, wet pussy."

That pink blush he'd grown to love painted her cheeks as she slowly parted her legs.

"Wider," Seth commanded.

As she inched her thighs farther apart, her feminine musk now saturated the air, compelling Beck to crawl between her knees.

"Brace yourself. She'll set your damn taste buds on fire," Seth growled.

For an unguarded moment, jealousy knifed Beck. He forced himself to yank out the blade. No more putting this petty shit above her. It wasn't a competition. There were no winners or losers. Time to exercise the same sage acceptance Seth had shown earlier so they could shower Heavenly with the passion and love she deserved.

"Wait until you feel her pretty mouth wrapped around your cock," he drawled without an ounce of malice.

"Beck!" She gaped in embarrassment.

"What?" He opened her wider and glided his palms up her thighs. "It's the truth. You've got a sinful tongue."

"Yeah?" Seth grinned. "I want that. I want that now."

God, the million things they could show her... The epic pleasure they could give her... The many ways they could twist her body—and her mind...

If she'd stay long enough to let them.

Beck refused to let worry creep in. Heavenly might have turned his life upside down, stolen his heart—then given him zero hope for the future—but he had to believe after tonight that she would want more. The wonder and awe lighting up her face were too bright to be snuffed so quickly.

Beck cleared his mind and focused on Heavenly spread out before him. Vaguely, he noticed Seth stacking pillows under her head before he aligned his cock against her mouth. She blinked up at him, uncertainty lining her face, before she bravely parted her lips.

The memory of her mouth surged through Beck. His blood thundered. Demand roared.

He focused on Heavenly's pouty, glistening folds, feeling like a kid on Christmas morning opening the special present he'd pinned all his hopes and dreams on. Inhaling her deeply, he filled his lungs with her thick, heady scent. Then he gripped her hips and lifted her to his mouth.

Beck trailed his tongue up the inside of her thigh, laving a shimmering path to her golden curls. Heavenly writhed, restless and seeking, as he parted her with his thumbs. Her juices seeped like warm syrup.

He couldn't wait. He swiped his tongue through her slit. Her tart essence made his taste buds sing. His body hummed. His cock wept. And his heart soared at the sheer perfection of his first taste of Heavenly.

With a growl, he latched onto her mound and began tongue-fucking her narrow, satiny walls without mercy. Her muffled cries and her undulating hips urged him to drive her higher.

"You look so fucking hot, angel," Seth groaned. "And your mouth feels insane."

Beck's cock pulsed impatiently against the sheet as he stared between her splayed thighs, watching Seth glide between her parted lips. The man fisted her hair as he shuttled in and out of her mouth. Heavenly looked beyond beautiful drinking in Seth's benevolent approval.

Determined to wring even more pleasure from her, he slid one finger inside her clutching walls and sucked her sensitive clit. When he pressed another finger inside her, she tensed, arched. The sounds of her muted suffering lit him up like a bonfire.

Twisting his fingers inside her sweltering core, he dragged them over the sensitive patch of nerves behind her clit. She bucked against his mouth again as a fresh torrent of liquid flooded his tongue.

Seth cursed and sucked in a hiss. "Angel. Christ…"

"Oh, my gosh," she panted in sweet desperation as she laved Seth's thick crest. "I love tasting you but…Beck. H-he's doing things, and I need…"

"You want to come for us?" Seth taunted as he plucked her nipple.

"Y-yes."

Her breathless reply was all the incentive Beck needed. He lashed her clit with his tongue while his fingertips toyed with the hyperaware spot inside her. Heavenly tensed. Her panting moans escalated into keening cries.

Heavenly was seconds from breaking into a million pieces.

"Give it to us," Seth insisted. "Come now!"

At his command, Heavenly's body bucked. She bore down and screamed. Beck felt her spasm, her hips jerk as she tossed back her head and splintered. He took her higher, circling her clit with his tongue and sliding his fingers through her fluttering pussy.

God, she was beautiful. Priceless. And right here, right now…she was theirs.

When climax released its grip on her, Beck stared into her smoldering, unfocused eyes. A fine sheen of sweat made her flushed skin glow. She whimpered, struggled to catch her breath again…and left him spellbound.

Seth dropped onto the bed next to her and stole her mouth in a long, passionate kiss.

Beck watched as he eased from her pussy. "Amazing, little girl."

Heavenly ended the kiss and cupped Beck's face with a sated smile. "That felt…incredible, way better than anything I can give myself." She blushed. "Even stronger than the orgasm you gave me at Angelo's."

"We can give you more, angel. First, we'll have to prepare you to take us both."

"Y-you're both going to be inside me…together? At the same time?"

Seth picked up the tube of lube Beck had left on the nightstand. "We'll take it as slow as you need. If, for any reason, you want us to stop, say the word."

Heavenly darted a glance between them, seeking, searching their faces. Then she nodded and lay back, exposing herself entirely to them. "Do whatever you need."

Her solemn show of trust undid him. Beck had to get inside her now.

He stood and held out his hand toward Seth for the lube.

Cooper shook his head and held out a condom instead. "I got this. You do the honors."

Beck stared at the little square foil in Seth's palm, his heart revving, his mind racing. Sweat beaded his brow. Sure, he'd fantasized about this over and over, but…

I don't do virgins!

Images of a different innocent girl from another lifetime assaulted his brain. The haunting apparition gripped his soul with icy fingers. He closed his eyes and tried to shove the memories away, focus on the moment. On Heavenly alone. If he wanted to make her his, this was the only way.

He swallowed. His hand shook as he reached for the condom. "You're sure?"

"Yeah. Are *you* okay with that?" Seth's brows furrowed in concern.

Of course the PI was too observant not to have noticed his hesitation. He'd no doubt ask questions later. Fuck.

Heavenly cupped his cheek, worry lining her face. "Beck, is everything—"

"All right?" He dragged in a breath, wiring his shit tight again. "No, little girl. Everything is perfect."

Then he brushed his mouth over hers before sinking past her swollen lips and savoring her.

He was going to take her virginity. Holy shit. The day he'd met her, he'd thought fleetingly that he'd break his rules to have her. He'd had no idea then that he'd be forced to shatter the one he'd held most sacred for two decades.

She smiled up at him as she wrapped her arms around his neck. Beck clutched her tight as he rolled onto his side in a tangle of arms and legs, dragging her with him.

The cap on the tube of lube opened with a pop. Seth wasn't wasting any time.

Beck didn't, either. He deepened the kiss, their tongues tangling as he slid his fingers between her warm thighs. Her saturated curls coated his digits as he penetrated her and thumbed her clit. Beck swallowed her erotic mewls as Seth worked to thin the rigid rim of her backside.

"Christ, she's so damn tight," Cooper growled.

The moment Seth worked a finger inside their girl, Beck felt him behind her vaginal wall. He absorbed every gasp and shudder and play of pleasure across her face. He strummed her clit and teased her G-spot, revving her…but he never let her sail over the edge.

Finally, Seth squeezed in a second finger. A tremor skittered through Heavenly. Her eyes grew unfocused. A wail rolled off her tongue. Beck smiled as Seth added more lube and quickly inserted a third finger.

"Relax and let him in." Beck held her quivering body and peppered her with kisses. "Once you do, we'll fill you with every burning, aching inch of our cocks. Then we'll all go up in flames."

Heavenly gave him a little nod as she rocked her hips between them. Her brows knit and the lush bow of her lips pursed as she processed the sensations he and Seth heaped on her. Beck let her set the tempo, unwilling to jerk her from the euphoria consuming her as Seth started seesawing his fingers back and forth. She dug her nails into his arms. Her soft, kitten-like mewls became pitiful moans.

She was going to come apart again.

For Beck, watching Heavenly was like watching a butterfly break free of its chrysalis. She was emerging more gorgeous than he'd imagined.

"Just one last finger to work inside you," Seth cooed.

"It burns." Her breathy voice shook. "It's so…"

"Good?" Beck snarled.

"Oh…" Her lashes fluttered shut. "So good."

"Can you imagine what it will feel like when we both squeeze our cocks inside you?"

"N-no. But I want to… I need… Oh. Please…"

"Ready to come again?" Seth asked, sweat dripping down his face.

Heavenly lifted her heavy lids as if trying to focus. "Y-yes. The fire…it's so hot. Overwhelming. I can't stop…"

Beck glanced Seth's way. He nodded.

The interminable wait was nearly over.

As he eased his fingers from Heavenly's pussy, she let out a frustrated howl.

With his teeth, Beck tore open the condom and dragged the latex over his pulsing shaft. He refused to think about the fact that he was violating the one tenet he'd always thought sacrosanct and merely thought about hearing her screams of ecstasy thundering through his ears.

The sound of ripping foil told him Seth was gloving up as well.

Then within seconds, they were again on the same page without exchanging a word, both driving their fingers into her body once more. Through her thin membrane, he brushed knuckles with Seth. Together, they drove her to the edge. Heavenly's high-pitched cries echoed off the walls and filled the air while she ground herself against their thrusting fingers.

"That's it, little girl," Beck growled. "Come!"

Heavenly screamed as rapture ripped through her. She clamped down, her walls fist tight and crushing his fingers. The sight of her squirming between them punched Beck in the chest.

"We need to move now, man," Seth barked, jerking his fingers from her virgin backside.

Digits still locked in place, Beck rolled her to her back. Ecstasy made her eyes glassy. Bliss transformed her face.

Beck had never seen any woman wear pleasure so absolutely and purely in all his life.

Swallowing hard, he hovered above her and kneed her thighs apart, then eased his fingers from her body and aligned his crest to her sweltering, still-pulsing opening.

It was time.

A lump of emotion clogged his throat. Tears stung the backs of his eyes.

He threaded his fingers through Heavenly's and dragged her arms above her head. She lifted her heavy lids and met his stare. She knew what he was about to do. Beck saw no hesitation or fear, just trust glowing from her blue eyes as she lay her soul wide open, somehow wrapping her entire being around his heart.

He loved her.

Beck couldn't explain or contain it. It just...was. And somehow he already knew that whatever happened next wouldn't be like any sex he'd ever had. He'd had an inkling once that if he ever fucked this girl, it would wreck him. He'd been right. She was going to both destroy and rebuild him in ways he couldn't fathom.

Locking his gaze to hers, he pressed his wide crest against her narrow folds. Heat crawled up his body. He shuddered with sensation. Jesus, he hadn't entered her yet, and she was already undoing him.

Beck dug for patience. Sweat ran from his temples. His arms trembled as he held himself above and slowly began to inch in.

Quickly, he reached her fragile barrier and paused, breath hot and harsh. As he gazed into her eyes, the gravity of the moment slammed him.

"Please," she begged with a beseeching stare.

Then she surged up and pressed her mouth to his, imploring him with her breath and her lips and every fiber of her being. How could he refuse her?

Clenching his jaw, Beck eased back, stared into her eyes, then plunged forward—and tore through her innocence.

The air rushed from their lungs. She tensed and panted rapidly, squeezing her eyes shut. Slowly, he tunneled deeper, watching pleasure and pain tangle on her face.

He was finally, completely inside her.

Though his cock was strangling inside her gripping heat, he remained unmoving, letting her adjust. Torturous seconds ticked by like hours. "Talk to me. Please tell me you're okay."

Academically, he knew he may have caused her something between discomfort and pain. But goddamn it, he needed her to be all right, to want him as deep inside her as he could get.

Finally, she opened her eyes and met his stare. Her pink tongue swept across her parted lips. Then she sent him a blinding, lazy smile. "I'm...wonderful. More?"

SETH RELEASED HEAVENLY and crawled onto the mattress beside her, breath held. Anticipation zipped up his spine as he watched the moment Beck rolled his hips and claimed her virginity. The air left Seth's lungs in a rush. Pleasure-pain rippled across her flushed face as she trembled, trying to adjust to the thick cock stretching her tiny pussy.

Fuck, he couldn't take his eyes off her. Seeing her cross into womanhood left him speechless.

Heavenly's breathless, raspy groan seeped under his skin, scored his flesh. His cock was on fire. The urge to drive deep and bestow on her every delicious, dirty, deviant pleasure he could think of deluged him. Seth already knew that once he got inside her, he wouldn't stop until she could feel him—feel them—all the way to her fucking soul.

"Talk to me." Beck's low demand filled the room. "Please tell me you're okay."

Her lashes fluttered lazily and opened. "I'm...wonderful. More?"

"As much as you can take," Seth rumbled.

She sent him a come-hither smile that shocked the hell out of him—and killed his patience.

"Get her in position. I can't wait." He grabbed the lube and slicked a layer over his cock.

"You got it." Beck rolled to his back, dragging Heavenly on top of him, his shaft still buried inside her as her slender legs straddled his hips.

Surprise skittered over her glowing face at the new sensations. Her mouth fell open. Then she wriggled on the doctor's dick with a gasp and a sigh, hands braced on his shoulders, as she sank impossibly deeper.

Her body undulated. Her back bowed. Her pale hair spilled down, draping over Beck's thighs. Even though he'd ten times rather be fucking her, too, Seth almost hated to stop watching.

Heavenly shocked him again when she opened her eyes and sent him an unfocused stare. "I'm ready."

Shit, had there been a vixen sleeping inside their virgin?

"Oh, angel… It's so on."

Seth raced to the foot of the bed and knelt on the mattress between Beck's legs. Wrapping an arm beneath her breasts, he pulled her against him, gratified when she melded herself to his chest.

Impatience rode Seth as he nipped at her ear and notched his cock against her ass, sliding his hard length back and forth between her plump cheeks. Heavenly moaned and rolled her hips back at him.

"You're fucking turning me on," he grunted as he gripped her and rubbed his skin—his scent—all over her.

"Me, too," Beck chimed in, his big hands engulfing her small waist. "Jesus… Hurry, Cooper."

Seth gave a sharp nod, but he was distracted by Heavenly swaying and surging against his dick. *Goddamn it…*

He jerked her against him even tighter, dragging her over the aching head and sensitive column. He dug his fingers deeper, knowing he'd leave bruises. The worry didn't stop him from straining for more, tendons popping in his neck, face contorting as he found a deliberate, demanding rhythm.

"She's so fucking tight," Beck bit out.

Seth was desperate to feel her for himself.

With an animal moan, he plowed his fist in her hair and tugged her face to his, gaze delving into her smoldering blue eyes. She panted, full of hunger, lips parting. The girl's half-lidded stare was fixed on his mouth.

Yeah, he wasn't refusing that invitation.

Seth devoured her lips, swallowing her raw cries. He cupped her breast, captured her beaded nipple, twisted and squeezed. She surged into his hand, into his kiss with a keening wail. He did the same to the other, torturing the bud until she whimpered and quivered and melted under his touch. He soaked in every one of her incoherent pleas. Oh, she was going to be a thrill to bend to his will.

He could hardly wait.

Peeling his mouth from hers, he scraped his teeth down her neck. "I'm going to fuck that pretty ass. While Beck is shoving his way up your cunt, I'm going to work every inch of my cock into your backside and plow you until you can't breathe."

"Fuck, yes," Beck moaned. "We're going to stretch you, make you burn hot and fast until you come for us. You'll still be bucking and shaking when we start all over. By the time we're done wringing pleasure from you, you'll be boneless and begging for mercy."

"And don't expect much of that," Seth added.

He caught the flutter of her lashes, watched her red, swollen lips form a sinful O as she twisted and wrapped her arm around his neck, her body flowing and rolling between them. A little smile played at her lips. "That sounds...perfect."

He stared. She was serious.

Seth swallowed hard, trying to contain his animal growl. "Head down. Ass up."

She gave him a little nod and began to lean onto Beck—but not fast enough. He propelled her against the man's chest, holding her flat with a palm between her shoulder blades. The doctor took full advantage, claiming her lips as he fucked up and into her. Seth couldn't stop staring, transfixed by the sight of Heavenly's parted thighs and Beck's thick stalk disappearing into her between. Her deep groan tangled with his panted breaths. The sounds were somehow muted yet magnified in the small room, spotlighting the intimacy of their passion.

His head swam. His heart roared. His dick screamed.

Fuck, he could barely breathe.

It was time.

Seth pressed his cock to her rosette. He gently squeezed his wide crest in, just against her tiny ring. His eyes nearly rolled into the back of his head. Hell, he'd be lucky if he didn't come like a teenager the second he felt her close around him.

"Seth..." She tossed her head back, skeins of her pale hair spilling everywhere.

"Hold on to me," Beck commanded. "Breathe out as he slides in.

Exhale and push down."

She arched, flattening her hips. "Like that? Is it going to hurt?"

"Just like that." Seth brushed his thumbs across the small of her back. "If it doesn't blow your mind, angel, I'm doing something wrong."

He rocked forward, pushing harder against her rim as he spread her cheeks with his hands. God, he'd never wedged his cock inside anyone so small. Sweat collected on his brow. His muscles screamed as he eased deeper.

Finally, his crest penetrated Heavenly's tight ring. A cry of shock tore from her throat as he submerged himself completely into her scalding heat. The air left his lungs as he bottomed out.

His heaven on earth had welcomed him completely inside her hot, silken body.

"No pain, angel?" he croaked.

"None." Her breath sounded uneven as she plunged and swayed between them experimentally. "I feel so full. It's…"

"What?" Seth barked. If she needed him to pull out, he'd have to do it now. He wasn't even moving yet, but the pressure and ripple of her narrow opening had every nerve in his cock lit up like fucking fireworks. His balls ached. He squeezed her hips tighter, fighting the compulsion to rock back, then thrust deeper. "What is it?"

Heavenly gripped Beck's shoulders and slid her lips up his neck until they rested near his ear. "Amazing. I feel"—she gasped when Beck fucked into her again—"taken."

And she clearly liked it.

Seth cursed. "Because you are."

Playtime was over. This newly awakened, sensually aware Heavenly was exciting the fuck out of him. He might have entered this bedroom believing he was going to claim her, but she clearly intended to claim them, too. Her little speech about not seeing a future with them? Yeah, he was calling bullshit. She belonged between them, igniting every power-hungry fuse in their Dominant brains.

He nodded Beck's way, letting the man know he was good to go. The doctor jerked his head in understanding and began to rock his hips. Then when he retreated, Seth surged. Back and forth, they worked wordlessly and found their rhythm.

Heavenly clutched and clung, making the most delightful and desperate noises. Seth bent and dragged his lips across her back as he hurtled himself inside her burning, velvety passage, digging his fingers into her soft hips and sinking his teeth into her neck.

She wailed in need, a shiver wracking her, before she flipped a glance over her shoulder at him. Their stares fused, her hooded eyes ravenous.

He gave her what she craved, filling her with stroke after ruthless stroke. Each thrust shoved her down onto Beck and forced her to take them both deeper. It sent her clit grinding against the man with a friction that had her fighting for breath. Her clasp tightened. The pressure became unbearable. Fuck, she was already shredding his control.

Seth caught the same agony contorting Beck's face. And when she arched and tossed her head, her hair tangled in his fingers. More aching need rushed to his cock. On the surface, she seemed so shy and delicate…but here she was, reveling in her blossoming sexuality like a force of nature. Her throaty cries, glowing skin, and tiny pulses… Her pheromones saturated the air. Christ, he felt drunk on her, like he was losing his mind for her. Like he would do anything to keep her.

Apparently her pussy wasn't the only thing voodoo about her.

"Fucking perfect," Beck choked out.

Seth agreed. Tonight felt nothing like the time he and Liam had sandwiched some forgettable sub between them and had a thoroughly awkward screw. Why did this feel so much righter? The answer dredged up implications he couldn't ignore.

"Christ, yes," Seth snarled, fucking her even harder than the stroke before. "I want more."

She bit her lip and sent him another stare. "Good. I love you both inside me."

Then she was milking them—deliberately or not—with a fiery hunger that made him feel wild and ready to crawl out of his skin. He fought impatience. He didn't want to hurt her, but she needed to stop inciting him. She needed to stop turning him on so much that she turned him inside out.

Suddenly, she arched and let out a long-suffering wail as she thrashed between them, clutching them both in a crushing, pulsing grip. "I'm… Oh… Coming!"

Heavenly's cries sliced through him as she bucked and shuddered. Seth closed his eyes, threw back his head, and gritted his teeth for restraint, fucking her through her orgasm with abandon.

She was euphoria, rapture—everything he hadn't dared to dream possible.

She was stripping his soul bare.

She was stealing his fucking heart.

For a fleeting moment, he locked eyes with Beck, wondering if he, too, felt the magnitude of their connection. A tear chased its way down the side of the man's face, disappearing into his hairline, and Seth had his answer.

"I know, man." He nodded in mutual understanding. Beck had been nothing but a thorn in his side for months. Now, they were inexplicably tied together by this woman who had sideswiped his defenses and captured him, body and soul. "Same for me."

No denying anymore that he was in love with Heavenly. They both were…and probably had been for a while. The realization was exhilarating…and terrifying. She had the power to hurt him—something he hadn't given any woman in eight long years. But then, no one else had managed to get under his skin. He didn't know how or when or why this one was different. All he knew for certain was that she belonged to them.

Neither man had wanted or planned to share Heavenly. But Seth didn't doubt this was how their relationship was meant to be. True, they might have stripped the choice from her. But in return, they'd chosen what would be best for them all.

As Heavenly continued to tremble and whimper, Beck thrust deep inside her. "Again."

Seth increased his tempo as he plucked her nipples and nipped at her neck. "Give it to us."

Heavenly withheld nothing as she shared their rhythm, sucking them in deeper than ever, a chorus of moans, grunts, and sighs melding around them.

"C'mon. I want your hot pussy melting all over my dick, little girl."

"I-I can't hold back. It's…too…much. I-I…need…" Her desperate words rang between them, a perfect searing plea that sent goose bumps rippling across Seth's skin and need shuttling straight to his cock.

His balls drew up tight and hard. "I can't hold back, either."

"Fuck. I'm losing it, too," Beck growled.

The man thrust up harder, his balls slapping with Seth's as he shoved inside her.

Heavenly went wild. Her screams became high-pitched howls. The tension straining and flowing between them pulsed like a living thing, setting Seth's every cell on fire. He clenched his jaw as the pleasure from her rippling, clutching tunnel, threatened to unravel him. Every muscle strained as he soared to the peak and detonated into a fucking million pieces with a mighty growl.

Heavenly followed him, screaming and clamping down around their cocks like a goddamn irresistible vise.

Beck's throaty roar and jerky thrusts said he'd followed them over.

Their mirrored shouts of ecstasy bounced around the room, lodged into both strong and soft flesh as they curled and clung together and rode out the storm.

When he came down from the euphoria, a whole pile of *oh, shit* should have been waiting for him. He was in love? Willing to engage in a long-term ménage? Yep. And weirdly, the realizations brought him nothing but peace. His earthly angel was everything. He and Beck were better men with her. Sure, nothing was perfect. They still had challenges—mostly her father and her promise to the dying man. But for the first time in what felt like forever, he was willing to go to the mat and do whatever it took to hold them together.

HEAVENLY SIGHED IN sublime, exhausted satisfaction. Seth pressed his lips to her shoulder, running his thumb over the slightly tender spot where he'd bitten her. Inspecting it? Beck cupped her face and looked into her eyes, his so dark and solemn. So full of gravity. So full of something that looked like love.

Her heart skipped and stuttered. "Beck?"

"Happy, little girl?"

A smile stretched across her face, wider than any she'd ever had, seeming to reach both ears. "I didn't know I could feel that good. I didn't even know what to want or hope my first time would be like, but you two gave it to me. It was perfect."

"I don't ever want you to regret giving your innocence to me." He nodded up at Seth. "To us."

"Impossible."

She dropped her head and kissed him, reveling in the fact that after long months of waiting and wondering, after everything they'd been through together, she was free to press her lips to his. That she could feel him still firm and filling her. Surrounding her.

Same with Seth. With a parting buss for Beck, she turned to meet his stare over her shoulder. She was used to seeing charming Seth, wry Seth, aroused Seth. This was the first time she could remember seeing just Seth—the man underneath. Nothing about his stare now was flirty or witty or excited. That look told her everything had changed, not only for him but for them all.

She felt that in her heart, too. It had been weeks since she acknowledged the girlish love she felt for them. Tonight, that love felt a lot less innocent and a lot more mature. Not strictly because they'd had sex but because she'd seen their true characters. These were men of honor, integrity, honesty. They were men she could rely on.

Now she just had to be brave enough to let herself do it.

Her father wouldn't like it…but he didn't understand. She hoped, in time, he would. It would take her a while to wrap her head around it, too. Especially since they were Dominants and they wanted her. She definitely wasn't ready for commitment—for marriage and babies— but she also didn't know how the heck she was supposed to walk away from these two men who had captured her heart and now cradled her soul in their hands.

"Angel?" Seth's stare searched her, full of concern.

She'd worry about the jumble of questions and problems later. After all, she didn't have to have answers today or even tomorrow. All she had to do was take things as she'd been doing, one day at a time…

"Everything is great," she promised. "I must be the luckiest girl in Los Angeles."

"I'm feeling pretty lucky, too." Seth pressed a kiss to the side of her neck, then gently withdrew from her backside.

She'd never given much thought to a man having sex with her…there. But she'd liked it. The slightly forbidden thrill of being taken, even ravished, still made her shiver. And Beck taking her virginity with such unexpected reverence, followed by stunning passion, had her feeling soft and needy again.

Tomorrow, she really would have to thank River for refusing her.

"Up." Beck tapped at her thigh. "Let's get you clean and talk."

"I'll get hot towels," Seth volunteered, thumbing toward the bathroom. "Everything I need in there?"

"Yeah. I can help you, man."

"I got it."

Heavenly gingerly lifted herself from Beck's softening penis, surprised to find she was more than a teensy bit sore. She was also surprised to see blood on the condom. "Let me. Please. I need to, um…use the ladies' room."

And despite every naughty, amazing thing they'd done with and to her tonight, she found herself blushing.

Beck rose and, like Seth, disposed of his condom. They both chuckled at her.

"Don't laugh…" She crossed her arms over her chest self-consciously.

"Don't hide." Beck uncrossed her arms and held her wrists firmly at her side. "I love that you're still my blushing little girl."

Her flush only turned hotter. "I don't think I'm a little girl anymore."

"To me, you always will be."

Beside him, Seth nodded. "He's right. My sweet heaven on earth."

When they both wrapped their arms around her and moved in for kisses, she backed away. "No more yet. I'm sticky and…" And she would have sworn she felt a trickle of something that was probably blood running down her thigh. "Sore. And hungry. I never got to eat the sandwich I packed for my dinner break."

Seth stepped back with a sigh. "Get clean. We'll rustle up food."

"I'll do it. I don't mind," she called as she plucked her clothes from the floor and headed toward the bathroom.

"The staples in the place are running a little low," Beck hollered from the refrigerator. "How about we call for pizza?"

"Give me a minute," she called.

She shut the door, flipped on the light, and fished out a few towels. As she waited at the sink for hot water, she looked in the mirror. Except for the tangled hair, she didn't look any different. But she felt different, like the universe had shifted and she suddenly understood so many of its best secrets.

She clutched a dry towel to her chest and smiled. Lots of things had gone so wrong lately...and yet she couldn't remember ever being so happy.

"Psst. Hey, man," Seth murmured. "Um, who the fuck was that?"

"You noticed it, too?"

"Kind of hard to miss. Man..."

Who were they talking about? Her?

"I had no fucking idea under all those blushes that she was a goddamn siren." Beck sighed. "I wasted months thinking I'd scare the hell out of her—"

"Me, too. And she turned into a vamp. I was balls deep inside her and she was *flirting*. She was almost demanding more. God, I can't wait to give it to her again."

"Think we can get in a quickie before the pizza comes?"

Heavenly covered her giggle behind her hand. So she'd surprised them? Delighted them a little bit, too, from the sounds of it. Thank goodness they weren't disappointed. In the back of her head, she'd worried she wouldn't know enough or be pretty enough to please them. But their eagerness to be with her again was far more than she'd expected. And it was a thrill.

"I think I'd like to give it a hell of a try," Seth drawled.

"You know, we have to keep a lid on this shit," Beck whispered. "If she figures out how damn hard we are for her, she's going to try to lead us around by our dicks."

"Good point."

She stifled another laugh. That hadn't actually occurred to her, but now that they'd suggested it...it did sound like fun.

Finally, the water in the basin started steaming. She doused the hand towel and wrung it out, then washed herself, gently wiping away layers of lube and blood and traces of semen from her thighs. Then she used the toilet, threw on her clothes, and tried to wrestle her hair into something that didn't look so wild.

But it was hopeless, so she gave up, deciding she'd rather have hot food than a pretty hairdo.

When she stepped out of the bathroom, they both stood in the bedroom in various states of undress. Seth had found his underwear among the pile of discarded clothing and donned them. The visual of his hard, ripped body had her holding in a sigh. Beck stood stark naked, reading his phone. His muscled derrière and wide, inked back made her wonder if food could wait just a bit longer…

They both turned, looked her way.

"Why are you dressed?" Seth didn't look pleased.

"I know Beck said he'd order a pizza, but I want real food, and I can't cook naked."

He paused and cocked his head as if he was envisioning that. Then he nodded. "Yeah, you can. I'd like that."

"I'm all about naked." Beck bobbed his head.

She gaped at them. "What on earth—"

The emergency tone on her phone rang. Her dad. Her heart stopped. He would only be calling this late at night if something was wrong.

Heavenly raced for her purse, panicked. Where had she left it? The noise was coming from somewhere near the foyer. Had she dropped it there when Seth's kisses had begun to overheat and overwhelm her?

As she darted around the corner, she found the little secondhand lavender shoulder bag on the floor and tore into it, yanking her phone free from the confines with trembling hands. "Dad?"

"Ms. Young?" asked an unfamiliar male.

In the background, she could hear what sounded like a commotion, footsteps pounding, machines beeping. "Yes. Where's my dad? What's going on?"

"He was trying to call you and…something's happened. We need you to come immediately."

Her breathing stopped. Her chest felt as if he'd stomped on it.

"What's wrong with him?"

"I don't know. But you may not have much time."

"I'll be there in five minutes." She managed to sound coherent.

Inside, she was falling apart. After a relapse, he never had another one this quickly. It was usually months, at least weeks. He'd usually rebound and feel better for a while and…

"Beck. Seth." She tried to yell. Her vocal cords didn't want to work. She ran toward the bedroom but turned to find them both standing in the kitchen, faces sober and grave.

They'd heard.

Heavenly tried not to cry, tried not to think the worst. "I need to go."

"We'll go with you," Seth assured. "I'll be dressed in one minute."

She shook her head. "No time. It's three blocks away. I can run and—"

"It's faster if we drive you." Beck shook his head. "I can make things happen. You want me there. No arguments."

The guys took off for the bedroom. She followed. Beck had a point.

She tried to drag in a breath, fought not to panic as they both looked through the discarded pile of clothes to find their own. She picked up the first pair of jeans she encountered. "Who do these belong to?"

"They're mine." Beck held out his hand.

As she tossed the denim his way and groped for a shirt next to her foot, a thick envelope tumbled to the carpet. Sheets of paper spilled free. She picked up the pages and absently tried to fit them back together. Something in her head told her it wasn't important and to set them aside. As she dropped them to the bed, three words at the top of the page screamed through her brain.

Marital Settlement Agreement.

Horror doused her like icy water as she read on. This agreement is made between Kenneth Edward Beckman, hereafter referred to as "husband" and Gloria Jane Beckman, hereafter referred to as "wife". The parties were married on… She scanned the date, did a quick calculation. Eighteen years ago?

Seth glanced at the papers. "Fuck."

He stiffened…but he didn't look surprised.

Beck paled. "I can explain."

Heavenly shook her head, grabbing the papers in her fist. "You're…married?"

The End…for now
Watch for the next installment in the Doms of Her Life:
Heavenly Rising saga. The Chase will begin in 2019!

ONE DOM TO LOVE
Doms of Her Life: Raine Falling (Book 1)
Now Available!

Raine Kendall has been in love with her boss, Macen Hammerman, for years. Determined to make the man notice that she's a grown woman with desires and needs, she pours out her heart and offers her body to him—only to be crushingly rejected. But when his friend, very single, very sexy Liam O'Neill watches the other Dom refuse to act on his obvious feelings for Raine, he resolves to step in and do whatever it takes to help Hammer find happiness again, even rousing his friend's possessive instincts by making the girl a proposition too tempting to refuse. But he never imagines that he'll end up falling for her himself.

Hammer has buried his lust for Raine for years. After rescuing the budding runaway from an alley behind his exclusive BDSM Dungeon, he has come to covet the pretty submissive. But tragedy has taught him that he can never be what she needs. So he watches over her while struggling to keep his distance. Liam's crafty plan blindsides Hammer, especially when he sees how determined his friend is to possess Raine for his own. Hammer isn't ready to give the lovely submissive over to any other Dom, but can he heal from his past and fight for her? Or will he lose Raine if she truly gives herself—heart, body, and soul—to Liam?

5 out of 5! "*Purest Delight* …an extraordinary journey into the lives of three passionate people. I was hooked from page one. The emotions jumped off the page. I was consumed by such an array of feelings I'm not likely to forget it anytime soon. This story is beautifully intense and complex." – **Guilty Pleasures Book Reviews**

5 out of 5! "This book is so hot it should come with its own fire extinguisher! Run...don't walk...buy this now!" – **The Romance Reviews**

5 O's... oh my! "One Dom to Love is rife with steamy hot sex, bondage, kinky play and lustful desires, but that is not the crux of the story. The real story is in the relationships of these three people. These three ladies have woven a wonderful story of love, sex and betrayal." – **Tasty Wordgasms**

THE YOUNG AND THE SUBMISSIVE
Doms of Her Life: Raine Falling (Book 2)
Now Available!

Raine Kendall has everything a woman could want...almost. Sexy, tender Dom Liam O'Neill is her knight in shining armor, but Raine keeps pinching herself. Is he too good to be true or is this growing connection one that could last a lifetime? She's constantly torn by her abiding feelings for her commanding boss, Macen "Hammer" Hammerman, especially in the wake of the mind-blowing night he cast aside the barriers between them and ravaged every inch of her body.

Hammer, Liam's former best friend, can't stop coveting Raine. But Liam is determined to hold and guide the woman he loves and see if she can be the submissive of his dreams. However, he's finding that her trust is hard won and he needs a bloody crowbar to pry open her scarred soul. So he risks everything to win her once and for all. But once he's put his daring plan in motion, will it cost Liam his heart if he loses Raine to Hammer for good?

5 STARS! "I would give 10 if I could. Brilliant! Outstanding! Dynamic!" **– Once Upon an Alpha**

5 STARS! "These three women once again take you on a sensual journey..." **– Smut Book Junkie**

5 out of 5! "What happens when you put together three amazing authors of erotic romance – magic!" **– Sizzling Hot Books**

THE BOLD AND THE DOMINANT

Doms of Her Life: Raine Falling (Book 3)
Now Available!

After spending weeks trying to reach Raine Kendall, Dominants Liam O'Neill and Macen Hammerman have finally broken past the walls to their submissive's wounded heart. Before they can enjoy their new-found closeness, Liam's past comes back to haunt him when his ex-wife drops in—with a secret that could tear his world apart. Forced to leave Raine in Hammer's care, Liam is stuck on the outside, stewing in frustration and insecurity...and wondering if Raine no longer needs him or if Hammer alone completes her.

Always the pillar of strength, Hammer tries to help Liam while sheltering their woman. But Raine soon discovers the truth that threatens the trio's chance of a happily-ever-after. Determined to hold them together, the two men cook up a scheme to uncover the ex's secret. When an old nemesis returns and targets Raine, can Liam and Hammer come together to slay the danger and save the woman they both love?

5 Stars! "Shayla Black, Jenna Jacob, and Isabella LaPearl have masterfully captured the feelings, the romance, and the intense passion... These three authors continue to blow me away... I couldn't be more in LOVE with this series..." **– Shayna Renee's Spicy Reads**

5 Hearts! "Be prepared for some scorching hot moments with these three along with some touching tender moments as well. I so love their story..." **– She Hearts Books**

5 Roses! "The Bold and the Dominant has everything you could wish for in a book. The passion and heat between the lovers caused my own heart to race. The emotions were so strong that my own eyes were tearing up. The writing is flawless." **– Sizzling Hot Books**

THE EDGE OF DOMINANCE
Doms of Her Life: Raine Falling (Book 4)
Now Available!

Since Macen "Hammer" Hammerman shares the bond he's long craved with Raine Kendall and his best friend, Liam O'Neill, he should be looking forward to a bright future. But a vengeful force from the past returns to cast a long shadow. As Hammer reels from a bombshell that exhumed struggles he'd buried after his late wife's passing, he learns her death may not be ruled a suicide after all.

Worse, a figure from Raine's childhood surfaces, determined to rip her away for good. As the threats against the trio multiply, Hammer must confront his demons while leaning on Liam to keep their new family intact. But with emotions running high and forces mounting against them, can their love survive so they can finally live happily ever after?

5 Shooting Stars! "This incredible fourth installment in The Doms of Her Life series was full of nail-biting drama and twists that I did NOT expect!" – **Marie's Tempting Reads**

5 Stars & Purest Delight! "A definite five star read and one with a satisfying conclusion to the entire series." – **Guilty Pleasures Book Reviews**

5 Stars! "This couldn't have been a better ending for these three. I was very happy with it." – **Alpha Book Club**

MORE THAN LOVE YOU
More Than Words, Book 3
By Shayla Black
Now Available!

I'm Noah Weston. For a decade, I've quarterbacked America's most iconic football team and plowed my way through women. Now I'm transitioning from star player to retired jock—with a cloud of allegation hanging over my head. So I'm escaping to the private ocean-front paradise I bought for peace and quiet. What I get instead is stubborn, snarky, wild, lights-my-blood-on-fire Harlow Reed. Since she just left a relationship in a hugely viral way, she should be the last woman I'm seen with.

On second thought, we can help each other...

I need a steady, supportive "girlfriend" for the court of public opinion, not entanglements. Harlow is merely looking for nonstop sweaty sex and screaming orgasms that wring pleasure from her oh-so-luscious body. Three months—that's how long it should take for us both to scratch this itch and leave our respective scandals behind. But the more I know this woman, the less I can picture my life without her. And when I'm forced to choose, I realize I don't merely want her in my bed or need her for a ruse. I more than love her enough to do whatever it takes to make her mine for good.

"Highly recommend! Shayla Black delivers once again with this passionate and sexy novel... A beautiful love story with a twist that you'll never see coming!" – **Meredith Wild, #1 New York Times Bestselling Author**

"Amazing! Everything I didn't even know I needed or wanted in a romance novel. Hot. Spicy. Addicting." – **Rachel Van Dyken, #1 New York Times Bestselling Author**

"Sexy, passionate and oh-so-clever! An intriguing love story!" – **Lauren Blakely, #1 New York Times Bestselling Author**

ABOUT SHAYLA BLACK

Shayla Black is the *New York Times* and *USA Today* bestselling author of more than sixty novels. For nearly twenty years, she's written contemporary, erotic, paranormal, and historical romances via traditional, independent, foreign, and audio publishers. Her books have sold millions of copies and been published in a dozen languages.

Raised an only child, Shayla occupied herself with lots of day-dreaming, much to the chagrin of her teachers. In college, she found her love for reading and realized that she could have a career publishing the stories spinning in her imagination. Though she graduated with a degree in Marketing/Advertising and embarked on a stint in corporate America to pay the bills, her heart has always been with her characters. She's thrilled that she's been living her dream as a full-time author for the past eight years.

Shayla currently lives in North Texas with her wonderfully supportive husband, her daughter, and two spoiled tabbies. In her "free" time, she enjoys reality TV, reading, and listening to an eclectic blend of music.

Connect with me online:
Website: shaylablack.com
VIP Reader Newsletter: shayla.link/nwsltr
Facebook Author Page: facebook.com/ShaylaBlackAuthor
Facebook Book Beauties Chat Group: shayla.link/FBChat
Instagram: instagram.com/ShaylaBlack
Book+Main Bites: bookandmainbites.com/users/62
Twitter: twitter.com/Shayla_Black
Google +: shayla.link/googleplus
Amazon Author: shayla.link/AmazonFollow
BookBub: shayla.link/BookBub
Goodreads: shayla.link/goodreads
YouTube: shayla.link/youtube

If you enjoyed this book, please review it or recommend it to others so they can find it, too.

Keep in touch by engaging with me through one of the links above. Subscribe to my VIP Readers newsletter for exclusive excerpts and hang out in my Facebook Book Beauties group for live weekly video chats. I love talking to readers!

OTHER BOOKS BY SHAYLA BLACK

CONTEMPORARY ROMANCE

MORE THAN WORDS

More Than Want You
More Than Need You
More Than Love You

Coming Soon:
More Than Crave You (September 18, 2018)

CONTEMPORARY EROTIC ROMANCE

THE WICKED LOVERS (COMPLETE SERIES)

Wicked Ties
Decadent
Delicious
Surrender to Me
Belong to Me
"Wicked to Love" (novella)
Mine to Hold
"Wicked All the Way" (novella)
Ours to Love
"Wicked All Night" (novella)
"Forever Wicked" (novella)
Theirs to Cherish
His to Take
Pure Wicked (novella)
Wicked for You
Falling in Deeper
Dirty Wicked (novella)
"A Very Wicked Christmas" (short)
Holding on Tighter

The Edge of Dominance

Coming Soon:
Heavenly Rising Collection
The Choice

THE MISADVENTURES SERIES

Misadventures of a Backup Bride

STANDALONE TITLES

Naughty Little Secret
Watch Me
Dangerous Boys And Their Toy
"Her Fantasy Men" (Four Play Anthology)
A Perfect Match
His Undeniable Secret (Sexy Short)

HISTORICAL ROMANCE (as Shelley Bradley)

The Lady And The Dragon
One Wicked Night
Strictly Seduction
Strictly Forbidden

BROTHERS IN ARMS MEDIEVAL TRILOGY

His Lady Bride (Book 1)
His Stolen Bride (Book 2)
His Rebel Bride (Book 3)

PARANORMAL ROMANCE

THE DOOMSDAY BRETHREN
Tempt Me With Darkness
"Fated" (e-novella)
Seduce Me In Shadow
Possess Me At Midnight
"Mated" – Haunted By Your Touch Anthology
Entice Me At Twilight
Embrace Me At Dawn

ABOUT JENNA JACOB

Bestselling author Jenna Jacob paints a canvas of passion, romance, and humor as her Alpha men and the feisty women who love them unravel their souls, heal their scars, and find a happy-ever-after kind of love. Heart-tugging, captivating, and steamy, Jenna's books will surely leave you breathless and craving more.

A mom of four grown children, Jenna and her Alpha-hunk husband live in Kansas. She loves books, Harleys, music, and camping. Her zany sense of humor and lack of filter exemplify her motto: Live. Laugh. Love.

Meet her wild and wicked family in her sultry series: **The Doms of Genesis**. Or become spellbound by the searing love connection between Raine, Hammer, and Liam in her continuing saga: **The Doms of Her Life** (co-written with the amazing Shayla Black and Isabella La Pearl). Journey with couples struggling to resolve their pasts and heal their scars to discover unbridled love and devotion in Jenna's contemporary series: **Passionate Hearts**.

CONTACT JENNA:
Website: www.jennajacob.com
E Mail: jenna@jennajacob.com
Facebook Fan Page: facebook.com/authorjennajacob
Twitter: twitter.com/@jennajacob3
Instagram: instagram.com/jenna_jacob_author
Amazon Author page: http://amzn.to/2Bmp0wP
Newsletter: bit.ly/JennaJacobNewsletter
Books+Main Bites: bookandmainbites.com/users/58

OTHER BOOKS BY JENNA JACOB

THE DOMS OF GENESIS

Embracing My Submission: (Book One) – FREE
Masters of My Desire: (Book Two)
Master of My Mind: (Book Three)
Saving My Submission: (Book Four)
Seduced By My Doms: (Book Five)
Lured By My Master: (Book Six)
Sin City Submission: (A Doms of Genesis Novella)
Bound To Surrender: (A Doms of Genesis Novella)
Resisting My Submission: (Book Seven)
Craving His Command: (A Doms of Genesis Novella)
Seeking My Destiny: (Book Eight)

HOTTIES OF HAVEN

Sin On A Stick: (A Hotties Of Haven Novella)
Wet Dream: (Book One)
Revenge On The Rocks: (A Hotties Of Haven Novella Coming Soon)
Beef Cake: (Book Two Coming Soon)

PASSIONATE HEARTS

Sky of Dreams: (Book One)

DOMS OF HER LIFE: Raine Falling
(by Shayla Black, Jenna Jacob, and Isabella LaPearl)

One Dom To Love: (Book One)
The Young And The Submissive: (Book Two)
The Bold and The Dominant: (Book Three)
The Edge of Dominance: (Book Four)

DOMS OF HER LIFE: Heavenly Rising
(by Shayla Black, Jenna Jacob, and Isabella LaPearl)

The Choice: (Book One)

ABOUT ISABELLA LAPEARL

Hello Friends! My name is Isabella and I write sexy, erotic romance. I'm a wife, mother, writer, reader and I love to ride my motorcycle.

To say it's been an extraordinary journey thus far would be an understatement…what a rush! What a thrill to realize dreams and see them go from a seed to fruition. So for all you aspiring Authors who like me, have a fire inside that burns brightly and demands to be sated by writing… Never give up.

Connect with me online:
Facebook: facebook.com/isabellalapearlpage
Twitter: twitter.com/IsabellaLaPearl

Made in the USA
Middletown, DE
28 July 2019